A COMPARATIVE STUDY
OF
ALL SANSKRIT GRAMMARS

A COMPARATIVE STUDY
OF
ALL SANSKRIT GRAMMARS

(With Special Reference to
Past Passive Participial Formations)

By

M. D. Pandit

Foreword
by
Prof. B.K. Dalai

BHARTIYA KALA PRAKASHAN
Delhi : : (India)

First Edition : 2009

Published by **C.P. Gautam**
BHARATIYA KALA PRAKASHAN
3421-A, IInd Floor, Narang Colony Tri Nagar,
Delhi-110035. Phone : 32967505, Telefax : 27393083
E-mail : bkp3421@yahoo.co.in

ISBN : 978-81-8090-222-2

Printed by :
D.K. Fine Art Press (P) Ltd.
Delhi

।। अथ नमस्काराञ्जलिः ।।

ॐ काररूपिणं वन्दे
सूत्ररूपं महेश्वरम्।
विवर्तं शब्दशास्त्रस्य
भगवत्पादपाणिनिम्।। १।।

प्रवर्त्तकं वार्त्तिकानाम्
कात्यायनमहामुनिम्।
तथाचार्यं नमस्कुर्वे
भाष्यकारं पतंजलिम्।। २।।

यैर्मे व्याकरणं विद्या
वैयाकरणभूषणैः।
पाठिता देवकृष्णाख्यान्
पितृपादान् नमाम्यहम्।। ३।।

—पण्डितोपाह्वः देवकृष्णसूनुः मनोहरशर्मा

To

The memory of

The Late Professor Dr. R.N. Dandekar,

the renowned Indologist,

to work under whom

for Ph.D. was my

pleasure and previledge.

Contents

Foreword

I feel great pleasure to introduce the present work by Prof. Dr. M.D. Pandit on the comparative study of all Sanskrit Grammars to scholars. As a matter of fact I am too small a person to introduce the work of Prof. Pandit who needs to introduction. The work is unique of its own kind in the sense that this type of comparative study of the Sanskrit grammars is rare. The treatment given to the subject by Dr. M.D. Pandit is from both grammatical as well as linguistic points of view. Dr. Pandit has written extensively on Sanskrit grammars. He is a specialist of grammar in general and Sanskrit grammar in particular. He has been writing for the last several years since 1961 when his first article titled 'Zero in Panini' was published in the M.S. University in Baroda journal (Humanities).

When a casual discussion with Prof. Pandit I learnt about this work, I requested him to publish the work. He handed over the manuscript of the work to me with pleasure and I am happy that such a learned piece of research of one of the senior-most scholar in the field is seeing the light of the day. There is again an emotional and personal aspect to my respect for Dr. Pandit. Dr. M.D. Pandit happens to be my teacher in linguistics when I was an M.A. student in 1979-80 in the university of Pune.

Now a few words on the present work: It is a comparative study of all available grammars, which is recorded by the author himself.

They are :

1. Panini's *Aṣṭādhyāyī* (650 B.C. or 400 B.C.)

2. Śarvavarman's *kātantra* (50-150 A.D.)
3. Çandragomin's *Cāndra Vyākaraṇa* (450-500 A.D.)
4. Devanandin's *Jainendra Vyākaraṇa* (450-500 A.D.)
5. Śākatāyana's *Śākaṭāyana Vyākaraṇa* (750-850 A.D.)
6. Bhoja's *Sarasvatīkaṇṭhābharaṇa* (1000-1050 A.D.)
7. Hemacandracaya's *Srisiddhahemacandra Vyākaraṇa* (1050-1100 A.D.)
8. Anubhūtisvarūpācārya's *Sārasvata Vyākaraṇa* (1200-1250 A.D.)
9. Vopadeva's *Mugdhabodha Vyākaraṇa* (1200-1250 A.D.)
10. Jaumāra's *Jaumāra Vyākaraṇa* (1200-1250 A.D.)
11. Saupadma's *saupadma Vyākaraṇa* (1300-1350 A.D.)

The attempt to study all grammars with a vision of comparison seems tough and very difficult; for, such comparative study can be made from the point of view of changes in the formations, if any, in historical perspective tracing such changes from the oldest work to the recent one. In the case of such grammars which are contemporary the changes in the formations can be viewed as dialectal differences of the authors of the grammars, who flourished in different parts of the country.

The difference in wording and its order also offers a very fascinating topic for a comparative investigation, revealing the style of the different authors and the change in the syntax of the sūtras. The change in the syntax of the sūtras, studied geographically and/or historically will give us an idea of the principles of the sūtra-system in different times and places.

Further, every grammarian and his works can be the a subject of subjected of a critical comparative study, and the findings will be really interesting.

In the present works, as Prof. himself writes, the study and comparison is mainly centered round the problem of finding out and comparing the grammatical principles of language-description and the techniques employed by the grammarians to arrive at the formations available in usages. An attempt is made to find out whether these grammars are distinguished from one another and are regarded as representing different schools of grammatical thought only because of the tradition and the difference in the authorship, or whether this is so done on account of the difference in their basic approaches and their grammatical and technical principles of description.

The main purpose in investigating and comparing the grammatical and technical principle of these grammas is to find out whether this long stream of grammatical activity in India, spreading over a period of more than two thousand years and thus creating a unique and unparalleled record in the field, has followed the same course with the same principle throughout all these years without any basic change or whether it displays at accepted or followed by Panini. To do justice to the problem, Prof. Pandit has selected only one major topic for investigation in the present study, that which deals with the description of the past passive participial formation in Sanskrit; technically called the *nisthā-prakaraṇa* or *ktādhikaraṇa* in grammar.

From the point of view of syntax of words in Sanskrit language, the past passive participial formations can be substituted for verbal forms, even though they are what is technically called as the *pratipadikas.* Though this tendency of using the past passive participles for verbal forms is reflected generally in all Sanskrit works of all the periods, the works like the *Pancatantra,* the *Hiitopadsa* etc. appear to be more distinct and largely inclined to use the past passive participles in the place of verbal forms of the corresponding roots. The importance of the past passive participles formations for the valuation and comparison of the styles of authors is, therefore, quite obvious. I am extremely happy to record that Prof. Pandit has very successfully handled such an important topic of grammar with ease and great perfection.

I am confident that the present work of Dr. Pandit will be well received, like his other works, equally by the students, teachers and research scholars in the field. I am sure it will certainly occupy an important place, which it rightfully deserves, in the works of research of the first order.

Prof. B.K. Dalai
Director and Head
Centre of Advanced
Study in Sanskrit
University of Pune

Preface

Traditionally, the linguistic and grammatical studies in India are taken to begin from the times of the Vedas. The Vedic pada-pāṭha, the prātiśākhyas, the Nighaṇṭu, the Nirukta and the śikṣās—all these Literature has done not only the pioneering work but even a detailed study of the phonetics, phonology, accent, semantics and even morphology in some cases of the vedic language. Yet, looking to the variety of the nominal and verbal formations, the *taddhita* and the *kṛdanta* derivatives, the different ways of the delcension of nouns and conjugation of verbs, the exactitude of the accent and syntax, the transformational procedures, the generative nature of the Sanskrit language and finally the versification with its rigid rules, the different metres and the accent-rules-all these characteristics of the vedic language show that though the Vedic linguists had done a sufficiently detailed study of the Vedic language, much remained to be done and the task was taken up by the post-Vedic grammarians.

The linguistic studies noted above, however, do not deal with the post-Vedic that is, the epic and classical language, though it can be said that the linguistic studies of the Vedas have definitely paved the way for the study of the later post-Vedic epic and classical Sanskrit language. We find that there is a great similarity between the principles of morpheme-segmentation of the *padapāṭhakāra* śākalya and of Pāṇini. So also, the phonetics and phonology of the *sikṣās* differ very little from that of the later grammarians. Just as the later post-Vedic linguistic and grammatical studies, pre-suppose the Vedic linguistics, we may venture to conjecture that there is every possibility of some linguistic activity in the pre-Vedic times which might have helped the Vedic scholars and writers. The legends of Indra and Bṛhaṣpati referred to by Patañjali in his Mahābhāṣya or that of gods invoking Indra to analyze the unanalyzed vāk in the Tait. Brāhmana are instances in this context. That the roots of Vedic linguistics (as are evident from various references to speech-analysis in the saṁhitās proper, the Brāhmaṇas and the Upaniṣads) go back to pre-Vedic times is not impossible, because just as the Vedic Sanskrit language, i.e. Old Indo-Aryan, has its history going back to Indo-Eruopean stage, the linguistic studies of the language cannot be the sudden off-shoot of the Vedic and pre-Vedic period alone. They also can be traced back to pre-Vedic times.

Even a simple thing as the versification and the metres is an instance in point. We find then the Vedas are nothing but verses in form composed in different metres. Thus, we have in the Veda the following metres chiefly. There is the Gāyatri of 24 syllables, the Anuṣṭubh of 32 syllables, the Triṣṭubh of 33 syllables, the Paṅkti of 40 syllables, and Jagati of 48 syllables. Besides we have other verieties of metres, which are of mixed type-of 28 syllables like Uṣṇih, Purusnih and kakubha; of 40 syllables like Sato-Brhati, of 60 syllables like Atiśakvari and of 68 syllables like Atyaṣṭi. Moreover, we have what are called strophic stanzas like pragātha, Kākubha Pragātha and Bārhata Pragātha. The composition of all these different types of metres presupposes a disciplined arrangement of letters by counting the number of syllables in the stanzas. Not only this, the stanza were sung with musical notes which had a melody rhythm and music. This again speaks for an advancement and study of music also in pre-Vedic times. This is the case of only a simple thing like the Vedic metres. What about all the linguistic studies in and after Vedic times, which show an advanced stage and knowledge in phonetics and phonology? It is, therefore, that all the post-Vedic linguistic studies are the product of only post-Vedic times. We are led to assume a long period even in pre-Vedic times for whatever development and advancement is seen in the Vedic and post-Vedic period.

It will, therefore, not be an exaggeration to say that the beginning of the linguistic activities of India go back even to pre-Vedic times. Unfortunately there is no literature of pre-Vedic times to support our conjecture of the pre-Vedic origin of the Indian linguistic studies and hence we cannot produce a documentary evidence or what the Naiyāyikas call as the pratyakṣa-pramāṇa. But, it should be noted, *pratyakṣa, pramāṇa* is not the only pramāṇas. There are at least four means of knowledge, viz-*pratyakṣa, anumāna upamāna and śābda.* And we can conjecture the pre-Vedic beginning of the linguistic studies with the help of common-sense judgement and the *anumāna pramāṇa.* If the Vedic language is what it is with all its richness of vocabulary, veriety of forms, exact syntax, the lofty thoughs, and high philosophy it must have taken a long period to evolve into its present states. Its linguistic studies also must have started and developed along with the development of the Vedic language, though we cannot produce a historical document in the form of writing of the pre-Vedic times to prove our point. The only evidence that we can cite is the mention of the many grammarians before Pāṇini's times in Pāṇini's grammar itself. The number of pre-pāṇinian grammarians, according to Yudhiṣṭhira Mimāṁsaka is well nigh 60. This figure speaks for itself.

If the line of reasoning given above about the pre-Vedic beginning of linguistic studies is correct, them what follows is that this very activity provided a base-may be rough or sound, scientific or otherwise to the post-Vedic linguistic activity in the form of the *padapāṭha,* the *Prātiśākhyas,* the *Nighantu,* the *Nirukta* and the *Śikṣās,* and later on in the form of the grammars of sixty and odd pre-Pāṇinian grammarians. We can see thus that the linguistic activity in India, which started from pre-Vedic times and was carried on by the post-

Vedic grammarians and linguistics like Pāṇini was further carried on even after Pāṇini's times in spite of the fact that Pāṇini's grammar was a master-piece in grammar composition and threw back all the pre-Pāṇinian grammars into total oblivion.

The number of Sanskrit grammars after Pāṇini's times is eleven. The latest grammar of Saupadma was written in about 1300 A.D-1350 A.D.

Besides the activity of proper grammar composition, there have been side-activities like the commentaries, adding supplements etc. to the grammars. The Vārtikas of Kātyāyana are a point in this connection. If all this literature swells into enourmous size. The Indians have thus a very tradition spreading over about 4000-5000 years and a very vast literature running in to thousands of pages on linguistics and grammar.

It is this vast size of the linguistic literature and long tradition of linguistics studies in ancient India, which has always attracted the linguists of the world to Indian linguistic, especially the grammatical activity. Grammar-composition is a very delicate and difficult task in the sense that it is both a science as well as an art. It is a science in the sense that it should be objective, formal and at the same time comprehensive of all the linguistic data. It is an art in the sense that the skill of framing grammatical rules (which are in the form of the *sūtras* in Sanskrit tradition) depends upon the individual grammarian. Pāṇini could achieve this difficult task. After studying Pāṇini's grammar, therefore, I became very much interested in knowing how the post-grammarians have done. It is this curiosity which led me to make a comparative study of all the Sanskrit grammars. I therefore, started working on this topic in 1964 and finished the spade work by about December of the same year. When I joined the Centre of Advanced study in Sanskrit in 1965, I showed the work done to the late Dr. R.N. Dandekar, the then Director who was very happy to see it and suggested me to work on comparative study of the grammars for my PhD. degree. He also agreed to my request to become my guide. Thus started the work on the comparative study of all Sanskrit grammars.

The subject was very vast. I, therefore, delimited the scope of the work to only the past passive participal formations and their treatment in all the grammars. I was awarded the Ph.D. degree for the work in 1972.

The present monography, though based on my Ph.D. thesis, is however not identical with the thesis. Nay, it cannot be identical if one wants to keep pace with growing research in the field. The thesis was written between 1965 and 1970; i.e. about 35-40 years ago. And since then much water has flown down through the Ganges. If, therefore, one wants to be up-to-date, one has to make the necessary changes in the writings of about 35 years back. And accordingly, I have imporved on the original a lot. Thus, there are additions of some more data; many of the highly technical details, which are required in the thesis but are not necessary in a readable book like this are dropped out; much of the text of the original Ph.D. thesis is newly drafted to suit to the demands of serious scholars.

And thus the whole subject of the comparative study of all Sanskrit grammars with special reference to past passive participles is treated on modern linguistic and not only on pure traditional grammatical level. This linguistic approach has given out certain interesting and important conclusions.

A word about my teachers. I was very fortunate to have learned persons as my teachers in my life. The first teacher I got was my father himself, the late Deokrishna Keshava Pandit. Himself a Vyakaranacarya, he got the whole Siddhanta Kaumudi memorized by me by the age of 12 itself. The next stalwarts in the field of Sanskrit, linguistic and Indological studies whom I got as my teachers and guides were the late Dr. S.S. Bhawe, the late Dr. N.G. Kalelkar, the late Dr. D.D. Mahulkar, Dr. S.M. Katre of the Deccan College Post-Graduate and Research Institute, Pune and lastly the renowned ideologist and Sanskritist, the late Dr. R.N. Dandekar of the Bhandarkar Oriental Research Institute, Pune. I am really deeply indebted to all these scholars for imparting highest training in the field of Sanskrit, Linguistics and Sanskrit Linguistics.

Actually I was very much reluctant to publish my thesis. But Dr. B.K. Dalai, the Director of the Centre of Advanced study in Sanskrit, University of Pune, however, was very much enthusiastic in seeing my thesis through printed form. I then finally submitted to Dr. B.K. Dalai's earnest request and agreed with him. I therefore, thank very sincerely Dr. B.K. Dalai for the interest he has taken in my work.

My thanks are also due to the students who prepared the subject-inde, the index of past passive particles discussed in the book and the bibliography. Last but not the least, the publisher, Bharatiya Kala Prakashan deserves my sinceremost thanks for the speedy and neat printing. But for their interest in pure academic and technical work like the present one, the work would have seen the light of the day.

Kārttika Śhukal Pratipadā, **M.D. Pandit**
(the Deepavali Day),
śake, 1929
10th November, 2007
PUNE

List of Abbreviations

ABORI	=	Annals of the Bhandarkar Oriental Research Institute.
B	=	Bhoja
BD	=	Bhaṭṭoji Dīkṣita
BDCPRI	=	Bulletin of the Deccan College Postgraduate and Research Institute.
BORI	=	Bhandarkar Oriental Research Institute
C	=	Candra
Conj.	=	Conjugation
Dhp. or dhp.	=	*Dhātupāṭha.*
H	=	Hemacandra
IL	=	Indian Linguistics, Deccan College, Poona 6.
J	=	Jainendra
Jaim. U. Br.	=	Jaiminīya Upaniṣad Brāhmaṇa.
JMSUB	=	Journal of the Maharaja Sayajirao University of Baroda, Baroda.
JMSUBH	=	Journal of the Maharaja Sayajirao University of Baroda, Baroda, Humanities Section.
JUP	=	Journal of the University of Poona, Poona - 7
JUPH	=	Journal of the University of Poona, Poona - 7, Humanities Section.

K	=	Kātantra
P	=	Pāṇini
RV	=	Ṛgveda
Ś	=	Śākaṭāyana
S	=	Sārasvata
ŚB	=	Śatapatha Brāhmaṇa
SK	=	Siddhānta Kaumudī
Tait. br.	=	Taittirīya Brāhmaṇa
V	=	Vopadeva
VIJ	=	Vishveshvaranand Indological Journal, Vishveshvaranand Vedic Research Insitute, Hoshiarpur, Punjab.

1
Introductory

1. Introduction

1.1 The history of linguistic studies in India goes back to a very remote past. Actually, according to Yāskācārya, the first great exponent of the science of etymology, and Ācārya Patañjali, the great Mahābhāṣyakāra, the study of language or speech (*vāk*) seems to have formed part of the compositions of the Ṛgvedic seers.[1] Besides the indirect references to the study of speech in Ṛgvedic times and their linguistic explanations by later authors, there are a good number of passages in the RV. itself which praise or invoke 'the Goddess of speech, *Vāk*.[2] It was but natural that speech formed part of the compositions and should not be left out of the considerations in such old times as the Ṛgvedic period because, the Vedic *mantras* were then not written down and read but were recited and heard and were handed down from generation to generation through oral tradition.

1.2 The Brāhmaṇas contain a lot of material which clearly aims at what may be called linguistic studies.[3] The innumerable mystic etymologies of the words set forth in the Brāhmaṇas under the pretext of the oft-quoted maxim, *parokṣapriyā ha vai devāḥ/pratyakṣadvisaḥ,*[4] fully bear testimony to the fact that linguistic activity, involving analysis and

1. cf. Yāska's linguistic explanations of the Ṛgvedic *ṛcs,* 10.71.4,5 and Patañjali's linguistic interpretation of the Ṛgvedic verses 1.164. 45; 4.58.3; 10.71.2, 4.
2. cf. RV. 1.164.42; 455; 53.15, 16; 8.100.11' 10.71 etc.
3. cf. ŚB. 4.1.3.15;17 etc., also Tait. Br. 1.5.12.1-7 etc.
4. cf. ŚB. 6.1.1.2 etc.; also Jaim. U. Br. 1.5.1 etc.

explanations of words and ideas was in full swing in the Brāhmaṇa-period.

This activity, however, does not seem to have been carried on in an organised way; it does not seem to have been based on any principles which can be characterised as strictly linguistic. But it certainly does seem to have paved way for a more systematic linguistic analysis in later times.

1.3 Next in line come the *Prātiśākhyas* and the *Śikṣās*. The *Prātiśākhyhas*, which are of the nature of treatises in phonetics, concentrate on the phonetic aspect of language and lay down rules pertaining to pronunciation. These rules are based on strong foundations of systematic phonetic analysis of Sanskrit sounds. Besides the phonetic aspect, the phonological aspect also is covered by the *Prātiśākhyas*, as could be seen from the rules governing sound-combinations or saṁdhi and also accent. The *Śikṣās* on the other hand deal exclusively with the phonetics of the Sanskrit language.

1.4 Yāska's *Nirukta*, which presupposes the collection of Vedic words in the *Nighaṇṭu*, can be said to be the first attempt in the direction of an organised and systematic etymological studies. Though many of the etymologies given by Yāska do not satisfy the scientific criteria and principles of etymological studies of modern times, there are some which clearly display a fine sense of phonetic and historical principles of linguistic studies.[1] The importance of Yāska as an etymologist lies in the fact that he is the first regular etymological of India whose work has come down to us.

All these movements, however, may be said to have been more or less disorganised, in the sense that no definite linguistic principles are found to be underlying them. They seem to be groping in the dark to evolve a scientific system of linguistic analysis with definite principles, scope and aim.

1.5 The period of scientific systematisation in linguistic

1. cf. Siddheshvar Varma, *Etymologies of Yāska*, p. 4ff.

studies is inaugurated by Pāṇini (about 650 B.C. according to S.K. *Belvalkar*[1] or about 400 B.C. at the lowest estimate[2]). This does not of course mean that linguistic studies were not pursued before. That they were pursued is clear from the existing Brāmaṇa texts, *Prātiśākhyas* and the work of Yāska. Besides Pāṇini himself refers to his pradecessors in the field of grammar. All these early works, however, are not as systematic, organised, logical and comprehensive as Pāṇini's *Aṣṭādhyāyī*. That the earlier work in the field of linguistic studies in general and of grammar composition in particular had not been so organised and systematic as Pāṇini's can be inferred from the fact that once Pāṇini's grammar came on the scene, all the pre-Pāṇinian grammars not only receded in the background but were almost thrown into oblivion. The existence of these works can now be deduced from indirect references.[3] Pāṇini's grammar must be said to herald a new epoch in the history of linguistic studies and grammar-composition in India. A comparison of the available pre-Pāṇinian work in the field of linguistics on the one hand and Pāṇinian grammar on the other will easily convince one of the superiority of the latter over the former from the point of view of objectivity, skill and technique of linguistic description, comprehensive-ness coupled with bravity and consistency, and formality. Indeed, Pāṇini's grammar is a unique phonomenon in the history of Sanskrit grammar.

---

1. cf. S.K. *Belvalkar, Systems of Sanskrit Grammar*, pp. 25-35.
2. For a detailed discussion of the times in which Pāṇini flourished, cf. V.S. *Agrawala, India As Known to Paṇini*, 1963 (2nd edition), pp. 458-478.
3. For a discussion of the pre-Pāṇinian grammatical thought in the matter of verbal roots, cf. G.B. *Palsule, The Sanskrit Dhātupāṭhas - A Critical Study*, University of Poona, Poona, 1961, Ch. I, Pp. 1-24; cf. also *Yudhiṣṭhira Mīmāṁsaka, Sanskrit Vyākaraṇa Śāstrakā Itihāsa*, Bhāratīya Prācya Vidyā Pratiṣṭhāna, Ajmer, parts I, 1963 (2nd edition) and II, 1962 (1st edition); cf. also B.K. *Ghosh*, 'Aspects of Pre-Pāṇinian Sanskrit Grammar', *B.C. Law Volume*, The Indian Research Institute, Calcutta, 1945, pp.334-345.

1.6 Fortunately whatever work on Sanskrit grammar was done after Pāṇini has come down to us more or less intact. They are known to be eleven principal grammars, including that of Pāṇini. In the choronological order, they are :

1. Pāṇini's *Aṣṭādhyāyī* (650 B.C. or 400 B.C.)
2. Śarvavarman's *Kātantra* (50-150 A.D.)
3. Candragomin's *Cāndra Vyākaraṇa* (450-500 A.D.)
4. Devanandin's *Jainendra Vyākaraṇa* (450-500 A.D.)
5. (Jain) Śākaṭāyana's *Śākaṭāyana Vyākaraṇa* (750-850 A.D.)
6. Bhoja's *Sarasvatīkaṇṭhābharaṇa* (1000-1050 A.D.)
7. Hemacandrācāya's *Śrīsiddhahemacandra Vyākaraṇa* (1050-1100 A.D.)
8. Anubhūtisvarūpācārya's *Sārasvata Vyākaraṇa* (1200-1250 A.D.)
9. Vopadeva's *Mugdhabodha Vyākaraṇa* (1200-1250 A.D.)
10. Jaumāra's *Jaumāra Vyākaraṇa* (1200-1250 A.D.)
11. Saupadma's *Saupadma Vyākaraṇa* (1300-1350 A.D.)[1]

2. Scope of the Present work.

2.1 The Point of View

2.1.1 The present work aims at a comparative study of all the eleven grammars mentioned above. There are many points of view from which such comparative study can be made. For instance, one can study these grammars from the point of view of changes in the formations, if any, in historical perspective and trace such change from the oldest work to the recent one. Or, as can be seen from the chronology of the

---

1. For a detailed historical information of all these different schools and their authors, cf. *Belvalkar, op. cit.* The chronology of these works is a matter for re-investigation. But as such re-investigation falls outside the scope of the present work. the chronology given by *Belvalkar* is accepted as the basis for the present study.

grammars given above, some grammars are almost contemporary. In the case of such grammars the changes in the formations can be viewed as not due to historical reasons, but due to dialectal differences of the authors of the grammars, who flourished in different parts of the country. These geographical differences can very well give a sound ground to view the differences in formations as arising out of regional peculiarities. Thus, both the historical as well as the geographical points of view can be applied to a comparative study of these grammars.

2.1.1 As will be seen from the grammars, the wording and the order of words in the *sūtras* is not the same in all the grammars. This difference in wording and its order also offers a very fascinating topic for a comparative investigation, revealing the style of the different authors and the change in the syntax of the *sūtras*. The change in the syntax of the *sūtras*, studied geographically and/or historically will give us an idea of the principles of the *sūtra*-system (or, axiomatics, if one can say) in different times and places.

2.1.3 Further, every grammarian and his work can be subjected to a very critical cultural-historical study, as has been so ably and remarkably done by V.S. *Agrawala* in the case of Pāṇini's grammar.[1] The cultural-historical data thus collected from all the grammars can again be subjected to a critical comparative study whose findings will be really greatly interesting.

2.1.4 The individual techniques-both linguistic and extra-linguistic-employed by the authors in describing the language, such as the *it-saṁjñā*, zero etc. and their historical evolution through the ages can also provide a very interesting field for study and comparison.

2.1.5 The present work, however, leaves all such questions out of consideration. It would view these works

1. cf. V.S. *Agrawala, India As Known to Pāṇini*, 1963.

primarily as works of grammar and would study and compare them from the point of view of only linguistic description. Naturally, therefore, the study and comparison would mainly centre round the problem of finding out and comparing the grammatical principles of language-description and the techniques employed by the grammarians to arrive at the formations available in usages. An attempt would be made to find out whether these grammars are distinguished from one another and are regarded as representing different schools of grammatical thought only because of the tradition and the difference in the authorship, or whether this is so done on account of the difference in their basic approaches and their grammatical and technical principles of description.

The main purpose in investigating and comparing the grammatical and technical principles of these grammars is to find out whether this long stream of grammatical activity in India, spreading over a period of more than two thousand years and thus creating a unique and unparalleled record in the field, has followed the same course with the same principles throughout all these years without any basic change in the fundamentals or whether it displays at some stage major diversions from the basic principles of grammatical description accepted or followed by the first known grammarian, viz. Pāṇini. In other words, it is to find out whether the general stock of grammatical principles as available at the end of this long journey has ramained mostly unchanged throughout from the beginning to the end or whether it reveals some broad and major improvements upon the initial principles as enunciated by Pāṇini.

3. The Data

3.1 Due to the enormous number of the *sūtras* in the eleven grammars and due to thousand-times enormous number of formations in Sanskrit, it is not possible in this work to study and compare these grammars in their entirety.

Only one major topic, therefore, is selected for investigation in the present study, namely, that which deals with the description of the past passive participial formations in Sanskrit; it is technically called the *niṣṭhā-prakaraṇa* or *ktādhikaraṇa* in grammar.

3.2 There are two main reasons for selecting only the past passive participial formations for the present comparative study.

3.2.1 From the point of view of syntax of words in Sanskrit language, the past passive participial formations can be substituted for verbal forms, even though they are what is technically called as the *prātipadikas* and are declined as nouns by applying what are called the *sup*-terminations. One can equally conveniently say *rāmeṇa rāvaṇaḥ hataḥ* instead of *rāmeṇa rāvaṇaḥ ahanyata*, by using the past passive participle *hataḥ* in the place of the verbal form *ahaṇyata.* Though this tendency of using the past passive participles for verbal forms is reflected generally in all Sanskrit works of all the periods, the works like the *Pañcatantra,* the *Hitopadeśa* etc. appear to be more distinct and largely inclined to use the past passive participles in the place of verbal forms of the corresponding roots.[1] The importance of the past passive participles formations for the valuation and comparison of the styles of authors is, therefore, quite obvious.

Secondly, the past passive participle is the only grammatical category which functions both as noun as well as verb. On the syntactical plane, therefore, the past passive participles are on par with the conjugated verbal forms.[2] From

1. cf. *J. Gonda, Remarks on the Sanskrit Passive,* Leiden, 1951, p.7: "Most 'passive' sentences in Sanskrit literature are formed by means of a verbal adjective in -ta- (or -na-)."
2. It is this syntactical or functional consideraion that had led the grammarians to group even forms like *śuṣka, kṣāma, pakva,* etc. under the category of past passive participles even though they do not exhibit the past passive participial suffix *-ta* or *-na.*

another point of view, the past passive participles lie on the borderline between the nouns on the one hand and the verbs on the other; because from the point of view of declension, it gets the nominal *sup*-terminations; yet from the point of view of function, it acts as a verb. We can, therefore, neither group them under the category of nouns or *prātipadikas* exclusively nor under that of the verbal forms or the *tiṅantas.* Being the pioneer of formal grammar, Pāṇini, however, has solved the difficulty by the criterion of the nominal declensional terminations applied to them, and grouped them under the category of nouns or *prātipadikas;* cf. his *sūtra, kṛttaddhitasamāsāś ca*, 1.2.46.

3.2.2 From the point of view of the grammatical description also, the past passive participles have been regarded by the grammarians as a very important category. As we shall presently see, all the past passive participial forms display a two-term structure invariably. They are composed of only two terms or morphenas-the *prakṛti* which is the verbal root or *dhātu* and the *pratyaya* which is the suffix-*ta* or its substitutes. The past passive participial forms can, therefore, be said to possess the minimum structure as compared to the greater, three-morpheme structures of verbs which contain the verbal root, the *vikaraṇa* and the conjugational termination.

Secondly, all the past passive participial formations, without any exception, are characterised by a complete absense of any modification in the root like *guṇa* or *vṛddhi;* they always show the roots in their weak grades. The significance of this phonomenon for a grammarian is that the past passive participles provide the best and the easier way to fix the basic norm of the verbal root or *dhātu*, than the fully conjugated verbal forms like *gacchati* or *bhavati* etc. which contain at least three morphemes. A two-morpheme structure without any modifications in the root is naturally more easily analysable than a three-morphems structure with different modifications.

The result of this minimum nature of the past passive participial formations must have been that their grammatical description was comparatively easier for the grammrians. This ease-this absense of any complications in the grammatical description-is likely to give us a faithful picture of the fundamental principles and techniques, the basic approach, involved in describing a language. The importance of the comparative study of the grammatical description of the past passive participial formations in Sanskrit by the different grammarians is that it is the shortest and the easiest way to arrive at the important assumptions, principles and techniques of the respective grammarians.

4. Some Self-imposed Limitations.

4.1 It is impossible, within the compass of the present work, to examine all the *sūtras* of all the grammarians which describe the past passive participial formations in Sanskrit. In all they total up to 1500 and describe the past passive participial forms, with all their options, of all the 2000 or more verbal roots. Moreover, some rules require the knowledge of previous rules and techniques, which have no direct connection with the topic in hand of the description of the past passive participial formations. Such rules are, therefore, excluded from the present study.

All the rules which describe the past passive participial formations in Sanskrit can be divided under the following seven heads :

1. Rules laying down the substitution for the root-morphems.
2. Rules laying down the substitution for the suffix-morpheme.
3. Rules laying down *nipātana* for the whole usable form.
4. Rules bringing about phonological and / or morphonemic changes in the root-morphems.

5. Rules laying down the *iḍ-āgama.*
6. Rules dealing with the formations of the transformed verbal bases, and
7. Rules dealing with Vedic forms.

4.2 Out of these seven types of rules, the present study restricts itself only to those which describe the past passive participial formation by the technique of

1. *ādeśa,* 'substitution', both for the root-morpheme or what is called the *dhātvādeśa* or more generally *prakṛtyādeśa,* as well as for the suffix-morpheme or what is called the *pratyavādeśa,* and of
2. *nipātana.*

4.3 The reasons for excluding the other rules in the remaining five heads are as follows :

The rules governing the phonological and/ or morphophonemic changes in the root-morpheme are excluded from discussion because they are more or less of a general nature, applicable not only in the present case, but also in the case of formations other than those of the past passive participles. In other words, these rules are framed primarilly to account for other formations. They cover the past passive participles only secondarily and are so framed to cover them only for the sake of brevity; cf. for example the phenomenon of *saṁprasāraṇa; yaj* displays *saṁprasāraṇa* in the form *iṣṭa.* no doubt, but the Pāṇinian *sūtra,* stating this phenomenon. 6.1.15[1], also states it in circumstances other than those of the past passive participial formations. The inclusion of such rules here, therefore, would have meant studying and comparing practically the whole grammars, since no formation is accountable by a single rule but requires a chain of rules.

---

1. cf. Pāṇini, 6.1.15; *vacisvapiyajādīnām kiti;*
cf. the corresponding *sūtras* of other grammarians also.

It is for the same reason as that mentioned above that the consideration of the past passive participles from the transformed verbal bases like the causal, desiderative etc. is left out from the present study. Their consideration would virtually amount to reproducing and comparing the whole of the process of transformation. Besides there are double and multiple transformation like *jigamiṣayati*, a causal from the desiderative of *gam.*[1] Actually the process of verbal transformation could theoretically be extended *ad infinitum.* It is, therefore, impossible to deal with all such possibilities in the present study.

The rules dealing with the prescription or negation of *iḍ-āgama* are excluded from the present investigation because they are of little use in finding out the basic principles or grammatical description. Moreover, they involve no highly complicated technique of description.

The rules describing the past passive participial forms from the Veda are left out of consideration in the present study for the simple reason that no grammar except that of Pāṇini treats them. Such rules, therefore, do not offer any scope whatsoever for comparison and contrast.

4.4 Before proceeding to the actual presentation of the relevant material, its study and comparison, and drawing general conclusions therefore, it is necessary to clarify certain technical terms like niṣṭhā etc. employed by the grammarians.

5. The Niṣṭhā

5.1 The Definition

As regards the past passive participles in Sanskrit, the gramarians have nowhere defined them from the point of view of the function or syntax of the participles. As grammarians, they are all strictly formal, and the past passive

1. For such double or multiple transformations, cf. the chapter entitled *tiṅante pratyayamālā* in BD's *Siddhantakaumudī.*

participial fromation according to them all is that verbal or primary derivative (the *kṛd-anta* in Pāṇinian terminology) which ends in *-ta*. This suffix *-ta,* as also another suffix *-tavat* (which is applied in an active sense as against the passive sense of the suffix *-ta*), is technically called *'niṣṭhā'* by some of them. Thus we have a purely formal and technical definition of the past passive participial formations and not a functional or syntactical definition. This very well speaks of the scientific outlook and cautiousness on the part of the grammarians and their awareness of the many logical difficulties a functional or syntactical or any other non-formal definition of the past passive participles would encounter.

The *sūtras* of the different grammarians defining niṣṭhā are as follows :

P.1.1.26 :	*ktaktavatū niṣṭhā*
K.4.1.84 :	*ktaktavatū niṣṭhā*
C.1.2.67 :	*bhāvāpyayoḥ ktaḥ*
J.1.28 :	*ktaktavatū taḥ*
Ś.4.3.204 :	*ktaktavatū*
B.1.4.136 :	*bhāvakarmaṇoḥ ktaḥ*
H.5.1.174 :	*ktaktavatū*
S.8.2.13 :	*ktaktavatū*
V.1050 :	*ktaktavatū bhūte ḍhabhāve ghe*

We thus find that only P. and K. introduce one more technical level called *niṣṭhā;* all other grammarians only speak of the past passive participial suffix *kta* and *ta*. However, from among these latter, J. seems to follow P. and K. in introducing one more technical level. But the symbolic title of the level, as given by him, is *ta* which is different from the title *niṣṭhā* mentioned by P. and K. It may also be noted that on the technical plane all the grammarians have attached the *it-* sound *k* to the past passive participial suffix *-ta* which is available on the linguistic plane.

5.2 Different Levels

The different levels of this definition on the past passive participial suffix *-ta* may be indicated as follows :

1. The linguistic level : Since *-ta* is available in actual usage, we may call *-ta* as representing the linguistic level in the definition; cf. the past passive participial formation like *kṛta, bhūta* etc. in all of which *-ta* is to be found.
2. The technical level : Besides laying down *-ta* as the suffix, the grammarians, except J., have added one more sound viz. *k* to it; and on the second, that is technical level, we find the past passive participial suffix assumes the phonetic form as *-kta.* This sound *-k* is termed as *it* by all the grammarians[1] and becomes accordingly zero. This is purely an extra-linguistic or technical level since the *it* sound *k* in the suffix *-kta* is nowhere available in any past passive participial form used in the language.

This extra-linguistic or technical level serves the purpose of a bridge between the formal categories and the non-formal categories in the language. It is a sort of 'artificial formal plane' with the help of which the grammarians have tried to account for the non-formal categories or phenomena like meaning, accent, *guṇa, vṛddhi* etc. in the formation.[2] We will discuss the propriety of the *it-* sound *k* in the next section.

---

1. For *k* to be *it*, cf. the sūtra of the greammarians
   P. 1.2.2 : *upadeśe aj anunāsika* it and
   1.3.7 : *laśakv ataddhite*
   K. :-
   C :- 1.1.5 : *anaṁśocihnam it.*
   J. :- 1.2.3 : *Kāryārthoprayogīt.*
   Ś. :- 1.1.5 : *aprayogīt.*
   B. :- 1.1.6: *anaṁsacihnam it.*
   H. :- 1.1.37 : *aprayogīt.*
   S. :- 6.1.8 : *kāryāyet.*
   V. :- : *it kṛte*
2. For a detailed discussion of the *it*-forms in Pāṇini, cf. M.D. *Pandit,* 'Pāṇinian *It-saṁnjñā* - A Symbolic Zero', Silver Jubilee Volume, *BDCPRI,* 1965, pp. 76-94.

3. The symbolic level : On the symbolic level the past passive participial suffix *-ta* or *-kta* assumes the title *niṣṭhā* the sounds in which (vis. *n, i, ṣ, ṭ, h* and *ā*) having nothing in common with either *-ta*, a linguistic category found in the language i.e. in the stage of what the grammarians call as the *laukika vākya*, or *-kta*, an extra-linguistic, technical category, available only on the grammatical level i.e. in the stage of what the grammarians call as the *alaukika vākya*. Nor does the meaning of the word *niṣṭhā* convey anything about the passive nature in the past tense of the participial suffix *-ta*. Thus the title *niṣṭhā* is a purely symbolic name of the suffixes *-ta* and *-tavat*. It thus represents a purely symbolic level, corresponding to the mathematical symbols, *x, y, z*, etc. or signs like plus (+), minus (-), multiplication (x) or division (ĭ) etc.[1] The symbolic title given to the past passive participial suffix *-ta* by J. is *ta* itself, while P and K call it by the title *niṣṭhā*. The other grammarians have not introduced a symbolic level in this case.

The introduction by P.K. and J. of pure symbols for the regular grammatical or linguistic categories, not only in this case but in many other cases, only shows that their whole attempt of the description of the language aims at describing it on a symbolic plane, that is to say, with the help of a language which is not, and cannot be, used in everyday communication. And truly, the language, in which the grammar of language is to be written, should and must fundamentally be different from the language used by the people; if the grammar is written in the ordinary language, the ordinary words or symbols, used by the people, are likely

1. While studying the grammars, especially the older ones like that of Pāṇini, one always gets an impression that the grammarians had some mathematical model before them; for a discussion of this topic, cf. M.D. *Pandit*, 'Mathematical Representation of Some Pāṇinian Sūtras', *JUPH*, 23, 1965, pp. 139-152; also 'Pāṇini va Gaṇitaśāstra' (in Marathi), *Saṁsjṛti Sugandha*, 1970, pp. 51-66.

to create confusion and ambiguity in the scientific description and discussion. It is in order to avoid any ambiguity and confusion that a scientific grammarian like Pāṇini has introduced many purely arbitrary symbolic titles like *prātipadika, bha, ghi, ghu,* etc. These titles are never likely to be confused with any symbols in the ordinary language used by people. Actually, the very utterrance of these symbolic names gives the hearer an idea about that he is hearing something which is not available in the daily language.

Pāṇini has fully succeeded in creating a symbolic metalanguage in the sense that no symbolic title introduced by him conveys any meaning in the ordinary language. So also Kātantrakāra; J. symbol *ta* for the suffix *-ta,* corresponding to P.'s and K.'s *niṣṭhā,* sounds from this point of view a little bit confusing, because *ta* as symbolic title is likely to be confused with *-ta* as past passive participial suffix.

This awareness on the part of P. and others of creating a purely symbolic metalanguage, which is totally different from the ordinary language, is definitely a long step and shows a tremendous advance in the desciptive technique in times as early as Pāṇini's.

5.3 The Propriety of the It-Sound k

According to the grammarians' definition of the *it,* the *it*-sounds in general and the *it*-sound *k* in particular have a specific function to perform.

As has been observed earlier, the verbal bases do not show a tendency to *guṇa* or *vṛddhi* in forming their past passive participial formation; they are all at their weak grades before the past passive participial suffix *-ta* or its alternants like *-na, -va, -ma, -ka* etc. The *it*-sound *k* in *-kta* is utilised by the grammarians for denoting this absence of *guṇa* or *vṛddhi* in the verbal bases. To put it in the form of a technical rule, we can say, the verbal base does not get either the *guṇa* or *vṛddhi* grade before a *kit*-suffix.

The *it k* in the suffix *-kta*, therefore, serves as a symbol of the absence or stoppage of any process like *guṇa* or *vṛddhi* in the verbal base just as a red signal stops the flow of traffic.

The sūtras of the grammarians, which prohibit the operation of *guṇa* and *vṛddhi* in the case of the *it*-sound *k* are as follows:-

P.1.1.5: *gkṅiti ca*
K. It has not used any *it-* sound
C.6.2.11: *kṅiti*
J.1.1.19: *gkṅiti*
Ś. It has not used any *it-* sound
B.6.2.11: *kṅiti*
H. It has not used any *it-* sound
S.7.4.65: *kṅity adyusi*

It will be seen from the above that most ot the grammarians follow Pāṇini's technique of inserting an *it*-sound *k* in the suffix and depriving it of the power of bringing about *guṇa* or *vṛddhi* in the verbal stem.

5.4 The Ktānta-Formations-Primary Derivatives

All those formations which are derived by applying the suffix *-ta* are primary derivatives, directly to be deduced from the verbal bases or *dhātus*. It is specifically laid down by every grammarian that the suffix *-ta* is directly applied to the verbal roots; of. the following *sūtras:*

P.3.1.91: *dhātoḥ*

K.4.2.1: *dhātoḥ*

C. does not define the term *dhātu*, because his is an *asaṁjñaka vyākaraṇa* (= a grammar without any *saṁjñā)*, term *dhātu* is indirectly or implicitly defined in his *sūtra*, 1.1.40: *ekāco halādeḥ krīyārthād bhṛśbhīkṣye yeṅ*, in which the word *kriyārtha* is identical in connotation with the Pāṇinian term *dhātu*. This word *kriyārthād* (abl.sg.) is to be understood in the case of applying the suffix *-ta* also; cf. the commentary on the C.*sūtra*, 1.2.67 (*bhāvāpyayoḥ ktaḥ*, quoted before):

'...*kriyārthāt kto bhavati,*' which borrows the word *kriyārthāt* (=verbal root) from the previous *sūtra*, 1.1.40, quoted above.

J.2.1.19: *dhor yaṅ kriyāsamabhihāre;* the sense of *dhoḥ*, abl. sg. of *dhu* (=pāṇinian *dhātu*) is to be enlarged to include the past passive participial suffix *-kta* also.

Ś.4.1.6: *dhātoḥ kaṇḍvāder yak,*which starts the *anuvṛtti* of the word *dhātoḥ* for all the *kṛt-* suffixes including the present *-kta*.

B. has not framed any saṁjñā for dhātu.

H. follows Ś.; cf. his *sūtra*, 3.4.8: *dhātoḥ kaṇḍvāder yak;* the word *dhātoḥ* is to be borrowed for all the *kṛt*-suffixes which start from the *sūtra*, 5.1.1: *ā tumo'tyādiḥ kṛt,* and include the present suffix *-ta*.

S. 8.1.1: *dhātoḥ,* where *dhu=pāṇinian* dhātu. V. follows J. in this respect.

While P., K., S. and V. frame independent *sūtras*, comprising only the word *dhātoḥ*, or *dhoḥ*, for laying down the rule that the *kṛt-* suffixes are to be directly applied to the verbal bases, others include the parallel word in bigger *sūtras*. The practice of P., K., S. and V. brings out more prominently the *adhikāra-* character of the *sūtra* than that of the others.

5.5 The Meaning of -kta

As we shall see later in greater detail,[1] every suffix or termination (the *pratyayas* and the *vibhakti pratyayas*)in P.'s grammar and consequently in all the post-Pāṇinian grammars, which have been taken here for study, is infused with a definite meaning. The practice of infusing a suffix with definite meaning is in sharp contrast with that of the pre-Pāṇinian[2] works. Yāska's cf. etymology in which the

1. cf. the last chapter.
2. Some are inclined, on the basis of evidence, to put Yāska after Pāṇini; cf. M.A. *Mehendale, Some Aspects of Indo-Aryan Linguistics,* University of Bombay, 1968 (Wilson Phil. Lectures, 1964), Ch. I, pp. 1-14. In any case, the contrast between the two descriptive techniques., namely,

termination or suffix is devoid of any meaning whatsoever.[1] The result is that while the entmological explanation given by Yāska look mechanical, without any life and substance, the derivations by the grammarians appear lively, animated and natural. Accordingly, the past passive participial suffix *-ta* is also invested with a definite meaning. The meaning that is laid down to signify is of two types: first, the meaning of the past tense and secondly, the meaning of the voice. In the second type of meaning there are three divisions corresponding to the three voices in Sanskrit : the passive sense, the active sense and the bhāve sense.

5.5.1 The Meaning of the Tense

The *sūtras* of the different grammarians which lay down the suffix *-ta* in the definite meaning of the past are:-

P.3.2.102: *niṣṭhā*, which comes under the *adhikāra, bhūte,* 3.2.84; the latter *sūtra* lays down that the *pratyayas* laid down hereafter upto the *sūtra,* 3.2.123, *vartamāne laṭ,* signify the sense of the past tense; cf. *kāśikā* on the *Pāṇinian sūtra,* 3.2.84: *bhūta ity adhikāro vartamāne laṭ iti yāvat/ yad ita ūrdhvam anukramiṣyāmo bhūta ity eva tad veditavyam//*

K.4.3.93: *niṣṭhā*, which comes under the *adhikāra, 'atīte'* (In the sense of 'what has gone'); the word *atīte* appears in the *sūtra,* 4.3.81: *karane' tīte yajaḥ.*

C.1.2.62: *bhūte.*

J.2.2.72: *bhūte.*

Ś. : The *adhikāra, bhūte,* starts from the *sūtra, vyabher bhuvo bhūte,* 4.3.186.

B.1.4.114: *bhūte*

H. : The *adhikāra, bhūte,* starts from the *sūtra,* 5.1.158: *karaṇād yajo bhūte.*

---

of Yāska on the one hand and of the grammarians beginning from Pāṇini on the other, does remain.

1. For a detailed comparison, cf. *M.D. Pandit*, 'Some Linguistic Principles in Pāṇini's Grammar', II. 23, pp. 50-70.

S. : The *adhikāra, atīte* (=bhūte) starts from the *sūtra*, 8.2.11: *ṇinir atīte*.

V. lays down this past tense in the same *sūtra* in which he lays down the suffix *-ta;* cf. 1050: *ktaktavatū bhūte ḍhabhāve ghe.*

Besides their sense of 'past', some participial formations with *-ta* signify under certain conditions the sense of 'present' also. These are also worth investigating. But since the scope of the paper is limited to a consideration of the past, passive participles only, those signifying the sense of 'present' are excluded.

5.5.2 The Meaning of Passive

As stated above, the voice-meanings that the suffix *-ta* is laid down as signifying are three (a) *bhāve,* (b) *karmaṇi* and (c) *kartari.* While the first meaning is signified in the case of roots which are intransitive,[1] the second meaning viz. *karmaṇi* is available in the case of transitive roots. The third meaning viz. *kartari* is found in the case of only some roots and under certain conditions. Since the scope of the thesis is to examine the treatment of only the passive participle in the past tense, the formations in the first and third meanings are left out of consideration.

The *sūtras* of the different grammarians which explicitly lay down the 'passive' meaning for the suffix *-ta* are as follows:—

P.3.4.70= *tayor eva kṛtyaktakhalarthāḥ,* in which the word *tayoḥ* refers to the meanings of *bhāva* and *karma* stated *cākarmakebhyaḥ.*

K. : 4.3.8 noted above

C. : 1.2.67, *bhāvāpyayoḥ ktaḥ,* in which the word *āpya* means '*karma*' (i.e. object); āpya is equivalent in meaning to *vyāpya;*

1. cf. *Kāśikā* on the Pāṇinian *sūtra,* 3.4.69 (*laḥ karmaṇi ca bhāve cākarmakebhyaḥ*) : *akarmakebhyo dhātubhyo bhāve bhavanti.*

cf. the *Candra-sūtra,* 2.1.43 *kriyāpye dvitīyā,* the commentary on which renders the word *āpya* in the *sūtra* with *vyāpya;* cf. wording of the *Candrarṛtti* on 2.1.43: *kriyāyā vyāpyā dvitīyā vibhaktir bhavati.*

J. : 2.4.55, *tayor vyaktakhārthaḥ,* in which the word *tayoḥ,* gen. du., refers to the two meanings of *bhāva* and *karma,* specified in the previous *sūtra* (2.4.54), *laḥ karmaṇi ca bhāve ca dheḥ.*

B. : 1.4.136 *bhāvakarmaṇoḥ ktaḥ.*

Ś. : no specific sūtra.

H. : 5.1.158, quoted above.

S. : 8.3.15: *bhāvakāryayoḥ ktaḥ.*

V. 1050: *ktaktavatū bhūte ḍhabhāve ghe,* in which the technical term *ḍha* (defined by V. in the sūtra, 281: *karma.... ḍham)* means 'object' and is equivalent to Pāṇini's *karman.*

5.5.3 Other Meanings

Besides the above two meanings, with which we are concerned in the present work, viz. of the past tense and of the passive, the verbal derivative formations in *-ta,* and consequently the suffix *-ta,* display other meanings also in the language. They are all noted down by the grammarians. Since all such formations also end in *-ta,* to which technically the term *niṣṭhā* (of Pāṇini and Kātantra) or *ta* of Jainendra can be applied, we simply note the other meanings of *-ta* also here, though the formations in *-ta* giving out all these meanings. (except the above two viz. past and passive) and the *sūtras* laying down or accounting for such formation, are excluded because, functionally or syntactically, they are not past passive participles although formally they end in the suffix *-ta.*

5.5.3.1 In the Sense of Present Tense

Certain formations in *-ta* give out the sense of the present tense also. Such formations are, to quote some examples, *minna, iṣṭa* etc. Kāśikā quotes a *Kārika*[1] which lists some of such examples:

śīlito rakṣitaḥ kṣāntaḥ
ākṛṣṭo juṣṭa ity api
ruṣṭaś ca ruṣitaś cobhāv
abhivyāhṛta ity api !! 1!!

hṛṣṭatuṣṭau tathā kāntas
tathobhau saṁyatodyatau!
kaṣṭaṁ bhaviṣyatīty āhur
amṛtaḥ pūrvavat smṛtaḥ !! 2!!

5.5.3.2 *In the Sense of Active Voice*

There are certain *ktānta* formations like *gata* etc. which are used in the active sense. These are generally from the roots like √*gam*, √*car* etc. which mean '*gati* ' or movement, going, etc.

5.5.3.3 *In the Sense of Adhikaraṇa*

We also meet with usages like *idam eṣāṁ yātam* (= this is the going of these people), *idam eṣām bhuktam* (= this is the eating or enjoyment of these people) etc. in which the *-tānta* forms have completely dissociated themselves from the passive or active, present or past meaning and have assumed a new function of a pure *prātipadika* devoid of any participial function. Pāṇini and all other grammarians have technically called this function as of '*adhikaraṇa*'.

Basides the above three non-passive, non-past meanings, the *Kāśika* in the *kārikā* quoted above notes a participle viz. *kaṣṭa* from √*kaṣ* or √*kaś* 'to destroy', 'to get tired' (cf. Pāṇinian *dhp. kaṣa ..... hiṁsārthāḥ*) which is used in language in the future sense also; cf. the remark in the Kāśikā on the Pāṇinian *sūtra* 3.2.188: *kaṣṭa iti bhaviṣyati kāle.*

All grammarians have described these formations also after defining their grammatical circumstances. But since

1. On the Pāṇinian *sūtra*, 3.2.188 (*matibuddhipūjārthebhyaśca).*

these formations are not past passive participles in the strict sense of the term, they are excluded from the present study. Also, the formations in these senses occur in a syntactical relation which is different from those which are strictly past passive participles.

6. The Syntactical Relation of *-ta*

The formations in *-ta,* which strictly convey the meaning of 'past' and 'passive', have definite syntactical relation (called *kāraka* in the terminology of the Sanskrit grammarians) in terms of the declensional suffixes (technically called the *sup*-terminations in Pāṇini's grammar) of the word which is the agent *(kartā)* of the action signified by the root in the formation. It is thus that the past passive participial formation in *-ta* is connected with the agent in an instrumental case (*tṛtīyā*). For instance, we find that *hata,* a past passive participle from √*han* 'to kill', is connected with *rāma,* agent, in the instrumental case; and we have usage *rāmeṇa hataḥ*.

All grammarians have explicitly noted this peculiar syntactical relation of the past passive participial formations with their agents. The *sūtras* are:

2.3.18 : *kartṛkaraṇayos tṛtīyā.* (P)

2.4.19 : *śeṣāḥ karmakaraṇasaṁpradānāpādānasvāmyādyadhi karaṇeṣu.* (K)

2.1.62 : *kartari tṛtīyā.* (C)

3.1.215 : *kartṛkaraṇayoś ca.* (J)

1.4.29 : *kartṛkaraṇe bhā,* where the term *bhā* is equivalent to Pāṇini's *tṛtīyā;* it is defined in 1.2.158. (B)

H.2.2.44 : *hetukartṛkaraṇetthaṁbhūtalakṣaṇe.*

Ś. follows Hemacandra in wording and defining the syntax;

cf. his *sūtra, hetukartṛkaraṇetthaṁbhūtalakṣaṇe,* 1.3.128.

S. 5.3.1: *kartṛkaraṇayos tṛtīyā.*

V. 288 : *sādhanahetuviśeṣaṇabhedaṁ ḍham kartā gha strī,* where *gha,* a technical term defined in the same *sūtra,* is the *kartā* or agent.

So one can see that the syntactical relation of a past passive participle, when it functions as a substitute for a verbal formation, is well defined by all the grammarians. The syntactic relation of these forms with the agents in the instrumental case is discussed here because, as we shall see in the sequel the functional aspect of these forms also is taken into consideration by the grammarians. This is clear from the fact thet even such forms as *pakva, kṣāma, śuṣka* etc. which do not end in *-ta* are taken as past passive participles by them.

7. The Accent of Formations in *-ta*

Fortunately the Vedic language has faithfully presever the original Indo-European accent in the case of formations in *-ta* in particular. The suffix *-ta* (accented) seems to have been accented right from the Indo-European period.[1] Any formation in *-ta,* not compounded with any other formation, is an oxytone with the suffix *ta* accented as *udātta.* Thus we have the formula, *R + ta = R-ta = R-tá* where *R* stands for root.

Pāṇini, who is the only grammarian who has accounted for the Vedic formations and accent has noted down the accent of the formations in *-ta* in the *sūtras, pratyayaḥ,* 3.1.1 and *ādyudāttaś ca,* 3.1.3; these *sūtras* supercede the rule *dhātoḥ,* 6.1.162, which lays down the accent on the root. Thus we get the past passive participal formations accented on the suffix *-tá.* For instance, we have the formations like *hatá,* RV. 1.182.4 etc., all accented on the last syllable i.e. the *a* of the suffix *-ta.*

1. cf. *J. Wackernagel, Alt-Indische Grammatik* Band Ii, 2, 432-434, pp. 576-582; cf. also *Carl D. Buck, Comparative Grammar of Greek and Latin,* pp. 306-309; cf. also *Karl Brugmann, Kurze Vergleichende Grammatik der Indogermanischen Sprachen,* Strassburg, 1903, Zweite Lieferung, pp. 317-318.

The compounds with past passive participial formations, however, display different accents. But this feature falls outside the scope of the present work.

In the post-Vedic language and literature, the accent seems to have dwindled in its importance while the accent in the classical period has not come down to us. We find that the rhetoricians have actually made it a rule that accent should not be necessary or should not be counted in poetry; cf. Mammaṭa in his *Kāvyaprakāśa*, 2nd chapter, verse 19: *indraśatrur ityādau veda eva na kāvye svaro viśeṣapratiītikṛt;* cf. also Viśvanātha in his *Sāhityadarpaṇa*, 2nd chapter verse 14: *svaras tu veda eva viśeṣapratītikṛn na kāvye, iti tasya viṣayo nodāhṛtaḥ;.....kāvyamārge svaro na gaṇyate, iti ca nayaḥ.*

8. The *-ta* in Greek and Latin

As the past passive participial suffix *-ta* is also found in other Indo-European languages, especially Greek and Latin, it would be interesting to consider briefly the form and function it assumes in them. Besides the Avestan language, Greek and Latin are the two Indo-European languages which are very close to Sanskrit in almost all repects.

8.1 *-ta* in Greek. The Sanskrit *-ta* is represented by *-to* in Greek (the Sanskrit *a* changing to *o*) ; it is accented and performes the function of verbal adjective and not necessarily of a participle. It is applied directly to the root which keeps its weak grade. As in Sanskrit, so also in Greek, it is a primary derivative like *klutó* (Sk. *śrutás), statós* (Sk. *sthitás)* all in just adjectival sense like 'hearing (man)', 'standing' etc. But there are others which signify either a passive sense, as in *graptó* 'written', or an active sense as in *rutós* 'flowing', or may imply a possibility as in *oratós* 'to be seen, visible' etc. The Greek participial *-tó* as signifying different active and passive senses, therefore, is well comparable to the *-tá* in Sanskrit.[1]

8.2 *-ta* in Latin:- The Sanskrit *-ta* is represented by *-tu* in

1. For details, cf. *C.B.Buck, op. cit.*, pp. 307-308.

Latin. Unlike in Sanskrit and Greek, the suffix in Latin is unaccented. Actually, the Latin language has not preserved any original accents. The Latin *-tu* performs the function of a participle, but with a difference. In some cases, the *-tu* suggests the function of the perfect passive participle. In such cases, however, the root does not exhibit the reduplication and change from weak to strong (esp. *guṇa)* grade. Thus we have the forms *status* (Sk. *sthitás), dictus* (Sk. *diṣṭás), inclutus* (Sk. *śrutás)* without *guṇa* or strong grade of the root-vowels. Though in such cases the *-tu* conveys the sense of perfect passive participle, there is complete absence of reduplication. These are thus formed from the verbal roots directly and are primary derivatives.

There are, however, other formations which display the strong grade of the root and hence which are formations from perfect i.e. reduplicated bases, with the reduplication amounting to zero.[1] This phenomenon is found in froms like *pōtus* 'having drunk', *scrīptus, fīsus, lēctus* etc. in which the lengthening of the vowels leads us to presume a perfect base with the loss of the reduplication. In majority of such formationsa in Latin, the meaning conveyed by the suffix is of passive, though formations like *pōtus* signify an active sense also. To quote from L.R.Palmer,[2] "Nor again does this verbal adjective originally refer to past events. Present reference is frequent with such participles from deponent verbs .... So it was that the perfect participle came to be used mainly of events taking place before that denoted by the main verb ..... Certain examples have an ambiguous temporal reference owing to the nature of the verbal action."

All these participial suffixes, viz. the Sanskrit past passive participial *-tá,* the Greek verbal adjectival *-tó* and the Latin

---

1. For the two types of perfect viz. reduplicated and non-duplicated, cf. *C. D. Buck, op. cit.,* pp. 291-293; cf. also, *L. R. Palmer, The Latin Language,* pp. 272-276.
2. cf. *L. R. Palmer, op. cit.,* p. 327.

perfect passive participial *-tu* go back to an Indo-European verbal adjective formed from the root with *-to*.

The fore-going discussion will make it clear that the variations of the tense and voice displayed by the Sanskrit past passive participial *-ta* have inherited the legacy from the old Indo-European stage and is not a phenomenon displayed in Sanskrit only.

2

Morphemic Substitution for The Base-Morpheme or Verbal Root, i.e. *Dhātvādeśa*

The Technique of Ādeśa or Substitution

1. Ādeśa as Opposed to Guṇa, Vṛddhi etc.

We shall begin our comparative study of the description of the past passive participial formations in the different Sanskrit grammars with the consideration of the technique of *ādeśa* or substitution employed by them to account for the changes which the verbal root or the participial termination *-ta* undergo in giving out their respective past passive participial formations. As is well-known, the technique of *ādeśa* was one of the most widely used techniques of grammatical description in ancient India. It was usually adopted when the form could not be accounted for by any other grammatical techniques like *guṇa, vṛddhi* etc. and when the adoption of procedures of *guṇa, vṛddhi* etc. led to cumbersome and lengthy description. It is true that the techniques like *guṇa* (i.e. *i* > *e*, *u* > *o*) or *vṛddhi* (i.e.*i* >*ai*, *u* > *au*) are basically of the nature of *ādeśa* itself, sinc the *guṇa*- or *vṛddhi*- grades are substituted in the place of the respective original sounds. Even the zero of a sound or morpheme is an *ādeśa;* cf *kāśikā* on the Pāṇinian *sūtra*, 1.1.58: *upadhālopasya sthanivattvāt. cf.* Patañjali: *lopaḥ api ādeśaḥ*, Mahābhāṣya on the *Sūtra*, 1.1.61 Yet, the technique of *ādeśa* is taken out here for a separate and independent study because of the following reasons:—

The *ādeśa*-technique that is here taken out for study refers to the morphemic substitution, that is to say, to a situation where a whole morpheme is substituted for another morpheme.[1] For example, if the morpheme *bhū* is substituted in the place of √*as* (to account for the formation of *bhūta*), it is a morphemic substitution. Such substitution is different from the substitution of, say, *e* for *i* (in the case of *guṇa)* or *ai* for *i* (in the case of *vṛddhi*) and certainly attains the status of an independent technique. As compared to this technique of morphemic substitution, the technique of *guṇa* and *vṛddhi* do not strike as being very important. The main reason why morphemic substitution is adopted in such cases is that the change, so brought about, cannot be accounted for on phonological level. Thus, the main difference between the two techniques of *ādeśa*, viz. *guṇa*, *vṛddhi* on the one hand and morphemic substitution on the other, lies not only in the fact that the one viz. the latter i.e. morphemic substitution is an extended form of the former i.e. the *guṇa* and *vṛddhi*, but chiefly involves the question of the levels of description on which the formation is sought to be described. While the adoption of morphemic substitution means that the description is laid down on morphological level, the adoption of *guṇa*, *vṛddhi* technique indicates that the description is on phonological level.

Secondly the rules of morphemic substitution are not general; they are particular in the sense that only a particular morpheme is substituted in the place of another particular morpheme. As opposed to this, the phenomena of *guṇa* and *vṛddhi* operate in a far wider field. Rules of a very general nature, covering a large number of instances, cases and conditions, can accordingly be laid down for *guṇa* and *vṛddhi*.

The chief characteristic of *ādeśa or* substitution is that it

1. For a defintion of morpheme, cf. *E.A. Nida*, *Morphology*, (2nd edition), The University of Michigan Press, 1963, p. 6; also L. *Bloomfield*, *Language*, 1933, p. 34.

totally dislodges the original morpheme or the phoneme, (called technically *sthānin)* and establishes as 'śatru' ('enemy') as opposed to the technique of *āgama* which is characterised as *'mitra'* ('friend") because it does not totally dislodge the original element but adjusts itself keeping the original element in tact. That is why it is often said, *ādeśaḥ śatruvat pravartate, āgamo mitravat.*

2. Definition

It is very difficult to define the term *ādeśa*. Pāṇini, in his famous rule, *sthānivad ādeśo 'nalvidhau,* 1.1.56, empowers the substitute to behave fully like the original i.e. *sthānin.* Patañjali, on the Pāṇinian *sūtra,* 1.1.56 defines it in the most general way as 'that which is prescribed for substitution'; cf. Patañjali on Pāṇini 1.1.56: *pacatu pacantu ime' pyādeśāḥ/ katham? ādiśyate yaḥ sa ādeśaḥ / ime cāpyādiśyante /;* cf. also his remark on the Pāṇinian *sūtra,* 1.1.20: *anāgamakānām sāgamakāḥ ādeśāḥ.*

This definition of ādeśa by Patañjali is similar to that of the commentator on *Tait. Prātiśākhya,* 2.20: *ādeśaḥ upadeśaḥ. RV. Prātiśākhya.* I.30.32 also seems to express the same view; cf. *yo'yaṁ svarādeśaḥ, antodāttam vadher ādyudāttatvam svaḥ svaritam ity ādeśaḥ.* But, as can be seen from different grammars, *ādeśa* seems to be different from 'that which is prescribed' (*upadiṣṭa*); it has a definite value and has grown into an independent and very important technique of grammatical description; and in this form it ceases to be mere 'that which is prescribed'.[1]

As to when this technique of *ādeśa* was first employed by the grammarians in linguistic description, it is very difficult to determine. Patañjali on his part ascribes the authorship and use of this technique to Pāṇini as his remark

---

1. cf. *L. Renou, Terminologie Grammaticale du Sanskrit* Paris, p. 84; cf. also *K. V. Abhyankar, A Dictionary of Sanskrit Grammar,* Gaekwad's Oriental Series, No. 134, Baroda, 1961, p. 54.

on the Pāṇinian *sūtra,* 1.1.20, shows: *sarve sarvapadādeśāḥ dākṣīputrasya pāṇineḥ*. But here the word *ādeśa* seems to have been used in the general sense of 'that which is prescribed', i.e. in the sense of *upadeśa* and not in the sense of *ādeśa* as 'the technique of substitution'.

3. Comparison With Mathematical Substitution

One is tempted at this stage to compare this technique of substitution viz. *ādeśa* in grammar with that used in mathematics. What the mathematicians do in certain circumstances is that if the sum given is very big but can be suitably adjusted by substituting suitable simple letters, the letters replace the sum. An example will make it clear. Suppose the following expression is given:-

$$(a+b+c+d)^2 + 2(a+b+c+d)\ (a+b+c+d)\ (a-b-c-d) + (a-b-c-d)^2.$$

It is very difficult, cumbersome and lengthy in such cases to find out the square of the big brackets. Some simple letters, say, x and y, are, therefore, substituted for (a+b+c+d) and (a-b-c-d) respectively. After substituting the letters x and y for the respective brackets, the whole expression, therefore, boils down to the following simple form:

$$x^2 + 2xy + y^2$$

Now, in this simple form, the expression can be easily comprehended as the square of the sum (x+y). Hence, we write

$$x^2 + 2xy + y^2 = (x+y)^2$$

The letters x and y are again substituted by their originals, viz. (a+b+c+d) and (a-b-c-d) and we get,

$= (a+b+c+d + a-b-c-d)^2$

$= (2a)^2$

$= 4a^2$, which is the answer.

Now, compare with this the situation in grammar. Let us take the example of *bhū* substituted for √*as*. We have,

as + ta
= bhū + ta
= bhūta, which is the answer.

A comparison of the two will reveal the following characteristics and differences:—

Just as the device of substitution in mathematics is adopted only for the sake of convenience and to avoid cumbersome and lengthy multiplications and divisions, it serves the same purpose in grammar also. Yet, there is something more in this device in grammar. While the substituting letters (x and y in the present case) are again substituted by the originals (*sthāṇin)* in mathematics, it is not so in grammar. An *ādeśa* is never substituted by the *sthānin* after serving the purpose. The purpose of substitution in mathematics is just convenience, while the purpose in grammar is to arrive at correct results found in spoken language. To clarify, *bhū,* which is substituted for *as,* is not again substituted by *as,* since the from *asta* is not available; only *bhūta* is available. In the mathematical expression, on the other hand, the result arrived at after substituting x and y, viz. $(x + y)^2$ is not the correct answer since the original does not contain x and y at all. Hence it requires the double substitution, or to be correct, both the procedures of substi tution and resubstitution. It is not so in grammar since the device of substitution is meant not only as device or an intermediary, artificial stage, but as a necessary, decisive stage to give out a result which must tally with the usage in language. Again, while the substituted symbols (x and y in the above case) in mathematics are purely arbitrary (one can easily put p and q or m and n for them respectively), the substituted morpheme in grammar is not arbitrary but real, available in the language. Thus, *as* can only be substituted by *bhū* alone and not by any other arbitrary morpheme. No doubt, a developed stage, while it is not so developed in grammar. Yet, stripped of all its complicated circumstances and employment in mathematics, the mathematical device of substitution resembles in principle fully with that used by the ancient Indian grammarians. We do not know whether Pāṇini and other grammarians knew mathematics; yet whatever devices Pāṇini has used in his grammar for describing the Sanskrit language resemble more or less basically with those used in mathematics. In this sense it can be said that the technique of *ādeśa* seems to have been borrowed by Pāṇini from mathematics. Or, it can be the other way also. We do not know for certain who borrowed from whom. Yet the similarity between the two is striking enough.[1]

4. Types of Ādeśa

There are two types of ādeśa in grammar: (i) the *ādeśa* or substitution of a sound for another sound, as in the case of *guṇa, vṛddhi* etc. in which the *i* or *u* are substituted by *e, ai* or *o, au* respectively. We can term this type of *ādeśa* as one on phonological level. (ii) The other type is on morphological level; that is to say, one in which a whole, completely new, morpheme is substituted for the original, whole morpheme. This is the case in situations like the substitution of the morpheme for the original, whole morpheme *bhū* or *jagdh* for √*as* or √*ad* respectively in forms *bhūta* and *jagdha.*

The second type, viz. the *ādeśa* on morphological level also gives us two more divisions, according as the substitution is laid down for (i) the base-morpheme i.e. the *prakṛti.* which is the *dhātu* or verbal root in the present case of past passive participial formations, and (ii) for the suffix or termination i.e. the *pratyaya,* which refers to the past passive participial termination viz. *-ta* in the present case. This division of the *ādeśa* implies that a usable form in

1. For a discussion and example of whether Pāṇini knew mathematics or not, cf. *M.D. Pandit*, 'Mathematical Representation.....' *JUPH.* 23, 1960, pp. 139-152. *cf.* also 'Zero in Pāṇini', CASS, Pune, 1990; also, 'Mathematics As Known To The Vedic Saṁhitās', Indian Books Centre, Delhi, 1993.

Sanskrit is divided into two, a *prakṛti* or base and a *pratyaya*, a termination, by the Sanskrit grammarians.

These two types of *ādeśa* can be grouped under one, common heading of 'morpheme-substitutes' as opposed to mere 'phoneme-substitutes' (*varṇādeśa*), which will be discussed later.

In the case of each of the divisions of 'morpheme-substitutes' we have to think of two classes: (i) one, in which the substitution takes place under certain semantic conditions and (ii) the other, in which no such semantic conditions are involved.

Table No. 1 on page 34 will give a complete idea of the different divisions or types of *ādeśa:*

5. Examples from the Grammar

We shall begin our discussion with the examples of *ādeśas*, substituted in the place of the verbal roots or *prakṛti* without any semantic, phonological or morphological conditions. We begin with Pāṇini.

(1) There is first of all the Pāṇinian *sūtra, sphāyaḥ sphī niṣṭhāyām*, 6.1.22, which lays down the morpheme *sphī* in the place of the root-morpheme *sphāy*, 'to grow', increase, swell' etc. (designated by Pāṇini technically as *sphāyī*, i.e. *īdit;* cf. Pāṇinian Dh.P *sphāyī opyāyī vṛddhau)*. Thus in the analytical stage, we get,

sphāy + *ta* (= *kta*, *k* as *it*, denoting no *guṇa* or *vṛddhi*)

= *sphī* + *ta* (*sphāy* > *sphī;* cf. P.6.1.22)

= *sphīta*.

The grammars of Kālantra, Candra, Jainendra, Bhoja, Hemacandra, and Sārasvata all follow Pāṇini in describing this from with the help of the ādeśa-technique.[1] Out of these

1. The respective *sūtras* of the different grammarians are : Kā. *sphāyas sphī*, 4.1.42; Candra : *sphāyah sphīh*, 5.1.32; Jainendra, *sphāyaḥ sphīte*, 4.3.17; Bhoja : *sphāyaḥ sphīḥ*, 6.1.37; Hemacandra : *sphāyaḥ sphī vā*, 4.1.92; Sārasvata : *sphāyaḥ sphīḥ*, 7.4.91.

Table No. 1

ādeśa (substitution)

- On morphological level
  - Substitution for the base or prakṛti
    - Under Semantic conditions
    - Not Under Semantic conditions
  - Substitution for the termination or pratyaya
    - Under semantic conditions
    - Not Under semantic conditions
- On phonological level
  - Under semantic conditions
  - Not Under Semantic conditions

Hemacandra gives an option for the substitute *sphī* for *sphāy*, which only speaks for the currency of the optional form *sphāta* (when *sphī* is not substituted for *sphāy)* in Hemacandra's times. So also, though the wording of the Candra *sūtra sphāyaḥ sphīḥ*, 5.1.32 dose not indicate any option, the *vṛtti* on the *sūtra* lays down the option in substitution; cf. the *vṛtti* on the C. *sūtra*, 5.1.32: *sphāyaḥ tatavatoḥ sphībhāvo bhavati vā/ sphītaḥ sphītavān/ sphātam iti vyavasthitavibhāṣayā niyataviṣaye prayogaḥ/* This option for the substitution can only be explained if we apply the principle of *anuvṛtti*, by which we may borrow the word *vā* (meaning 'optionally') from the previous *sūtra, vābhyavayāt,* 5.1.31.

Similarly Bhoja's rule does not contain the option; cf his *sūtra, sphāyaḥ sphīh*, 6.1.37; yet *Hṛdayahāriṇī*, the commentary on Bhoja's grammar, understands the option, most probably on the basis of the *anuvṛtti* of *vā* from the previous rule *vābhyavābhyām*, 6.1.36.

Kātantra also implies that the substitution is optional, as is clear from his technical reconstruction of the root *sphāy* as *sphāyi*, the final short *i*, which is *it*, suggesting that any substitute for *sphāy* is to be taken as *anitya*, i.e. not compulsory, cf. the *vṛtti* on the Kā. *sūtra*, 4.1.42: *sphāyīti / idanuvbandha balād ādeśo 'yam anitya iti /sphātaḥ, sphātavān /*

This leads us to the conclusion that, in Pāṇini's times, only one form was current, viz. *sphīta*, whereas the post Pāṇinian period saw the emergence of two forms *sphīta* and *sphāta*, which were optionally used.[1] The Caitr., a comentary on the Kātantra, also gives the example, *sphātīkṛtāni vimalayaśāṁsi* (source not traceable) to show that the substitute is optional.[2]

1. Another Ms. of Kātantra vṛtti, which J. Eggeling marks as B, gives the past passive participial form of √*sphāy* as *sphita* i.e. with short *i*. This short *i* goes well with the phonological substitution adopted by Śākaṭāyana (see the discussion above further) for treating the form. It, however, is not consistent with the wording of Kātantra which clearly states the long *ī*.
2. cf. J. *Eggeling's* edition of Kātantra, Notes, p. 540.

Jaumāra's remark on 3.505, viz. *sphātās taṇḍulāh iti sphātir ity asya matvarthīyāt pratyayena,*[1] does not show his inclination towards the option definitely. Actually the option should well have been supported by Jaumāra who came later than C. and B.,[2] for the use of the optional form *sphāta* had become current already in the times of C. and B. In this case, Jaumāra clearly seems to follow Pāṇini in making the substitute compulsory.[3] We must, however, leave this dicussion here since the purpose of the present thesis is surely not to study historically the availability or otherwise of a form in the language, but to examine the descriptive techniques of the different grammarians.

One thing, howerver, is clear from the above discussion, namely that, all the grammars, with the exception of that of Śākaṭāyana explain the from *sphīta* with the technique of morphemic substitution or *prakṛtyādeśa;* in other words they treat the phenomenon on morpholgical plane. Śākaṭāyana on the other hand describes the form on phonological level. What he does is that he substitutes long *ī* for the sound group *āy* in *sphāy.* So we get (*sphāy* + *ta* =) *sphīta* as the desired from; cf. his *sūtra, sphāyaḥ,* 4.1.129; for the lengthening of the substituted short *ī*, cf. his *sūtra,* 4.1.135. It is to be remebered here that the long *ī* which he substitutes is a substitute for the sounds *ā* and *y* both and not only for the sound *y;* hence it is not the Pāṇinian *saṁprasāraṇa;* cf. the *vṛtti* by Cintāmaṇi on the Ś. *sutra,* 4.1.129: *sphāyāiṅ ity asya dhātoḥ ktayoḥ sācaḥ pūrveṇācā yañaḥ ig bhavati;* the *anuvṛtti* of *yañaḥ ig* and *sācaḥ* is implied by the *sūtra,* 4.1.108: *ig yañaś sācor yyājyam,* which runs up to the *sūtra,* 4.1.135, thus covering in all 28 *sūtras.* The *sūtra,* 4.1.108, may, therefore, be designated as the *adhikāra-sūtra* of Śākaṭāyana.[4] It is to be noted here that the

1. cf. *S. K. Belvalkar, ibid.,* pp. 108-110.
2. cf. *S. K. Belvalkar, ibid.,* p. 109.
3. cf. also *K. C. Chatterjee, Cāndravyākaraṇa of Candragomin,* part II, p. 131, notes on the *sūtra,* 5.1.32.
4. *anuvṛtti* is one of many grammatical principles which resemble with the mathematical principle of taking out the highest common factor;

substitution of long *ī* for *āy* is not optional according ot Śākaṭāyana; and in that respect he follows Pāṇini.

Not only in the case which has been treated so far, but also in the case of many other roots like √*pyai*, √*styai* etc. Śākaṭāyana invariably adopts, as we shall presently see, this method of phonological substitution.

(2) The second form which Pāṇini explains with the help of the ādeśa- technique is *pīna* from √*pyāy* (Pāṇinian *opyāyī*). The *sūtra* is *pyāyaḥ pī*, 6.1.28, which optionally[1] substitutes the morpheme *pī* for the verbal base *pyāy*. Thus,

pyāy + *ta*

= *pī* + *ta*

= *pī* +*na* (*ta* > *na* according to the *sūtra*, *oditaś* ca, 8.2.45)

= *pīna.*

Without the substitute *pī*, the form is *pyāna.*

The grammars of Candra, Jainendra, and Sārasvata follow Pāṇini in every detail. They treat the form on the level of pure morphemic substitution. And all of them describe the form on purely formal level, without bringing in any other non-formal considerations such as meaning etc. cf. Cāndra: *pyāyaḥ pīḥ*, 5.1.34; Jainendra: *pyāyaḥ pī*, 4.3.23; Sārasvata: *pyāyaḥ pī*, 7.4.90: It is to be noted that according to Candra, Jainendra, and Sārasvata the substitute is compulsory and not optional, which fact explains the use of the form *pīna* alone in their times.

The grammars of Bhoja and Hemacandra on the other hand lay down by way of a condition for substitution of *pī* for *pyāy* that the verbal root √*pyāy* should be without any

---

for a discussion, cf. *M. D. Pandit*, 'Mathematical Representation of Some Pāṇinian *Sūtras*', JUPH, No. 23, 1996, pp. 147-151. *cf.* also, 'Zero in Pāṇini', ch. on *avavṛtti*-zero, CASS, Pune, 1990.

1. cf. BD on the *sūtra*, 6.1.28: *vā syān niṣṭhāyām*; cf. also Kāśikā... *dhātor niṣṭhāyām vibhāṣā pītyam ādeśo bhavati.* The option is carried here from the *sūtra*, 6.1.26: *vibhāsābhyavapūrvasya.*

upasarga as far as its past passive participial form is concerned; for Hamacandra, the root √*pyāy* can be substituted by *pī* without any condition in the case of its perfect and frequentative forms; for Bhoja, *upasarga* is not adimssible; cf. Hemacandra: *pyāyaḥ pīḥ* 4.1.91 and *ktayor anupasargasya*, 4.1.92; Bhoja: *pyāyaḥ pīr anupasargasya*, 6.1.40.

The Kātantra grammar lays down a semantic condition for the substitute *pī* for *pyāy*. The condition is that the substitution takes place only if the meaning '*svāṅga*' (= 'one's own i.e. human body') is intended; cf. the *sūtra*, *pyāyaḥ pī svāṅge*, 4.1.43 and the *vṛtti* thereon: *svam aṅgam svāṅgam / svāṅge vartamānasya pyāyater dhātor niṣṭhāyāṁ ca pīr bhavati*. Thus according to the Kātantra view, the use *pīnaṁ mukham* is fully permissible if the word *mukha* refers to 'the mouth' of a *human being*. As opposed to this, in cases like *mukham śālāyāḥ* (= 'front part of the school') where *mukha* refers not to 'the mouth' of a human being, but implies secondarily by *lakṣaṇā* 'the front part', the form noted by Kātantra is *pyāna;* thus *pyānaṁ devadattasya*.

It may thus be pointed out that in the case of past passive participle of √*pyāy*, Kātantra found it necessary to acount for the form only by a reference to its semantic circumstances, which only gives us a picture of the form in Kātantra's times.[1] The *vṛtti* further quotes the usages *pyānaḥ svedaḥ*, *pyānā buddhiḥ*, thus emphasising the point that semantic circumstances govern the formation of the past passive particles.

It seems that, though only the form *pīna* was current in Pāṇini's times, it gradually came to be alternated with the form *pyāna* after his times. This is clear from the fact that,

1. A collection of such forms which are accounted for differently by different grammarians deserves to be historically studied. Such a study would help us to have a general idea about the change - semantic, phonological, morphological, or syntactic - which the language has undergone.

besides the evidence of Kātantra, Bhaṭṭojī also finds it necessary to add the remark that since the option for the substitution given by Pāṇini is well-defined (*vyavasthita vibhāṣā*), it can give out the form *pīna* only when the meaning of *svāṅga* is intended; cf. BD on the Pāṇinian *sūtra*, 6.1.28: *vyavasthitavibhāṣeyam / tena svāṅge nityam pīnaṁ mukham*. Yet, unlike Kātantra, Pāṇini's *vyavasthita vibhāṣā* will give two equally optional forms viz. *pyāna* and *pīna* if the meaning of *svāṅga* is not intended; cf. again BD on Pāṇini 6.1.28: *anyatra pyānaḥ pīnaḥ svedaḥ*.

So far as the condition of 'being accompanied by *upasarga*' is concerned (which is the condition for the substitution of *pyāy* by *pī* according to Hemacandra and Bhoja), Bhaṭṭoji remarks that the substitute *pī* occurs only when the root is not accompanied by any *upasarga*; cf. BD on 6.1.28: *sopasargasya na*. This remark, especially when the Pāṇinian *sūtra* does not provide for any such conditions, semantic or morphological, clearly speaks for the weight of the usage of the form in the circumstances defined by grammarians other than Pāṇini, like Hemacandra, Bhoja and Śākaṭāyana.

As in the case of the previous form *sphīta* from √*sphyāy*, in the present case also, Śākaṭāyana follows the method of substitution on phonological, and not on morphobgical, level. According to him, the vowel *ā* together with the final *y* of the root *pyāy* is changed to *ī* (which is then lengthened according to *dīrgho'co'vaḥ*, 4.1.135); cf. his *sūtra, ktayor anupasargasya*, 4.1.127. He also follows Hemacandra and Bhoja in laying down the condition for substitution that the form should be without an *upasarga*; cf. the word *anupasargasya* in his *sūtra*.

The semantic condition of the primary meaning of *svāṅga*, explicitly laid down by Kātantra and implicitly interpreted by BD., is, however, notably absent in Śākaṭāyana's description. Thus like Pāṇini, Śākaṭāyana seems to follow a purely formal explanation of the form as far as possible.

A small point in connection with the past passive participial form with *upasarga* and the meaning of *svāṅga* needs to be noted here.

All grammars except those of Pāṇini, Kātantra and Sārasvata, incorporate one more rule in regard to √*pyāy*, namely that, when preceded by the *upasarga ā* (i.e. *āṅ*), the root gets the substitute of *pī* in the case of the words *andhu* and *ūdhas*, even if they do not refer to human body, and are accompanied by an *upasarga ā*. Thus we get the form *āpīna* as qualifying *andhu* and *ūdhas.*

cf. Candra: *āṅo'ndhūdhasoḥ,* 5.1.35; Śākaṭāyana: *āṅo'ndhūdhasoḥ,* 4.1.128; Bhoja: *āṅo'ndhūdhasoḥ,* 6.1.41: Hemacandra: *āṅo'ndhūdhasoḥ,* 4.1.93. Jainendra frames two *sūtras* for this purpose; cf. *āṅaḥ,* 4.3.24 and *andhūdhasoḥ,* 4.3.25.

Pāṇini, however, is corrected by Kātyāyana in this respect; cf. the latter's *vārttika* on the Pāṇinian *sūtra,* 6.1.28: *āṅpūrvasyāndhūdhasoḥ,* though it is to be noted that he has not corrected Pāṇini so far as the condition of *anupasargatva* is concerned, which condition is made clear by Bhaṭṭoji by the remark *sopasargasya na* and by the example *pyāy* equally optional in any circumstances in Pāṇini's times; and the different restrictions put on that substitution came only after him, presumably from Kātyāyana's times onwards.

(3) The next formation in question is *hlanna,* past passive participle from theroot √*hlād* (Pāṇinian *hlādī).* In the *sūtra, hlādo niṣṭhāyām,* 6.4.95. Pāṇini lays down that the long *ā* in *hlā-* is shortened to *-a,* thus the whole morpheme *hlād* is changed to *hlad* before past passive participial termination *ta* (which also changes to *-na* according to Pāṇinian *sūtra, radābhyāṁ niṣṭhāto naḥ pūrvasya ca daḥ,* 8.2.42); and the form is *hlanna.* The process is simple and the form is accounted for by Pāṇini on the phonological, and not morphological level. Some other grammarians, however, have treated the form on the level of morphemic substitution. It is very surprising in this connection that, besides Kātantra,

Jainendra, and Sārasvata, Śākaṭāyana, who has treated the previous two forms on phonological level against Pāṇini's morphological plane, also follows Pāṇini in this case; cf. the respective *sūtras: Kātantra: hlādo hrasvaḥ,* 4.1.18. The Sārasvata grammar has no *sūtra* for this purpose and the shortening is laid down by a *vārttika* type statement viz. *niṣṭāyāṁ hrasvo vācyaḥ* pertaining to the root √*hlād āhlādane.*

The mode of statement of Jainendra and Śākaṭāyana, though both of them follow Pāṇini, is a little bit different. Jainendra is more careful and definite in that he specifically lays down the penultimate position of the vowel *ā.* cf. the Jainendra *sūtra, hlādas te,* 4.4.89, which has the *anuvṛtti* of the words *uṅ* (= penultimate sound) from the *sūtra, goher uṅaḥ,* 4.487.[1]

Similarly, though Śākaṭāyana means shortening and treats the form on phonological level, his wording of the *sūtra* is different from that of Pāṇini as well as Jainendra. What he does is that, instead of laying down the shortening of *ā* into *a,* he enjoins *a-kāra* for the penultimate sound *ā* of √*hlād.* Though this *at-karaṇa* in effect is the shortening of *ā* into *a,* from purely technical point of view it is a phonological substitution of *a* for *ā.* This method of description brings into foreground an important difference between Śākaṭāyana on the one hand and Pāṇini and Jainendra on the other, namely, that while for Śākaṭāyana the substitution means the substitution of a sound for another sound, for Pāṇini and Jainendra it is the substitution of the short or *hrasva* grade of

1. The technical terminology of the Jainendra *vyākaraṇa* is peculiar, and differs from that of Pāṇini and others. The penultimate sound, which is termed by Pāṇini and others as *upadhā* or *upāntya,* is termed as *uṅ* (cf. the Jainendra *sūtra, upāntyāl uṅ,* 1.1.66) and the short grade which is termed as *hrasva* by other is termed as *pra* (cf. the Jainendra *sūtra, ākālo'c pra-dī-paḥ,* 1.1.11 in which *pra* = *hrasva* or short, *dī* = *dīrgha* or long and *pa* = *pluta* or prolated); cf. the *Mahāvṛtti,* commentary on Jainendra's grammar, on the Jainendra *sūtra,* 4.4.89: *hlādas te parata uṅaḥ pro bhavati.*

a sound for its long or *dīrgha* grade. In other words, while Śākaṭāyana describes the form on purely phonological level, without bringing in the phonetic characteristics of the sound in question, Pāṇini and Jainendra bring in the phonetic characteristics of the sound. Thus to be exact one can say that while Śākaṭāyana's description is purely on phonological or even phonemic level, Pāṇini and Jainendra describes the form on phonetic level. And this point raises an important question whether phonetic studies can be brought in into the field of grammar.

As is clear, grammar restricts its scope only to morphophonemics, morphology, and syntax.[1] Patañjali clearly states that the science of grammar represents a stage later than phonetics and phonemic.[2] It seems that for Pāṇini and jainendra there is no harm if a form can be more briefly explained by resorting to its phonetic characteristics. Though, therefore, the scope of grammar is different from that of phonetics, phonetic considerations cannot be totally avoided in grammar; nay, they are sometimes useful for a briefer description of a language. Śākaṭāyana, however, nowhere seems to have subscribed to this view at least so far as the description of past passive participles is concerned. Otherwise, if he had so intended, he could have easily framed the *sūtra, hlādo hrasvaḥ ktiḥ,* in the place of *hlādaḥ aḥ ktiḥ,* 4.1.244, which is its present reading. The term *hrasva* is not unknown to Śākaṭāyana (cf. his many *sūtras* like, *hrasvaḥ,* 2.2.79; *hrasvasya halaḥ,* 4.2.18; *hrasve,* 3.4.99 etc. in which he uses the term *hrasva),* though unlike Pāṇini and others, he has nowhere defined it. This lends further support to the above reasoning that the resort to *at-karaṇa,* instead of to *hrasvīkaraṇa,* by Śākaṭāyana is a purposeful attempt not to describe the form on phonetic level and to adhere strictly to the boundaries of grammatical studies.

---

1. cf. *G. Trager, Studies in Linguistics,* 1958.
2. cf. Patañjali on the Pāṇinian *sūtra,* 1.2.32 *(=tasyādita udāttam ardhahrasvam): vyākaraṇaṁ nāmeyam uttarā vidyā / so'sau chandaḥśāstreṣv abhivinīta upalabdhā'dhigantum utsahate//*

It is to be noted here that the substitution of *a* for *ā* is on phonological and not morphological level.

The *anuvṛtti* of the words 'penultimate vowel' in the *sūtra,* 4.1.244 is taken from a previous *sūtra,* 4.1.202.

The next grammar which follows Pāṇini in substituting a short grade for a long grade is Sārasvata which only makes a *vārttika*-type statement under the root √*hlād;* cf. Sārasvata: *niṣṭhāyāṁ hrasvo vācyaḥ,* which does not specify the root, the place or even the sound in which the shortening is to be brought about. This speaks for the looseness of the *sūtras* and the technique, both aximoatic as well as descriptive.

The other line of linguistic description of the past passive participial form of √*hlād* is provided by the grammars of Candra, Bhoja and Hemacandra. All the three grammars account for the form *hlanna* on the level of morphemic substitution of *hlad* for *hlād*. The relevant *sūtras* are: Candra: *hlādo hlad,* 6.3.92; Bhoja: *hlādeḥ hlat ktinniṣṭhayoḥ,* 7.1.83 and Hemacandra: *hlādo hlat kyayoś ca,* 4.2.67.

Though Pāṇini does not lay down any condition as to whether the root is accompanied by any *upasarga* or not while giving out its past passive participial form, BD. gives the example of *prahlannaḥ,* which shows that the root √*hlād* gives out the form *hlanna* in anycircumstances irrespective of the accompaniment of any *upasarga*. The commentaries on Kātantra, Jainendra, and Candra also cite the example of only *hlannaḥ,* without an *upasarga,* given by Śākaṭāyana, Sārasvata, and Hemacandra, however, do not make the point clear. Can we assume that by citing only *hlanna,* they implicitly suggest that, with an *upasarga,* √*hlād,* gives out a different form? Actually we have no evidence either for or against such supposition. And the matter has to be left at that.

We have three ways of describing the form: (1) substitution of a grade for another grade, followed by Pāṇini, Kātantra, Jainendra and Sārasvata; this may be called description on phonetic level. (2) Substitution of a sound for another sound, followed by Śākaṭāyana alone; this may be called substitution on phonological level; and (3) substitution of a morpheme for another morpheme, followed by Candra, Bhoja and Hemacandra; this may be termed substitution on morphological plane.

(4) The next form to be considered is *hita*, the past passive participle from √*dhā* 'to hold, to bear', etc. (3rd conj. *Ubhayapadin*).

According to the Pāṇinian *sūtra*, *dadhāter hiḥ*, 7.4.42, the root morpheme *dhā* is substituted by the morpheme *hi* before the past passive participial termination *-ta*. Thus we have,

dhā + ta
= *hi + ta*
= *hita*

It is to be noted that in the matter of explaining the past passvie participial form of √*dhā*, all grammarians, surprisingly enough, agree with, and follow the method of description of, Pāṇini. All have treated it on the level of morphemic substitution; cf. the different *sūtras:*

Kātantra: *dadhāter hiḥ*, 4.1.78.

Candra: *dhāño hiḥ*, 6.2.94.

Jainendra: *dhāño hi*, 5.2.146.

Śākaṭāyana: *dhāño hiḥ*, 4.2.116.

Bhoja: *dadhāter hiḥ*, 7.2.94.

Hemacandra: *dhāgaḥ*, 4.4.15, the *anuvṛtti* of *hi* being followed from the previous *sūtra*, 4.4.14, *hāko hiḥ ktvi*, which lays down the substitute *hī* for √*hā* 'to abandon' thus giving out the form *hīna*.

Sārasvata: *dadhāter hir niṣṭhāyām*, 7.4.92.

(5) Another case in which all grammarians except one have adopted the same method of explanation pertains to the forms hīna (from √*hā* 'to abandon'), pīta (from √*pā* 'to drink') and *gīta* (from √*gai*)

Pāṇini in the *sūtra, ghumāsthāgāpājahātisām hali,* 6.4.66 lays down that the *ā* of the roots √*hā*, √*pā* and √*gā* (< √*gai*) is substituted by long *ī* before the *kit-terminations.* And we have the forms *hīna* (*ta* > *na* according to Pāṇini *oditaś ca.* 8.2.45) *pīta* and *gīta.*

In this case also, Śākaṭāyana, who usually adopts a method different from pāṇini's, follows Pāṇini by adopting the method of phonological substitution. All except Sārasvata follow Pāṇini. The *sūtras* are:

Kātantra: *dāmāgāyatipibatisthāsyatijahātīnām īkāro vyañjānādau,* 3.4.29

Jainendra: *īd ye,* 4.4.64 and *bhumāsthāgāpāhāksām hali,* 4.4.65.

Śākaṭāyana: *ghumāsthāgāpāhāksaḥ,* 4.2.86 and *ī haly apye,* 4.2.87.

Candra: *īd yati,* 5.3.76 and *māsthāsāgāpiba hāgdādhāṁ hali,* 5.3.77.

Bhoja: *īd yati,* 6.3.75 and *māsthāsāgāpibahāgdādhāṁ hali,* 6.3.76.

Hemacandra: *gāpāsthāsādāmāhākaḥ,* 4.3.96 and *īvyañjane'yapi,* 4.3.95

Only Sārasvata strikes a different note by adopting the method of morphemic substitution, but it gives out a totally different form viz. *hita* from √*hā* to abandon', against the one used in the language, viz. *hīna;* cf. the Sārasvata *sūtra, jahāteś ca kiti;* the *vṛtti* on the *sūtra* explains it as: *jahāter dhātoḥ kiti pratyaye pare hirādeśaḥ syāt / tena pūrvaṁ hitvā / hīyate smāsau hitaḥ / ahāsīt iti hitavān.*

Thus according to the Sārasvata grammar, the form *hita* can be derived both from √*dhā* as well as √*hā,* while according to others, *hita* is the past passive prticiple from √*dhā* alone. Does it mean that *hita* was used as the past passive participle of √*hā* in Sārasvata's times? But no usage in Sanskrit language up-to-the-present day supports such a conclusion, the past passive participle from √*hā* being *hīna* only. The *sūtra* is, therefore, either a clear mistake on the part of the author of Sārasvata grammar or is an interpolation added by others afterwards. The latter conclusion is supported by the fact that the *sūtra* has no number at all in terms of *adhyāya*, *pāda* and *sūtra*. It, therefore, seems possible that taking advantage of the looseness in arrangement of the *sūtras*, somebody has added it afterwards. The interpolation is, of course, for the sake of proving that the Sārasvata grammar is also as comprehensive as other grammars.

Another explanation is also possible. The *sūtra* in question is perhaps framed in order to account for the gerundive form in *tvā* of the root √*hā*, the form given out being *hitvā*, which is the form used in language and accounted for by other grammarians also. This is supported by the fact that the wording of the *sūtra* closely follows that of the corresponding *sūtras* by other grammarians; cf. the *sūtras*:

Pāṇini:	*jahāteś ca ktvi*, 7.2.43.
Kātantra:	*ij jahāteḥ ktvi*,
Jainendra:	*hākaḥ ktvi*, 5.2.147.
Śākaṭāyana:	*hākas tvi*, 4.2.117.
Candra:	*hākas tvi*, 6.2.95.
Bhoja:	*jahāteḥ ktvi*, 7.2.95.
Hemacandra:	*hāko hiḥ ktvi*, 4.4.14.

The similarity between the wording of Sārasvata and other *sūtras* is so apparent that it needs no comment. It is because of this similarity that one feels inclined to think that the Sārasvata *sūtra*, *jahāteḥ kiti* was primarily intended to explain the gerundive form in *tvā*, viz. *hitvā* from √*hā*. But soon the looseness of sūtra-arrangement led its supporters and commentators to believe that it also explained the past passive participle from √*hā*. The *sūtra* from this point of view came to be read in a wrong context and was consequently misinterpreted.

On the other hand, we do not get any *sūtra,* which enjoins the form *hīna.* Indeed, we are constrained to say that the past passive participle from √*hā* remains unnoticed or unexplained in the Sārasvata grammar. Secondly, the forms *pīta* and *gīta* also remain unaccounted for in the school.

(6) The next form to be discussed is the past passive participle of √*dā;* two morphemic substitutes are laid down: (a) substitute before the past passive participial termination, and (b) substitute for the root accompanied by *upasargas* which end in vowels.

In the first case, the root-morpheme *dā* is substituted by the morpheme *dat* or *dath* and in the second case it is replaced by the simple sound *t.* Though the substitute *t* in the second case is a simple sound, it is treated here as morpheme because it is substituted in the place of a morpheme viz. √*dā* and from the point of view of morphological analysis, the value and status of *t* is on par with that of the morpheme *dā.* The following discussion and examples will make the point clear.

(a) *Dat* or *Dath* Substitued for *dā*

The Pāṇinian *sūtra* is *do dad ghoḥ,* 7.4.46, which lays down that the root √*dā,* which is technically termed as *ghu,*[1] get the *ādeśa dath*[2] before the past passive participial termination. So

1. For the definition of the Pāṇinian technical term *ghu,* cf. Pāṇinian *sūtra, dādhā ghu adāp,* 1.1.20, which excludes the roots √*dāp* and √*daip* from the province of *ghu.* For a general historical information on the term, cf. *K. C. Chatterji, Technical Terms and Technique of Sanskrit Grammar,* Calcutta, 1948, pp. 49-51.

2. That it is *dath* and not *dat* or *dad* or *dadh* is discussed in the *Tattvabodhinī* on BD's *SK,* though BD. accepts all the possibilities; cf. BD's remark on the *sūtra,* 7.4.46: *tānto vā'yam ādeśaḥ---dāntovā dhānto vā/* (see p. 35)

   BD refutes all the objections and difficulties that would arise if the substitute for *dā* is taken to be any other than *dath* i.e. *thānta* 'ending in *th*'; cf.BD on the *sūtra,* 7.4.46. Kāśikā quotes a *kārikā* which sums

we have *datta* (*dā + ta = dath + ta = dat + ta = datta; th > t according to the Pāṇinian sūtra, khari ca,* 8.4.55) as the past passive participle of √*dā,* which is termed as *ghu* according to the Pāṇinian *sūtra,* 1.1.20.

The purpose of the technical term *ghu* is to exclude the other roots which are homophonous with √*dā* but which do not give out the past passive participle *datta.*[1] Such roots are technically reconstructed by Pāṇini differently. They are two: √*dāp* 'to purify' (2nd Conj; cf. Pāṇinian Dh P. : *daip śodhane).* Here then we have the clue to decide whether or not the form *datta* is from √*dā* 'to give' or from √*dā* 'to cut'.

It is to be noted that in the case of the descriptive technique of the past passive participle of √*dā,* all have agreed with Pāṇini and adopted the method of substitution on morphemic level; cf. the different *sūtras.* Kātantra: *dad do' dhah,* 4.1.80; Jainendra: *do dad bhoḥ,* 5.2.148; Śākaṭāyana: *ghor daḥ,* 4.2.112; Candra: *do dat,* 6.2.96; Bhoja: *do dat,* 7.2.96; Hemacandra: *dat,* 4.4.10 and Sārasvata: *do datti,* 8.4.33.

(b) Substitution of *t* for *ā* for √*dā*

The condition for this supstitution is that the root must be preceded by an *upasarga* which ends in a vowel and must be followed by the past passive participial termination *-ta.*

---

up all the objections that would be taken against accepting the *ādeśas, dat, dad* and *dadh* as againt *dath;* cf. the *kārikā:*
tānte doṣo dīrghatvaṁ syāt,
dānte doṣo niṣṭhānatvam
dhānte doṣo dhatvaprāptiḥ,
thānte adoṣas tasmāt thāntam//

1. The other grammars also have adopted the same technique for excluding the roots which do not give out the form *datta,* though their technical terms are different. They are : Kātantra : *dā* (cf. *adāp dādhau dā,* 3.1.8); Jainendra: *bhu* (cf. *dādhā bhvapi,* 1.1.27); Candra : *dā* (cf. *do'paḥ,* 1.1.4); Śākaṭāyana : *ghu* (cf. *dādhā ghvap,* 1.1.23); Bhoja : *dā* (cf. *do'paḥ,* 1.1.5); Hemacandra : *dā* (*avau dādhau dā,* 3.3.5); Sārasvata : *dā* (cf. *dā dhā ghvap,* 1.1.23); Mughdhabodha : *dā* (cf. *dā dhā dā,* 537); Saupadam : *ghu* (cf. *dā dhā ghu ap,* 1.1.23).

Here again we meet with two types: (1) √*dā* with *upasargas* which end only in any vowel and (2) √*ḍā upasargas* which end only in *iganta*[1] vowels i.e. *i, u, ṛ* and i.

(1) √*dā* with *Upasargas* Ending in any Vowel

In this case also all the grammars follow Pāṇini in treating the forms on *ādeśa* level. The Pāṇinian *sūtra* is, *aca upasargāt taḥ,* 7.4.47, which states that the final vowel of √*dā,* as satisfying the criterion of being *ghu,* is substituted by *t* before a *kit* suffix beginning with *ta.* And we have

pra + dā + ta

= *pra + d.t +* ta

= *pra + t.t + ta* (*d > t* according to 8.4.55)

= *prattam.*

The corresponding *sūtras* of other grammarians are:

Kātantra: *svarāntād upasargāt taḥ,* 4.1.81.

Jainendra: *ges*[2] *to'caḥ,* 5.2.149.

Śākaṭāyana: *śto'ca upasargāt,* 4.2.113.

Candra: *prāder acas taḥ,* 6.2.97.

Bhoja: *upasargād acas taḥ,* 7.2.97

Hemacandra: *svarād upasargād das ti kityadḥaḥ,* 4.4.9.

Sārasvata: *svarātto vā,* 8.4.34.

The forms of √*dā* with the vowel-ending *upasargas,* which these *sūtras* aim at accounting for, are *pratta, avatta, apatta,* etc. The forms with consonant-ending *upasargas* like *nir, dur*

1. *ik* is the *pratyāhāra* representing the vowels *i, u, ṛ* and *ḷ* in Pāṇini's grammar; for the formation of *pratyāhāra,* cf. the Pāṇinian *sūtra, ādir antyena sahetā,* 1.1.71; for a possible mathematical principle underlying the *sūtra,* 1.1.71. cf. *M. D. Pandit,* 'Mathematical Representation of Some Pāṇinian *Sūtras*', JUPH, Vol. 23, 1966, pp. 139-142.

2. *gī* is the technical name given by Jainendra to what are known as *upasargas* in grammars of Pāṇini and others; cf. the Jainendra *sūtra, kriyāyoge gi,* 1.2.130, which defines *gi.*

etc. will be according to the *sūtras, do dat ghoḥ* (Pāṇini, 7.4.46) etc. discussed previously; thus we have *nirdatta, durdatta, saṁdatta* etc.

In the language, however, forms like *avadatta, vidatta, pradatta* etc. are also found (cf. the stanzas quoted by Patañjali, Kāśikā and BD: *avadattaṁ vidattaṁ ca pradattaṁ cādikarmaṇi / sudattam anudattaṁ ca nidattam api ceṣyate//* Kāśikā explains these forms in two ways: (i) that they are to be regarded as *nipātanas,* not accountable by the Pāṇinian *sūtras* or (ii) that the morphemes *ava, vi, anu* etc., which are there, do not function as *upasargas* at all, but that they function as regular words; cf. Kāśikā on the *sūtra,* 7.4.46. aca *upasargātta iti prāpte nipātyante/ anupasargā vā ete avādayaḥ kriyāntaraviṣayā veditavyāḥ* // BD. only remarks *caśabdād yathāprāptam,* which clearly shows his submission to the linguistic usage which cannot be accunted for by Pāṇini's rules. Jainendra also resorts to this explanation only; cf. the *Mahāvṛtti* on the Jainendra *sūtra,* 5.2.149: *avādīnāṁ gamyamāna kriyāntaraviṣayatve ca dadātiṁ praty agittvāt siddham/ ..... avahīnaṁ avagataṁ vā dattam avadattam iti kriyāntaraviṣayatvaṁ yojyam //*

Tattvabodhinī, a commentary on BD's *SK* explains the meaning of *pradatta* as: *dātuṁ prakrāntam ārabdham ityasyaivārthaḥ/* which means that by resorting to the sense of *ādikarma* (=beginning of the work), these forms could be explained. In doing so, it perhaps has in view either the Pāṇinian *sūtra, ādikarmaṇi ktaḥ kartari ca,* 3.4.71 or the *vārttika, ādikarmaṇi niṣṭhā vaktavyā,* on the Pāṇinian *sūtra,* 1.2.19. But this sense can obviously be signified by only the form *pradatta,* as the author of *Tattvabodhinī* himself is aware (cf. his remark: *ādikarmaṇi ity etat pradattam ity asyaiva viśeṣaṇam netareṣām. asaṁbhavāt/).* The other forms still remain unexplained. They can only be explained as *prādisamāsas* as the commentary on Jainendra (cf. the *vṛtti* on Jainendra 5.2.149 quoted above) or on Kātantra would like to explain (cf. the *vṛtti* on Kātantra, 4.1.81: *ādikarmaṇi prādisamāso nipātā vā*); so also the *vṛtti* on Candra, 6.2.97 (cf. *dattaśabdena prādisamāso bhaviṣyati*).

Śākaṭāyana has surmounted the difficulty of explaining these forms by framing two separate *sūtras*. The *sūtra, prād dāñas ta vāraṁbhe*, 4.2.114 lays down the option for substitution of *dā* by *t* when the sense of *āraṁbha* is present, while the *sūtra, nivisvanvavāt*, 4.2.115, lays down the option for substitution of *dā* by *t* without reference to the meaning.

Bhoja follows Śākaṭāyana in this respect. While he lays down only the optional substitution for *dā* with *upasargas, su, vi, ni, ava* and *anu* (cf. the *sūtra, suvinyavānubhyaḥ kta vā*, 7.2.98), he makes the semantic condition of *ādikarma* essential for optional substitution of *dā* with the *upasarga pra* (cf. the *sūtra, prād ādikarmaṇi*, 7.2.99). It is notable that he has improved upon both Pāṇini and Candra whom he follows in linguistic description and descriptive technique respectively.

Hemacandra also adopts the same technique as that of Bhoja and Śākaṭāyana. He resorts to the meaning of *ārambha* for the optional substitution of *dā* by *t*; cf. his *sūtra, prād dāgastta ārambhe kte*, 4.4.7. In the case of √*dā* with *upasargas, ni, vi, su, anu* and *ava*, however, no such semantic condition is laid down by him; cf. *nivisvanvavāt*, 4.4.8; cf. the *vṛtti* on the *sūtra*, 4.4.7: *ārambhārthasya prapūtvasya dāgaḥ..... ta vā syāt/* , while it does not mention the meaning in the explanation of the sūtra, 4.4.8; cf. *ebhyaḥ parasya dāgaḥ kte tto vā syāt*.

The Sārasvata grammar, on the other hand, without entering into any controversy of the above type, lays down straightaway the option for substitution, without referring to meaning or *upasargas*: cf. the Sārasvata *sūtra; svarātto vā*, 8.4.34.

One may suggest an alternative way of describing this form. Instead of substituting *t* or *tt* (as Hemacandra does), for the whole morpheme *dā* or for the final sound *ā*, as all grammarians have done, if only the final *ā* would have been elided, the same result could have been achieved; thus,

pra + *dā* + *ta*
= *pra* + *d* + *ta* (ā = o)
= *pra* + *t* + *ta* (*d* > *t*, according to 8.4.55, khari ca)
= *pratta*

Similarly in all other forms like *avatta, apatta,* etc. But it should be remembered here that Pāṇini and all other grammarians are not following the structural method of description in the case of the past passive participles.

At least Pāṇini, who follows a structural way of description,[1] was expected to follow this method of *lopa,* which would have brought greater brevity in description. That even Pāṇini, apart from all others, did not follow this method of zero of *ā* in *dā* shows that they have not analysed the past passive participial forms in the structural way. Instead of starting with the usable form, they started with given hypothetical root-norms and terminations and tried to account for the formation and the necessary morphophonemic changes in the process. They have taken the roots and terminations, arrived at after analysis, and juxtaposed them and explained the usable form with the help of morphophnemic rules and semantic condition. The method of description in the case of the past passive participial forms is in sharp contrast with that of description of the conjugated forms of roots and declined forms of many nouns. This is further supported by the fact that not only in the case of the forms *pratta, avatta,* etc; but, in general, in the case of all the past passive participial forms, nowhere do we find the

1. For the structural approach of linguistic description by Pāṇini, cf. *M. D. Pandit,* 'Zero in Pāṇini', JMSUBH, Vol. XI, No. 1, 1962, pp. 53-66; also, CASS. Pune, 1990 cf. also *M. D. Pandit,* 'Some Linguistic Principles in Pāṇini's Grammar', *Indian LInguistics,* Deccan College, Vol. 24, 1963, pp. 56-61.

important technical device of *lopa* or zero used. Zero, it should be noted, can only come when the approach to linguistic analysis and description is structural.[1] That all the grammarians do not follow the structural way of analysis and description in the case of the past passive participles will be clear when we come to study the insertion of *āgamas* like *iṭ* etc. below.

(2) √*dā* with *Upasargas* Ending in only the Vowels *i, u, r, i,* (i.e. *iganta* vowels)

The root √*dā,* when accompanied by *upasargas* ending in vowels *i, u, ṛ* and *i* however, gives out a different past passive participial formation. The characteristic feature of this formation is that though the final *ā* of *dā* is substituted by *t* (as Pāṇini would describe it) or though the whole root-morpheme *dā* is substituted by *t,* the final vowel of the preceding *upasargas* is lengthened.

Thus, for example,

ni + dā + ta
= ni + d.t. + ta
= ni + t.t + ta
= ni + tt + ta
= nītta.

So also with *upasargas* ending in *u* like *anu, su* etc. since there is no *upasarga* ending in the vowels *ṛ* and *i* the only examples available are of *upasargas* ending in *i* and *u.*

The Pāṇinian *sūtra,* which notes this phenomenon, is *dasti,* 6.3.124.

The corresponding *sūtras* of other grammarians are:

Jainendra: *dasti,* 4.3.225.

Candra: *dasti,* 5.2.143

---

1. cf.f *W. S. Allen,* 'Zero and Pāṇini' IL, 16, 1955, pp. 106-113; cf. also *W. Hass,* 'Zero in Linguistic Description', *Studies in Linguistic Analysis,* Special Volume of the Philological Society, Oxford, 1957, pp. 33-53.

Bhoja: *dasti*, 6.2.181.

Hemacandra: *dasti*, 3.2.88.

Sārasvata: It has no independent *sūtra;* the lengthening in brought about by a *vārttika*-type statement on the *sūtra*, 8.4.34. (*svarātto vā*); cf. *nāmyantopasargasya bhavati.*

Śākaṭāyana: *kāśattīkaḥ*, 2.2.89.

The Kātantra grammar, however, has no such *sūtra*, which lengthens the final vowel of *iganta upasargas.* The *vṛtti* by Durgasiṁha on Kātantra, 4.1.81, perhaps cites the Pāṇinian sūtra, *dasti* 6.3.124 when it says: *dasti kvacin nāmino hrasvasya dīrghatā.* But another manuscript of the *Vṛtti*, which J. Eggeling designates as A has the reading *asti* in the place of *dasti*, which seems to be original since it completes the sentence of the *vṛtti* quoted above. The fact that there is no such *sūtra* as *dasti* in Kātantra is sufficient to show that the grammar is incomplete in this respect and the *sūtra, dasti*, which the *vṛtti* cites is a later addition by the followers of the Kātantra school. In the absence of such a *sūtra*, we can safely presume that the Kātantra has no technique which lengthens the final vowels of *iganta upasargas*, though, it is to be noted, the *vṛtti* quotes the examples *nittam, parīttam* with lengthened *ī*.

In this light the explanation of Trilocanadāsa in his *Pañjikā*, a commentary on Kātantra, viz. *dastīti/ dāsaṁjñakasya sthāne yas takārādeśas tasmin nimitte nāmina*[1] *eva dīrghaḥ*, is lame and without any ground.

Or, did the Kātantra originally have any such *sūtra*, lengthening the final vowels of *iganta upasargas*, which was lost later on?

(7) We take *jagdha* next for consideration. It is explained as the past passive participle of √*ad* 'to eat' (2nd Conj., Parasmaipada) by all Sanskrit grammarians.

---

1. *nāmin* is a technical term referring to all the vowels except *a;* cf. the Kātantra *sūtra, svaro'varnajo nāmī*, 1.1.7.

The Pāṇinian *sūtra,* which substitutes the morpheme *jagdh* for the root-morpheme *ad* is *ado jagdhir lyapti kiti,* 2.4.36. The conditions for such a substitute are that the root must be followed by the gerundive termination *-ya* (Pāṇinian *lyap*) or by terminations which begin with *-ka* and are *kit.*

The grammatical procedure to arrive at the form according to Pāṇini's grammar is :-

ad + ta

= *jagdh + ta*

= *jagdh + dha* (t > *dh according to 8.4.20)*

= *jagdhdha* or *jagdha,* the first *dh* optionally amounting to zero according to the Pāṇinian *sūtra, jharo jhari savarṇe,* 8.4.65

All the grammars follow Pāṇini in resorting to the method of substituting *jagdh* for *ad* for accounting the past passive participial form *jagdha* from √*ad.* And, it may be added that no other method is possible in this case, because, from the point view of historical development of Sanskrit, √*ad* has no forms in past passive participle and in some tenses; thus we find that while √*ghas* replaces √*ad* in perf. etc. (cf.the Pāṇinian *sūtras* for detailed information; *sūtras,* 2.4.35-40) √*jagdha* replaces it in past passive participle and gerund in *-ya.* Thus in order to be able to account for all the possible formations of √*ad* in the language, one has to assume that the root is replaced by two different substitutes.

The corresponding *sūrtas* of other grammarians are:

Kātantra: *yapi cādo jagdhiḥ,* 4.1.82.

Candra: *ti kity ado jagdhaḥ,* 5.4.85.

Bhoja: *lyapi kity ado jagdhiḥ,* 6.4.92.

Jainendra: *ti kit pye'do jagdhiḥ* 1.4.110.

Śākaṭāyana: *jagdhadah pye ca,* 4.2.118.

Hemacandra: *yapi cādo jagdh-,* 4.4.16.

Sārasvata: *ado jagdhuḥ,* 7.4.89.

It is to be noted that Bhoja, who usually follows Candra in descriptive methods and Pāṇini in the wording of the *sūtras,* has followed Pāṇini in wording the *sūtra* in this case also; cf. Pāṇini's *ādeśa jagdhi* with Bhoja's *jagdhi* as against Candra's *jagdha.*

It is also to be noted that, instead of laying down the *ādeśa jagdh,* the Sārasvata grammar has reconstructed the *ādeśa, jagh.* The process according to the Sārasvata grammar is, therefore, is as follows:—

ad + ta

= *jagh + ta*

= *jagh + dha* (*t > dh* according to *sūtra, tathor dhaḥ,* 4.429)

= *jag + dha* (*gh > g* according to *jhabe jabāḥ,* 4.4.26)

= *jagdha.*

Sārasvata thus strikes a different note in the matter of arriving at the form and of reconsturcting the substitute for *ad.* It must, however, be said, that the Sārasvata process neither explains the form more briefly nor shows any improvement on the methods of Pāṇini and others.

All other grammars have followed the same process and reconstruction of substitutes as Pāṇini.

Historically speaking, the form *jagdha,* which represents the past passive participle of √*ad* in Sanskrit, or more accurately in old Indo-Aryan, has evolved out of the form * *jagzdha,* in which the interconsonantal *z* totally disappears in Sanskrit and represents an earlier *s* in the Indo-European. The form **jagzdha,* therefore, could originally be **jagh-s-ta* (*s* >t and *-ta* > *-dha*). Now this form **jagh-s-ta* could be nothing but the past passive participle of the reduplicated root √*ghas* 'to eat' with the loss of the vowel *a* in the root-part of the reduplication.[1]

1. This reduplicated stage of √*ghas* with the loss of *a* has given rise to an altogether independent root viz. √*jakṣ* 'to eat' (2nd Conj., Parasmaipada); cf. *W.D. Whitney, The Roots, Verb-Forms and Primary Derivatives of the Sanskrit Language,* 1945, pp. 42 and 51.

Though, therefore, superficially √*ad* seems to have been substituted by two root-morphemes viz. *ghas* (in perf. etc) and *jagdh* (in past passive participle), it may be regarded as having been basically substituted right from the Indo-European stage, by only one root-morpheme viz. *ghas*.[1] The Sanskrit grammarians, however, do not concern themselves with such a historical inquiry of the form since they are all doing a synchronic, and not a diachronic, study of the Sanskrit language; they therefore are fully justified in laying down two different substitutes in different formations for √*ad*.

One thing, however, is quite clear; √*ad* does not retain its phonetic contents viz. *a* and *d* (or *t*) in all its formations of all the tenses and derivatives; for example, the derivative of √*ad* in *tvā* should have been regularly as *attvā*, but it is not found in the language. Hence the necessity of substitution of *ghas* or *jagdh* for √*ad*.

A point to be noted here is that the basis for such a substitution of *jagdh* for √*ad* is purely semantic, viz. the identity of meaning between the two roots.

(8) The next root-morpheme to be entirely substituted by an altogether different root- morpheme, which bears neither phonological nor morphological similarity, much less identity, is the √*as* 'to be' (2nd Conj. Parasmaipada).

This root is substituted by the morpheme *bhū* in all its forms of the *ārdhadhātuka* conjugations and primary derivetives. Thus we have,

as + *ta*
= *bhū* + *ta*
= *bhūta* as the past passive participle of √*as* 'to be'.

1. For a detailed historical treatment of this phenomenon, cf. *J. Wackernagel,Altindische Grammatik,* Band I, pp. 131, 230, 239; Band II, 1, pp. 195 and Band II. 2, pp. 551, 572, 629, 723; cf. also *T. Burrow, Sanskrit Language,* p. 94.

The *sūtras*, enjoining this substitution, of the different grammarians are:-

Pāṇini: *aster bhūḥ*, 2.4.52.

Kātantra: *aster bhūr asārvadhātuke*, 3.4.87.

Candra: *aster bhūḥ*, 5.4.79.

Bhoja: *aster bhūh*, 6.4.84.

Jainendra combines two substitutions for two rules into one *sūtra*, of course, for the sake of greater brevity; cf. *astibrūñor bhūvacī*, 1.4.124, for the substitution of *vac* for √*brū*, see the next section No. 9.

Hemacandra follows Jainendra in combining two *sūtras* into one; cf. *astibruvor bhūvacav aśiti*, 4.4.1.

So also Śākaṭāyana; cf. *astibruvor bhūvacau*, 4.2.91.

Sārasvata, however, follows Pāṇini; cf. the *sūtra*, *aster anapi bhū vaktavyaḥ*, which is a *vārttika* -type statement and no regular number is assigned to this *sūtra* in the *sūtra-pātha*. This shows the incompleteness of the grammar.

It must be remembered, however, that as in the case of √*ad*, in this case also, the semantic identity of the two roots viz. √*as* and √*bhū* is taken into consideration and is made to form the basis for the substitution.

Similarly, such an uneven substitution is necessitated by the fact that √*as* does not show its forms in all the *ārdhadhātuka* tenses, moods and primary derivatives.

All have followed Pāṇini in treating this form on the level of morphemic substitution and , we may say, even in the wording of the *sūtras*.

Jainendra, Hemacandra and Śākaṭāyana are certainly briefer than Pāṇini and others in laying down two *ādeśas* for two morphemes in single *sūtra*. Two independent *sūtras* for √*as* and √*brū* as given by Pāṇini and others seem to be unnecessary in so far as the conditions for the substitutions are almost the same in both the cases.

(9) As indicated above, √*brū* (2nd Conj. Ubhayapada) gets the substitute *vac* in all its *ārdhadhātuka* forms. The Pāṇinian process to arrive at the past passive participle of √*brū* is:-

brū + ta

= *vac + ta*

= *uc + ta* (*saṁprasāraṇa* of *v* into *u* according to the Pāṇinian *sūtra, vacisvapiyajādīnāṁ kiti,* 6.1.15); *a* merges into *u* according to 6.1.108.

= *uk + ta* (*c* > *k* according to *coḥ kuḥ,* 8.2.30)

= *ukta.*

The *sūtras* of the grammarians are:—

Pāṇini: *bruvo vaciḥ,* 2.4.53.

Kātantra: *bruvo vaciḥ,* 3.4.88.

Candra: *bruvo vac,* 5.4.80.

Bhoja: *bruvo vac,* 6.4.85.

Jainendra: *astibruvor bhūvacī,* 1.4.124.

Hemacandra: *astibruvor bhūvacav aśiti,* 4.4.1.

Śākaṭāyana: *astibruvor bhūvacau,* 4.2.91.

Sārasvata: *bruvo vaciḥ,* which seems to be a *vārttika* in the grammar since no number is assigned to this *sūtra* in the *sūtrapāṭha.* Or, otherwise it is clearly a brorrowing from Pāṇini's grammar by later commentators of Sārasvata. This confirms the assumption regarding the incompleteness of the grammar.

As in the previous two cases of √*ad* and √*as,* in this case also, the only basis for the substitution is semantic similarity between the roots √*brū* and √*vac.* Again, such a substitution was necessitated by the fact that √*brū* did not display all its formations.

All grammarians have followed Pāṇini in the technique of describing this form and even in the wording of their respective *sūtras.*

(10) The next form for discussion is the past passive participle of the root √*cakṣ* (Pāṇinian *cakṣin* 'to speak, to tell' etc.), 2nd Conj. Ātmanepada.

The substitute for this root in the *ārdhadhātuka* formations, according to the Pāṇinian rule, is *khyā*.

Hence the past passive participle of √*cakṣ* will be:

cakṣ + ta

= *khyā + ta*

= *khyāta*

But in this connection we face a difficulty. The substitute *khyā*, which acts as a full original root, though here it is a substitute,[1] ends in *ā*, has a conjunction of *kh* and *y* in the beginning and contains *y* (one of the sounds from the *pratyāhāra yaṇ);* it, therefore, satitsfies the conditions for the change of the *t* into *n* according to the *sūtra, saṁyogāder āto dhātor yaṇvataḥ*, 8.2.43. Thus, strictly according to the Pāṇinian rules, the past passive participial formation from *khyā* will be *khyāna* and not *khyāta*.

But the formation *khyāna* as a past passive participle is nowhere available in the language. Perhaps it is on account of this fact that Patañjali initiates a discussion on whether the *ādeśa* for √*cakṣ* is *khyā* or *kśā/khśā*.[2] If the *ādeśa* is taken to be *kśā* or *khśā*, the *ś* has to be optionally changed to *y* by introducing a new *sūtra* to that effect in the *asiddha-prakaraṇa* i.e. in the *tripādī* beginning with the *sūtra*, 8.2.1., *pūrvatrāsiddham* and the form that might then become available would be the regular *khyāta*, which is attested in the language; cf. the *vārttika* in the *bhāṣya* on Pāṇini 2.4.54: *asiddhe śasya yavacanaṁ vibhāṣā*.

1. cf. the Pāṇinian sūtra, *sthānivad ādeśo'nalvidhau*, 1.1.56, and Patañjali's excellent discussion on the same.
2. cf. Patañjali on the Pāṇinian *sūtra, cakṣiṁaḥ khyāñ* 2.4.54; *kim ayam kaśādir āhosvit khayādih?* etc.; cf. also the *vārttika* on the Pāṇinian *sūtra*, 2.4.54: *cakṣiṁaḥ kśāñkhyāñau*.

This whole complicated discussion and the suggested procedure seem to have originated from the contingency of *ta* being changed to *na* and thus giving the form *khyāna*, which,however, is not found in the language. This is clear from the *vārttika, niṣṭhānatvam ākhyāte,* in the *bhāṣya* on Pāṇini 2.4.54.[1] Actually the whole discussion seems unnecessary and an attempt on the part of Patañjali and the Vārttikakāra Kātyāyana to improve on Pāṇini is futile because Pāṇini, anticipatting this difficulty has himself prohibited the change of *ta* into *na* for roots √*khyā* etc. in the *sūtra,* 8.2.57: *na dhyākhyāpṛmūrcchimadām.*

It may, however, be pointed out that, as the author of *pradīpa*, a commentary on the *Mahābhāṣya,* says, Kātyāyana and Patañjali take the root √*khyā* in the *sūtra,* 8.2.57 (for which the change of *ta* into *na* is prohibited) to be the regular root √*khyā* listed by Pāṇini in the 2nd conjugation as *khyā prakathane,* and not the *khyā* which is an *ādeśa* for √*chkṣ.*[2]

The reason for such an argument is that since √*khyā* is listed by Pāṇini in 8.2.57, it should refer to the regular root √*khyā* listed (by Pāṇini himself) in the *dhātupāṭha;* in other words, one *upadeśa* (i.e. *pratipadokta)* should refer to another *upadeśa* only[3] and not to any other entity, which becomes secondary (i.e. *lākṣaṇika)* in comparison with the *upadeśa; upadeśa* or *pratipadokta* is regarded as primary. The substitute *khyā* for √*cakṣ* from this point of view is secondary and √*khyā* is primary,[4] because in the case of the former *khyā,* the y is a substitute for *ś* according to the Vārttikakāra and Patañjali. So, the substitute *khyā* being secondary, and not being referred to in the *sūtra,* 8.2.57, will give out the past passive participial formation as **khyāna* and not *khyāta.*

---

1. For other difficulties in accepting the *ādeśa khyā* for √*cakṣ,* cf. *vārttikas* 1-9 in the bhāṣya on the Pāṇinian *sūtra,* 2.4.54.
2. cf. Pradīpa : *'na dhyākhye'ti tu pratiṣedhaḥ, 'khyā prakathana' ity asyaiva pratipadoktatvāt.*
3. cf. the paribhāṣā : *lakṣaṇapratipadoktayaḥ pratipadoktasyaiva grahaṇam.*
4. cf. Pradīpa : *asya tu śasya yatvena lākṣaṇikatvād iti manyate.*

In order to get over this difficult situation, Patañjali and the Vārttikakāra take the substitute originally *kśā* or *khśā*[1] and then suggest the framing of a new *sūtra* in the *asiddha-prakaraṇa* (after the *sūtra* which changes *ta* into *na)* which will lay down the change of *ś* into *y*. Thus the procedure thought of by them would be:

cakṣ + ta

= *khśā + ta*

= *khśāta*

= *khyāta*, changing *ś* to *y*.

The Vārttikakāra has achieved two purposes by this process: (i) he has accounted for the perfect forms like *cakṣe*, etc. in which the root *kśā* is evident, and (ii) he has prohibited the undesirable change of *ta* into *na* by proposing substitute *kśā* or *khśā* for *caks*.

Another *vārttika* on the same *sūtra*, viz, *varjane pratiṣedhaḥ* imposes on the substitution a semantic condition, viz. *varjana* 'exclusion, avoidance' etc. If this sense is present, √*cakṣ* is not substituted by *khyā;* thus we have the circumstances like *durjanāḥ saṁcakṣyāḥ* (=wicked people should be avoided) in which the substitution of *cakṣ* by *khyā* does not take place.

There is yet another condition laid down by Kātyāyana under which the substitution becomes null and void. It is morphological. If the morphemes *-as* and *-ana* follow the root √*cakṣ*, giving rise to primary derivatives *cakṣas* and *cakṣaṇa*, the root is not substituted by the morpheme *khyā;* cf. the *vārttika, asanayoś ca* on the Pāṇinian *sūtra*, 2.4.54.

Kātantra and Candra follow Pāṇini *ad verbatim;* cf. the *sūtras, cakṣiṅaḥ khyāñ*, 3.4.89 and *cakṣaḥ khyāñ*, 5.4.81 from Kātantra and Candra respectively.

---

1. cf. *udyota*, another commentary on the Mahābhāṣya by Nāgeśa : *asya tatrāgrahane 'ākhyānaṁ' ityapi syad iti tadvyāvṛttyartham khaśāditvaṁ iti bhāvah.*

Kātantra does not note the semantic condition of *varjana* and the morphemes *-as* and *-ana* for the absence of the subsitution, though the *vṛtti* by Durgasiṁha on Kātantra, 3.4.89, takes the froms *saṁcakṣya, nṛcakṣas* and *vicakṣaṇa* into consideration; cf. the *vṛtti* : *kathaṁ saṁcakṣyo durjano/ varjanīya ityarthaḥ/ nṛcakṣā rākṣasaḥ/ ....vicakṣaṇaḥ.../*

Candra notes the sense of *varjana*, as well as morphological condition of terminations *-as* and *-ana* which prohibit the substitution of *cakṣ* by *khyā;* cf. his *sūtra, nāsanavaraneṣu,* 5.4.83.

Bhoja follows Candra; cf. his *sūtras, cakṣiṅaḥ khyāñ avarjane,* 6.4.86 and *nasasaneṣu,* 6.4.88. He, however, adds one more termination viz. *u* (i.e. *us),* giving out the formation *cakṣuḥ* ('eye' form *cakṣ* + *us*), to the list of terminations which do not necessitate the substitution of *cakṣ* by *khyā.*

Jainendra lays down the substitute as *khśāñ* i.e. *khśā,* and then by another *sūtra, khśaḥ śo yo* vā, 5.4.124 changes the *ś* into *y.* He thus seems to follow very carefully all the objections and suggestions made on the Pāṇinian *sūtra,* 2.4.54, by Kātyāyana (cf. Kāyāyana's *vārttika* on the Pāṇinian *sūtra,* 2.4.54: *asiddhe śaṣya yavacanam vibhāṣā)* and Patañjali's remark: *asiddhe śasya vibhāṣā yatvaṁ vaktavyam.*

He notes the sense of *varjana* also as prohibiting the substitution; cf. his *sūtra, na varjane,* 1.4.126. The prohibitory morphological conditions of -as and *-ana* are, however, not noted by him, though the Mahāvṛtti on the *sūtra,* 1.4.126, tries to exclude the two terminations *-as* and *-ana* by an interpretation of the *sūtra,* 1.4.125, for which the technique of *yogavibhāga* of the *sūtra,* 1.4.126, into *na* and *varjane* is resorted to; cf. the *vṛtti* on 1.4.126: *neti yogavibhgāgād asi yuci ca pratiṣedhaḥ/ nṛcakṣāḥ rākṣasaḥ/ vicakṣaṇaḥ/*

Jainendra, therefore, seems to follow Kātyāyana more closely than Pāṇini.

Hemacandra has only one *sūtra*, viz. *cakṣo vāci kśāṅg*, 4.4.4, which restricts the *ādeśas kśāṅg* and *khyāṅg* only to the sense of *vāci* i.e. 'speaking, telling' etc. This excludes the other senses like *varjana* atc. for such a substitution. cf. the *Svopajñalaghuvṛtti* on Hemacandra's *sūtra,* 4.4.4: *vācīti kim? bodhe vicakṣaṇah?* ('why vāci only? In the sense of *bodha,* the form is *vicakṣaṇah*'); cf. also the *Prakriyāvṛtti* on Hemacandra's grammar by Śrivinaya vijayagaṇi: *vāgarthasyaiva kśāṅg khyāṅgau tena varjanārthād ghyaṇi sañcakṣyāḥ parisañcakṣyāḥ avasañcakṣyāḥ durjanāḥ/ varjanīyā ity arthaḥ / bhakṣaṇārthād anati cakṣaṇam / ..... asmād as ....cakṣaḥ khyāḥ rakṣonāmanī / .... aṇe vicakṣaṇah, jñānārthatvād atra kśāṅg-khyāṅg-abhāvaḥ/ cakṣeḥ....kity usi cakṣuḥ paricakṣuḥ avacakṣuḥ avasañcakṣuḥ/*

This gives us in all four meanings in which the root √*cakṣ* was used in the language since the times of Kātyāyana.

The meanings are:[(A)] (1) to speak, to tell, (*vyaktāyāṁ vāci*) which all the grammarians note for the root; (2) to avoid to exclude (*varjane*), which is noted by all except Pāṇini and which gives rise to the prohibition of the substitution of *kśā/ khyā* for the root, (3) to eat, to enjoy (bhakṣaṇārthe), noted by Śrīvinayavijayagaṇi's commentary on Hemacandra's grammar (cf. the quotation above); and (4) to know (*jñānārthe or bodhe*), noted by the author of the *Svopajñalaghuvṛtti,* who according to the tradition is none other than Hemacandra himself,[1] and of the *Prakriyāvṛtti,* named Śrīvinaya-

A. In the above is reproduced a column of the Table of the different *dhātus* from*A Concordance of Sanskrit Dhātupaṭhas* by Dr. G. B. Palsule (p. 41). The *dhātus* are collected from the various *dhātupāṭhas* of the different grammarians. The purpose in this reproduction is to facilitate easy reference to the root *cakṣ* as available in the different *dhps.* The numerical figure refers to the serial number of the root in the particular class and the English alphabet A (A=Ātmanepada) against it shows the *pada* to which the root *cakṣ* belongs *(cf. G.B. Palsule, ibid.* Introduction, p. ii). Abbreviations— B=Bohtlingk, C= Candra, H= Hemacandra, J = Jainendra, KK = Kāśakṛtsna, Kṣ = Kṣīrasvāmin, Kt = Kātantra, M = Mitreyarakṣita, P = Pāṇini, S = Sāyaṇa, Śa = Śarvavarman, Śā = Śākaṭāyana, V = Vopadeva; Vs arrangement of the root is alphabetically; so no number is given.

1. cf. The edition of *Śrī Siddha Hemacandra śabdānuśāsanam,* edited by Muni Hemāṁśuvijaya, Jain Advocate Press, Ahmedabad, 1934,

Table No. 2

(√cakṣ as occuring in different *dhātupāṭhas*)

	P		Śa	C	J	KK		Kt	Śā		H	V
B	Ks	M S	-	-	-	-		-	-		-	-
cakṣ	117A	7A	7A	7A	7	37A	46A	39A	41A	43A	64A	A

vijayagaṇi, on the Hemacandra *sūtra*, 4.4.4. It is very surprising, however, that all the grammars note only the first meaning, the other meanings being lost in the language.

An important point to be noted here is that Hemacandra unhesitatingly admits the morpheme *kśā* as the regular substitute for √*cakṣ* along with the substitute *khyā*. He thus, seems to follow Kātyāyana's view-point.

Moreover, in laying down that the substitution of *cakṣ* by *kśā* and *khyā* takes place only when the sense of 'speaking, telling' is intended, Hemacandra automatically excludes the cases, characterised by the semantic condition of *varjana*, *bhakṣana* etc. in which the substitution does not take place. He, therefore, is much briefer than Kātantra, Candra, Bhoja and Jainendra in describing the different forms of *cakṣ*, with and without the sense of 'speaking' etc.

Śākaṭāyana agrees with Hemacandra and Jainendra in laying down both the *ādeśas*, viz. *khśā* (>*kśā*) and *khyā*. But his method is a little diffrerent. What he does is that he first enjoins the substitute *khśā* in the *sūtra*, *cakṣaḥ khśāñ vāci*, 4.2.92, and then in the *sūtra*, *śo yaḥ*, 4.2.94, optionally substitutes the *ś* of *khśā* by *y*, giving rise to another *ādeśa khyā*. This incidentally supports our former observation that Śākaṭāyana as far as possible tries to build up his system of grammar on phonological level. Thus we have both the forms *khyāta* and *kśāta*, besides *cakṣita* when the sense of *'vāci'* ('speaking') is not present.

Introduction, p. 14, Section of *Laghuvṛtti*; cf. *atra mudritā laghuvṛttiḥ sūtrakartrā Hemacandrarṣiṇaiva viracitā*.

The Cintāmaṇivṛtti on Śākaṭāyana's grammr notes in all four meanings of the root: (1) to speak, to tell, which is his regular meaning for the root, noted in his *dhātupātha;* cf. *cakṣi vyaktāyāṁ vāci* (2) to know *(bodhe);* in *cakṣuḥ, vicakṣaṇaḥ;* cf. the *Cintāmaṇivṛtti* on Śākaṭāyana 4.2.92; *cakṣuḥ vicakṣaṇaḥ/ atra bodhe;* (3) to avoid, (varjane); cf. the *vṛtti : avasañcakṣyāḥ parisañcakṣyāḥ/atra varjane;* (4) to kill, destroy, (hiṁsāyām); cf. the *vṛtti: nṛcakṣaḥ rākṣasaḥ/atra hiṁsāyām.* Thus the *vṛtti* adds one more meaning to the total number of four meanings, viz. of *hiṁsā,* noted for the root.

Like Jainendra, Śākaṭāyana follows the view and method of Kātyātana in accepting the substitute of √*cakṣ* primarily as *kśā* and then changing the *ś* into *y* by an independent *sūtra,* viz. 4.2.94.

Sārasvata follows Hemacandra, Śākaṭāyana and Jainendra in laying down both the ādeśas viz. *khyāñ* and *kśāñ* for the root *cakṣ;* cf. the *vārttika-type* statement on the root √*cakṣ : cakṣiṅo'napi khyāñkśāñau ṇādau vā vaktavyau.* The fact that this statement is not numbered makes it clear that it does not form part of the regular body of the grammar and is added later on by the commentators; secondly, it shows a very loose and incomplete nature of the grammar.

Sārasvata, it may be further pointed out, neither notes the semantic situations of *varjana* etc. nor the morphological conditions of terminations *-as, -us, -ana* etc. in which the substitutes do not take place. This is indicative of the superficiality of description and lack of details in the grammar.

In general we may say that Pāṇini, Kātantra, Candra, and Bhoja lay down only one *ādeśa* for √*cakṣ;* and that is *khyāñ;* Jainendra, Śākaṭāyana, Hemacanra, and Sārasvata follow Kātyāyana in enjoining both the *ādeśas* viz. *kśā* and *khyā.* Secondly Hemacandra and Śākaṭāyana incorporate Kātyāyana's suggestion of the prohibition of the substitution in only the semantic conditions concerned into the regular body of the grammar, while Candra, Bhoja, and Jainendra incorporate both the semantic as well as morphological conditions of the prohibition. Kātantra does not follow Kātyāyana. Sārasvata follows Kātyāyana in only admitting both the ādeśas viz. *kśā* and *khyā* but does not note conditions for their absence.

As in the previous cases of √*as* and √*bhū*, in the present case of √*cakṣ* also, the basis of its substitutions by *khyā* or *kśā* is the semantic similarity between the two. It is on this basis that we may say that Pāṇini is fully justified in giving the substitute as *khyā* and not *kśā* since √*kśā* is nowhere available in Sanskrit while √*khyā* is available and that Kātyāyana's suggestion of substituting *khśā/kśā* and then turning the *ś* into *y*, followed by many other grammarians, is unrealistic and artificial. Perhaps in the case of morphemic substitutes, Pāṇini seems to have been guided by considerations of meaning, phonetic change etc. which were admissible in the languae itself and hence when he substituted *khyā* and not *kśā*, it was semantically similar root √*khyā* which must have been in his mind; this is clear from the fact that the *sūtra, na dhyākhyāpṛmūrchimadām*, 8.2.57, automatically excludes the *ādeśa khyā* also (besides the root √*khyā*) from the scope of *sūtra, saṁyogāder āto dhātor yaṇvataḥ*, 8.2.43, which would have changed the *-ta* into *-na* in the case of *khyā*. This shows that for Pāṇini there is basically no distinction between the root khyā and the substitute *khyā*. Even technically both are *pratipadokta* or *upadiṣṭa* and not *lākṣaṇika* as Kātyāyana would maintain.

In opposition to this suggestion of Kātyāyana to substitute *khśā/kśā* initially and then change the *ś* into *y* is not only not supported by language, as √*kśā*/√*khśā* is nowhere available but is against linguistic structure of Sanskrit; the combination of *k* and palatal *ś* is nowhere available in Sanskrit; much less the combinations of *kh* and palata *ś*. In this sense Kātyāyana's substitutes seem to be arbitrarily set up, as against Pāṇini's which are real and allowed by the usage in language by the linguistic structure.

Unlike in the cases of √*ad*, √*brū*, √*bhū*, etc, whose past passive participial formations are not at all available in the language, in the present case the substitution of √*cakṣ* by *khyā* is necessitated by the fact that besides the regular forms *cakṣita*, the form *khyāta* is also used as the past passive participle of √*cakṣ*.

(11) We may now take up for discussion the form *vīta* from √*aj* 'to go, to drive' etc. (cf. Pāṇinian *dhātuhātha, aja gatikṣepaṇyaḥ*, 1st Conj. Parasmaipada). The substitute for this root in all *ārdhadhātuka* formations except those with the Pāṇinian terminations *ghañ* and *ap*[1] is *vī*. This √*aj* belongs to the first conjugation and not to the nineth conjugation which latter is technically reconstructed as *añjū* by Pāṇini; cf. Pāṇinian *dhātupāṭha : añjū vyaktimrakṣaṇakāntigatiṣu;* this is clear from the wording of the Pāṇinian *sūtra, ajer vy aghañapoḥ*, 2.4.56, which uses the word as *ajeḥ* and not as *añjeḥ* or *anakteḥ*. The Pāṇinian *sūtra*, which lays down this substitute *vī* is *ajer vy aghañapoh* 2.4.56. This gives the past passive participle from √*añj*, 9th Conj as *vīta*.

The grammatical process to arrive at the formation is simple:

aj + *ta*
= *vī* + *ta*
= *vīta*

The corresponding *sūtras* of other grammars are :

Kātantra : *ajer vī*, 3.4.91.

Candra : *ajer vy ayughañapkyeṣu*, 5.4.84.

---

1. Patañjali in his *bhāṣya* on the Pāṇinian sūtra, 2.4.56, *(ajer vy aghañapoḥ)* interprets a point of view which says that the *ap* in the *sūtra* refers, not to the termination *ap* alone, but to the *pratyāhāra* formed by the first letter *a* of the termination *ap* in the Pāṇinian *sūtra, ṛdor ap*, 3.3.57 and the last letter *p* in the termination *kyap* laid down in the Pāṇinian *sūtra, vrajayajor bhāve kyap*, 3.3.98. Thus the *pratyāhāra* ap representes all the terminations like *ṇa* (cf. 3.3.60), *ktri* (cf. 3.3.68) etc. included in the sūtras 3.3.57-3.3.98.

Bhoja : *ajer vy aghañapkyapsu*, 6.4.89.

Jainendra : *vy ajo'ghañacoḥ*, 1.4.128.

Śākaṭāyana : *valane'co vī*, 4.2.129 and *akyabghañaci*, 4.2.130; thus he has two sūtras; this reflects *gaurava* as against *lāghava* of Pāṇini and other grammarians who describe the form in only one sūtra.

Hemacandra : *aghañkyabalacy ajer vī*, 4.4.2.

Sārasvata : It has no independent *sūtra* for describing this form and the commentators describe it by the *vārttika*-type statement : *ajer ārdhadhātuke vī vaktavyaḥ vasādau vā*, which, with no numbering, is clearly a later addition and again implies the incompleteness of the grammar.

All grammarians follow Pāṇini in describing the form. There seems to be no difference of opinion, nor of usage, in the morphological conditions under which √*aj* is replaced by the morpheme *vī*.

The semantic similarity between the two roots which is the basis for the substitution of *anj* by *vī*, seems to be restricted only to the meaning of 'going'. Out of the other meanings, only this meaning is shared by the two in common; cf. Pāṇinian *dhp.* √*vī* (2nd conj. Parasmaipada)—*gativyāpti-prajanakāntyasanakhādaneṣu*.

The substitution of √*aj* by *vī* is necessitated by the fact that no past passive participial forms from √*aj* 'to go' are available; instead, only the form derived from √*vī* viz. *vīta*, is used in the language.

(12) The next form for discussion is *kṣīṇa* or *kṣita*, the past passive participle from √*kṣi* 'to go, to dwell, or to wane' (cf. Pāṇinian *dhp. kṣi kṣaye*, 'to wane', 1st Conj. Parasmaipada, which is intransitive; cf. BD's remark: *akarmakaḥ: kṣi hiṁsāyām*, 5th Conj. Parasmaipada, which is transitive; *kṣi nivāsagatyoḥ*, to dwell, to go, 6th Conj. Parasmaipada; intransitive in the first and transitive in the second sense. The Pāṇinian *sūtra, niṣṭhāyām aṇyadarthe*, 6.4.60 (with the

anuvṛtti of *kṣiyaḥ* from *sūtra* 6.4.59), lays down that the final short *i* of √*kṣi* gives place to a long *ī* before the past passive participial termination *-ta* (Pāṇinian *kta*), when the past passive participle thus formed, has not the sense of *bhāva* and *karma*.[1] In other words, short i is changed to long *ī* when the active sense *(kartari)* is present. The *-ta* can be added to intransitive √*kṣi* according to the Pāṇinian *sūtra*, 3.4.72 in an active sense as opposed to its normal passive sense.

Thus when the active sense is present, the past passive participle from √*kṣi* will be *kṣīṇa* (with long *ī*, and *ta* > *na* accrding to Pāṇini, 8.2.46). In the *bhāva* and *karma* senses, however, the short *ī* will not be lengthened; consequently *ta* will not change to *-na;* and the form will be simply *kṣi* + *ta* = *kṣita*.

It will be clear (i) that Pāṇini treats this phenomenon on phonological level, or to be more precise on phonetic level since the description is given in terms of a phonetic term *dīrgha* (to be borrowed from the previous *sūtra*, 6.4.58); and (ii) that he explains the forms *kṣīṇa* and *kṣita* with a reference to the grammatical meaning of *bhāva*, *karma* and *kartari* of the past passive participial termination —*ta*. The reference, it is to be noted, to linguistic meaning of the whole form is totally absent in this case of the substitution of a long grade for a short grade.

The linguistic meaning, however, is referred to in the case of optional substitution of the long grade, laid down for the root in the next *sūtra*, viz. *vā'krośadainyayoḥ*, 6.4.61, which states that if the meanings of (i) *ākrośa* i.e. cursing and (2) *dainya* i.e. miserable plight are present, the short *i* is

1. This is the meaning of *aṇyadartha;* the word *ṇyadartha* means the sense of *bhāva* and *karma* in which senses alone the terminations called *kṛtya* (cf. Pāṇini : *kṛtyāḥ prāṅ ṇvulaḥ*, 3.1.95, BD reads only *kṛtyāḥ*) in Pāṇini's grammar are laid down; for *ṇyadartha* = the senses of *bhāva* and *karma*, cf. kāśikā on the Pāṇinian *sūtra*, 6.4.60: *ṇyataḥ kṛtyasyārtho bhāvakarmaṇī;* cf. also BD. on 6.4.60: *ṇvadartho bhāvakarmaṇī*.

optionally substituted by long *ī*. Thus we have two forms in the sense of *ākrośa* and *dainya.* viz. *kṣīṇa* (short *i* > long *ī*) and *kṣita* (since short *i* does not change to long *ī*, the *-ta* is not changed to *-na*), as in *kṣitaḥ kṣīṇaḥ vā tapasvī*, 'what a plight; (to convey the sense of *ākrośa* or *dainya*) the sage has grown very thin.'

We can, thus, see that the form is expalined by Pāṇini with the help of a reference to grammatical meanings of *bhāva, karma* and *kartari*, as well as to linguistic i.e. contextual meanings and on phonetic level.

It must be made clear here that though the *sūtra* treats the forms on phonetic level, it is included here in the chapter dealing with morphemic substitutes because some grammars like Candra, Bhoja and Hemacandra describe them on the level of *Prakṛti-ādeśas.*

It should also be noted that the linguistic meaning that is taken here for the explanation of the form is not of the root √*kṣi* but of the whole form like *kṣīṇa* and *kṣita.* Any √*kṣi* in Pāṇinian *dhātupātha* can, therfore, be taken as an illustration and the termination *-ta* can be applied to it; cf. *Tattvabodhinī* on BD's *SK* which makes this point clear; *kṣi kṣaye / kṣi nivāsagatyoḥ / dvayor api grahaṇam;* the third root √*kṣi* in the sense of *hiṁsā* (5th Conj. Parasmaipada) is not included by *Tattvabodhinī* obviously because it, being transtitive, is not likely to yield any form like *kṣīṇa* in a *kartari* i.e. active sense; Pāṇini specifically mentions the exclusion of the grammatical meaning of *bhāva* and *karma;* cf. the word *aṇyadarthe* in the *sūtra*, 6.4.60, to be carried to *sūtra*, 6.4.61 also.

The corresponding *sūtra* of other grammarians who follow Pāṇini in describing the past passive participial form of √*kṣi* are :

Kātantra : *niṣṭhāyāṁ* ca, 4.1.41 with the words *kṣer dīrghaḥ* to be borrowed from the previous *sūtra, kṣer dīrghaḥ*, 4.1.40. The grammar, however, does not note the grammatical meaning of *abhāvakarma,* nor does it refer to the optional substitution of *i* by long *ī* in linguistic environments, though the commentaries elaborate the point; cf. Durga's *vṛtti* on Kātantra, 4.1.41 : *dīrgha ti saṁjñā-pūrvakatvād anityārthaḥ / tena bhāvakarmanor na syāt / .... ākrośadainyayoś ca vā //* The *vṛtti* by Chaitr. reads the meaning of *bhāva, dainya* and *ākrośa* in the word *ca* in the *sūtra*, 4.1.41; cf. *cakāraḥ kim? bhāva-dainyākrośeṣu vikalpārtham.*

Jainendra : *te'nye,* 4.4.59, with the word *dī (=dīrgha;* cf. for the defination of the technical term *dī* meaning *dīrgha* the Jainendra *sūtra, ākālo'c pradīpaḥ,* 1.11.11) to be borrowed from the previous *sūtra, kṣiyo dīḥ,* 4.4.58; for the semantic consideration of *ākrośa* and *dainya*, cf. the *sūtra, vā danyākrośe,* 4.4.60.

Śākaṭāyana : *kṣer aghye,* 4.1.252, in which *ghya* refers to the termination *ghyaṇ* = Pāṇini's *ṇyat.* cf. also for optional substutition on the basis of linguistic meaning of *dainya* and *ākrośa*, the *sūtra, dainyākrośe vā,* 4.1.253. The word *dīrgha* is to be borrowed from the previous *sūtra, dugvor dīrghaś* ca, 4.1.251.

Sārasvata has no *sūtra* in this connection in the *sūtrapāṭha;* the form is expalined by the *vārttika* type statement *kṣiyo niṣṭhāyāṁ kartari dīrgho vācyaḥ* and *dīrghādeva kṣiyaḥ niṣṭhāyās tasya ṇo vācyaḥ.* The word *kartari* excludes the *bhāve* and *karmaṇi* sense; cf. commentary *bhāvakarmaṇos tu kṣīyate sma tat kṣitaṁ tena.* The grammar, however, does not note the linguistic meanings of *ākrośa* and *dainya;* even the commentary does not mention anything on this. This speaks for the incomplete and loose nature of the grammar.

As opposed to all the above five grammars, the grammars of Candra, Bhoja and Hemacandra treat the form on the level of morphemic substitution. What they do is that they substitute the morpheme *kṣī* (with long *ī*) for *kṣi* (with short *i*); cf. the *sūtra:* Candra : *kṣeḥ kṣī ca,* 6.3.81 ; *vā bhāvā-krośadainyeṣu,* 6.3.82. Bhoja : *kṣeḥ kṣī ca,* 7.3.92; *vā bhāvākrośadainyeṣu,* 7.9.93. Hemacandra : *kṣeḥ kṣī cā'ghyārthe,* 4.2.74; *vā'krośadainye,* 4.2.75.

3
Morphemic Substitution for the Suffix-Morpheme *-ta*, i.e. *Pratyayādeśa*

1. Functional and Formal Consideration

As is well known, besides the past passive participial forms which end with the termination *-ta*, there are also other past passive participial forms which end in *-na*, *-ma*, *-la*, *-ka*, and *-va*. What is worth noting in this connection is that all these latter formations function or behave in the language exactly in the same way as the past passive participial formatins in *-ta*. The formations, which end in *-na*, *ma*, *-la*, *-ka*, and *-va*, are, therefore, also naturally treated as past pasive participles by the grammarians. And we must say that in doing so the grammarians are all fully justified. Because a formation is what it is only with reference to its relation with other words or its function in the language. This gives us an insight into the approach of the grammarians to the study, analysis and descriptions of Sanskrit language, viz. that all of them have analysed the language only after carefully taking into consideration the functional, relational or syntactical, and other types of environments in which the form accours. The anaysis and description of the forms in the language in general and of past passive participial formations in particular by the Sanskrit grammarians, therefore, is not arbitrary depending on the whim of an individual, but is based upon the accurate factual knowledge of the place and function of the form in the language. It must be noted also that while doing the functional study of the form, they have not only not neglected the formal aspect but have admirably and carefully preserved and pursued it to such an extent that the whole description and linguistic analysis seems to be purely formal, devoid of any functional or non-formal aspect. The suggestions that the syntactic or functional aspect is considered by the grammarians only in what is called the *Kāraka* section and that it is conspicuously absent in any other section of grammar will have to be discarded after a study of the section on past passive participles. The only principle underlying the treatment of all the forms ending in *-ta, -ma, -na, -la, -ka* and *-va* under one single category, viz. of past passive participles or what is technically termed as *ktānta* or *niṣṭhānta* is their functional consideration. They are set against different environments; their functions are carefully determined; they are then taken out of thesee environments and analysed as far as possible formally. In the event of the formal aspect coming in opposition to the functional aspect, the functional aspect is given preference. That seems to be the process of analysis of all the forms.

2. Technique of Description

The technique of description of all such formations, however, is different - may, it is likely to be different according to different individuals - and should not be confused with the underlying principle. What the grammarians have done is that they have assumed the morpheme *-ta* as basic, representing the past passive participial function of the form and then substituted the different morphemes like *-ma, -na, -la, -ka* and *-va* in its place in the case of roots concerned. And this is quite natural because from the point of view of the statistical count of all the past pasive participal forms, those ending in *-ta* are far greater in number than those ending in *-ma, -na, -la, -ka* and *-va*. From the point of view of brevity in statement, therefore, it is more convenient to lay down a general rule which is applicable to as greater a number of cases as possible and then note down the exceptions to or variations from them. This process, however, may differ according to individual technique and the subject treated; but this process seems to have been adopted by all the grammarians as far as the present topic of past passive participles is concerned.

The most general and basic or primary termination that is laid down as denoting the function of past passive participle is *-ta* or technically *-kta,* with the initial *k* being zero. This *-ta* is afterwards substituted by *-na, -ma, -la, -ka, -va* etc. That is the technique followed by all the grammarians without exception. All have thus adopted the method of morphemic substitution in the case of the terminations also, as they have done in the case of some roots *(vide* ch. II*)*. This would account for the title of the present chapter, viz. *pratyayādeśa.*

3. A Small Point Requires a Little Explanation

In the phenomenon of the substitution of *-ta* by *-na, -ma, -la, -ka* or *-va,* what is actually substituted is only the sound *-t,* and not the whole termination *-ta* (*t* with *a*), by the respective sounds *n, m, l, k* or *v.* And that is also how the grammarians have enjoined. It, therefore, apparently seems improper to characterise this phenomenon as morphemic substitution, instead of phonemic substitution. This also creates an impression that the phenomenon of substitution in the case of the past passive participial termination *-ta* is treated on phonological, and not morphological, level.

Yet, though apparently it seems that this is a case of phonemic or sound-substitution, it provides us a good example of how even a single sound or phoneme can attain the status of a full-fledged morpheme. The sounds *-t, -n, -m, -l, -k, -v* are all theoretically minimal meaningful units.[1] They are, therefore, full morphemes in every sense of the term.

1. cf. *E. A. Nida,* loc. cit., p. 6.

Secondly, in the spoken language, what is really substituted for *ta*, is not merely the sound *-n*, *-m*, etc. Thus the substitution of *-ta* by *-na*, *-ma*, etc. by the speaker is done not on the phonemic basic but on morphemic basis, though after analysis we get the difference of only one sound for *-t*.

The point will be clear by an illustration. Pāṇini, for example, analysed the form with √*pac* (> *pak*) + *va* in analogy with the form *kṛta* with √*kṛ* + *ta*. Put in the equational manner with the help of symbols, the forms and their analysis are:

kṛta = *kṛ* + *ta* = R_1S_1 (R = root, S = suffix)

and *pakva* = *pac* + *va* = R_2S_2.[1]

This gives us $S_1 = S_2$ so far as their function, status and values are concerned; the whole *va* is identical with the whole *ta*, and not only *t* = *v*. Even in the technique of phonemic substitution, what they are actually substituting is one morpheme for another. They are both identical from the point of view of their position (which is posterior to the root), function (which is past passive participle) and meaning, both grammatical (i.e. *niṣṭhā*) and linguistic (in the sense of past passive participle). One is, therefore, fully justified in describing this phenomenon as morphemic substitution and not as phonemic substitution.

4. Substitution of *-ta* by *-na*

We first take up the substitution of *-ta* by the morpheme *-na* because, statistically the number of cases ending in *-na* comes next to those ending in *-ta*. The problem is handled by the grammarians by different methods which may be summarised as follows :—

---

1. For a representation of all Sanskrit forms in terms of N.S. (Nucleus-Satellite) symbols, *cf. M. D. Pandit*, 'Pāṇini —A study in Non-compounded Word-Structures *VIJ*, Vol. I, Pt. II, 1963, pp. 324-338; also 'Pāṇini— A Study in Compound Word-Structures', *JMSUB*, Humanities, Vol. 12, No. 1, 1963, pp. 81-99. *cf.* also 'A Concordane of Vedic Compounds Interpreted by Veda,' CASS, Pune, 1989.

4.1 They have accomplished the substitution by determining the formal — phonological or morphological- environments; we may call this the formal plane.

4.2 Sometimes the semantic considerations, with or without formal considerations are brought in; this may be called a semantic or non-formal plane.

4.3 Some grammarians, who have employed the technique of *it-saṁjñā*,[1] have resorted to it for explaining some forms. This may be termed artificial formal plane.

4.4 Lastly when all these methods have failed, they have resorted to enumeration of all such cases as are not covered by the above three methods. We may call this enumeration plane.

The four general divisions mentioned above should not be taken to mean that all grammrians have adopted all these four methods; nor is it suggested that when one follows a particular method, say, that in 4.1, in a particular case, all follow the same methods in that case. All that is implied in the above statement is that all the methods that have been adopted in identical or different cases by different grammarians can be divided into the four general types noted above.

4.1 Formal Conditions for ta > na

The Pāṇinian *sūtras* that lay down the formal or in particular phonological conditions for the change of *-ta* into *na* are two : (i) *radābhyām niṣṭhāto naḥ pūrvasya ca daḥ*, 8.2..42 and (ii) *saṁyogāder āto dhātor yaṇvataḥ*, 8.2.43.

The former *sūtra*, viz. 8.2.42 states that when the past passive participial termination *-ta* is placed after the consonantal sound *r* and *d*, it changes to *na;* moreover, the sound *d* also changes to *n*. Thus the past passive participle

1. For a study of Pāṇinian *it-saṁjñā cf. M.D. Pandit* 'Pāṇinian It-Saṁjñā—A Symbolic Zero', *BDCPRI*, Vol. 25, 1966, pp. 76-94. *cf.* also 'Zero in Pāṇini', CASS, Pune, 1990.

from √*śṝ*, 'to whither away, to fall down, to scatter, to destroy or kill', which changes to *śīr* (i.e. ṛ > īr) according to the *sūtra*, *ṝta id dhātoḥ*, 7.1.100 is :

ṣṝ + ta

= śīr + ta

= śīr + na

= śīrna

= śīrṇa (*n* > *ṇ* according to 8.4.1)

So is the case in the situation when the *-ta* is confronted with the sound *d*. Take, for example, the root √*bhid* 'to cut'. The process is :

bhid + ta

= bhid + na

= bhin + na

= bhinna

As *Kāśikā* says the sound *r* in the *sūtra* does not include the vocalic sound *ṛ* also; because the *ta* in *kṛ+ta* does not change to *na;* cf. *Kāśikā* on the *sūtra* 8.2.42 : *ra ity atra śrutisāmānyaṁ nopādīyate, kiṁ tarhi vyañjanamātram / rephasāmānyanirdeśe'pi sati rephāt parā yā'jvibhaktis tadvyavadhānan natvaṁ na bhavati.*

A second point to be noted in this connection is that the sound *d* does not automatically change to *n* according to the *sūtra, yaro'nunāsike 'nunāsiko vā,* 8.4.45; it is specifically stated to change to *na* because the *sūtra,* 8.4.45 requires that the *d* must be at the end of a *pada;* cf. the word *padānṭāt* to be borrowed in the *sūtra,* 8.4.45, from a previous *sūtra,* 8.4.42.

The *sūtras* of other grammarians, corresponding to Pāṇini's *8.2.42*, are :

Kātantra : *rān niṣṭhāto no'pṝmūrchi madikhyādhyābhyaḥ,* 4.6.101, and *dād dasya ca,* 4.6.102.

Candra : *radāt tatavator daś ca,* 6.3.74.

Bhoja : *radābhyāṁ nisṭhāto daś ca naḥ*, 7.3.84.

Jainendra : *drāt tasya to naḥ pūrvasya do' pṝmūrchimadām*, 5.3.59.

Hemacandra : *radād amūrchamadaḥ ktayor daysa ca*, 4.2.69.

Śākaṭāyana : *ktayor draśyauditsūyatyāder dasya cāmanmṝchaḥ*, 4.1.246.

Sārasvata : *raḥ*, 7.4.28; *das tasya no daś ca*, 7.4.36.

Kātantra and Sārasvata agree in framing two independent *sūtras* for the phonological conditions of the precedence of sound *r* and *d* to *ta* and the consequent change of *ta* and *d* into *n*.

Jainendra, Hemacandra, and Śākaṭāyana agree in combining two *sūtras* of Pāṇini viz. 8.2.42 and 8.2.57.

Candra and Bhoja, however, fully agree with Pāṇini in respect of the wording and the meaning of the *sūtra*.

4.1.2 The second Pāṇinian *sūtra* which lays down the formal or phonological conditions for the change of *t* to *n* is *saṁyogāder āto dhātor yaṇvataḥ*, 8.2.43. The rule states that if the *dhātu* or root-morpheme begins with a conjuction or cluster[1] of consonants with any of the semi-vowels (cf. the words *yaṇvataḥ saṁyogādeḥ*, in the *sūtra* 8.2.43) and ends in -*ā* before the past passive participal termination *-ta*, the termination changes to *-na*. It is to be noted that both the conditions. viz. beginning with cluster of consonant with a semi-vowel and ending in *-ā* before the termination *-ta*, must be statisfied simultaneously or concurrently. If, therefore, a root only begins with the conjunction of a consonant with a semi-vowel, say for example, the root *dru* 'to go, to run' (cf. Pāṇinian *dhp. dru gatau*, 1st conj. Parasmaipada), and does not end in *ā*, or if a root only ends in *-ā* and does not begin with the conjunction of a consonant with a semi-vowel, like the root √*vā* 'to go' (cf. Pāṇinian *dhp. vā gatau*, 2nd conj.

1. *Saṁyoga* or cluster is defined by Pāṇini in *halo' nantarāḥ saṁyogaḥ*, 1.1.7.

Parasmąipada), the change of *ta* into *na* does not take place; thus the past passive participles from the two roots, √*dru* and √*yā*, will respectively be *druta* and *yāta*, and not *druṇa* and *yāna*.

Moreover, a root to have its *-ta* changed to *-na* must satisfy both these conditions before the past passive participial termination only and not in any other situation; otherwise, the *ta* does not chnge to *na*. The root *styai* with *pra*, for example, which changes its *-ai* to *-ā* in many other situations (cf. the Pāṇinian *sūtra, ādeca upadeśe'śiti*, 6.1.45), does not change to *ā* but undergoes the *saṁprasāraṇa* and changes to *pra* + *stī*; hence the *ta* does not change to *na* and the formation is *prastīta* (for the *saṁprasāraṇa* of √*styai*, cf. the Pāṇinian rule, *styaḥ prapūrvasya*, 6.1.23).

The corresponding *sūtra* of other grammarians are :

Kātantra : *āto'ntaḥsthāsaṁyuktāt*, 4.6.103.

Candra : *yaṇsaṁyogād ātaḥ*, 6.3.75.

Bhoja : *yaṇsaṁyogāder ātaḥ*, 7.3.85.

Jainendra : *sphāder āto dhātor yaṇvato'dhyākhyaḥ*, 5.3.60

Hemacandra : *vyañjanāntaḥsthā 'to'dhyākhyaḥ*, 4.2.71

Śākaṭāyana : *halo yaña āto 'dhyākhyaḥ*, 4.1.247.

Sārasvata : As in many other cases, in the present case also, the Sārasvata grammar has no *sūtra* in the *sūtrapāṭha*, and the need of a rule of this type is fulfilled by the *vārttika*-type statement of the later commentators; *cf. varalavasaṁyogāder ādantān niṣṭhātasya no vācyah*. As is clear, this shows incompleteness of the Sārasvata grammar.

All grammrians have followed Pāṇini, excepting Jainendra, Hemacandra, and Śākaṭāyana, who, instead of framing an independent rule for the formal conditions for the change of *ta* into *na*, have included certain exceptions also in the same rule - might be for the sake of greater brevity. Pāṇini perhaps thought it more convenient to mention these exceptions in an independent *sūtra*, viz. 8.2.57.

4.1.3 Exceptions to the Above Rules

The two sūtras of Pāṇini (and the corresponding *sūtras* of other grammarians), viz. 8.2.42 and 8.2.43, laying from the formal or phonological conditions for the change of *ta* to *na* cover a good number of cases of roots. Yet, the language, refusing to be dictated or channelised by the rules of grammarians, provides certain exceptions. These exceptions are of the types in which the roots in spite of satisfying all the conditions for the change of *ta* into *na* noted very carefully in the above two rules viz. 8.2.42, 43 do not give us forms with *-na* but with only *ta.* The exceptions of such roots are listed by Pāṇini in the *sūtra, na dhyākhyāpṝmūrchimadām,* 8.2.57, which notes the roots √*dhyā,* √*khyā,* √*pṝ,* √*mūrch* and √*mad* as giving out their past passive participles as *dhyāta, khyāta, pūrta, mūrta* and *matta* and not as *dhyāna, khyāna, pūrṇa, mūrṇa* and *manna.*

The relevant *sūtras* of other grammrians are :

Kātantra : *rān niṣṭhāto no'pṝmūrchimadikhyā-dhyābhyaḥ,* 4.6.101.

Candra : *na dhyākhyāpṝmūrchimadām,* 6.3.95.

Bhoja : *na pṝmūrchi madikhyādhyādevatrābhyaḥ,* 7.3.103, which adds two more roots viz. √*deva* and √*trā* to the list.

Jainendra : Instead of making an independent rule, Jainendra lists the exceptions in the rules laying down the formal conditions for *ta* > *na;* while the *sūtra, drāt tasya to naḥ pūrvasya to'pṝmūrchimadām,* 5.3.59 lists the exceptions of roots √*pṝ,* √*mūrch* and √*mad,* the *sūtra, sphāder*[1] *āto dhor yaṇvato'dhyākhyaḥ,.* 5.3.60, notes down the roots √*dhyā* and √*khyā* as exceptions.

Hemacandra follows Jainendra in discribing the exceptions in the rules stating the formal conditions

---

1. Jainendra's technical terms *spha* and *dhu* refer respectively to 'conjuction of consonants' and 'root'; *cf.* his *sūtras halo'nantarāḥ sphaḥ,* 1.1.3 (for *spha*) and *bhūvādayo dhuḥ,* 1.2.1 for *dhu.*

themselves; cf. *radād amūrcha madaḥ ktayor dasya ca,* 4.2.69. He, however, does not note the root √*pṝ*, whose past passive participle form is given as *pūrṇa* by Hemacandra's own commentary called *Svopajñalaghuvṛtti;* cf. the forms *pūrṇah, pūrṇavān* given in the *vṛtti* on 4.2.69. So also the commentary *prakriyāvṛtti* by *Śrīvinayavijayagaṇi; cf. pūrnaḥ, pūrṇvān/pūraici ity asya rūpam/*

Śākaṭāyana also agrees with Hemacandra in excluding the root √*pṛ* as exception to the general rules; he notes only the roots √*murch*, √*mad*, √*dhyā*, and √*khyā*; cf. his *sūtras, ktayor draśyauditsūyatyāder dasya cāmanmūrchaḥ,* 4.1.246 and *halo yaña āto'dhyākhyaḥ,* 4.1.247. It is to be noted that even the commentaries do not note the root √*pṛ* as exception or otherwise. Śākaṭāyana follows Hemacandra in not framing an independent *sūtra* for the exceptions.

Sārasvata : As in many previous cases, in this case also Sārasvata has no sūtra; the *vārttika*—type statement of the commentator, however, follows Pāṇini in noting all the five exceptions; *cf. dhyākhyāpṝmūrchimadām ktasya natvābhāvo vācyaḥ.* This is one more instance which brings out the incompleted character of the Sārasvata grammar.

Besides these, there are other exceptions also, which, in spite of not satisfying the formal conditions laid down in the two general rules, betray the change of *ta* to *na*. There are yet other cases in which the change of -*ta* into -*na* takes place optionally. Moreover, there are those which require the help of meaning to account for the change of -*ta* to -*na*. All such cases are treated under suitable headings below.

4.2 Semantic Conditions for the Change of ta into na

Certain forms undergo certain phonological, morphological, or syntactic changes under the influence of semantic environments. And the proces of substitution of one morpheme for another is no exception to this rule. In the case of the substitution of the terminationn *ta* by *na* also, there are cases which exhibit a tendency in which semantic considerations are unavoidable.

4.2.1 The form in question is *śīna,* alternated with *śīta;* both are past passive participles from *syai* 'to go' (*cf.* Pāṇinian *dhp. śyaiṅ gatau,* 1st conj. Ātmanepada). Yet the former i.e. *śīna* is used in circumstances in which the meaning of 'touch' is neither intended nor present, while the latter is used if the meaning of 'touch' is either present or implied. Thus we have the contexts like *śīnaṁ ghṛtam* (i.e. frozen or cold ghee), *śīnaṁ medaḥ* (i.e. the increased fat) etc. in which one's knolwedge of the state of the things signified does not depend upon 'the touch' of those things, and, therefore, in those circumstances *-ta* is changed to *-na.* In other contexts, however, like *śīto vāyuḥ* (i.e. the cold wind), *śītaṁ jalam* (i.e. cold water) etc. the quality of being cold can be judged or known only through the sense of touch. In such circumstances, *-ta* does not change to *-na.* In other words, where the *sparśānumeyatva* is present, *-ta* does not change to *-na;* where it is absent, *ta > na.*

The Pāṇinian *sūtra,* stating this rule, is *śyo'sparśe,* 8.2.47; the *saṁprasāraṇa* of *śyai* into *śi* is accomplished by the *sūtra, dravamūrtisparśayoḥ śyaḥ,* 6.1.24; the lengthening of *i* into *ī* is stated in *halaḥ,* 6.4.2.

In this connection, a reference may be made to a small point of discussion which has been raised by the Kāśikā. The √*sparś,* which gives out the primary derivative *sparśa* used in the *sūtra,* seems, according to the Kāśikā to have two meanings : (i) 'to touch' (cf. Pāṇinian dhp. *śpṛśa saṁsparśane,* 6th conj. Parasmaipada) and (ii) 'to be affected with disease' which meaning is nowhere found in any of the Sanskrit *dhātupāthas;*[1] this meaning is also noted by the Kātantra-vṛtti by Drugasiṁha in the *sūtra* corresponding to Pāṇini's 8.2.47 (cf. the *vṛtti* on Kātantra, 4.6.107, *śyo'sparśe); cf.* Kāśikā on the

1. cf. G. B. Palsule, *A Concordance of Sanskrit Dhātupāṭhas,* Deccan College Dissertation Series No. 14, Deccan College, Poona, 1955, p. 155.

Pāṇinian *sūtra*, 8.2.47: *śītam udakam ity atra guṇabhūto'pi sparśo natvapratiṣedhasya saṁprasāraṇasya ca nimittaṁ bhavati/ guṇe ca sparśe pratiṣedho'yam, na roge; tena pratiśīna ity atra natvaṁ bhavaty eva;* the same wording is repeated in Durgasiṁha's *vṛtti* on Kātantra, 4.6.107, with the additional remark : *na tu roge.*

This fact of the availability of another meaning viz. 'to become diseased' for the root √*spṛś*, which, according to all Sanskrit *dhātupāṭhas*, is stated to have only one meaning viz. 'to touch' raises many problems. That Pāṇini and all other grammarians are aware of another meaning for the root is clear from the fact that they have excluded that meaning in substituting *-na* for the past passive participial *-ta.* Then is the other meaning totally lost to us? Or, are all Sanskrit *dhātupaṭhas* incomplete in that they have not given this meaning also for the root √*spṛś?* As there is no evidence available in support of either of these two alternatives, one has to leave this question undecided.

All other grammarians follow Pāṇini in treating this phenomenon of *ta* > *na* in the case of the past passive participle from √*syai* on semantic level. The corresponding *sūtras* are :

Kātantra	:	*śyo'sparśe*, 4.6.107.
Candra	:	*śyo'sparśe*, 6.3.83.
Bhoja	:	*śyo'sparśe*, 7.3.94.

Jainendra combines into one three rules of Pāṇini viz. 8.2.47, 48, 49; cf. his *sūtra, śyāñcidivo'sparśānapādānājaye*, 5.3.65. The *Mahāvṛtti* on Jainendra explicitly remakrs: *śītam udakam ity atra śparśābhidhānadvāreṇaiva dravye vṛttiḥ.* It, however, quotes the root √*spṛs* meaning 'to become diseased'; *cf. nanu spṛśa upatāpe ity etasya sparśo rogaḥ / tatra pratiśīnaḥ /* The Jainendra *dhātupāṭha*, however, gives only one meaning for the root; cf. *spṛśa sparśe.*

Hemacandra combines into one the two Pāṇinian rules,

viz. *dravamūrtisparśayoḥ śyaḥ*, 6.1.24 and *śyo 'sparśe*, 8.2.47. He, however, strikes a point of difference in that he treats the change of *śyai* to *śī*, not on phonetic i.e. *saṁprasāraṇa* level, but on the level of morphemic substitution;[1] he straightaway substitutes *śī* for *śyai*. Yet, he follows Pāṇini in treating the substitution of *ta* by *na* on the semantic level; cf. his *sūtra* : *śyaḥ śīr dravamūrtisparśe naścāsparśe*, 4.1.97.

Śakaṭāyana : *ktayor draśyauditsūyatyāder dasya cāmanmūrchaḥ*, 4.1.246, only substitutes the *ta* by *na* without referring to semantic conditions under which the change takes place. The *Cintāmaṇivṛtti* on Śākaṭāyana's grammar, however, significantly gives the examples of *śīnaṁ ghṛtam / pratiśīnam*. Unlike Hemacandra, Śākaṭāyana accomplishes the base *śī* with the help of phonological substitution of *y* by *i*, which is lengthened according to the *sūtra*, *dīrgho 'co'vaḥ*, 4.1.135. The substitution corresponds to Pāṇini's *saṁprasāraṇa*. The *sūtra* laying down *i* for *y* is *dravamūrtau śya*, 4.1.131, in which also the meaning *sparśa* is absent. Thus a reference to semantic condition of *sparśa* is totally absent in both these *sūtras* of Śākaṭāyana.

The Sārasvata grammar does not explain the form in the regular *sūtra-pātha;* what is, however, still more surprising is that even none of the commentators on that grammar has taken the trouble to explain or even refer to it. This speaks for the incompleteness as well as the looseness of the Sārasvata grammar.

4.2.2 The next form for discussion on semantic level is the past passive participle from √*añc* (Pāṇinian *añcu gatau yācane ca*, 1st conj. Parasmaipada) 'to go, to beg, to ask for' etc. The Pāṇinian *sūtra*, *añco'napādāne*, 8.2.48, which explains the forms *akna* and *akta*, both from √*añc* is not connected with

1. Hemacandra thus seems to be consistent in adopting morphemic substitution in the case of *śyai* as he has done in the previous two cases of √*pyai* and √*sphāy*, while Pāṇini adopts the morphemic substitution only in the case of √*pyai* and √*sphāy*.

an *apādāna* which always takes the ablative case (cf. the Pāṇinian *sūtra, apādāne pañcamī,* 2.3.28); the *ta* changes to *na*. The *apādāna* is defined by Pāṇini in the *sūtra, dhruvam apāye'pādānam,* 1.4.24. If it is connected syntactically with an *apādāna* in the ablative case, the *ta* does not change to *na*. The illustration given by Kāśikā and BD, namely, *udaktam udakaṁ kūpāt* ('the water is well drawn out of the well'), in which the form *-akta* with the *upasarga* ud is connected syntactically with the ablative sing. *kūpāt* and hence does not get the substitute *-na* for *-ta,* well illustrates the point. As against this, the context *samaknau śakuneḥ pādau,* ('the feet of śakuni are very good or very well gone') has no syntactic relation with an *apādāna* and hence the form *samakna* gets *-na* in the place of *-ta*. If, however, we find the form *-akta* (as in *vyakta),* not connected with an *apādāna* and still retaining its *-ta,* the form must be derived from √*añj* and not from √*añc;* cf. Kāśikā: *vyaktam ity añjeḥ rūpam.*

All other grammars have also noted this form in the context of its syntactic relation with other elements of the structure; cf. the corresponding *sūtras:*

Kātantra : *anapādāne'ñceḥ,* 4.6.108.

Candra : *añco'navadhau,* 6.3.84; Candra's *avadhi*[1] is the same as Pāṇini's *apādāna, cf.* Candra *sūtra, avadheḥ pañcamīm* 2.1.81.

Bhoja : *añco' napādāne,* 7.3.95.

Jainendra : *śyāñcidivo'sparśānapādānājaye,* 5.3.65.

Hemacandra combines the two Pāṇinian *sūtras* viz. 8.2.48 *(añco'napādāne)* and 8.2.49 *(divo'vijigīṣāyām)* and the *vārttika,*

1. Though about Candra's grammar it is said that it does not contain any technical terms (cf. *candropajñam asaṁjñakam vyākaraṇam*), it is true only in a narrow sense; because if the word *avadhi* used here and in 2.1.81 is not a technical term, what else is it? It exactly behaves like a technical term though it is not defined. The usual primary linguistic meaning of the word *avadhi* as 'limit' etc. is true only in a narrow sense in the *sūtra,* 2.1.81.

pūño vināśe (on the Pāṇinian *sūtra,* 8.2.44 : *tvādibhyaḥ)* into one *sūtra;* cf. *pūdivyañcer nāśādyūtānapādāne,* 4.2.72.

Śākaṭāyana, like Hemacandra, combines the three roots, √*pū,* √*añc* and √*div* into one *sūtra;* cf. his *sūtra: pūdivyañcer nāśājigīsānapādāne,* 4.1.248.

The Sārasvata grammar has neither any *sūtra* nor any *vārttika*-type statement which explains the subtle semantic and syntactic difference between the two past passive participial formations *akta* and *akna.* This shows incomplete and loose character of the Sārasvata grammar.

4.2.3 The next form in which the change of *-ta* to *-na* is explained by all on the bais of semantic consideration is *dyūta,* alternated with *dyūna,* from √*div* 'to play dice, to go' etc., which is a multi-vocal root; *cf.* Pāṇinian *dhātupāṭha: divu krīḍāvijigīṣādyutistutimodamadasvapna-kāntigatiṣu,* 4th conj. Parasmaipada. Out of all these meanings, only the meanings (i) to play dice and (ii) 'to desire to win' *(vijigīṣā)* display difference in formations according as the root conveys this or that meaning.

The Pāṇinian *sūtra, divo'vijigīṣāyām,* 8.2.49 states that if the meaning 'to desire to win' the game (of dice) is not present or intended, the *-ta* is substituted by *-na.* Thus, we have the two forms: (i) *dyūta,* signifying 'played with the desire to win' the game (of dice) and (ii) *dyūna* signifying simply 'play', the desire to win being absent on the part of the player.

All grammarians have noted this semantic difference underlying the formal difference of the two forms. All have followed Pāṇini. The corresponding *sūtras* by other grammarians are :

Kātantra :	*avijigīṣāyāṁ divaḥ,* 4.6.109.
Candra :	*adyūte divaḥ,* 6.3.85.
Bhoja :	*divo'vijigīṣāyām,* 7.3.96.
Jainendra :	*śyāñcidivo'sparśānapādānājaye,* 5.3.65.

Hemacandra : *pūdivyañcer nāśādyūtānapādāne*, 4.2.72.
Śākaṭāyana : *pūdivyañcer nāśājigīṣānapādāne*, 4.1.248.

As is often the case Sārasvata does not describe this form.

4.2.4 Besides the formations discussed above, which are noted and described by almost all grammarians in the body of their grammars, there are others which are treated by some grammarians only, while the others do not note them at all. The present section, therefore, is meant to study all such formations. In the case of these formations also, the semantic import for the explanation of the substitution of *-ta* by *-na* is predominant throughout.

4.2.4.1 One of the forms is *pūta*, alternated with *pūna* with a change of *ta* into *na*, from √*pū* 'to flow, to purify' etc.; *cf.* Pāṇinian *dhātupāṭha : pūṅ pavane*, 1st conj. Ātmanepada and *pūñ pavane*, 9th conj. Ubhayapada.

Besides these two meanings, as Vārttikakāra Kātyāyana says, we get a third meaning for the root; and that is 'to destroy'. In this sense of the root, the past passive participial termination *-ta* gives place to *-na* as the *vārttika, pūño vināśe*, on the Pāṇinian *sūtra, lvādibhyaḥ*, 8.2.44, notes. Pāṇini, however, does not note the meaning 'to destroy' for the root nor does he explain the change of *-ta* to *-na* in its past passive participial formations. Thus we have the two forms *pūna* and *pūta*, the former in the sense of 'destruction' and the latter in the sense of 'flowing or purifying'.

The Kātantra grammar also follows Pāṇini in not describing the form *pūna*, though the *vṛtti* by Durgasiṁha on the Kātantra *sūtra*, 4.6.104 *(lvādyodanubandhaś ca)* notes the form and says : *pūño nāśe, pūnā yavāḥ, vinaṣṭāḥ ity arthaḥ* and further brings out its semantic difference from the alternative form *pūta* by the remark : *nāśa iti kim? pūtaṁ dhānyam, kampitam ity arthaḥ*. The commentary *Chandrikā* on the Kātantra sūtra adds as a sort of *vārttika* the statement : *punāter vināśe iti vaktavyam.*

Jainendra, on the other hand, notes the form *pūna,* not on the level of morphemic substitution of the termination but on *nipātana*-level. In the *sūtra, vittabhittadūnagūnapūnasitarṇāni,* 5.3.74, he mentions the form *pūna* itself without explaining the procedure of its derivation. As the *Mahāvṛtti* on Jainendra says *(cf. pūño vināśe natvaṁ, pūnā yavāḥ/vināśa iti kim? pūtā yavāḥ, pūtam dhānyam),* the meaning of *pūna* requires the environment of *'vināśa'* i.e. destruction.

Candra notes and treats the form on the level of morphemic substitution of *-ta* by *-na;* cf. his *sūtra : pūño nāśe,* 6.3.77.

So also Bhoja who usually follows Candra : *cf.* his *sūtra, pūño nāśe,* 7.3.87.

Hemacandra and Śākaṭāyana follow Candra; *cf.* Hemacandra : *pūdivyañceḥ nāśādyūtānapādāñe,* 4.2.72 and Śākaṭāyana : *pūdivyañceḥ nāśājigiṣānapādāne,* 4.1.248.

Neither the Sārasvata *sūtrapāṭha* nor the commentaries note the form *pūna;* the grammar, however, in the *sūtra, pūño vā ktaḥ seṭ,* explains the form *pūtaḥ.*

Actually no Sanskrit *dhātupāṭha* records the meaning 'to destroy' for the root √*pū,* especially for the one which is in the 9th conj. and Ubhayapadin, viz. *pūñ.* The only explanation for such a meaning is, as Kaiyyaṭa in his Pradīpa says : *anekārthatvād dhātūnām;* cf. Kaiyyata's *Pradipa* on the *vārttika, pūño vināśe* on the Pāṇinian *sūtra,* 8.2.44.

4.2.4.2 The next form, noted by some but not others, is *sina,* alternated with *sita,* a past passive participle from √*si* 'to bind'; cf. Pāṇinian *dhātupātha, ṣiñ bandhane,* 5th conj. Parasmaipada.

Pāṇini does not note the form *sina* on any level. The vārttikakāra, however, adds the supplement *sinoter grāsakarmakartṛkasyeti vaktvyam,* which states that the *-ta* changes to *-na* in the case of the root √*si* 'to bind' when it is used in a reflexive sense of becoming a morsel fit for consumption or swallowing. Thus the form *sina* in the context, *sino grāsaḥ svayam eva*, means that a morsel has bound itself (note the reflexive sense), whereas the context like *sito grāsaḥ devadattena* ('the morsel is bound by Devadatta) requires the form *sita*, and not *sina*, as the sense is not reflexive but passive; cf. *Tattvabodhinī* on the *sūtra*, 8.2.44: *piṇḍīkriyamāṇo grāso yadā dadhyā-divyāñjanavaśād bandhane'nukūlo bhavati tadā karmaṇa eva kartṛtvaṁ iti bodhyam;* cf. also Kaiyyaṭa's *Pradīipa* and Nāgeśa's *Udyota*, both commentators on the *Mahābhāṣya* of Patañjali.

The Sārasvata grammar follows Pāṇini in not describing the form. So also Kātantra and its commentaries none of which notes this form.

Candra : *ser grāse*, 6.3.79.

Bhoja : *ser grāse karmakartari*, 7.3.89.

Hemacandra : *ser grāse karmakartari*, 4.2.73.

Śākaṭāyana : *seḥ karmakartari grāse*, 4.1.249.

Jainendra notes the form on the *nipātana* level; *cf. vittabhittadūnagūnapūnasitarṇāni*, 5.3.74.

There seems to be some mistake in the reading of the *sūtra*, which notes the form as *sita* and not *sina*. Surprisingly enough, even the *Mahāvṛtti* on the Jainendra grammar totally misses the form *sina;* it actually explains the form *sita* in the context of reflexive sense in which, according to other grammarians, *sina* should be used; cf. the *Mahāvṛtti : sita iti sinoter grāsakarmakartṛkasya bhavati; sito grāsaḥ svayam eva / grāsa iti kim? sitā pāśena sūkarī / karmakartṛkasyeti kim? sito grāso devadattena*. Thus there is no mention of the form *sina* at all either in the *sūtra* or in the commentary. One important point may be noted here. The *sūtrakāra* does not specify the semantic conditions under which the two forms *sina* and *sita* are to be distinguished. The absence of the specification of semantic conditions is notable especially in cases which are treated by Jainendra on *nipātana* -level.

4.3 Forms Treated by Enumeration

The third method followed by the grammarians in making their grammar as comprehensive as possible is enumeration. This method is followed when a form or a group of forms displays a structure totally different from that of those which are treated in generalised rules. Thus if a form cannot be accounted for by general rules, the form is specially treated in an independent *sūtra*.

There are two ways of enumeration : (i) If all the forms which cannot be explained by general rules display individual characteristics different from one another and if they cannot be comprehended in a single *sūtra,* each and every form of this type requires to be explained singly and individually in an independent *sūtra*. This is *gaurava* obviously; but it has also got to be resorted to in some cases. (ii) The other type of enumeration becomes applicable, when, out of all the formations which defy general rules, some display characteristics which are common pattern already noted by general rules. Such formations can be enumerated in groups. We may, therefore, term the former enumeration as 'enumeration of individual items' and the latter as 'enumeration of groups'. We start with the first type of enumeration.

4.3.1 Enumeration of individual items for the morphemic substitution of *ta* by *na* :— The semantic considerations are totally absent here. All cases in which the semantic aspect is taken into consideration are already dealt which in previous section viz. 4.2.

4.3.1.1 One such form which is noted in isolation, since it cannot be fixed in any general rules, is *kṣīṇa* the past passive participle of √*kṣi* 'to wane, to dwell' etc. The form is already discussed in Chapter 2; but there the point of emphasis was of the substitution of the root morpheme *kṣi* by another morpheme viz. *kṣī*. Here the point of interest is the substitution of the termination-morpheme *-ta* by the morpheme *-na* under certain conditions.

The Pāṇinian *sūtra* which lays down the formal condition for the change of *ta* into *na* is *kṣiyo dīrghāt*, 8.2.46 which states that the *ta* changes to *na* in the case of the root √*kṣi* which is lengthened; the lengthening is accomplished by the *sūtras, kṣiyaḥ*, 6.4.59 and *niṣṭhāyām aṇyadarthe*, 6.4.60 discussed in chapter 2. Since the lengthening is stated to take place when the sense of *bhāva* and *karma* (cf. the word *anyadarthe* in the *sūtra*, 6.4.60) are not intended, the meaning of the past passive participle of √*kṣi* formed by lengthening and the change of *ta* into *na* is also not in *bhāva* and *karma* but active. Thus :

kṣi + *ta*

= *kṣī* + *ta*

= *kṣī* + *na*

= *kṣīṇa* (*n* > ṇ according to 8.4.2).

When however, the *i* of *kṣi* is not lengthened, the *-ta* does not change to *-na;* this situation arises when the meaning is of *bhāva* and *karma*. We have thus two forms : *kṣita* (in the sense of *bhāva* and/or *karma*) and *kṣīṇa* (in the active sense).

The corresponding sūtras of other grammarians are :

Kātantra : *kṣer dīrghāt*, 4.6.106.

Candra : *kṣeḥ kṣī ca*, 6.3.81.

Bhoja : *kṣeḥ kṣī ca*, 7.3.92.

Jainendra : *kṣīṇaḥ*, 5.3.64.

Hemacandra : *kṣeḥ kṣī cāghyārthe*, 4.2.74.

Śākaṭāyana : *kṣer aghye*, 4.1.252.

Sārasvata has no regular *sūtra* and the change of *-ta* into *-na* is accomplished by the *vārttika*-type statement : *dīrghād eva kṣiyo niṣṭhāyās tasya no vācyah*, added obviously by later commentators. This speaks for the incompleteness of the grammar.

We see now that for the form *kṣīṇa*, there are two statges : (i) the change of short *kṣi* into long *kṣī;* this is accomplished by Pāṇini, Kātantra, Jainendra, Śākaṭāyana, and Sārasvata on the phonetic basis of the substitution of a short grade by a long grade; Candra, Bhoja, and Hemacandra, on the other hand, accomplish it by the substitution of the morpheme *kṣi* (with short *i*) by the morpheme *kṣī* (with long *ī*). Both the groups of grammrians, however, account for the phonetic or morphemic substitution with the help of the grammatical meaning of 'active' (*cf. aṇyadartha* or *aghyartha* i.e. non-*bhāva* and non-*karma* meaning). (ii) The second stage is the substitution of *-ta* by *-na.* Thus both, the base morpheme as well as the termination-morpheme undergo change in the case of the form *kṣīṇa.*

Thus superficially both the points of view seem indentical. Yet there is a subtle difference between the two approaches. While Pāṇini, Kātantra, Jainendra and Sārasvata connect the change of *-ta* into *-na* with the lengthening of the previous vowel *i* of √*kṣi* (which is accomplished on semantic basis), Candra, Bhoja, Hemacandra and Śākaṭāyana connect the change with semantic difference between the forms *kṣita* and *kṣīna;* cf. the respective *sūtras.*

Now the problem is which procedure is in greater agreement with the principle of grammar composition? Granted that every grammarian is at full liberty to follow his own method of linguistic description; yet strictly from grammatical point of view, only a description which is based on formal consideration is the most natural to grammar, if grammar is to be as formal as possible. If we now compare the form *kṣīṇa* and *kṣita,* devoid of their semantic counterparts, we notice that the most conspicuous formal factor responsible for the change of *ta* into *na* is the lengthening of the previous vowel. It is therefore more natural to connect this lengthening rather than the change of *-ta* into *-na,* with the semantic consideration. Pāṇini has done exactly the same thing. From grammatical point of view, therefore, Pāṇini's description is more natural than that of Candra, Bhoja, Hemacandra and Śākaṭāyana who connect the change of *-ta* into *-na* with meaning.

Jainendra's description of the form *kṣīṇa* seems to have been treated on the level of *nipātana* (cf. his *sūtra, kṣīṇaḥ,* 5.3.64), though the *Mahāvṛtti* does not explain it as a *nipātita* form; on the other hand, it explains that the *ta* changes to *na* before the lengthened *ī* of *kṣī;* cf. the *Mahāvṛtti: kṣī ity etasmāt kṛtadītvāt parasya takārasya no bhavati.*

4.3.1.2 The other forms which are described by individual enumeration are *dūna* and *gūna* from root √*du* 'to go' (1st conj. Parasmaipada; Pāṇinian *du gatau,* and not ṭudu upatāpe, 5th conj. Parasmaipada[1]) and √*gu* 'to void feces' (cf. Pāṇinian *dhātupāṭha, gu purīṣotsarge,* 6th conj. Parasmaipada) respectively. Pāṇini, however, has not noted these forms and it is left to Kātyāyana to improve on Pāṇini. The *vārttika* of Kātyāyana on Pāṇini 8.2.44 *(lvādibhyaḥ),* which notes these forms is *dugvor dirghaś ca.* Since these forms are noted by other grammarians in the regular body of their grammar, they are taken here for discussion, in spite of their non-observance on the part of Pāṇini.

Kātantra follows Pāṇini in not describing the forms, though the vṛtti by Durgasiṁha on the Kātantra *sūtra,* 4.6.104, *(lvādyodanubandhāc ca),* notes them; cf. the *vṛtti : dūnaḥ, dūnavān/vidūnaḥ, vidūnavān/vigūnaḥ, vigūnavān,* adding the remark that the group of *lvādi* is flexible (cf. the *vṛtti : ganakṛtasya anityatvāt)* and that the word *ca* in the sūtra, 4.6.104 includes even those roots which are not included in the *gaṇa;* cf. the *vṛtti : cakāro'nuktasamuccayārthaḥ.* It perhaps quotes the *vārttika* of kātyāyana when it remarks : *dugvor*

1. That √*du* refers to one in the 1st conj. and not to the one in the 5th conj. is clear from the absence of the *it* sound *ṭu,* the *it*-sounds *ṭu* are applied to the latter, cf. BD's remark on the *vārttika, dugvor dīrghaś ca,* on Pāṇini 8.2.44: *ṭudu upatāpe ity ayaṁ na tu gṛhtyate, sānubandhakatvāt.* Secondly, if √*du* from 5th conj. were intended, at least some such form as *'dunoteḥ'* would been used in the *vārttika.*

dīrghaś ca. The Candrikā, another commentary says : *dugvour dīrghaś ceti vaktavyam.*

Candra and Bhoja lay down the substitution of (long) *ū* for (short) *u* of the root √*du* and √*gu;* cf. Candra : *dugvour ū ca,* 6.3.78 and Bhoja : *dugvor ū ca,* 7.3.88. Actually Candra, who does not use any technical terms, uses the term *dīrgha* (cf. the *sūtras,* 5.1.72; 112; 6.1.33; 6.2.122; 141; 6.4.147 all of which contain the term *dīrgha*); he could have stated the phenomenon in terms of phonetic grades of *hrasva* and *dīrgha* (he also uses the term *hrasva;* cf. the *sūtras,* 6.2.119; 6.4.87 etc.). The purpose in not using the term *dīrgha* here is perhaps brevity because *dugvor dīrghaś ca,* contains five syllables as against four of the statement *dugvour ū ca.* Bhoja follows Candra.

Jainendra notes the forms by way of *nipātana* in the *sūtra, vittabhittadūnagūnapūnasitarnāni,* 5.3.74, though the *Mahāvṛtti* does not fail to remark: *dugvor dītvaṁ natvaṁ ca nipātyate.*

Hemacandra follows Candra; cf. his *sūtra: dugor ū ca,* 4.2.77. He, however, takes the root √*du* to refer to the one form the 5th conj. (cf. Hemacandra's *dhp. tuduṇṭ upatāpe);* cf. the Prakriyāvṛtti by Śrīvinayavijayagaṇi; *ṭuduṇṭ upatāpe, svādiḥ.* What is more surprising is that he full well knows BD's point of view that √*du* does not refer to the one from the 5th conj., as is clear from his remark: *kaumudyāṁ tu... tudu upatāpe ity ayaṁ na tu gṛhyate, sānubandhakatvā.* He, however, has not advanced any reasons for his view.

Śākaṭāyana : *dugvor dīrghaś ca,* 4.1.251. His example *gūno vatsaḥ,* however, suggests that the form is used in an active sense. He follows Kātyāyana.

Sārasvata's commentary only notes the form *dūna* from √*dū* (with long *ū*) which is reconstructed as √*dūṅ,* yet which has two meanings; cf. *dūṅ parityāge,* and *dūṅ duḥkhe.* We do not yet know to which conjugations they belong. The form *gūna* is not noted in the commentary. Sārasvata follows Pāṇini in not noting the forms.

This exhausts the list of forms which are listed individually in independent *sūtras*, for the change of *-ta* into *-na* without any semantic considerations.

4.3.1.3. There is yet another form viz. *vṛkṇa* from √*vraśca* 'to cut' (Pāṇinian *ovraścū chedane*), which Pāṇini and all other grammarians, except the author of Kātantra grammar, have not enumerated independently. Since the Kātantra grammar specially notes this form for the change of *ta* into *-na* as well as for the substitution on the final *-śc* by *k*, it is taken here for study. The Kātantra *sūtra* that lays down both these changes is *vraśceḥ ka ca*, 4.6.105. The process according to the Kātantra, therefore, is

vraśc + ta

= *vṛśc + ta (saṁprasāraṇa* of *r* into *ṛ* by 3.4.2)

= *vṛśc + na (ta > na* according to 4.6.104.)

=*vṛk + na (śc > k* according to 4.6.105).

=*vṛkna*

= *vṛkṇa*

According to Pāṇini the change of *-ta* to *-na* is accounted for by the Pāṇinian *sūtra oditaś ca*, 8.2.45, the change of *vraśc* to *vṛk* is also accounted for, not by substitution of *-śc* by *-ka*, but by another grammatical process. The grammatical process to arrive at the formation according to Pāṇini is :

vraśc + ta

=*vṛśc + ta* (*r > ṛ* according to 6.1.16)

= *vṛc + ta* (*ś* = o according to 8.2.29)

=*vṛk+ ta* (*c > k* according to 8.2.30)

=*vṛk + na* (*ta > na* according to 8.2.45)

= *vṛkna*

= *vṛkṇa* (*n > ṇ* according to 8.4.2).

Similar is the process of other grammarians also, who treat this form on phonological level by regular grammatical procedure. Since the Kātantra has no such procedure for the change of *-śc* to *k*, it has to make an independent *sūtra* for that purpose.

4.3.2. *Enumeration by Forming Groups for the Change of* ta *into* -na.

4.3.2.1 One such group is the *lvādi* group, i.e. the group of roots with √*lū* in the beginning. The enumeration, it is clear, is by forming a group, because of the simple reason that all the roots in the group display identical grammatical behaviour in forming their past passive participial formations, though they do not follow either the formal or semantic conditions for the change of *-ta* into *-na*, which are laid down in the sūtras discussed in section 4.1 and 4.2 before. The Pāṇinian *sūtra* is *lvādibhyḥ*, 8.2.44 and the total number of roots in the lvādi group is 21[1] beginning with the root √*lū;* all roots are from the 9th conjugation. The *sūtra*, 8.2.44, states that in the case of the roots beginning with √*lū*, the past passive participial termination *-ta* changes to *-na*.

All the 21 roots can be divided on the basis of their endings into two broad groups: (i) all those which end in vowels other than ṛ and (ii) those which end in ṛ.

(i) The former includes the following 7 roots :

1. √*lū* 'to cut' (cf. Pāṇinian *dhp. lūñ chedane*).
2. √*jyā* 'to grow old' (cf. Paṇinian *jyā vayohānau*)
3. √*rī* 'to go' (cf. Paṇinian *rī gatireṣaṇayoḥ*).
4. √*lī* 'to stick' (cf. Pāṇinian *lī śleṣaṇe*).
5. √*vlī* 'to choose, to cover' (cf. Pāṇinian *vlī varaṇe*)
6. √*plī* 'to go' (cf. Pāṇinian *plī gatau*)
7. √*dhū* 'to tremble' (cf. Pāṇinan *dhūñ kampane*)

(ii) The latter group contains the following 14 roots :

1. √*stṛ* 'to cover' *(stṝñ ācchādane)*

---

1. cf. BD. on Pāṇini 8.2.44: *ekaviṁśater lūñādibhyaḥ*.

2. √kṝ 'to destroy' *(kṝñ hiṁsāyām)*
3. √vṝ 'to choose, to cover' *(vṝñ varaṇe)*
4. √śṝ 'to destroy' *(śṝ hiṁsāyām)*
5. √pṝ 'to fill, to protect' *(pṛ pālanapūraṇayoḥ)*
6. √vṝ 'to choose, to feed' *(vṝ varaṇe,[1] bharaṇe ity eke)*
7. √bhṝ 'to condemn' *(bhṝ bhartsane)*
8. √mṝ 'to destroy' *(mṝ hiṁsāyām)*
9. √dṝ 'to break open' *(dṝ vidāraṇe)*
10. √jṝ 'to grow old' *(jṝ vayohānau)*
11. √nṝ 'to lead, to train' *(nṝ naye)*
12. √kṛ 'to destroy' *(kṝ hiṁsāyām)*
13. √ṝ 'to go' *(ṝ gatau)*
14. √gṝ 'to speak, to praise' *(gṝ śabde)*

The corresponding *sūtras* of other grammarians are :

Kātantra : *lvādyodanubandhāc ca*, 4.6.104, which combines into one the two Pāṇinian sūtras, viz. 8.2.44 and 8.2.45.

Candra : *ṝlvādibhyaḥ ktinaś ca*, 6.3.76 followed by

Bhoja : *ṝlvādibhyaḥ ktinaś ca*, 7.3.86.

What is notable is that the *sūtras* of Candra and Bhoja mention separately the roots ending in *ṝ*, besides those that are in the *lvādi*-group. This may be taken to mean that either the *lvādi-group* in their *dhātupaṭhas* does not include the *ṝ*-ending roots or they are aiming to explain the *kṛt*-formations in *-ti* i.e. *ktin* also; in the latter case they follow Kātyāyana who specially for the purpose of accounting for the *kṛt*-formation in *-ti* frames a *vārttika* on Pāṇini 8.2.44, viz. *ṝkāralvādibhyaḥ ktin niṣṭhāvad bhavatīti vaktavyam.*

Jainendra follows Pāṇini, cf. his *sūtra, lvādeḥ*, 5.3.61.

---

1. The difference between *vṝñ* and *vṝ* is that while the former, being reconstructed as *ñit*, is conjugated in both the *padas* (cf. Pāṇinian *sūtra, svaritañitah kartrabhiprāye*, 1.3.72), the latter viz. *vṝ* is conjugated only in Parasmaipada; similar also is the difference between √kṝñ and √kṛ.

Hemacandra follows Candra and specially includes the ṝ-ending roots in the *sūtra* mainly for the purpose of accounting for their formations in *-ktin*, cf his *sūtra, ṝlvāder eṣāṁ tono'praḥ*, 4.2.68. He, however, excludes the root √*pṝ* whose past passive participle will then be *pūrta* and not *pūrṇa.*

Śākaṭāyana follows Hemacandra, Candra, and Bhoja in mentioning the ṝ-ending roots independently besides the *lvādi*-group; cf. his *sūtra, ṝlvādeḥ ktaktināṁ no apraḥ*, 4.1.245. Like Hemacandra, he excludes the root √*pṝ* for the change of *-ta* into *-na.*

Śārasvata follows Pāṇini in not mentioning the *ṝ*-ending roots seperately besides the *lvādi*-group. From his point of view, therefore, the *lvādi*-group contains the *ṝ*-ending roots also. He, however, follows Kātantra in combining into one the two Pāṇinian *sūtras*, viz. 8.2.44 and 8.2.45; cf. the Sārasvata sūtra, *lvādyoditaḥ*, 8.4.37.

4.3.2.2 In the case of another group of roots which are enumerated, the change of *-ta* into *-na* is optional. These are noted by Pāṇini in the *sūtra, nudavindondatrāghrā-hrībhyo'nyatarasyām* 8.2.56, which lists the roots √*nud*, √*vind*, √*und*, √*trā*, √*ghrā* and √*hrī*. We have two optional forms of the past passive participles of each of these roots, viz. *nunna/ nutta, vinna/vitta, unna/utta,/ trāna/trāta, ghrāna/ghrāta* and *hrīṇa/hrīta.* The pecullar feature of these forms is that they display optional formations (without change of *-ta* into *-na*) in spite of satisfying the formal conditions for the change of *-ta* into *-na*, covered up by Pāṇini in his *sūtra* 8.2.42 and 8.2.43. This clearly is a case of dialectal difference.

The corresponding sūtras of other grammarians are :

Kātantra : *hrīghrātrondanudavidāṁ vā*, 4.6.110

Candra : *ghrātrārtihrīnudondavido vā*, 6.3.87, which adds one more root viz. √*ṛ* to the list; the root √*ṛ*, therefore, gives out the two optional formations as *ṛta* and *ṛṇa.* Though Pāṇini does not list the root √*ṛ* for the optional change of *-ta* to *-na*, he has suggested by implication the optional form *ṛta* besides *ṛṇa,* which he notes by way of *nipāntana* on the basis of semantic considerations in the *sūtra, ṛṇam ādhamarṇye,* 8.2.60.

Bhoja, who usually follows Candra, however, excludes the root √ṛ from the list of Candra; cf. his *sūtra hrīghrātrondanudavinattibhyo vā,* 7.3.99.

Jainendra follows Pāṇini in the enumeration of roots; cf. his *sūtra, trāghrāhrīnudondavinter vibhāsā,* 5.7.73.

Besides following Candra in nothing the root √ṛ, Hemacandra lists one more root viz. √*dhrā;* cf. his *sūtra, ṛhrīghrādhrātrondanudavinter vā,* 4.2.76. The total number of roots in the case of which the *-ta* is optionally changes to *-na* thus swells to 8 which in Pāṇini's times is only 6.

Śākaṭāyana adds one new root to the six roots of Pāṇini, the new root is √*drā.* Thus, according to Śākaṭāyana, there are in all 7 roots in whose case *ta* optionally changes to *-na* without any semantic bearing, cf. his *sūra, hrīghrādrātrondanudvinteḥ,* 4.1.254. The roots √ṛ and √*dhrā* of Hemacandra are totally absent here. According to Pāṇini, however, the root √*drā* gives out only one form viz. *drāṇa* (according to the sūtra, 8.2.43); *drāta* is not possible in his grammar.

Can it be that Śākaṭāyana's √*drā* is the same as Hemacandra's √*dhrā?* But then, besides being phonetically different, these two roots display a semantic difference also; while Śākaṭāyana's √*drā* means 'to censure' to blame, to rebuke' (cf. *Śākatāyana's dhp. drā kutsāyām*), Hemacandra's *dhrā* means 'to satisfy, to be satisfied' etc. (cf. Hemacandra's *dhp. ḍhraiṅ trptau*). The root √*drā* and √*dhrā,* therefore, do not seem to be identical.

The Sārasvata *sūtra* which notes the optional substitution of *-ta* by *-na* in the case of the above roots is: *trāṇādyā vā,* 8.4.38. The *traṇādya* roots, according to the commentary are:[1]

---

1. cf. the commentary: ete *trāṇādyā jñeyāḥ.*

√*trā*, √*ghrā*, √*hrī*, √*nud*, √*vid*, √*und* and √*vā*, which adds the new root √*vā* to the Pāṇinian list of 6 roots. But it is to be noted that the examples of √*vā* that are given by the commentary are with the *upasarga nir;* cf. *nirvāti sma vā nirvāyate smāsau nirvāṇah, nirvātaḥ*. Out of these two, the form *nirvāṇa* is noted by Pāṇini on *nipātana*-level with the help of meaning in the *sūtra, nirvāṇo'vāte*, 8.2.50.

It may be noted that in all the cases discussed in the present section, no semantic considerations are resorted to by the grammarians for the explanation of the forms.[1]

4.4 Forms Accounted for With the Help of it-sounds

One of the most widely used and hence presumably the most favourite techniques of all Sanskrit grammarians in general and of Pāṇini in particular is the technique of *it-saṁjñā*, defined by Pāṇini in the *sūtras*, 1.3.2-1.3.8. The *it*-sounds in Pāṇini's grammar are attached anywhere and to any category of *dhātu, pratyaya*, or *prātipadika* according as it is found to have been accompanied by different categories.[2] The *it*-sounds, attached to terminations distinguish themselves from those attached to roots in that those in the former case are all from the group of consonants whereas those in the latter case are mainly from the group of vowels; also there are four *it* sound-groups viz. *ñi, ṭu, ḍu* and *ir* attached to the *dhātus*, which is in sharp contrast to those attached to the terminations which are all single-sound *it*-symbols. Grammatically, the purpose, as is well-known, of these it-sounds attached to *dhātus* is two-fold : (i) to

1. For details, cf. *M. D. Pandit*, 'Pāṇinian *It-Saṁjñā* — A Symbolic Zero' *BDCPRI*, 25, 1966, pp. 77-94; cf also, 'Zero in Pāṇini', ch-2, CASS, Pune, 1990 cf also for the *it*-soundss attached to the roots, *G. B. Palsule, The Sanskrit Dhātupāthas — A Critical Study*, University of Poona, 1961, Chapter III, pp. 57-58.
2. cf. for example the termination *-ya-* with different *it*-sounds as *yak, yat, yaṅ, yañ, kyac, kyaṅ* etc.; also the *it*-sound *c* accompanying different terminations *ac, ituc, imanic, śānac, kānac, cānaś, khac*, etc. cf. M.D. Pandit, Zero in Pāṇini, CASS, Pune, 1990. pp 56-58.

distinguish the apparently similar or homophonous terminations, *dhātus* etc. and (ii) to bring out the necessary grammatical modifications either in *prakṛti* or base, or in *pratyaya* or termination, or in both.

Logically the purpose of the *it*-sounds seems to be to create an artificial formal plane with reference to which the grammatical i.e. formal and non-formal categories could be bound together.

The technique is a very useful one and Sanskrit grammarians without any exception have resorted to it when the circumstances have demanded.

In the present case of the past passive participles also, the substitution of *ta* by *na* is sought to be explained with a reference to this artificial formal plane created by the *it*-sounds, which acts as a substitute for an alternative method of enumeration.

What Pāṇini and others have done is that they have attached some arbitrary *it*-sounds to roots; the roots are then recognised by these *it*-sounds. Thus there are *ādit, idit, īdit, udit, ūdit, ṝdit, ḷdit* and *odit* roots. This only means that the roots concerned are accomplished by the it-sounds *ā, i, ī,* etc.

Now, besides the roots, which have been studied before, and in whose case the *-ta* changes to *-na,* there are others which also display the same phenomenon but which are not covered up by the general rules. Such roots, therefore, are reconstructed by Pāṇini and others on the technical plane with the *it*-sound O and are termed as *odit* roots. This technique has made matters certainly easy for attaining brevity, the next step being to frame a *sūtra* stating that, in the case of *odit* roots, the past passive participial termination *-ta* is substituted by *-na.* And that is what exactly Pāṇini and others have done. The Pāṇinian *sūtra* for a change of *-ta* into *-na* with th help of the technique of *it-saṁjñā* is *oditaś ca,* 8.2.45. Thus the root √*ruj* 'to break', which is reconstructed technically as *rujo* gives out its past passive participial form as *rugṇa* and not *rukta*.

According to the enumeration of Pāṇini and others, the total number of *odit* roots is 21 (with 4 in the 1st conj., 2 in the 3rd, 5 in the fourth, 7 in the 6th, and 3 in the 7th conjugation).

The *sūtras* of other grammarians, corresponding to the Pāṇinian *sūtra*, 8.2.45 *(oditaś ca)* are :—

Kātantra : *lvādyodanubandhāc ca*, 4.6.104.

Candra : *oditaḥ*, 6.3.80.

Bhoja : *oditaḥ*, 7.3.90.

Jainendra : *oditaḥ*, 5.3.63.

Hemacandra : *sūyatyādyoditah*, 4.2.70.

Śākaṭāyana : *ktayor draśyauditsūyatyāder dasya cāmanmūrchaḥ*, 4.1.246.

Sārasvata : *lvādyoditaḥ*, 8.4.37.

It will be seen that while Kātantra and Sārasvata combine into one the two Pāṇinian *sūtras*, viz. 8.2.44 and 8.2.45, Śākaṭāyana combines four *sūtras* of Pāṇini into one, viz. 8.2.42; 45, 47 and 57. What is still more suprising to note is that the Sārasvata grammar, which has not laid down or defined the *it*-sounds in the case of the other non-*dhātu* category like the terminations, follows the technique of *it-saṁjñā* in the case of the roots; This fact combined with the other viz. that all the grammarians have resorted to the techniques of *it-saṁjñā* in the present case makes it clear that either all have followed the Pāṇinian *dhātupāṭha* in attaching the *it*-symbol O to all the 21 roots called *odit* or that all, including Pāṇini, have drawn from a common source of *dhātupāṭha* in which the roots were accompanied by the *it*-sound O. The only function that the *it*-sound O performs is the substitution of *ta* by *na;* there is no other function ascribed to it.

Besides the above 21 roots in whose case the past passive participial terminations *-ta* changes to *-na* there are other roots also which show a similar change of *-ta* to *-na* in thier past passive participles, but which neither satisfy the formal or semantic conditions nor are enumerated nor are *odit*. In the case of such roots Pāṇini and others have followed a different technique. What they have done is that they have arbitrarily termed these roots as *odit* even though the roots are not accompanied by the *it*-sound O.[1] The number of such roots is 9 and they are all from the 4th conj. They are :—

1. √*sū* 'to procreate' (cf. Pāṇinian *dhp. ṣūṅ prāṇiprasave*)
2. √*dū* 'to trouble' (cf. *dūṅ paritāpe*)
3. √*dī* 'to wane, to decrease' (cf. *dīṅ kṣaye*)
4. √*ḍī* 'to fly' (cf. *ḍīṅ vihāyasā gatau*)
5. √*dhī* 'to support' (cf. *dhīṅ ādhāre*)
6. √*mī* 'to destroy' (cf. *mīṅ hiṁsāyām*)
7. √*rī* 'to hear' (cf. *rīṅ śravaṇe*)
8. √*lī* 'to stick' (cf. *līṅ śleśaṇe*)
9. √*vrī* 'to choose' (cf. *vrīṅ vṛṇotyarthe*)

It is to be noted that all are Ātmanepadin roots ending as they are in the *it*-sound *ṅ*, according to the Pāṇinian *sūtra*, *anudāttaṅita ātmanepadam*, 1.3.12.

The technique of naming arbitrarily any group by a technical term such as *odit*, *ṅit*, etc. facilitates the lessening of the number of *sūtras*. In the case of the present 9 roots, otherwise, which could not be covered up by any previous *sūtras* stating the change of *ta* into *na*. Pāṇini and others

1. Pāṇini has followed this technique in many places; cf. for example, the *āgama*, *yāsut*, which, even though it does not contain the sound *ṅ* as *it*, is termed as *ṅit*, so that the purpose which the *it*-sound *ṅ* serves should be served here also; cf. the Pāṇinian *sūtra*, *yāsuṭ parasmaipadeṣūdātto ṅic ca*, 4.3.103. Such cases are examples of 'double artificiality', which is an indication of the language being so evasive of generalization.

would have been compelled to frame at least one *sūtra* more dealing with these roots. Those who follow Pāṇini in resorting to this technique of 'double artificiality' in which a category of group is arbitrarily named (here as *odit*) after a term which itself is already arbitrary or artificial (cf. the *it*-sounds *o*, *ṅ*, etc.) are :— Kātantra, Jainendra, Candra and Sārasvata; cf. their respective remarks:

Pāṇini : Kāsikā on the *sūtra*, 8.2.45: *svādayaḥ oditah;* BD. on the root √*vrī : svādaya oditaḥ; tat phalaṁ tu niṣṭhānatvam;* also on the *sūtra*, 8.2.45: *svādaya odita ity uktam.*

Kātantra : *vṛtti* by Durgasiṁha on 4.6.104: *svādaya odanubandhāḥ.*

Jainendra : Mahāvṛtti on the *sūtra*, 5.3.63: *ātideśikāḥ svādaya oditaḥ; sūñ prāṇiprasava ityādayo vrīṅ vṛnotyarthe ityevamantā daivādikaḥ.*

Candra, who generally does not follow Pāṇini surprisingly enough follows him in the present case; cf. the *vṛtti* on the *sūtra*, 6.3.80: *svādaya odita iti vacanāt.*[1]

Sārasvata: It lists all the 9 roots; cf. the commentary on the *sūtra*, 8.4.37: *ṣūṅ, dūṅ, ḍīṅ, dhīṅ, rīṅ, mīṅ, dīṅ, līṅ, vrīṅ ete nava oditaḥ.*

Those who have not used this type of technique of naming a group arbitrarily as *odit* even though it is not *odit* are:

Bhoja, who usually follows Candra and sometimes Pāṇini also, has followed neither of them in the present case; he, therefore, had to frame a new independent *sūtra* to describe these nine forms; cf. the sūtra, *sūyatyādibhyo navabhyaḥ*, 7.3.91.

Hemacandra and Śākaṭāyana, after forming a group of

---

1. This is one more example, in which the technical term *it* (defined by Candra in *anaṁśacihnam it*, 1.1.5) is employed by Candragomin, which proves false the claim *candropajñam asaṁjñakam vyākaraṇam*. One more result of being an *odit* is that these do not take the *āgama iṭ* in Candra's grammar; cf. the *vṛtti* on the *sūtra*, 6.3.80: *odittvād eva liṅgād iḍabhāvaḥ.*

these nine roots called *sūyatyādi,* include them in the *sūtra* which changes *-ta* into *-na* in the case of *odit* roots; cf. Hemacandra: *sūyatyādyoditaḥ,* 4.2.70 and Śākaṭāyana : *ktayor draśyauditsūyatyāder dasy cāmanmūrchaḥ,* 4.1.246.

Here ends the list of *sūtras* which prescribe the substitution of *ta* by *na.* If we study all the caes of roots which end in vowels and in whose case *-ta* changes to *-na* except that of the root √*kṣi* 'to dwell, to wane', etc. which ends in a short vowel viz. *i,* we find that the vowels preceding the termination *-na* are invariably all long. Pāṇini, therefore, is right in connecting the change of *-ta* into *-na* with the lengthening of the final vowel of √*kṣi* (cf. the discussion before on the Pāṇinian *sutra, kṣiyo dirghāt,* 8.2.46) and not with the semantic aspect as has been done by some grammarians.

5. Substitution of *-ta* by *-ka*

The next substitute of the past passive participial termination *-ta* is *-ka,* the formations with which also function as past passive participles. Historically speaking such a formation is just a verbal derivative with the termination *ka* having the sense of past passive participial form. The Indian grammarians are, therefore, justified in treating the substitute *ka* as an allomorph of the major termination *-ta.*

There is only one formation in which the termination *-ta* is substituted by *-ka* and that is of the form *śuṣka* 'dried' from √*śuṣ* 'to dry up'; cf. Pāṇinian *dhp. śuṣa śoṣaṇe,* 4thconj. Parasmaipada. The Pāṇinian *sūtra* that lays down this substitute is *śuṣah kaḥ,* 8.2.51.

The corresponding *sūtras* of other grammarians are :

Kātantra : *kṣaiśuṣipacām makavāḥ,* 4.6.111, which combines the three Pāṇinian *sūtras* viz. 8.2.51, 52, 53 into one, obviously for the sake of greater brevity.

Candra : *śuṣaḥ kaḥ,* 6.3.90.

Bhoja : *śuṣaḥ kaḥ,* 7.3.102.

Jainendra : *śuṣipaceḥ kvau,* 5.3.67 which combines two *sūtras* of Pāṇini, viz. 8.2.51 and 8.2.52.

Hemachandra follows Kātantra in combining three Pāṇinian *sūtras* into one cf. *kṣaiśuṣipaco makavam,* 4.2.78.

Śākaṭāyana follows Jainendra in combining only two Pāṇinian *sūtras;* cf. *śuṣpacaḥ kvam,* 4.1.257.

Sārasvata follows Pāṇini, Candra and Bhoja; cf. his *sūtra, śuṣeh kaḥ,* which has no regular serial number in the *sūtra-pāṭha* of that grammar. It seems to be an addition made by the commentators. An another example of the incomplete and loose character and composition of the grammar.

There are very few primary derivatives in *-ka* in Sanskrit. T. Burrows[1] notes only three, viz. *śuṣka, śloka* (<*śroka* from √*śṛ* 'to hear') and *atka,* 'garment'. To this list one may did not another, viz. *muṣka* (from √*muṣ*) also.[2] It is, however, significant that no formations other than *śuṣka* function as past passive participles. The termination *-ka,* however, is found abundantly in secondary derivatives; cf. *dūraka, vamraka, arbhaka, kumāraka, bālaka*[3] etc.

6. Substitution of *-ta* by *-va*

Like the previous substitute *-ka,* the substitute *-va* also, which replaces the past passive participial morpheme *-ta,* is available in an isolated case, viz. in the form *pakva,* from √*pac,* 'to cook'; cf. Pāṇinian *dhp. ḍupacaṣ pāke,* 1st conj. Ubhayapada. The root is also available in other senses, viz. 'to make clear'. (cf. Pāṇinian *dhp. paci vyaktīkaraṇe,* 1st conj. Ātmanapada) and 'to elaborate' (cf. Pāṇinian *dhp. paci vistāravacane,* 10th conj. Ubhayapada); in both these cases, the root gets the *num-āgama* (according to the *sūtra, idito num dhātoḥ,* 7.1.58) since they are both reconstructed as *idit* by Pāṇini on the technical

1. cf. *T. Burrow,* ibid., p. 196.
2. For others, cf. *A. A. Macdonell,* Vedic Grammra, p. 120.
3. For a detailed historical treatment of the suffix *-ka,* both in primary as well as secondary derivatives, cf. *J. Wackernagel, ibid.;* Band I, p. 225; Band II. 1, p. 230; Band II. 2, pp. 533f, 541, 552, 566, 751.

plane. The form *pakva*. however, goes back to the root √*pac* in the first sense of 'cooking' (i.e. to the root *ḍupacaṣ)* and not to the other two because, first, semantically it is found to have been used in the language in the sense of 'cooking' and secondly formally the past passive participial derivations from the other two will be *pañcita* and not *pakva.*

Since the form *pakva* functions as past passive participle in the language, it is treated as *niṣṭhānta* by grammarians.

The different *sūtras* of the grammarians which lay down the substitution of *-ta* by *-va* are :

Pāṇini :	*paco vaḥ,* 8.2.52.
Kātantra :	*kṣaiśuṣipacām makavāḥ,* 4.6.11.
Candra :	*paco vaḥ,* 6.3.91.
Bhoja :	*paco vaḥ,* 7.3.103.
Jainendra :	*śuṣipaceḥ kvau,* 5.3.67.
Hemacandra :	*kṣaiśuṣipaco makavam,* 4.2.78.
Śākaṭāyana :	*śuṣipacaḥ kvam,* 4.1.257.
Sārasvata :	*paco vaḥ,* 8.2.15.

There are quite a number of roots in the Sanskrit language which form their primary derivatives in *-va;* cf. *ṛkva* (from √*ṛc* 'to praise) *dhruva* (from √*dhru* 'to be firm'), *ranva* (from √*raṇ* 'to be glad') etc.[1] It seems very strange that out of all these formations only the form *pakva* is selected as representing the past passive participle of √*pac.* and others are rejected. The reason seems to be that while *pakva* functions in the language as past passive participle, the others do not. the inclusion of this form, therefore, as past passive participle supports our earlier observation viz. that for the grammarians functional or syntactic relations seem to be the base on which the various formations are sorted out.

---

1. For details, cf. *T. Burrow, ibid.,* p. 185; 369; cf. also for detailed treatment of the form *pakva, J. Wackernagel, ibid.,* Band I, p. 153, Band II. 1, p. 136, 230, 239, and Band II. 2, p. 552, 866f; cf. also *A. A. Macdonell,* ibid., p. 131.

7. Substitution of *-ta* by *-ma*

The next substitute of the past passive participial termination is *-ma*. There are only two forms with this suffix, which may be regarded as past passive participles. They are : (1) *kṣāma* (from √*kṣai* 'to wane, to decrease'; cf. Pāṇinian dhpd. *kṣai kṣaye,* 1st conj. Parasmaipada) and (2) *prastīma* (from pra + √*styai* 'to speak, to group' etc. cf. Pāṇinian *dhp. styai ṣṭyai śabdasaṅghātyoḥ,* 1st conj. Parasmaipada). There is a difference in the substitution of the termination *ma* in the case of these two forms. While for √*kṣai,* no formal or semantic condition in necessary, for √*styai* certain conditions are laid down.

7.1 The form kṣāma

The Pāṇinian *sūtra* that enjoins the substitution of -ta by *-ma* in the case of √*kṣai* is *kṣāyo maḥ,* 8.2.53.

The grammatical process to arrive at the formation according to Pāṇini is :—

kṣai + ta

= *kṣā + ta (ai > ā* according to *ādeca upadeśe'śiti,* 6.2.45)

= *kṣā + ma (ta > ma* according to 8.2.53*)*

The corresponding sūtras of other grammarians are :

Kātantra : *kṣaiśuṣipacām makavāḥ,* 4.6.111.

Candra : *kṣaḥ,* 6.3.89.

Bhoja : *kṣāyo nityam,* 7.3.101.

Jainendra : *kṣai maḥ,* 5.3.68.

Hemacandra : *kṣaiśuṣipaco makavam,* 4.2.78.

Śākaṭāyana : *kṣaḥ,* 4.1.256.

Sārasvata : *kṣāyo maḥ,* which seems to be a statement of the commentators since it has no number in the regular *sūtrapāṭha.* An example of the incompleteness of that grammar.

No formal or semantic conditions are laid down for the substitution of *-ta* by *-na*. Again, the substitution is not optional; it is compulsory, which is explicity stated by Bhoja ; cf. the word *nityam* in his *sūtra*, 7.3.101.

7.2 The form *prastīma*

There are three conditios for the root √*styai* giving the form *prastīma* : (i) It must be accompanied by the *upasarga pra;* (ii) In that case it gets the *samprasāraṇa, styai* changing to *sti,* which is lengthened into *stī* according to the Pāṇinian *sūtra, halaḥ,* 6.4.2 and (iii) it gets the substitute *-ma* for *-ta* only optionally.

Pāṇini first lays down the *saṁprasārana* which is connected with the formal condition of the accompaniment of the *upasarga pra.* The sūtra is : *styaḥ prapūrvasya,* 6.1.23. Then in the *sūtra, prastyo'nyatarasyām,* 8.2.54, he lays down the optional substitution of *-ta* by *-ma.* The grammatical process according to Pāṇini is:

pra + styai + ta

= *pra + sti + ta (saṁprasāraṇa* and *i + ai > i* according to *saṁprasāraṇāc, ca,* 6.1.108).

= *pra + stī + ta* (*i > ī* according to *halaḥ,* 6.4.2).

= *pra + stī + ma (ta > ma)*

= *prastīma.*

Since the substitution is optional, the *-ta* retains its existence and we have the optional form *prastīta.*

If, however, the root √*styai* is not accompanied by the *upasarga pra,* or is accompanied by any *upasarga* other than *pra,* the *saṁprasāraṇa* and the consequent substitution of *-ta* by *-ma* will not take place. And the form is :

styai + ta

= *styā + ta (ai > ā* according to 6.1145*)*

= *styā + na (ta > na* according to 8.2.43*)*

= *styāna,*

or with any *upasarga* other than *pra* like *vi, sam,* etc., *(vistyāna=) viṣṭyāna, saṁstyāna* etc.

For all practical purposes, the root √*styai* is the same as *ṣṭyai;* cf. Kāśika's remark on the Pāṇinian *sūtra,* 6.1.23: *styai ṣṭyai śabdasaṅghātayor dvayor apy etayor dhātvoḥ styārūpam āpannayoḥ sāmānyena grahaṇam.* The ditinction between the two roots will have to be made in forms like *tiṣṭyāsati* (des.), *atiṣṭyapat* (caus. aor) etc. where the original *ṣ* in *ṣṭyai* will be retained; cf. BD's remark on the roots √*styai* and √*ṣṭyai* : *ṣopadeśasyāpi satve kṛte rūpaṁ tulyam; ṣopadeśaphalam tu tiṣṭyāsati, atiṣṭyapad ity atra ṣatvam.*

The corresponding *sūtras* of other grammarians are :

Kātantra : *vā prastyo maḥ,* 4.6.112.

Candra : *prastyo maḥ,* 6.3.88, the option *(vā)* to be borrowd from the preceding *sūtra,* 6.3.87.

Bhoja : *prastyo maḥ,* 7.3.100, *vā* to be borrowed from previous *sūtra,* 7.3.99.

Jainendra : *prastyo vā,* 5.3.69.

Hemacandra : *prāt taś ca mo vā,* 4.1.96.

Śākaṭāyana : *prastyo maḥ,* 4.1.255, *vā* to be borrowed from 4.1.253.

The Sārasvata grammar which notes the other form *kṣāma* fails to note this form. Even the commentary on the grammar has nothing to say on this form.

That the sole reason to treat only these two forms with -*ma* suffix as the past passive participles is their function in the language; this is clear from the exclusion of many other primary derivatives in *-ma* like *tigma, dasma, bhīma, ajma, idhma, gharma, dhūma, rukma* etc. which do not function as past passive participles.[1]

---

1. For many other formations ending in *-ma,* cf. *A. A. Macdonell, ibid.,* pp. 127-128; cf. also *T. Burrow, ibid.,* p. 174; cf. also *J. Wackernagel, ibid.,* Band I, p. 239, Band II. 2, pp. 130, 552, 750f.

8. Substitution of *-ta* by *-la*

The only formation that ends in *-la* which is treated by the grammarians is *phulla* from √*phala* 'to blossom, to burst' (cf. Pāṇinian *dhātupāṭha, ñiphalā, viśaraṇe*, 1st Conj. Parasmaipada). Actually the form *phulla* from √*phal* is treated by Pāṇini and others on the level of *nipātana*. But since the form after its analysis into the *prakṛti-pratyaya* elements can be compared with other similar forms with past passive participial suffixes, with the suffix *-ta* in other forms alternating with *-la* of this form and also, since it is treated so by Bhoja, it is treated here under the heading of the substitution of *ta* by *la*. Thus after its analysis into

phul + la,

it can be compared with the analysis of other formations like

kṛ + ta, bhid + na, pac + va, śuṣ + ka, etc.

and the equivalence, both from the point of view of the type of formal category and meaning, between the *-ta* and -*la* can be established. Secondly some grammrians like Bhoja have treated this form on the level of morphemic substitution of *-ta* by *-la* and not on the level of *nipātana*.

The Pāṇinian *sūtra* that treats this form on the level of *nipātana* is *anupasargāt phullakṣībakṛśollāghāḥ*, 8.2.44. The regular grammatical procedure to arrive at the formation *phulla* according to Pāṇini can be laid down as follows :

phal + ta

= *phul + ta* (ā > u according to *ti ca*, 7.4.89)

= *phul + la* (*t* > *l* according to 8.2.55 quoted above)

=*phulla*

The formal condition for the change of *-ta* into *-la* in the case of this form is that it should not be accompanied by any *upasarga*. Thus the root √*phal* with the *upasarga pra* will give out its past passive participle as *praphulta*, *a* of √*phal* changing to *u* according to 7.4.89, the *āgama iṭ* being not applied since the root is *ādit* according to the *sūtra, āditaś* ca, 7.2.16 and *-ta* not changing to *-la*.

Kātyāyana, the *vārttikakāra*, however, notes two *upasargas* viz. *ut* and *sam* as an exception to the Pāṇinian condition of *anupasartva; cf.* his *vārttika* on Pāṇini 8.2.55: *utphullasaṁphullayor iti vaktavyam*, which gives out two more forms viz. *utphulla* and *saṁphulla* in whose case the *-ta* changes to *-la* in spite of having the *upasargas ud* and *sam*.

The corresponding *sūtras* of other grammarians are :—

Kātantra : *anupasargāt phullakṣībakṛśollāghāḥ*, 4.6.115. The form *sampraphulla, utpraphulla* are, however, derived by the *vṛtti* of Durgasiṁha from √*phull* 'to blossom' and not from √*phal*. This is contrary to the fact that Durgasiṁha usually follows the suggestions of Kātyāyana.

Candra : *phullakṣībakṛśollāghāḥ*, 6.3.94. Though the word *anupasarga* is absent, it is so be understood since the *nipātana* is devoid of any *upasargas;* cf. the *vṛtti : prādirahitānām nipātanād iha na bhavati praphultāḥ*. Neither the grammar of Candra nor the *vṛtti* follow the suggestion of Kātyāyana and the *vṛtti* explains the forms *utphulla, samphulla* as the *prādi* compounds from *ud+phulla* and *sam+phulla*.

Bhoja, however, includes all the suggestions of Kātyāyana and treats the form *phulla* on the level of the morphemic substitution of *-ta* by *-la* and not on the level of *nipātana;* cf. his *sūtra: phaler anupasargāllaḥ*, 7.3.104; *samudbhyām ca*, 7.3.105.

Jainendra follows Pāṇini in treating the form on the level of *nipātana*. He, however, also accepts the suggestion of Kātyāyana for including the forms *samphulla* and *utphulla;* cf. his *sūtras: phullaḥ*, 5.3.70 and *samudaḥ*, 5.3.71. Neither the *sūtra* nor the *Mahāvṛtti* contain any condition for *anupasargatva;* it is to be implied by the rule that since the *nipātana* is without any *upasarga*, except the *upasargas sam* and *ud* stated in 5.3.71, the form *phulla* is allowed by grammar only when it is without *upasargas*.

Like Jainendra, Hemacandra alfo follows Pāṇini in describing the form *phulla* on the level of *nipātana*, yet includes the suggestion of Kātyāyana in the regular *sūtra*; cf. his *sūtra* : *anupasargāḥ kṣībollāghakṛśaparikṛśaphullot-phullasamphullāḥ*, 4.2.80.

Śākaṭāyana agrees with Hemacandra in every detail of description; cf. his *sūtra*, which is identical with that of Hemacandra: *anupasargāḥ kṣībollāghakṛśaparikṛśa-phullotphullasaṁphullāḥ*, 4.1.258.

Sārasvata has no *sūtra* describing this form. Even the commentary fails to note these forms. Another example showing the incomplete and loose character of the Sārasvata system.

4
Morphemic Substitution by the Technique of *Nipātana*

1. One of the techniques for describing the language widely used by Pāṇini and other grammarians is the technique of *nipātana.* This technique is resorted to when other techniques of regular formative rules fail. Thus, the form *dhvānta* from the root *Vdhvan* cannot be easily explained with the help of the normal formative rules; it would require some special rule or rules to describe it; cf. the famous maxim, *śāstrāntarāprāptasya mukhata uccāraṇam nipātanam,* in which *śāstrāntara* means the regular formative rules. To frame new rule or rules for the description of such individual forms would be *gaurava* as against *lāghava* which latter was keenly aimed at by the ancient Indian grammarians. In order to avoid *gaurava,* therefore, this technique of *nipātana* was employed by the Sanskrit grammarians.

We do not know the state of affairs concerning the technique of *nipātana* in pre-pāṇinian grammatical works, since no work, which can be called as strictly grammatical belonging to a time prior to Pāṇini, can be assumed to have come down to us. It may, therefore, be safely presumed that the first Sanskrit grammarian to employ that technique in his work was Pāṇini. All other post pāninian grammarians simply followed suit. It would be, therefore, quite apropos if we critically examine this technique vis-a-vis the other techniques like *ādeśa,* morphophonemic changes, *it-saṁjñā,* etc. employed by Pāṇini himself.

One of the most outstanding point of difference between

the technique of *nipātana* and all other techniques employed by Pāṇini, which strikes us even at cursory galnce, is that the former is so simple in contrast with the latter which are very complicated in nature. While the former looks, at least on the surface, like simple enlisting or enumeration of forms, the latter ones require a good deal of labour and study for being mastered.. Indeed one wonders whether the great grammarian, viz. Pāṇini, who in his masterly manner, worked out and employed such complicated techniques such as *ādeśa, it-saṁjñā* etc. could have thought of such pedestrain method of simple enumeration of forms. The significant difference between the two kinds of techniques tends to create a doubt in one's mind as to the authenticity of Pāṇini's authorship in regard to the technique of *nipātana.* In other words one is inclined to think that the technique of *nipātana* was a non-Pāṇinian, or, better, a pre-Pāṇinian technique which Pāṇini himself may have borrowed it and introduced into his grammar with the relevant *sūtras* with a view to making the Aṣṭādhyāyī sufficiently comprehensive.

Such a reasoning is not without evidence. As we learn from the legend of Bṛhaspati and Indra, referred to by Patañjali in his *Mahābhāsya* the only method of writing a grammar of a language (cf. the phrase *vācaṁ vyā+kṛ)* was to collect different words, list them and recite them by heart *(pratipadokta śabdas).* It was this method that was followed in pre-Pāṇinian times by Bṛhaspati to teach Indra to write grammar.[1] This legend clearly shows that one of the simple ways of composing grammar in pre-Pāṇinian times was enumeration of the forms. The technique of *nipātana* basically resembles the technique of simple enumeration. It will thus be seen that the technique of *nipātana* has its roots, not in Pāṇinian skill, but in pre-Pāṇinian pedestrian way of

1. cf. Patañjali's *Mahābhāsya, paspaśāhnika,* on *vārttika* no. 1, *atha śabdānuśāsanam: kiṁ śabdānām pratipattau pratipadapāṭhaḥ kartavyaḥ? evaṁ hi śrūyate / bṛhaspatir indrāya divyaṁ varṣasahasram pratipadoktānāṁ śabdānām śabdapārāyaṇaṁ provāca/*

enumeration, which was perhaps the only descriptive technique adopted for the description of a language in pre-Pāṇinian times.

There is yet another fact which points to the conclusion that the method of enumeration (technically called *nipātana* later on) belongs to pre-Pāṇinian days and is not Pāṇini's own innovation We have the Nighaṇṭu which has collected a number of Vedic words whose meaning had become mostly unintelligible and whose etymology was beyond any type of grammatical explanation. And it was only when Yāska tried his scientific hand at the explanation of Nighaṇṭu words that a fairly scientific method and outlook became discernible.

Besides the above mentioned factual evidence which is external to Pāṇini's grammar, there is some internal evidence also which would point to non-Pāṇinian character of the *nipātana-sūtras*. If we study critically the nature of the Aṣṭādhyāī, we find that the work betrays a lot of complicated techniques and heavey interdependence of *sūtras*. No *sūtra*, which falls in the category of formative rules, is independent by itself in the sense that it does not pre-suppose a chain of *sūtras* for its adequate understanding. Take, for example, the simple *sūtra* enjoyining *saṁdhi*, viz., *iko yan aci*, 6.1.77. It contains three padas: the gen. sing. *ikaḥ;* the nom. sing. *yaṇ*, and the loc. sing. *aci*. All the three padas are primarily what are called the *pratyāhāras*. In order to understand the term *pratyāhāra*, therefore, one would be required to know the *sūtras*, *ādir antyena sahetā*, 1.1.71 and *halantyam*, 1.3.3. So too, to understand the significance of the different case-terminations of gen. sing, nom. sing. and loc. sing. one would be required to have full knowledge of the *sūtras*, *ṣaṣṭhī sthāneyogā*, 1.1.49, (for gen. sing. *ikaḥ)* and *tasminn iti nirdiṣṭe pūrvasya*, 1.1.66 (for the loc. sing *aci)*. Also the knowledge of the *sūtra*, *sthāne'ntaratamaḥ* would be necessary for determining as to which *ādeśa* out of *y*, *v*, *r* and *l* takes place in the place of *i, u, ṛ* and *ḷ*. Thus, a simple saṁdhi-sūtra like the above require a previous knowledge of at least five *sūtras.*

Such is not the case with the *nipātana-sūtras*. Even if they are read by themselvs, they give out their meaning fully and very clearly. Thus, when it is stated that *nirvāṇo'vāte,* 8.2.50, we understand, without the previous knowledge of any other *sūtras* in the whole *Aṣṭādhyāyī,* that the word *nirvāṇa* (from *nir+vā*) is to be used when the sense of *avāta* is present. The same is the case with the other *nipātana-sūtras;* they do not require any previous knowledge of other *sūtras* or techniqus of Pāṇini.

In other words the *nipātana-sūtras* do not seem to have what may be called an organic relationship with the rest of the *Aṣṭādhyāyī*. They seem to be extraneous and to have been admitted into the Pāṇinan fold out of sheer practical necessity.

2. The word *nipātana* is derived from *ni* + *pat* (causal) 'to fall down, to cause to fall down' etc. with the *kṛt* suffix *ana* (Pāṇinian *yuc* according to *ṇyāsaśrantho yuc,* 3.3.107; *yu* > *ana* according to the *sūtra, yuvor anākau,* 7.1.1) and literally means 'laying down' or even 'that which is laid down'. Thus, when a form, say, *phulla* or *kṣība* (discussed in the previous Chapter 3; cf. the Pāṇiniam *sūtra,* 8.2.55) is 'laid down', without its grammatical analysis into *prakṛti* and *pratyaya,* in the form in which it is used in the language, it is said to be *'nipātita';* no grammatical analysis of the form is given nor could the form be arrived at by the existing grammatical procedures. The only alternative to the device of *nipātana* is to lay down the grammatical procedure of the form; but since such a grammatical procedure involves elaboration, the short-cut is found out by adopting the technique of *nipātana.*

Patañjali has nowhere defined *nipātana*. L. Renou[1] explains it as 'the way of falling upon by chance' (obviously

1. cf. L. Renou, *Etudes vedique et Pāṇineennes,* I. p. 103. Paris, 1955: *le fait de tomber par hasard.*

from *ni* + √*pat* 'to fall') in the grammatical process instead of treating under general formative rules. Vāsudeva Dīkṣita, the author of the *Bālamanoramā*, regards it as 'a statement of a form whose grammatical procedure is self-established *(siddhaprakriyasya nirdeśah nipātanam)*. Kāśikā on Pāṇini 3.1.123 remarks; *yadiha lakṣaṇenānupapannaṁ tat sarvaṁ nipātanāt siddham/śāstrāntarāprāptasya mukhataḥ uccāraṇaṁ nipātanam.*

If, however, we study the *nipātana-sūtras* of Pāṇini and others, of course, from the section describing the past passive participles only—we find that when a whole or finished form is laid down, without the analysis into its components viz. *prakṛti* or nucleus and *pratyaya* or satellite, it is called *nipātana.* Thus, when instead of laying down the grammatical procedure of the form *nirvāṇa* (from *nis* + √*vā)* in terms of its analysis into the component and/or in terms of the change of *-ta* into *-na,* the whole ready-made form *nirvāṇa* is laid down, it becomes a *nipātana*. In almost all cases, the components of the form are easily discernible; for example, in the present case, they are *nis* + √*vā*. If, however, we apply the formative rules to these components and follow up the usual grammatical procedure, we get a form which is totally different from the one laid down in the *nipātana-sūtra.* Take the components *nis* + √*vā* themselves. By applying the rules to get the past passive particles the regular past passive participle from *nis* + √*vā* that we get it *nirvāta* which is different from *nirvāṇa* laid down by Pāṇini in the *sūtra, nirvāno'vāte*, 8. 2. 50.

One thing is, therefore, clear from the *nipātana sutras,* namely, that the form which is *nipātita* has also another corresponding form used in the language; and secondly—and this is perhaps more important- the form corresponding to the one which is *nipātita* can be easily arrived at by applying the regular formative rules (or, what we technically call *lakṣaṇa* or *śāstrāntara)* applicable to the general cases. In other words, the *nipātita* form implies the existence of a corresponding form. In the case of the form *nirvāṇa,* for example, we get a corresponding form *nirvāta* also, which can be easily deduced by applying the regular rules of the formative procees. So also is the case with many other forms like *vitta* (from √*vid*), *bhitta* (from √*bhid*), etc. all of which have corresponding forms like *vinna, bhinna* etc. This fact throws a new light on the phenomenon and gives us a new point of view. Instead of just saying that a *nipātita* form implies the existence of another form which can be arrived at by regular formative process, we can say that a *nipātita* form is a sort of substitute laid down for a regular form which can be easily derived according to the stated rules of grammatical procedure. Thus, the forms *nirvāna, vitta, bhitta* etc. which are treated on the level of *nipātana* can be viewed as substitute for the forms *nirvāta, vinna, bhinna* etc. respectively under certain phonological or semantic conditions. That every *nipātita* form has a corresponding regular form is proved by the fact that the commentators on the grammars mention invariably the other regular forms while commenting on the *nipātita* ones; to cite an instance, cf. *Kāśikā* on the Pāṇinian *sūtra,* 8.2.50 *(nirvāṇo'vāte) : nirvāṇo'gniḥ/nirvāṇaḥ pradīpaḥ/.. avāta iti kim/ nirvāto vātaḥ/ nirvātam vātena/;* cf. also the other commentaries on the different grammars.

3. *Nipātana* and *Ādeśa*—a Comparison

The interpretation of *nipātana* as a substitute for the form arrived at by regular formative process brings into focus the technique of *ādeśa,* especially morphemic and not phonetic *ādeśa* or substitution, for comparison. As has been seen, the *ādeśa* is a substitution of one morpheme for another, which may be either *prakṛti* i.e., nucleus or *pratyaya* i.e. satellite; *nipātana,* on the other hand is a substitution of one whole form for another which, under certain phonological, semantic or accentual conditions, mentioned in the *sūtras* specifically and explicitly, is not used in the language when the conditions are not existing. The form *nirvāṇa,* for example, is not used in the langauge when the semantic condition of *avāta* i.e. *'not-blowing'* does not exist. In the same way, a morphemic subsitute does not take place when the conditions under whichi it is stated to take place do not exist; thus, the form *dyūta* (from √*div* 'to play dice') does not display the morphemic substitution of *ta* by *na* since the semantic condition of *'avijigīṣā'* is absent; cf. the Pāṇinian *sūtra, divo'vijigīṣāyām,* 8.2.49. These are exmaples of semantic conditions for *nipātana.* For accentual *nipātana,* cf. the Pāṇinian *sūtra, kṣayo nivāse,* which states that the word *kṣaya* is *ādyudātta* if the meaning *nivāsa* i.e., 'dwelling' is intended.

It can thus be seen that every *nipātita* form has one corresponding non-*nipātita* form, which latter can be arrived at by the regular formative process. In other words, a nipātita form is a conditional (the conditions may be semantic, phonological or accentual) substitute for a corresponding finished form. This means that the techniques of both, the *nipātana* and the *ādeśa,* involve fundamentally the same principle, viz. that of substitution of something by some other thing.

Yet, there is a great difference between the two techniques. In the case of *nipātana,* the substitution is of a whole, finished or unfinished, form for another whole, finished or unfinished, form; *nirvāṇa* is substituted for another whole unfinished, form *nirvāta.* In the case of *ādeśa,* however, the substitution in only of a part for a part of the word; thus, only -ta which is a part of the word *dyūta* is substituted by another part viz. *na* in *dyūna.* The part may be either a single phoneme or morpheme, or a *prakṛti* or a *pratyaya.* In the case of the form *dyūna,* it is the *pratyaya* morpheme *ta* that is substituted by *-na;* in the case of forms like *jagdha* (from √*ad*), *bhūta* (from √*as*) etc. it is the *prakṛti*-morpheme that is substituted by *Jagdh, bhū* etc. respectively.

If, therefore, the technique of *nipātana* is viewed as an extended form of the general technique of substitution, we get the following three stages through which the technique of substitution has evolved gradually.

1. phonological substituition or *varṇādeśa*
2. morphemic substitution, displaying two divisions—(a) for *prakṛti*-morpheme and (b) for *pratyaya*-morpheme, and finally.
3. *nipātana,* morphemic substitution for the whole form which may be referred to as *rūpādeśa* and which may be finished or nufinished one.

Thus there appears to be regular graded evolution in the technique of substitution, namely, from the simple, rudimentary substitution of a single phoneme through that of a morpheme to finally that of the whole form. Thus logically the gradation-cycle is complete. Since there cannot be any bigger morpheme than a finished form on morphological plane and since Pāṇini and others have described the language on only phonological and morphological planes, the technique of substitution has inherently no scope at all to evolve further beyond these planes.

The gist of the whole discussion above can be stated symbolically as follows :—

From Patañjali's explanation of the Pāṇinian assumption underlying the analysis of the Sanskrit language,[1] namely that any usable form is composed of two elements, viz. *prakṛti* i.e. nuclesu and *pratyaya* i.e. satellite, any usable (i.e. one without the *sup*-terminations) past passive participial formation in Sanskrit can be symbolically represented as :

Form = Nucleus + Satellite,[2] i.e.

1. cf. Patañjali on the Pāṇinian *sūtra,* 1.2.45 *(arthavad adhātur apratyayah prātipadikam): nityasaṁbandhāv etāv arthau prakṛtiḥ pratyayaś ceti; pratyayena nityasambhandhāt.*
2. For a symbolic representation of Sanskrit formations, cf. *M. D. Pandit,* 'Pāṇini — A Study in Non-Compounded Word-Structures', *VIJ,* Vol.

$$F = N + S,$$

in which F stands for the form ready for applying the declensional terminations, N stands for the Nucleus or *Prakṛti* and S for the Satellite or *pratyaya*. Thus in the form *kṛta, kṛta* is F; *√kṛ* is N and *ta* is S. The S in the present case represents the past passive participial suffix *-ta*. The declensional terminations or what are called *vibhakti-pratyayas* by Pāṇini[1] follows the S in the above formula and may be represented by the same or different symbol.

Now, in this formula, if N is substituted by N1, as in the case of the substitution of *bhū* for *as* (cf. the Pāṇinian *sūtra*, *aster bhūḥ*, 2.4.52) or if S is substituted by S1, as in the case of the substitution of *-na* for *-ta* (e.g. *bhinna, d* of *√bhid* changing to *-na* according to the Pāṇinian *sūtra*, 8.2.42), it will be an example of *ādeśa*, since the substitution is only partial in the sense that it relates to one part of component out of many parts of components. Thus, for the formula

$$F = N. S$$

both the substitutions, viz.

$$F = N_1. S, \text{ or}$$

$$F = N. S_1$$

are examples of morphemic substitutions or *ādeśa*. If however, the whole form represented in the above formula by F is substituted by another, say, F1, without its analysis into the components (represented in the above formula by N and S) it becomes the symbolic representation of nipātana i.e. substitution for the whole. Thus, for the formula,

$$F = N.S,$$

I, pt. 2, Sept. 1963, pp. 324-338; also, 'Pāṇini — A Study in Compound Word-Structures', *JMSUBH*, Vol. XII, No. 1, 1963, pp. 81-99. *cf.* also, 'A Concordance of Vedic Compounds Interpreted by Veda', CASS, Pune, 1989

1. cf. the Pāṇinian *sūtra, vibhaktiś ca*, 1.4.104; cf. BD on the *sūtra*, 1.4.104 : *suptiṅau vibhaktisaṁjñau stah*. The *sup-pratyayas* are listed by Pāṇini in 4.1.2 and the *tiṅpratyayas* in 3.4.78.

We get the formula as

$$F1 = N.S, \text{ or } N1.S \text{ or } N1+S1 \text{ or } N_1+S_1$$

where the components N and S are the same, yet the form (F1) is different from the previous one (F). To take a concrete example,

nirvāta (F) = *nir* + √*vā* (N)+ *ta* (S),

while

nirvāṇa (F1) = *nir* + √*vā* (N)+ ta >na (S).

The N and S in the second formula may, in some cases (as in the case of *nirvāṇa*) be easily discernible,while in some other cases (as in the case of *nasatta* stated by Pāṇini in the *sūtra*, 8.2.61) they may not be so easily recognizable. But one thing is certain, namely that the form F1 seems to be a substitute for the form F, though this fact is not stated explicitly in term of an *ādeśa;* secondly either F1 cannot be accounted for by the usual grammatical procedure or by formative rules (cf. the form *nasatta* in Pāṇini 8.2.61) or it is not used in conditions in which F is used (cf. the forms *nirvāta* and *nirvāṇa* above).

An objection may be raised against the statements that the techniques of *nipātana* and *ādeśa* are basically the same, both involving substitution; and that the difference between *nipātana* and *ādeśa* is only of degree and not of kind, a new, whole form being substituted in the case of *nipātana* and only a part —that is, either the root-morpheme or the suffix-morpheme-being substituted in the case of *ādeśa.* The objection pertains to the *sthānin* in whose place the substituted word i.e. *ādeśa* takes place, which is specifically and explicity mentioned by the grammarians; cf. for example, the Pāṇinian *sūtras, aster bhūḥ,* 2.4.52, *bruvo vaciḥ* 2.4.53, *ado jagdhir lyapti kiti,* 2.4.36 etc. in which the substitution of √*as,* √*brū,* √*ad* by *bhū, vac, jagdh* etc. is laid down; it is clear that the *sthānins* viz. √*as,* √*brū,* √*ad* etc. which are substituted by the *ādeśas bhū, vac, jagdh* etc. respectively are specifically and explicitly mentioned in the *sūtras* themselves. There is no *sūtra* in any grammar which describes a form on the level of *ādeśa,* and yet which does not specifically and explicity mention the *sthānin* for which are *ādeśa* is laid down.

In the case of the *nipātana* techniques, however, the *sthānin* is not at all mentioned in the *sūtra;* only the *nipātita* form is stated.

This distinction between *ādeśa* and *nipātana,* however, is not so real as to dissuade one from assuming the essential identity of the two techniques. Though it is true that in the case of *nipātana* the *sthānin* for which the *nipātita* form is substituted is not mentioned, it can be easily inferred. Actually it has been the practice of all commentators on all grammars to state the *sthānin* for which the *nipātita* form is laid down in the *sūtra.* Moreover, the way the *nipātana* is done is itself so clear that one can easily know or infer the *sthānin* for which the *nipātita* form is substituted. This will be clear when the *nipātana sūtras* dealing with past passive participial formatios which will be discussed below individually.

The mention of the *sthānin* in the case of *ādeśa* and its non-mention in *nipātana* is, therefore, no bar to say that the two are basically identical techniques. The non-mention in *nipātana* of the *sthānins* seems to be the result mainly of the tendency of the Sanskrit grammarians towards proverbial brevity. To take an example, to say simply *nirvāno avāte* is certainly briefer than, and yet as accurate as saying *nirvātasya nirvāno'vāte,* the *sthānin, nirvāta,* being left to be understood. Fundamentally, therefore, there seems to be no difference between the technique of *ādeśa* and that of *nipātana;* both seem to be based on the basic idea of substitution. What makes for the distinction between the two is not the basic principle involved but the difference in the form of statement; the one viz. *ādeśa* mentions the *sthānin;* the other viz. *nipātana* does not. The former deals with the substitution of the components; the latter with what of the whole form.[1]

It will be seen from the foregoing discussion that, though superficially the technique of *nipātana* seems to be non-Pāṇinian, basically it involves the same principle, viz. of substitution, which underlies the technique of *ādeśa*. One may say, therefore, that though the *nipātana* of forms might be one of the methods of linguistic description in pre-Pāṇinian and/or non-Pāṇinian schools or grammar, Pāṇini still adopted it and raised it to the status of a grammatical technique of *nipātana* which thereafter ceased to be simple enumeration or enlisting of forms. In this sense, the *nipātana* as a technique seems to be Pāṇini's own invention; as a simple enumeration of forms, it might be non-Pāṇinian or pre-Pāṇinian.

4. After these preliminary remarks, we may begin by pointing out that the study of all the *nipātana-sūtras* laying down the past passive participal formations falls into three broad categories;

4.1 Those *sūtras*, which lay down with the help of *nipātana* only the form of the participle, no other categories such as meaning, accent etc. being taken into consideration. We may call this 'formal *nipātana*.' The study of purely formal morphological conditions can also be included in this category.

4.2 Those *sūtras*, which lay down the form of the participle by bringing out the semantic difference also. The semantic

1. A fuller light will be shed on this problem only when all the *nipātana-sūtras* of all the grammarians are subjected to a critical examination. The present conclusion is based only on the study of the few *nipātana-sūtras* which come under that section of grammar which describes the past passive participle in Sanskrit. It may be mentioned in this connection that a full study of all the types of *nipātana-sūtras* was undertaken by Saudamini Bahulikar, and was being done by the late R. M. Rishi, both of the Centre of Advanced Study in Sanskrit, University of Poona, Poona 7.

difference is without any exception accompanied by formal difference. We may call this type 'semantic *nipātana*', since the *nipātana* is intended more specifically for semantic purposes.

4.3 Those *sūtras*, which lay down the form for the sake of explaining its accent which deviates from the general pattern and hence cannot laid down by the general formative rules. We may call this type of *nipātana* as 'accentual *nipātana*'. The accentual *nipātana* may or may not be accompanied by formal or semantic *nipātana*. Actually it is the *nipātana* of accent.

The accentual *nipātana*, however, is not included in the preset study; and this for two obvious reasons; (a) Since no grammarian other than Pānini treats the accent, there is no scope for comparison and contrast regarding the accentual *nipātana-sūtras*. (b) Secondly, no grammarian other than Pāṇini describes the Vedic forms in which alone the accent is available. No comparison or contrast of the descriptive techniques of all the grammarians is, therefore, possible. As the present study aims chiefly at a comparative study of the different techniques and principles or grammatical and linguistic description, adopted by the different grammarians, the enumeration of the *sūtras* of Pāṇini who alone treats the Vedic forms and accent would become pointless.

4.1 Formal Nipātana

As has been suggested above, this type of nipātana does not refer to or take into consideration any non-formal category like meaning, accent etc. in describing the form; it only lays down the form. All the *sūtras* stating only the forms can be further divided into two sub-types according to the levels on which they treat the formations; the levels are two : one, the non-transformational level and two, the transformational level.

4.1.1 Formal Nipātana on the Non-transformational Level

This type obviously excludes the past passive participal

formations derived from verbal bases transformed into causal, desiderative, frequentative etc. This section may include the following examples :

4.1.1.1 The Pāṇinian *sūtra*, *anupasargāt phullakṣībakṛśollāghāḥ*, 8.2.55, explains the forms *phulla*, *kṣība*, *kṛśa* and *ullāgha* with the help of the technique of *nipātana*. The forms, as is clear, can by no technique of formal analysis be explained as past passive participles since they do not contain any of the past passive participial suffixed such as *-ta*, *-na*, *-va* or *ma*. That these forms need to be treated as past passive participles from the relevant roots implies that they function in the language as past passive participles. This lends strong support to our earlier observation that the usage or functional considerations cannot be totally ignored even in strictly formal grammar. Not only this. The functional considerations for decideing whether a form fits into a particular grammatical category or not are also as essential as the considerations of formal analysis. Mere formal analysis cannot be regarded as the sole deciding factor. This shows a very high regard for the spoken language on the part of the Sanskrit grammarians. They believe—and rightly so—that every form, besides having formal structure, is also related to other forms in the language under certain other conditions like function, meaning, accent, gender, etc. and cannot be explained entirely in isolation with only a reference to its formal structure. In case of certain forms, on the contrary, only these non-formal considerations play a predominant role in the explanation. Such forms, therefore, must be explained with reference to their non-formal characteristics. The non-formal characteristics in the present case of forms play an important role in their functioning as past passive participles.

The Pāṇinian *sūtra*, 8.2.55, therefore, means that, although the forms are not analysed and accounted for by the usual general formative rules and that although the forms, even after their analysis, do not give out any of the usual past passive participial suffixes, they are to be taken as past passive participles or *siddhaniṣṭhāntarūpāṇi*, accompanied by any upasargas, the past passive participial forms which they will give out will be respectively *praphulta* (from *pra* + √*phal* > *phul* according to the Pāṇinian *sūtra, ti ca* 7.4.89), *prakṣībita* (from *pra* + √*kṣīb*), *prakṛśita* (or *prakṛṣta*, from *pra* + √*kṛś*), and *prollāghita* (from *pra* + *ud* + √*lagh?*)[1]. Out of these four forms, the form *phulla* could have been treated on the level of morphemic substitution of *-ta* by *-la*, instead of on the level of *nipātana*. A possible reason for not treating *phulla* on the level or morphemic substitution by regular formative process may be that, though it functions as past passive participle, it also functions as past active participle in the sense in which its past active participle in *-tavat* i.e. *phullavān* would function. But the past active participal form *phullavān* is nowhere available in the language. Instead of treating a single form by itself by the regular formative process, therefore, the grammarians chose to describe the form *phulla* on the level of *nipātana*. In the case of the other three forms viz. *kṣība*, *kṛśa*, and *ullāgha* also, this reasoning, viz. the absence of the corresponding past active participal form in *-tavat*, is quite acceptable.

A minor point regarding BD's remark, *niṣṭhātasya latvaṁ nipātyate*, on the Pāṇinian *sūtra*, 8.2. 55, for the form *phulla*, deserves consideration. In one sense BD. is right when he says that *-la* replaces *-ta* in this case. The point is that he thereby suggests that the form could have been treated on formaive level rather than on *nipātana*—level. But one cannot agree with him if he means to suggest that the substitution of *-ta* by *-la* can be taken as a sort of *nipātana* for a part; because, as has been seen above, the *nipātana* can never be partial; it is always for the whole form. If it were partial, there would have been no distinction whatsoever between the *nipātana* technique and the *ādeśa* technique.

1. Cf. BD. on the Pāṇinian *sūtra, ti ca*, 7.4.89.

Whatever has been said above also applies to BD's other remark, viz. that the form *phulla* is a partial *nipātaṇa* for its past active form **phullavān;* cf. BD. on the Pāṇinian *sūtra,* 8.2.55: *ktavatveka-deśasyāpīdaṁ nipātanam iṣyate.* To interpret the Pāṇinian *nipātana* or *phulla* to stand for a part in the form **phullavān* is all right so far as the ordinary *vyavahāra* is concerned. But strictly from point of view of scientific technique and statement, it is doubtful how far a *sūtra* can be interpreted to give out such a meaning. Secondly, the form **phullavān,* for which, according to BD., the *nipātana* of *phulla* stands, is nowhere attested in the language, since *phulla* itself functions both as past active participle and past passive participle. We may find the usage like *kusumam phullam* or *kusumena phullam* but nowhere do we find *kusumam phullavat.* BD's above remark, therefore, is pointless.

There is yet another important point regarding the other three forms. It is brought into focus by BD's remark, *kṣībādiṣu tu tapratyayasyaiva lopaḥ* (on the Pāṇinian *sūtra,* 8.2.55). What this remark implies is that the forms *kṣība, kṛśa* and *ullāgha* can be formed by eliminating the sound *t* in the past passive participal termination *-ta;* thus,

√*kṣīb* + *ta*

= *kṣīb* + a (since *t* = o)

= *kṣība.*

So also in the case of the forms *kṛśa* and *ullāgha.*

The suggestion is quite intelligent and convincing. Yet in his over-enthusiasm to lay down an alternative explanation of the form or to explain the different constituents of the form which are laid down by *nipātana,* BD. seems to have lost sight of one very important side of linguistic analysis which Pāṇini and other grammarians have followed in the case of the description of the past passive participles. What Pāṇini (as also consequently other grammarians) does is that he takes the root, the basic norm of which is already fixed by him in his *dhātupāṭha,* and then applies the past passive participial suffix *-ta* to that basic norm. While adopting this procedure, he simply states the rules regarding the morphophonemic or phonetic or substitutional changes which would thereby take place. This whole procedure shows that Pāṇini starts with a hypothetical root-norm and goes to describe the formation. He does not start with the usable formation first and then find out the missing links. In other words his approach is not structural, as is seen in the case of the description of the conjugated verbal forms. The description of the verbal form *atti* (pres. 3rd pers. sing. of √*ad* 'to eat', 2nd conj. Parasmipada) is, for example, based on the structural approach. The form *atti,* according to him, is not an isolated one, to be divided into the two constituent morphemes as *ad+ti,* but it is part of a whole gamut of forms like *bhavati, gacchati* etc. which are divided into three morhemes, a root, a *vikaraṇa,* and a conjugation (i.e. *vibhakti*) termination. Viewed from this point of view, the form *atti* seems short of a *vikaraṇa* which he has arranged to be elided according to the *sūtra adiprabhṛtibhyaḥ śapaḥ,* 2. 4. 72. In symbols, we can say that if

$$bhavati = R + S_1 + S_2,$$

atti also must have the same three-morpheme structure. And since S_1 in *atti* is not found, it is supposed to have elided.[1] Thus in the case of atti, the symbolic formula is

$$\begin{aligned} & R + S_1 + S_2 \\ = & R + O + S_2 \ (S_1 = O) \\ = & R + S_2 \end{aligned}$$

The description of the past passive participial formation, however, follows a different grammatical procedure. Symbolically put down, it is as follows :—

1. For details, cf. *M. D. Pandit,* "Zero in Pāṇini", *JMSUBH.* Vol. XI, No. 1, 1961. pp. 53-66; cf. also "Some Linguistic Principles in Pāṇini's Grammar", *IL,* 1963, pp. 57-62; *cf.* also, CASS, Pune, 1990.

√*kṛ* + *ta*
= *kṛta*
i.e. = R + S.

From a comparison of the two symbolic formulas, it will become clear that the description of the past passive participial formations is based on a footing different from the one followed in the case of the conjugated verbal forms; the method in the case of the latter is structural, since the description starts with the usable structure of the form, while in the case of past passive participles, the description starts with a hypothetical root-norm.

There is yet another point of difference between the two approaches. The form *atti* is described with reference to the form *bhavati;* and since the form *bhavati* contains three morphemes, viz. the root, the *vikaraṇa* and the termination, the form *atti* also is also assumed to contain three morphemes, this is the basic logic involved in the description of the form *atti.* This logic naturally must culminate in stating the loss or zero of the *vikaraṇa-* morpheme which is missing in atti and present in *bhavati.* The question of eliding or zeroing a particular phoneme or morpheme can come only in the case of the description of a form with reference to another; zero is inevitable when a comparison betwen two forms is implied.

No such comparison exists in the case of the description of the past passive participial formations; and hence there is no scope for a zero in that case. Again one past passive participial form is not explained with reference to another past passive participial form. The description in this case follows a non-comparative and non-referential approach.

In the light of the foregoing discussion about the difference between the two appraoches in general and about the non-structural and non-referential approach in the case of the descriptions of the past passive participal formations, BD's suggestion of the zero of *-t* in the case of forms *kṣība,* *kṛśa* and *ullāgha* could never have been followed by the grammarians. There is no instance—indeed, there cannot be any—in the description of the past passive participles in which the technique of zero is adopted, if the approach to description is what we have mentioned above.

At interesting point which may be noted here that, though it is strictly laid down that the form should be without any *upasargas*, the form *ullāgha* itself which is enumerated in that very *sūtra* is characterised by the upasarga *ud* (with the root √*lāgh*).

The corresponding *sūtras* of other grammarians are given in the previous chapter while discussing the form *phulla* on the basis of morphemic substitution, and need not be repeated here. Some grammarians, however, have treated the forms *kṣība, kṛśa,* and *ullāgha* in a separate *sūtra.* They are:

Bhoja : *kṣībakṛśaparikṛśollāghāḥ,* 7.3.106, in which the form *parikṛśa* (*kṛśa* with the *upasarga pari*) is also included and explained as a compound of *pari* and *kṛśa.*

Jainenedra: *kṣībakṛśollāghāḥ,* 5.3.72.

The Sārasvata grammar has no *sūtra* which describes these forms either on the level of *nipātana* or of morphemic substitution. This confirms incompleteness of the system.

3.1.1.2. The next example of the *nipātana* of the past passive participial forms on the non-transformational level, without reference to any non-formal categories like meaning, accent etc. is of the forms *pratistabdha* and *nistabdha,* both from √*stabh* 'to obstruct' (Pāṇinian *stanbhu*)[1], 9th Conj. with the *upasargas prati* and *ni.* The purpose of the *nipātana* of these two forms is not to state that they are past passive participles, since obviously they can be regularly formed as such by the general formative rules, but to state that the initial *s* of the

1. It is a *sautra dhātu* in the sense that it is mentioned only in the Pāṇinian *sūtra,* 3.1.82 and not listed in the regular Pāṇinian *dhp.*

root √*stanbh* does not change to its cerebral counter part when preceded by the *upasargas*. The general pāṇinian rule regarding this root is that when an *upasarga* precedes the root, the initial *s* is changed to *ṣ*; cf. the Pāṇinian *sūtra*, *stanbheḥ*, 8.3.67. The present *sūtra* laying down the forms *pratistabdha* and *nistabdha*, viz. *pratistabdhanistabdhau ca*, 8.3.114, therefore, nullifies the operation of the change of *s* into *ṣ* laid down in the *sūtra*, 8.3.67.

A small point requires an explanation here. The two forms considered above are derived from the root √*stanbh* of the 9th Conj. and not from the root √*stabh*> √*stambh* (pāṇinian *ṣṭabhi* which is an *idit*) of the 1st conjugation. This is clear from the fact that the *sūtra*, *stanbheḥ*, 8.3.67, clearly states the change of *s* into *ṣ* with reference to the root √*stanbh* with *n* in the pen-ultimate position, whereas the root √*stabh*> √*stambh* has *m* in the pen-ultimate position; cf. BD's remarks on the root *ṣṭabhi*, 1st Conj. : *tad bījaṁ tūdasthāstambhor iti pavargīyopadhapāṭhaḥ; stanbher iti tavargyopadhapāṭhaśceti mādhavaḥ*. The result of this distinction is firstly, that, the past passive participial form from the root √*stabh*> √*stambh* (with *m* in the pen-ultimate position) will be *stambhita* (and not *stabdha*) and secondly that if the form is accompanied by the upasargas *prati* and *ni*, the initial *s* will change to *ṣ* according to the Pāṇinian *sūtra*, *iṇkoḥ*, 8.3.57 Thus the relevant forms from the latter root will be *pratiṣṭambhita* and *niṣṭambhita* if the *upasargas prati* and *ni* precede it.

Instead of explaining these two forms on the basis of *nipātana*, Pāṇinin could have treated them on the level of morphophonemic change; that is to say, he could have prohibited the change of *s* into *ṣ* in the case of the root √*stanbh* if it was accompanied by the *upasargas prati* and *ni*, in a *sūtra* immediately after a *sūtra stanbheḥ*, 8.3.67, as has been actually done by Candra, Bhoja and others.

The relevant *sūtras* of other grammarians are:

Kātantra does not note the form.

Candra in the *sūtra, niprateḥ stabdhaḥ*, 6.4.4, treats the form on the phonological level by prohibiting the change of *s* into the cerebral *ṣ* in the case of *stabdha* preceded by the *upasargas, ni* and *prati.*

Bhoja follows Candra in treating the forms on phonological level; *cf.* his *sūtra, nipratibhyām stabdhasya*, 7.4.100.

Jainendra follows Pāṇini in adopting the technique of *nipātana* in the case of these two forms; cf. his *sūtra, nistabdhapratistabdhau ca*, 5.4.80. The change of order of the words is notable.

Hemachandra does not note these forms, though he notes the root √*stambh* (with *m* in the penultimate position) in the *sūtra, stambhūstumbhū-skambhūskumbhūskoḥ śnā ca*, 3.4.78.

Śākaṭāyana follows Candra and treats the forms on the phonological level; *cf.* his *sūtra, stambho'ṅa-pratistabdhanistabdhe*, 4.2.222. In reality, however, the utterance of the forms in the *sūtra* clearly shows that they are treated on the level of *nipātana.*

Sārasvata does not note these forms, which constitutes additional evidence to show that the grammar is incomplete.

4.1.1.2. The next form by *nipātana* on the non transformational level is *apacita*, from *apa* + √*cāy* 'to worship', 1st Conj. Parasmaipada (Cf. Pāṇinian *dhp. cāyṛ pūjāniśāmanayoḥ*). The purpose of the *nipātana, apacita*, is to show the optional application or otherwise of the *āgama iṭ*. The other optional form with *iṭ* will, therefore, be *apacāyita.* The presence of the *upasarga apa* in the *sūtra* makes it clear that—without it, the mere root will give out only one from viz. *cāyita* with *iḍāgama.* The Pāṇinian *sūtra* that lays down the *nipātana* is *apacitaś ca*, 7.2.30.

The Kātantra grammar has no *sūtra* which treats this form either by *nipātana* or by any other technique. The *vṛtti* on the Kātantra *sūtra*, 4.6.95 *apacāyita* and *apacita; cf.* the *vṛtti* on 4.6.95: *apacāyitaḥ/apacita iti cāyinā cinā ca pūjāvṛttinā siddham/*

Candra notes the form *apaciti*, one in *-ti*-and not *apacita* in *-ta;* actually there is no mention of either the form *apacita* or of apacāyita. Candra perhaps seems to have been guided by Patañjali's remark that the *iṭ* is not to be applied to the root √*cāy* in the case of the *kṛt* feminine termination *-ti* cf. Patañjali on Pāṇini 7.2.30; *ktini nityam iti vaktavyam.* According to Candra, therefore, the past passive participle of √*cāy* with apa is only *apacāyita* and not *apacita.* It is also possible that by *nipātana* of a form of the root √*cāy* in *-ti*, Candra might have suggested the same *nipātana* (viz. *cāy* > *ci*) for the past passive participial formation also.

The Candra *sūtra* is *apacitiḥ*, 5.4.157. The commentary on the *sūtra*, viz. *apapūrvasya cāyeḥ ktini parataś cibhāvo nipātyate*, however, creates an impression that the form is treated on the level of morphemic substitution of √*cāy* by *ci;* but the form of the *sūtra* does not allow such an interpretation. The *sūtra* clearly follows the technique of *nipātana.*

Bhoja, surprisingly enough, follows neither Pāṇini nor Candra; he treats the form on the level of morphemic substitution of *cāy* by *ci;* c. his *sūtra kter apāc cāyaḥ ciś ca*, 6.4.174. There is, however, no indication either in Candra or Bhoja that the *nipātana* or the substitution is optional.

Jainendra follows Pāṇini in noting the form by *nipātana;* he, however, combines into one the two Pāṇinian *sūtra*, viz. 7.2.29; 30. The Jainendra *sūtra* is *hṛṣṭāpacitau*, 5.1.125.[1]

Hemachandra follows Pāṇini and Jainendra, both in noting the past passive participle *apacita* and not *apaciti* as

---

1. It may be noted that the *Mahāvṛtti* on Jainendra remarks : *cakāro'nuktasamuccayārthaḥ;* this shows that the *Mahāvṛtti* assumes a *ca* in the *sūtra*, 5.1.125, it shows that it takes the *sūtra* to be *hṛṣṭāpacitauca.* Actually, however, the *sūtra*, as it has come down to us does not have *ca.* This means that either the *ca* in 5.1.125 is lost to us or the *Mahāvṛtti* is thinking, in this context, of the *ca* in the Pāṇinian *sūtra, apacitaś ca*, 7.2.30. Is the commentary referring to a version of Jainendra other than the present one which is commonly known?

well as in adopting the technique of *nipātana; cf.* his *sūtra, apacitaḥ,* 4.4.77.

Śākaṭāyana and Sārasvata do not note the form.

4.1.2 Formal Nipātana on the Transformational Level

Besides the forms discussed in the previous section, there are certain forms which agree in structure with those on the non-transformational plane and yet give out a transformational meaning. Thus, for example, we have the form *dānta,* from √*dam* 'to control' (4th conj.), which has a causal sense viz. 'made to control, in its formation; the form is a non-causal one though by its function in the language it is causal. The regular past passive participial form from √*dam* in the causal should be *damita* did not *dānta.*

There are a few other formations like this, which Pāṇini and other grammarians have treated by the technique of *nipātana.* Such forms constitute the topic of the present section.

It should, however, be noted in this connection that of all the types of transformation, only the causal transformation, and that too in the case of a few forms, displays such a discrepancy in form and meaning. Hence the examples noted by the grammarians are all only from the sphere of causal transformation. No other transformation, such as the desideraive. frequentative etc., betrays a characteristic formal feature different from the one arrived at by regular, general formative process.

All these example could have been discussed under the heading of semantic *nipātna* (which is the topic of the next section) since they are discussed in the grammar chiefly to bring out their semantic (i.e. causal meaning) differences. But the meaning that all these formations give out is causal e.g. grammatical and not social or linguistic.

The chief distinction between the grammatical meaning and linguistic meaning rests on the fact that, while in the case of the former the meaning of the form is based on the meaning of the basic root, in the latter the meaning of the derived form signifies a meaning totally different from that of the root in the language. Again, the grammatical meaning is chiefly based upon the grammatical category like the *vikaraṇa, pratyaya,* etc. whereas the linguistic meaning depends upon the usage of the form in the language. If, therefore, a grammatical category is elided or lost in the formation, the formation ceases to convey the definite grammatical meaning; this loss of the grammatical category, however does not affect the linguistic meaning. Take, for example, the formations *kṣība, kṛśa,* etc. discussed in the previous section. The grammatical category of the past passive participial termination *-ta* is absent in these formations. Yet, they function as past pasive participles in the language and they convey the meaning based on the respective roots. In other words, though the absence of *-ta* in these formations does not affect their linguistic meaning in usage, from the point of view of formal grammar, it is as a general rule capable of denying them their character as past passive participles.

This whole discussion is meant to bring out the point that, since the grammatical meaning based on the application or loss of a grammatical category does not bring about a change in the linguistic or social meaning of the formation, such formations should generally be treated on the formal, and not purely on semantic, level. It is on this consideration that the examples, discussed below, of the *nipātana* on the transformational level find a place under formal, and not semantic, *nipātana*.

4.1.2.1 The forms which are non-causal in appearance and yet convey a causal meaning in the language are : *dānta* (from *√dam*), *śānta* (from *√śam*), *pūrṇa* (from *√pūr*, 4th and 10th Conj.), *dasta* (from *√das*), *spaṣṭa* (from *√spaś*), *channa* (from *√chad*) and *jñapta* (from *√jñap*). They are laid down by Pāṇini in the *sūtra, vā dāntaśāntapūrṇadastaspaṣṭachannajñaptāḥ,*

7.2.27. As the option (cf. the *word vā*) shows, we have also optionally the forms *damita, śamita, pūrita, dāsita, spāśita, chādita* and *jñapita* respectively, used in the language besides the above forms. The *nipātana* aims at the the optional application of *iṭ* in causal; cf. Kāsikā on the *sūtra*, 7.2.27: *dam ity eteṣāṁ ṇyantānāṁ dhātūnāṁ vā aniṭtvam nipātyate.*

The *nipātana* is the shortest way to account for these formations because any other technique of substitution or general formative rules would have been very clumsy and elaborate. Secondlly, each of the forms would have required an independent *sūtra* for explanation because no two of them can be fitted into a general rule; that would have meant on unnecessary addition of seven *sūtras.*

The corresponding *sūtra* of other grammarians are :

Kātantra : *dāntaśāntapūrṇadastaspaṣṭacchannajñaptāś cenantāḥ*, 4.6.100.

Candra : *vā dāntaśāntapūrṇadastaspaṣṭacchannajñaptāḥ*, 5.4.155.

Bhoja : *vā dāntaśāntapūrṇadastaspaṣṭacchannajñaptāḥ*, 6.4.169.

Jainendra : *dāntaśāntapūrṇadastasoaṣṭacchanajñaptaḥ*, 5.1.124.

Hemacandra : *ṇau dāntaśāntapūrṇadastaspaṣṭacchanna jñaptāḥ*, 4.4.74.

Śākaṭāyana : *dāntaśāntapūrṇadastaspaṣṭacchannajñaptā vā*, 4.2.102.

The Sārasvata grammar does not note these forms, which speaks for the incomplete character of the system.

It is so be noted that all the grammarians in every detail have followed Panini in respect of these seven forms, that is, in adopting the method of *nipātana*, in the number of forms, and even in the order of enumeration of all of them.

In can be easily seen that in all the above examples, the

absence or presence of *iḍāgama* does not affect their linguistic meaning as derived from the meanings of their basic roots √*dam*, √*śam* etc.

4.2 Semantic Nipātana

As has been already pointed out, the purpose of semantic *nipātana* is to bring out the semantic difference of the *nīpātita* form from the other one which can be arrived at by regular formative process. The difference is to be seen in the social or linguistic meaning and not in the grammatical meaning. Thus, for example, a form, say *niṣṇāta,* is derived from the root √*snā,* 'to bathe', with the *upasarga ni* and its regular lingustic meaning based on the meaning of the root would be 'that which has bathed', but in actual linguistic usage the form conveys the maning of 'an expert'; and in this sense, the form displays the change of the initial dental *s* of √*snā* into the cerebral *ṣ*.

One can easily see that in such cases the derivative from the basic root totally abandons its meaning and signifies in the language a sense which has very title or sometimes absolutely no relation whatsover to that of the basic root. Such *nipātana* is, therefore, treated on purely semantic level, since, besides the fact that the *nipātita* word cannot be easily derived with the help of the existing set of rules of formative process, the sole guiding factor behind such *nipātana* is the difference in mening. It must, however, be mentioned that the semantic difference is often accompanied by a formal diffference also; but the latter is so insignificant that the semantic differenc alone becomes conspicuous. Hence such forms are treated under the title of 'semantic-*nipātana*'.

Actually semantic *nipātana* forms part of a larger category called 'non-formal *nipātana*', that is, a *nipātana* which is based on considerations of purely non-formal categories like meaning, gender, number, accent, tense, etc. But since no category other than that of meaning provides any example in the sphere of past passive participles, the category of meaning alone is taken for study. This would explain the title of the section, namely 'semantic *nipātana*', and not 'non-formal *nipātana*'.

In the case of the semantic *nipātana* also we get two sub-divisions :

4.2.1 Semantic *nipātana* on non-transformational level, and

4.2.2 semantic *nipātana* on transformational level

While in the former sub-division, both the base, which is described by *nipātana,* the meaning of which is given explicitly in the *sūtra,* and the alternative form derived by the regular formative process remain formally not-transformed, in the latter, that is, in that of semantic *nipātana* on the transformational level, either the base itself or the form derived by the regular formative process is transformed.

Thus, for example, in the case of forms *ṛṇa* (which is *nipātita*) and *ṛta* (which is arrived at by regular formative process), both from √*ṛ*, the base morpheme *ṛ* does not undergo any transformational change in connection with any of the two forms. On the other hand, in the case of the forms *vṛtta* (which is *nipātita*) and *vartita* (which can be arrived at by regular formative process), both from √*vṛt*, the base morpheme *vṛt* undergoes the causal transformational change in the case of the form *vartita*.

4.2.1 Semantic Nipātana on Non-transformational Level

4.2.1.1. The Pāṇinian *sūtra, kṣubdha-svāntadhvānta-lagna-mliṣṭa-viribdha-phāṇṭa-bāḍhāni mantha-manas-tamaḥ sakta-avispaṣṭa-svara-anāyāsa-bhṛśeṣu,* 7.2.18 lists in one single class the following 8 forms by *nipātana,* which display semantic differences from the corresponding forms available by regular formative process.

4.2.1.1.1. *kṣubdha :* √*kṣubh* 'to move, to get angry (cf. Pāṇinian dhp. *kṣubha saṁcalane,* 4th conj. Par. pada) gives out two forms namely with and without *iḍāgama,* which display a difference in meanings. Thus the form *kṣubdha* (without *iḍāgama*) means as the *sūtra* states, 'the churning rod' *(mantha)*, whereas the form *kṣubhita* (with *iḍāgama*) conveys the regular root-meaning, viz. 'one who is moved or angry'.

These meanings, however, seem to have been in vogue only in Pāṇini's times : because in later classical literature we find that the form *kṣubdha* is also used in the sense of 'one who is angry, agitated, shaken' etc.

4.2.1.1.2. *svānta:* √*svan* 'to produce sound' (cf. Pāṇinian dhp. *svana śabde*, 1st Conj. Par. pada) gives out two forms, *svānta* (without *iḍāgama*) and *svanita* (with *iḍāgama*). The former, viz. *svānta*, noted in the *sūtra*, means 'mind', whereas the latter signifies the sense of 'the noise, that which is spoken' etc.

It may, however, be noted that *svānta*, meaning 'mind', may also be split up as a compound of *sva* (one's own) +*anta* ('end, inferior part) to give out the sense of 'mind' stated in the Pāṇinian *sūtra*.

4.2.1.1.3. *dhvānta :* √*dhvan* 'to make sound' (cf. Pāṇinian dhp. *dhvana śabde*, 1st conj. Para.pada) gives out the two forms, *dhvānta* (without *iḍāgama*) and *dhvanita* (with *iḍāgama*). While the former means 'darkness', the latter means 'that which is uttered, spoken, suggested' etc.

4.2.1.1.4. *lagna :* √*lajj* 'to be ashamed, to blush' etc. (cf. Pāṇinian dhp. *olasjī vrīḍāyām*, 6th Conj. Atm. pada) gives out two different *ktānta* derivatives, namely, *lagna* (without *iḍāgama*) and *lajjita* (with *iḍāgama*); while the form, viz. *lagna*, as the *sūtra* states, means 'that which is attached', the latter conveys the regular root-meaning 'one who is ashamed of' etc.

The author of *Kāśikā*, however, assumes two semantically different roots for these two past passive participial forms; while he derives the form *lagna* from the root √*lag*, 'to be attached, stuck' etc. (cf. Pāṇinian dhp. *lage saṅge*,1st Conj. par. pada), he assumes the root √*lag* 'to taste', for the form *lagita* (with *iḍāgama*); √*lag* is given in the *dhp.* as *laga āsvādane*, 10th Conj. Ubhayapada. This derivation,however, sounds a little strange coming as it does from an authoritative commenatator of *Aṣṭādhyāyī*. The very motive of *nipātana* is to show the semantic difference between the two forms derived from the same root with a single meaning; if the roots are different and have different meanings, there is no propriety in stating a derivative from another root. The roots √*lag* (Ist conj.) and √*lag* (10th conj.) differ in meaning basically though their phonetic structure is the same. One feels, therefore, that in the present case both the chief commentators on Pāṇini's Aṣṭādhyāyī, namely BD. and Kāśikākāra, have missed the point or the principal motive underlying the technique of *nipātana*.

4.2.1.1.5. *mliṣṭa* : √*mlecch* 'to produce unclear sound' (cf. Pāṇinian *dhp. mleccha avyakte śabde*,1st conj. Parapada) gives out the two derivatives, *mliṣṭa* (without *iḍāgama*) and *mlecchita* (with *iḍāgama*). The former means 'not clear, ambiguous', whereas the latter, viz. *mlecchita* means 'that which is not spoken clearly' or to put it in other way,'that which is spoken not-clearly like a *mleccha*'.

4.2.1.1.6. *viribdha* : *vi* + √*ribh*/ √*rebh*, 'to speak, to sing' etc. (cf. Pāṇinian *dhp. rebhṛ śabde*, 1st conj. Ātm.pada) has two derivatives, *virebhita* (with *iḍāgama*) and *viribdha* (without *iḍāgama*). While the former means 'that which is spoken or sung, i.e. a word or hymn', the latter means, according to the *sūtra*, '*svara* i.e. voice, tone' etc.

The alternative form by regular formative process with *iḍāgama* can also be *viribhita* without *guṇa* of *i* into *e* if √*ribh*, a *sautra dhātu*, is assumed as the base; cf. Kāśikā on the Pāṇinian *sūtra*, 7.2.18: *anye tu viribhitam anyad iti paṭhanti; ribhim sautram dhātuṁ paṭhanti te viribhitam itipratyudāharanti.*

4.2.1.1.7. *phāṇṭa* : √*phaṇ* 'to go' (cf. Pāṇinian *dhp. phaṇa gatau,* 1st conj. par.pada), gives out two derivatives : *phāṇṭa* (without *iḍāgama,* with cerebralisation of the past passive participial termination *-ta,* due to the presence of *ṇ* in √*phaṇ* and with the *vṛdhi* of *a* into *ā*) and *phaṇita* (with *iḍāgama*). While the former means 'a kind of pungent preparation, easily prepared' 'a kind of bitter drink' (*cf.* BD. *anāyāsasādhyaḥ kaṣāyaviśeṣah;* the Kāśikā explains it as : *phāṇṭam iti bhavaty anāyāsaś cet yad aśṛtam apiṣṭam ca kaṣāyam udakasaṁparka-mātrād vibhaktarasam īṣaduṣṇam tat phāṇṭam; tad alpaprayanasādhyatvād anāyāsena lakṣyate),* the latter form, viz *phaṇita* means 'that which has gone.' Both are derived from the same root. (Is this *phāṇta* related with, or is the same as, the 'fanta-drink' available to-day?)

4.2.1.1.8. *bāḍha :* This is the last form mentioned in the *sūtra;* the sense conveyed by it is *bhṛśa* i.e. excessive, very much' etc. The form can be derived from √*bāh* or √*vāh,* 'to try,to attempt' etc., cf. Pāṇinian *dhp. vāhṛ prayatne* (or even *bāhṛ prayatne; cf.* BD. on the root: *antyaḥ kevaloṣṭhyādiḥ; ubhāv apy oṣṭhyādītyeke),* 1st conj. Ātm.pada. The form *bāḍha* is without *iḍāgama;* the corresponding form by regular formative process with *iḍāgam* is *vāhita* or *bāhita;* the sense conveyed by *vāhita* or *bāhita* will be regular root-meaning, viz. 'tried, attempted' etc. The indeclinable *bāḍham* may also be noted in this connection. It does not seem to be different from the one noted in the *nipātana-sūtra* 7.2.18 quoted above, though Pāṇini has not listed it in the enumeration of the indeclinables *(avyayas)*in the *sūtra, svarādi nipātāam avyayam,* 1.1.37. Of course, since the *svarādigaṇa* is taken as *ākṛtigaṇa,* the past passive participle *bāḍham* can be included in the group of indeclinables.

It will be seen that, in the *sūtra* 7.2.18, both the forms and the meanings of the different past passive participles, are different from those derived by the the normal fomative process. Also, the purpose of *nipātana* in the case of the present form is, first, to emphasize the non-application of *iḍāgama* on the formal plane; formally speaking, all these participles in the *sūtra*, 7.2.18, donot exhibit the existence of *iḍāgama*. Secondly, on the semantic plane, it is to stress the difference in linguistic or social meaning.

The meaning conveyed by both the types of forms, namely those that are laid down by *nipātana* as well as those that can be arrived at by the normal, regular formative process,are essentially social or linguistic meanings; no non-linguistic or technical meaning is available in the case of any types of forms out of the two types viz. *nipātita* and *non-nipātita*. Thirdly it will also be seen that the linguistic or social meaning, which the *nipātita* forms without *iḍāgama* convey, have no intrinsic relation to the meaning of the basic roots from which they are normally traditionally derived. This may mean that the derivation of these *nipātita* forms that is traditionally given may be totally wrong. In that case their etymologies will have to be sought somewhere else. Or, as one view claims,[1] such *nipātita* words, whose meaning has no intrinsic relation with the meaning of the basic roots from which they are derived, might be borrowed words form non-Indo-European languages.

The relevant *sūtras* of other grammarians are : Kātantra frames only two *sūtras* which include all the forms noted by Pāṇini in three *sūtras*,viz.7.2.18,22 and 23. The *sūtras* are : *kṣubhivāhisvanidhvaniphaṇi-kaṣighuṣām kte neḍ manthabhṛśamanastamo'nāyāsakṛcchrā-viśabdaneṣu*, 4.6.93, and *lagnamliṣṭaviribdhāḥ saktāvispaṣṭasvareṣu*, 4.6.94. It is also noted that while the five forms *kṣubhda, bāḍha. svānta, dhvānta* and *phāṇṭa* are treated by Kātantra on the level of morpho-phonemic changes (viz. the absence of *iḍāgama*), the three forms *lagna, mliṣṭa* and *viribdha* are treated on the level of *nipātana*.

Candra on the other hand splits the Pāṇinian *sūtra*, 7.2.18

1. cf. *Joshi V. L.* "Treatment of Loan-words in Sanskrit Grammar', *IL*, Vol. 32, No. 2, 1971, pp. 113-122.

and frames two independent *sūtras* laying down by *nipātana* only the seven forms, viz. *kṣubdha, svānta, dhvānta, viribdha, phāṇṭa, bāḍha* and *mliṣṭa;* the form *lagna* is not only omitted here but is not noted anywhere else; *cf.* the two Cāndra *sūtras: kṣubdhasvāntadhvāntaṁ manthamanastamaḥ,* 5.4.145 and *viribdhaphāṇṭabāḍha mliṣṭāni svarānāyāsabhṛśāspaṣṭesu,* 5.4.146. All the forms are treated by *nipātana.*

Bhoja follows Pāṇini in every detail viz. in laying down all the 8 forms by *nipātana,* in including them in a single sūtra, in the wording of the *sūtra* and the order of the forms; cf. his *sūtra* which is identical with the Pāṇinian one :

kṣubdhasvāntadhvāntalagnamliṣṭaviribdhaphāṇṭabāḍhāni manthamanastamaḥsaktāvispaṣṭasvarānāyāsabhṛśeṣu, 6.4.160.

Jainendra on the other hand combines the Pāṇinian 8 *sūtras*(viz. 7.2.18-23; 25; 26) into one and lays down by *nipātana* in all 16 forms. His *sūtra* reads as follows :

kṣubdhasvāntadhvāntalagnamliṣṭaviribdhaphāṇṭabāḍha viśastadhṛṣṭaghuṣṭadṛḍhaparivṛḍhābhyarṇavṛttāḥ, 5.1.126. He, however, does not note the meaning in which the different forms are used in the language. Not only here, but in the case of all the forms which Pāṇini describes by *nipātana* with the help of semantic considerations, Jainendra is strictly formal and does note in the *sūtra* itself the semantic import the forms carry. The explanation of the meanings of these forms is done by the commentary, which well agrees with those given by Pāṇini.

Hemacandra's *sūtra,* 4.4.70 *(kṣubdhaviribdhasvāntadhvānta lagnamliṣṭaphāṇṭaphāṇṭabāḍhaparivṛḍham-manthasvaramanas-tamassaktāspaṣṭānāyāsa bhṛśaprabhau),* adds one form more viz. *parivṛḍdha,* to the Pāṇinian list of 8 forms.

Śākaṭāyana follows Hemacandra in every detail, *cf. his sūtra, kṣubdhasvāntadhvāntaparivṛḍhalagnamliṣṭaviribdhap-hāṇḍabāḍham manthamanastamaḥprabhusasktāspaṣṭas-varānāyāsabhṛśe,* 4.2.150.

The Sārasvata grammar does not note these forms at all, which, incidentally, speaks for the incompleteness of the system.

Except the Kātantra, all the grammars have treated the forms by the technique of *nipātana* and explained them with the help of semantic considerations. The Kātantra grammar, however, describes some forms on the formal level by prohibiting the application of *iḍāgama.*

4.2.1.2. The next form on the non-transformational level described by semantic *nipātana* is *dṛḍha,*a past passive participle without *iḍāgama* from √*dṛh* / √*dṛṁh,* 'to grow, to increase' *(cf.* Pāṇinian *dhp. dṛha dṛhi vṛddhau,* 1st Conj. Par.pada). The meanings given for the form are two : (i) *sthūla* i.e. fat and (ii) *bala* i.e. strong (i.e. *balavān; cf.* BD's paraphrase *balavati).* The corresponding forms with *iḍāgama* are *dṛhita* or *dṛṁhita* and retain the root-sense of 'growing, increasing'.

The sūtras of the different grammarians are :

Pāṇini : *dṛḍhaḥ sthūlabalayoḥ,* 7.2.20.

Kātantra combines the two Pāṇinian *sūtras* viz. 7.2.20 and 21 into one; cf. *parivṛḍhadṛḍhau prabhubalavatoḥ* 4.6.95 which notes only one meaning for the form *drdha,* viz. *balavān.*

Candra : *dṛḍhaḥ sthūlabalinoḥ,* 5.4.148.

Bhoja : *dṛḍhaḥ sthūlabalinoḥ,* 6.4.162.

Jainendra does not note the meaning of the forms *cf.* his *sūtra,* 5.1.126, given in the previous section.

Hemacandra : *balisthūle dṛḍhaḥ,* 4.4.69.

Śākaṭāyana : *dṛḍhaḥ sthūlabalinoḥ,* 4.2.149.

Sārasvata does not note the form which shows the incompleteness of the system.

All the grammars have described the form by semantic *nipātana.* Pāṇini's use of a substantive *bala* for an adjective *balavān* is noteworthy in this connection; all other grammars have used the regular adjective *balin* or *balavān.* The *nipātana* aims at showing the absence of *iḍāgama.*

4.2.1.3. The form *parivṛḍha*, from *pari* + √*vṛh* / √*vṛṁh* 'to grow, to increase', 1st Conj. Par.pada., is laid down by *nipātana* in the sense of 'lord, master,capable of' etc. The Pāṇinian *sūtra* is *prabhau parivṛḍhaḥ* 7.2.21.

Though the from is from √*vṛh* / √*vṛṁh*, as the word *parivṛṭha* shows, the Pāṇinian dhp. has no such roots; what it has are the roots *bṛh/bṛṁh*; cf. Pāṇinian *dhp. bṛhabṛhi vṛddhau*, 1st Conj. Par.pada; the initial *b* of √*bṛh* alternates with *v* and the root changes to √*vṛh*. This is why BD. specifically mentions the roots √*vṛh*/√*vṛṁh* in his explanation of Pāṇini 7.2.21, cf. BD. *vṛha vṛhi vṛddha*, suggesting thereby that the roots √*bṛh* / √*bṛṁh* are the same as √*vṛh* / √*vṛṁh*.

The other forms of the roots with *iḍāgama* will be *parivṛhita* and *parivṛṁhita* and will convey the basic root-sense of 'one which has grown or increased'. *parivṛhita*, with *iḍāgam*, may have a transformational, causal sense like *parivardhita*.

The corresponding *sūtras* of other grammrians are :

Kātantra : *parivṛḍhadṛḍhau prabhubalavatoḥ*, 4.6.95, which combines Pāṇinian 7.2.20 and 21.

Candra : *prabhau parivṛḍhaḥ*, 5.4.149.

Bhoja : *prabhau parivṛḍhaḥ*, 6.4.163.

Jainendra does not specify the meanig, *c.f.* his *sūtra*, 5.1.126 noted earlier.

Hemacandra notes this form along with *kṣubdha, svānta, dhvānta* etc. cf. his *sūtra*, 4.4.70 noted earlier in the section 3.2.1

Śākaṭāyana follows Hemacandra in noting the form along with *kṣubdha, svānta* etc; *cf.* the *sūtra*,4.2.150 noted in the section 3.2.1

The Sārasvata grammar has not noted this form which indicates incompleteness of the system.

The *nipātana* aims at the absence of *iḍāgama* and presence of the *upasarga pari* with the root √*vṛh* / √*vṛṁh*.

4.2.1.4. The next form treated by semantic *nipātana* on the non-transformatinal level is *nirvāṇa,* from *nir* + √*vā* 'to blow' (cf. Pāṇinian *dhp. vā gatigandhanayoḥ,* 2nd Conj. Par.pada). The form employed to denote an idea other than the one connected with *vāta* i.e. wind, blowing etc. Thus we have the usages *nirvāṇāḥ agniḥ,* 'the fire is extinguished', *nirvāṇaḥ pradīpaḥ,* 'the lamp is blown out' etc. If, however, the context of 'wind' is present, the form would be *nirvāta* as in *nirvātaḥ vātaḥ* 'the wind has blown' etc.

The Pāṇinian *sūtra* that treats this form by *nipātana* is *nirvāṇo'vāte,* 8.2.50. Pāṇini could have treated form on the level of morphemic substitution of *-ta* into *-na* under the specified semantic conditions.

The corresponding *sūtras* of other grammarians are :

Kātantra : *nirvāṇo'vāte,* 46.113.

Candra : *avāte nirvāṇaḥ,* 6.3.86.

Bhoja : *avāte nirvāṇaḥ,* 7.3.97.

Jainendra : *nirvāṇo'vāte,* 5.3.66.

Hemacandra : *nirvāṇam avāte,* 4.2.79.

Śākaṭāyana : *nirvāṇo'vāte* 4.1.250.

Sārasvata does not note in complete agreement about the method of *nipātana* in the description of the form and the meaning.

The *nipātana* aims at the substitution of *-ta* by *-na* under the specified semantic condition of *avāta.*

4.2.1.5. The Pāṇinian *sūtra, vitto bhogapratyayayoḥ,*8.2.58, describes the form *vitta* by *nipātana* in the two senses of (i) *bhoga* i.e. enjoyment and (ii) *prataya* i.e. knowledge, conviction etc. The root from which this form is derived is obviously √*vid,* which is conjugated differently in different *gaṇas* and in diferent senses.[1] The most interesting fact, moreover, is

1. Cf. BD. on/vid, 10th Conj. : *sattāyām vidyate, Jñāne vetti, vinte vicāraṇe // vindate vindati prāptau śyan-luk-śnam-śeṣv idaṁ kramāt//,* though it must be noted that he forgets to include in the list the root √*vid* from the 10th Conj. itself on which he is writing the *kārikā.* This shows

that the different roots in different *gaṇas* with different meanings give out different forms in their past passive participial derivatives. This fact necessiated the grammarians to note the different forms and their meanings. Secondly, the root √*vid* is already mentioned in an earlier Pāṇinian *sūtra,* 8.2.56 *(nudavidondatrāghrāhrībhyo'nyatarasyām)* as optionally getting the morpheme *-na* in the place of *-ta* in its past passive participial formation. The meanings of the forms *vitta* and *vinna* require to be distinguished, which is done in the present *sūtra.*

According to Patañjali, the root √*vid* gives out different past passive participial formations according as it occurs in one or the other conjugations; *cf.* his *kārikā* on the Pāṇinian *sūtra,* 8.2.58 :

vettestu vidito niṣṭhā vidyater vinna iṣyate/
vinter vinnaś ca vittaś ca bhoga vittaś ca vindateḥ//

The present form *vitta* in the sense of *bhoga* can, on the authority of Patañjali, be safely taken as derived from √*vid-vind* 'to obtain', of the 6th Conj. (Pāṇinian *vidḷu lābhe*); cf. also BDs remark, which clearly states the above point; *vindater niṣṭhāntasya nipāto'yam bhogye pratīte cārthe.*

The corresponding *sūtras* of other grammarians are :

Kātantra combines into one the three Pāṇinian *sūtras* viz. 8.2.58, 59 and 60; *cf.* the Kātantra *sūtra bhittarṇavittāḥ śakalādhamarṇabhogeṣu,* 4.6.114. He, however, notes only one meaning viz. *bhoga* for the derivative.

Candra notes both the meanings, *cf.* the *sūtra, vittaḥ pratītabhogayoḥ,* 6.3.96.

Bhoja : *vitto dhanapratītayoḥ,* 7.3.108, which prefers the concrete meaning *dhana* i.e. wealth to the abstract one viz. *bhoga* i.e. enjoyment.

---

that the root belongs to the 10th Conjugation only secondarily — perhaps a causal formation from any of those from other conjugations, displaying an independent and non-causal meaning, *cf.* for meaning Pāṇinian *dhp. : vida* (10th Conj.) *cetanākhyānanivāseṣu.*

Jainendra does not note the meaning of the form at all, which shows that he strictly adheres to the formal procedure, cf. his *sūtra, vittabhittadūnagūna-pūnasitarṇāni,* 5.3.74. The commentary, however, gives the same meanings viz. *bhoga* and *pratīta* for the form as those given by Pāṇini.

Hemacandra follows Bhoja in laying down the concrete meaning of *dhana* in preference to *bhoga* for the form, cf. his *sūtra, vittaṁ dhanapratītam* 4.2.82. Hemacandra, however, notes one more form from √*vid* with *ni,* which no other grammrian has either described grammatically or noted by *nipātana;* the form is *nirviṇṇa* and the *sūtra* is *nirviṇṇaḥ,* 2.3.89. The meaning of the form, however, is not given, though the commentary *Svopajñnalaghuvṛtti* derives it form √*vid* in the sense of (i) *sattā, 'to be'* (4th Conj.), (ii) *lābha* 'to obtain' (6th Conj.) and (iii) *vicāraṇa* 'to think' (7th Conj.). The meaning of the form *nirviṇṇa* will, therefore, be any one of these three.

Śākaṭāyana follows Bhoja and Hemacandra in giving the concrete meaning *dhana; cf.* his *sūtra, vittam dhanapratītam,* 4.1.260.

Sārasvata has no *sūtra* which describes this form in this sense. This indicates the incomplete nature of the grammar.

4.2.1.6. The next non-transformed form treated by semantic *nipātana* is *bhitta* from √*bhid* 'to cut open' (cf. Pāṇinian *dhp. bhidir vidāraṇe,* 7th Conj. Par. pada) noted by Pāṇini in the *sūtra, bhittam śakalam,* 8.2.59 with the meaning 'a broken piece'. The other past passive participial formation from the same root is *bhinna* which in its root-sense means 'that which is cut'. The difference between the meanings of the forms *bhitta* and *bhinna* is more functional than semantic. While the former can function absolutely as a noun (*viseṣya*) and never as an adjective *(viśeṣaṇa),* the latter viz. *bhinna* can function only as an adjective or participle. The changes of *ta* into *na* in the case of the form *bhinna* is brought about according to the Pāṇinan *sūtra,* 8.2.42.

The corresponding *sūtras* of other grammarians are

Kātantra : *bhittarṇavittāḥ śakalādhamarṇabhogeṣu*, 4.6.114.

Candra : *bhittam śakale*, 6.3.97.

Bhoja : *bhittam śakalam*, 7.3.109.

Jainendra does not note the meaning of the form; *cf.* his *sūtra, vittabhittadūnayūnapūnasitarṇāni*, 5.4.74.

Hemacandra : *bhittam śakalam*, 4.2.81

Śākaṭāyana : *bhittam śakalam*, 4.1.259.

The Sārasvata does not note the form, which again shows its incomplete nature.

The *nipātana* aims at the absence of the change of *-ta* into *-na* based on the semantic change.

4.2.1.7. The next form is *ṛṇa*, from √*ṛ* 'to go' in the sense of 'debt', as against *ṛta* (from √*ṛ* 'to go') meaning 'that which has gone'. The Vedic concept of *Ṛta* is to be derived from this same root √*ṛ* 'to go'.

The different *sūtras* of the different grammarians are :

Pāṇini : *ṛṇam ādhamarṇye*, 8.2.60

Kātantra : *bhittarṇavittāḥ śakalādhamarṇa-bhogeṣu*, 4.6.114.

Candra treats this form on the level of optional morphemic substitution of *-ta* by *-na* and not by the technique of *nipātana;* cf. his *sūtra, ghrātrārtihrīnudondavido vā*, 6.3.87. The *sūtra,* however, does not give the meaning of the form; only the commentary says : *ṛṇam śodhyam*.

Bhoja, who usually follows Candra, follows Pāṇini in the present case *cf.* his *sūtra ṛṇam ādhamarṇye*, 7.3.98, which resorts to the technique of *nipātana*.

Jainendra does not note the meaning of the form, though he adopts the method of *nipātana*, *cf.* his *sūtra*, *vittabhittadūnagūnasitarṇāni*, 5.3.74.

Hemacandra follows Candra in treating this form by the technique of optional morphemic substitution of *-ta* by *-na*, which does not leave any scope for noting its meaning also; *cf.* his *sīra, ṛ-hrī-ghrā-dhrā-trā-unda-nuda-vinter vā*, 4.2.76.

Śākaṭāyana adopts the technique neigther of *nipātana* nor of mophemic substitution. According to his school of grammar, the form can be accounted for by a *sūtra* viz. *ṛṇe*, 1.3.155 (in a different context) by resorting to the technique of *jñāpana;* the *Śākaṭāyana-sūtra*, 1.3.155, is therefore, is *jñāpaka* of the form *ṛṇa*, *cf.* the commentary *Cintāmaṇi* on the *sūtra*,. 4.1.246: *ṛṇam dhārayati iti ṛṇe iti nipātanāt siddham*, which terms this as *nipātana;* yet from strictly technical point of view it is *jñāpana*.

Sārasvata does not note the form, which again shows in completeness of the system.

The *nipātana* aims at the change of *-ta* into *-na* based on the difference in meaning.

4.2.1.8. The next form that is treated by the technique of semantic *nipātana* on non-transformational level is *pratiṣṇāta*, from *prati* + √*snā;* the semantic context in which the form occurs in the language refers to 'a thread' or '*sūtra* of grammar'. The regular meaning of the form would be 'that which has taken bath' from √*snā* 'to bathe' (2nd Conj. Par. pada). In this case, the form with *prati* will be *pratisnāta* and will not show the change of s into its corresponding sibilant cerebral ṣ. When, however, the s change to ṣ, the form signifies the meaning 'purification of a thread or a *sūtra* of grammar'.

The Pāṇinian *sūtra* that treats this form is *sūtram pratiṣṇātham*, 8.3.90. Though BD. explains the *sūtra* in such a way as to create an impression that the form is treated on the level of phonetic substitution of ṣ (*cf.* BDs explantion : *prateḥ snāteḥ ṣatvam*), the Pāṇinian *sūtra* does not create that impression. It clearly states it by *nipātana*.

The corresponding *sūtras* of other grammarians are :

Kātantra does not note the form.

Candra in his *sūtra*, *prateḥ sūtre*, 6.4.78, describes the form with the help of the phonological change of s into ṣ.

Bhoja follows Candra : *cf.* his *sūtra, prateh sūtre*, 7.4.80.

Jainendra follows Pāṇini in describing the form by *nipātana*, but does not specify its meaning *cf.* his *sūtra, niṣṇāta nadīṣṇātapratiṣṇātābhiniṣṭānakapiṣṭha lapraṣṭhaviṣṭaraviṣṭāraga-viṣṭhirayudhiṣṭhirāḥ*, 5.4.75, which, besides the form *pratiṣṇāta*, treats the forms *niṣṇāta* and *nadīṣṇāta* also by *nipātana*. It should be noted that the latter two are described by Pāṇini on the basis of phonological change of *s* into *ṣ*; *cf.* the Pāṇinian *sūtra, ninadībhyām snāteḥ kauśale*, 8.3.89.

Hemacandra, following Candra, describes the form on the basis of phonological change of *s* into *ṣ*. *cf.* his *sūtra, prateḥ snātasya sūtre*, 2.3.21.

Śākaṭāyana follows Candra, Bhoja and Hemacandra, *cf.* his *sūtra prateḥ snātam sūtre*, 2.2.152.

The Sārasvata does note the form. It will be seen that only Pāṇini and Jainendra treat the form by *nipātana*, all others have treated it by adopting the technique of the phonological change of *s* into *ṣ*, which Pāṇini and Jainendra also could have done, especially in view of the fact that they have treated the forms *niṣṇāta* and *nadīṣṇāta*, other derivative from the same root √*snā* with the *upasargas ni* and *nadī*, on the basis of phonological changes of *s* into *ṣ*.

The chief aim of the *nipātana* is to 'show the presence of *ṣ* when the semantic context is of the '*sūtra*'.

4.2.1.9. The next form to be explained with the help of semantic *nipātana* is *śṛta*, a past passive participle from √*śrā* 'to cook' (*cf.* Pāṇinian *dhp. śrāi pāke*, 1st Conj. Par. Pada, or *śrāi pāke*,[1] 2nd Conj. Par. pada). Actually the regular past

1. Actually √*śrai* and √*śrā* are the same roots; *cf.* BDs remarks at *śrai pāke*, 1st Conj. : *śrai iti kṛtātvasy śrā ity ādādikasya ca sāmānyenānukaraṇam; lugvikaraṇā lugvikaraṇayor alugvikaraṇasya, lakṣaṇapratipadoktayoḥ pratipadoktasyaiva grahaṇam iti paribhāṣābhyām.* It is included in the list of roots which are technically termed by Pāṇini as *mit*; the causal form, therefore, will be *śrapayati* in the sense of *pāka* and *śrāpayati* in a sense other than that of *pāka*; *cf.* BD. *śrapayati/ vikledayatīty arthaḥ / pākād antyatra śrāpayati / svedayatīty arthaḥ/*

passive participial form which the root should give out is *śrāṇa* (i.e. **śrāta*, the *-ta* > *-na* according to the Pāṇinian *sūtra*, 8.2.43), non-causal and *śrapita*, causal. But the root gives out the form *śṛta* under the semantic conditions of *pāka* i.e. cooking done with reference to *kṣīra* i.e. milk or *havis* i.e. oblation. The Pāṇinian *sūtra* that lays down this form by *nipātana* is *śṛtam pāke*, 6.1.27. The *sūtra*, however, does not contain the words *kṣīra* and *havis;* the commentaries of BD. and Kāśikā supply the elipsis; *cf.* BD. *śrātiśrapayatyoḥ kte śṛbhāvo nipātyate kṣīrahaviṣoḥ; cf. als* Kāsikā : *vyavasthita-vibhāṣeyam; tena kṣīrahaviṣoḥ nityam śṛbhāvo bhavati.* With reference to the cooking of *kṣira* and *havis*, therefore, the usage admissible is *śṛta* (as in *śṛtam kṣīram, śṛtam havīḥ*); in other cases, the form *śrāṇa* alone is admissible (as in *śrāṇā yavāgūḥ*, non-causal, and *śrapitā yavāgūḥ*, causal; *cf.* Kāśikā).

There is one more subtle point in the case of this form. Besides being used in the context of *kṣīra* and *haviṣ* alone, the participle *śṛta* can be used both in the non-causal as well as causal senses; *cf.* BDs wording: *śrātiśrapayatyoḥ; cf.* also Kāśikā : *ṇyantasya aṇyantasya ca*. Thus this form is different from all other forms in that, while the other forms, under the given semantic conditions, are used only in either a transformational or in a non-transformational meaning, the present form conveys both non-tranformational as well as transformational meanings. Secondly, its *nipātana* points to its peculiarity of signifying both the linguistic or social meaning of *pāk* as well as the grammatical meaning of '*causal*'.

It is also to be noted that, instead of laying down only the semantic context of *kṣīra* and *havis* and the participial form, that is to say, instead of composing a *sūtra* like *śṛtam kṣīrahaviṣoḥ* (as he has done in the case of the forms *nirvāṇa* etc.), Pāṇini has chosen to lay down the meaning of the root *śrā* (viz. *pāke*) along with the *nipātita* form. The reason for such a wording of the *sūtra* seems to be that the meaning of the root viz. *pāka* would definetely specify the root to be √*śrā*. If no meaning was stated and if the wording of the *sūtra* was simply *śṛtaṁ kṣīrahaviṣoḥ,* there would have been some ambiguity as regards the basic root. The *nipātita* form *śṛta* might have been easily misunderstood to have been derived from √*śru* 'to hear', (since the form *śṛta* is the closest to *śruta* in hearing, the *nipātana* might have been misunderstood as for substituting the vowel *ṛ* for the sound-group *ru* in √*śru*), if the meaning *pāka* would not have been specified. The statement of the meaning of the basic root thus easily suggests the basic root and leaves no scope for any ambiguity or misunderstanding as regards the basic root from which the *nipātita* form should be derived.

The form could have also been explained on the basis of morphemic substitution of the base *śrā* by *śṛ*.

The corresponding *sūtras* of other grammarians are :

Kātantra does not note this form.

The Cāndra grammar does not note the meaning of the root √*śrā*, but states the semantic context of *kṣīra* and *havis; cf.* the Candra *sūtra, śṛtam kṣīrahaviṣoḥ,* 5.1.33. The *Cāndravṛtti* seems to mention a root √*śrā* of the 10th conjugation as its wording, viz. *śrapayater vā caurādikasya ṇyantasya,* would imply. So also the *Tattvabodhinī* on BDs *Siddhānta Kaumudī; cf. Tattvabodhinī; śrā pāke ity adādau paṭhyate; curādāv api ghaṭādiṣv api paṭhyate mittvārtham;* Pāṇinian *dhp.* has no such root in the 10th Conjugation. The form *śrapayati* which BD. and *Cāndravṛtti* mention seems to be the causal of √*śrā.* It is on the basis of the presumed root √*śrā* in the 10th conjugation that the *Cāndravṛtti* remarks : *prayojakavyāpāre tu yo ṇic tadantasya na bhavati; śrapitaṁ kṣīraṁ devadattena.* This goes against Kāśika's explanation (cf. the word *ṇyantasya*), and the usage marks a departure from the one in vogue in the times of Pāṇini and Kāśikākāra.

Bhoja is quite precise in framing the *sūtra* to explain the form; he mentions the root, its form by *nipātana,* and the semantic context in which the latter is used; *cf.* his *sūtra, śrāteḥ śṛtam kṣīrahaviṣoḥ,* 6.1.88.

Jainendra : *kṣīrahaviṣoḥ śṛtam*, 4.3.22, which leaves the root to be understood from the usage.

Besides laying down the form *śṛta* for the root √*śrā* in a non-causal sense, Hemacandra explicitly notes the causal sense also in an independent *sūtra; cf.* his two *sūtras: śraḥ śṛtam haviḥkṣīre*, 4.1.100 and *śrapeḥ prayoktraikye*, 4.1.101. His second *sūtra*, viz. 4.1.101, therefore, follows Kāśika's explanation viz. in the case of a double causal, the root √*śrā* gives out only the form *śrapita* and not *śṛta;* cf. Kāśikā on Pāṇini 6.1.27: *yadāpi bāhye prayojake dvitīyo ṇij utapadyate tadāpi neṣyate.* This is the meaning of Hemacandra's condition *prayoktṛ-aikya.*

Śākaṭāyana : *śṛtam pakve haviḥkṣīre*, 4.1.134. He also makes a distinction between a single-causal and double-causal formation; *cf.* the Cintāmaṇi-vṛtti on Śākaṭayana-*sūtra*, 4.1.134; *prathamaṇyantasya dvitīyaṇyantāt ktaḥ.*

Sārasvata does not note the form, which only shows the incomplete nature of the grammar.

The *nipātana* aims at substituting the morpheme *śṛ* for the root-morhpheme *śrā*. The form would have been equally well explained on the level of morphemic substitution. All have treated the form on the *nipātana* level.

4.2.2 Semantic Nipātna on Transformational Level

We get only one form of this type viz. *vṛtta*, from the causal of √*vṛt* 'to be, to remain' (*cf.* Pāṇinian *dhp. vṛtu vartane*, 1st Conj. Ātm. pada; *cf.* also *vṛtu varaṇe*, 4th Conj. Ātm.pada, which probably is not meant here because of its meaning viz. *varaṇa* i.e. choosing; there is yet another root √*vṛt* 'to speak', noted by Pāṇini in the 10th Conj; *cf. vṛtu bhāṣārthaḥ*, which has closer semantic affinity with the meaning *adhyayana* i.e. study which the form *vṛtta* signifies. If, therefore, the word *ṇeḥ* in the Pāṇinian *sūtra, ṇer adhyayane vṛttam*, 7.2.26, which treats the form, refers to the root *vṛt* from the 10th Conj. and does not mean the causal of √*vṛt*, 1st

Conj. the form could well be taken as treated on the non-transformational plane.

The meaning in which √*vṛt* gives out the form *vṛtta* is of *adhyayana* or study. Thus, we have the usage *vṛttam chandaḥ chātreṇa*, 'the metre is studied by the pupil', as opposed by *vartitā rajjuḥ*, 'the rope is rolled'.

The Kātantra grammar has no *sūtra* which explains this form, though the *vṛtti* on the Kātantra *sūtra*, 4.6.95 (*parivṛḍhadṛḍhau prabhubalavatoḥ*, discussed earlier) noted it and remarks : *katham vṛttam pārāyanaṁ vipreṇa / vṛtto guṇaś chātreṇeti / antarbhūte' narthavṛtter bhaviṣyati/ inantasyāpi*[1]*/ vartito guṇo'neneti bhavitavyam iti matam*[2]*/ anye tv ino'dhyayane vṛttam iti nipātayanti//* The *anye* obviously refers to the followers of the Pāṇinian school of grammar.

The whole discussion in the *Kātantravṛtti* shows that the Kātantra-school does not seem to agree about the causal nature of the form *vṛtta* and its meaning of 'study'.

Candra : *ṇer vṛttam granthe*, 5.4.154, which says *granthe* in the place of the Pāṇinian *adhyayane*. Does it mean that the word *grantha* means the study of the whole book, implying thereby that in the case of the study of the part of a book, the form *vṛtta* could not be used? Such a conjecture, however,is not supported by any evidence. On the contrary, Candra's example *vṛttam pārāyaṇam devadattena* is the same as given by Kāśikā (*cf. vṛttam pārāyaṇam devadatten* in Kāśikā) which is writing on the Pāṇinian word *adhyayana*. This shows that the two words *adhyayana* and *grantha* cannot mean the same activity. It also shows that the form *vṛtta* can be used in both the contexts, viz. of the *grantha* as well as of the *adhyayana*.

Bhoja follows Candra in the wording of his *sūtra; cf.* his *sūtra*, *ṇer vṛttam granthe*, 6.4.168.

---

1. Kātantra's *inanta* is the same as Pāṇini's *ṇijanta*, causal.
2. This is the opinion or Vararuci, as the commentary on the Kātantra-*sūtras* by Trilocanadāsa shows; *cf.* the word *vararuceḥ* added after the word *matam*.

Jainendra lays down only the form *vṛtta* and not its meaning; cf. his *sūtra,* 5.1.126, noted earlier. The meaning *adhyayana* is supplied by the commentary; *cf. vṛttam ity adhyayane'rthe nipātyate... vṛttas tarkaḥ devadattena, vṛttam Jainendram.*

Hemacandra follows Candra ; *cf.* his *sūtra vṛtter vṛttam granthe,* 4.4.56. The commentary *Svopajñalaghu-vṛtti* by Śrīvinayavijayagaṇi, however, remarks that the form *varttita* is used with reference to a *grantha* also according to some people; *cf. anye tu granthe'pi varttitam iti prayogam ādriyante.* Who these *anye* are, is not explained in the commentary. This only shows that though in the days of Pāṇini the form *vṛtta* might have been used strictly in the sense of *adhyayana* or grantha, the form *varttita* also might have been used in the same sense and context later on presumably in the times of Hemacandra.

Śākaṭāyana, surprisingly enough, does not note this form.

So also Sārasvata.

The nipātana is meant to show the absence of *iḍāgama* and the consequent *guṇa,* as well as of the causal termination (cf. BD. *ṇiluk*). All grammars agree in laying down the form by *nipātana.*

5. Form Noted by Some Grammarians Only

Besides the forms discussed above, which are noted by almost all grammarians, excepting the author of the Sārasvata grammar, there is one form which is described by some and not even noted by others. The form in question is *nirviṇṇa,* from the root √*vid* 'to think', 7th Conj. Ātm.pada with the *upasarga nis.*

Those who have neither described nor noted the form are Pāṇini, Kātantra, Jainendra and Sārasvat. According to these grammarians, therefore, the form could be well accounted for by the general regular rules of formative process.

But the difficulty in deriving this form by regular grammatical process lies in the change of *n*, which replaces the *-t*, into cerebral *ṇ*. Hence one can say that the form is not accounted for by the above-listed four grammarians. The *vārttika, kṛtsthasya ṇatva nirviṇṇasyopasaṁkhyānam,* on the Pāṇinian *sūtra,* 8.4.29 *(kṛty acaḥ)* therefore, tries to bring this omission to the notice of the Pāṇinian school.

Those who have noted this form are :

Candra : *nirviṇṇaḥ*, 6.4.123.

Bhoja : *nirviṇṇaḥ*, 7.4.135.

Hemacandra : *nirviṇṇaḥ*, 2.3.89 and

Śākaṭāyana : *nirviṇṇaḥ*, 4.2.252.

It should be noted that the form is unanimously described by resorting to the technique of *nipātana;* also that the meaning of the form is not given and is left to the usage. The *nipātana* aims at bringing about the change of the dental *n* (< *-ta*) into the cerebral *-ṇ*.

5
General Linguistic and Descriptive Principles

1. The various forms of the past passive participles, which have been collected in the preceding chapters from different grammars and discussed in detail are adequate enough, both in quality and quantity, to enable us to formulate a broad idea of the general principles—linguistic, descriptive, technical, grammatical, etc— underlying the description of those forms by the different grammarians. These principles may be divided into two main categories for the sake of the convenience of critical examination and study:—

(1) **General Principles :—** This category will include all such principles as are generally accepted or followed by all the grammarians. A critical study of these principles will facilitate our arriving at the commom core of principles underlying the different grammars.

(2) **Special Principles :—** Besides the principles in the first category, there are certain features of methods of descriptive analysis which seem to be special to the individual authors of the different grammars. A study of these features and methods will enable us to identify the individual characteristics of the different schools of grammar. Such a study will also help us to mark out the differentiating features of the principal schools of grammars.

1. **General Principles :—** The general principles are here examined under the following four heads :—

1. Principles of Language-Analysis;

2. Principles of Descriptive Analysis;
3. Principles of Morpheme-Indentification; and
4. Principles of Derivation.

It is obviously more logical, more convenient and perhaps also safer to begin with finding out the general principles of the analysis of language followed by the different grammarians. Some indications of the principles of language-analysis are given already in the previous chapters while dealing with some cases (cf. for example, the discussion of the two principles of linguistic descriptin; in one case, the concept of zero is inevitable; in the other it can never come in the field at all; cf. Ch. 4. dealing with *Nipātanas)*. They are, however, discussed here again in greater detail.

1.1 Principle of Language-Analysis

As has been already seen in connection with all the past passive participial formations described by the grammarians, every grammarian starts with a hypothetical (hypothised by himself) verbal root and lays down the past passive participle termination *-ta* to be applied to it. In the combination of these two, namely, the verbal root and the termination, certain morphophonemic changes naturally take place, and they too are set forth. The spring-board of grammarian for the description of these formations, therefore, is the principle of a basic verbal root, the form of which is determined by himself, to be followed by the past passive participal suffix -*ta.* This principle can be easily represented in the form of a symbolic formula like,

$R + S = F$, where R =the basic verbal root,

S = the past passive participial suffix *-ta,* and

F = the past passive participial formation ready for use in the language after the application of the *sup*-terminations for nominal declension. It may be thus seen that the whole description of the past passive participial formation assumes, *a priori*, the existences of the basic root-norms and the exact form of the suffix to be applied.

This practice of assuming, in the case of the description of the past passive participial formations, a theoretical root-norm in the initial stage and then applying to it a fixed suffix-norm is in sharp contrast with the one followed in the case of many other formations. Take, for example, the conjugation of verbs. The root √*ad* 'to eat', belongs to the second conjugation. The form of the root in present, 3rd person, sing. is *atti*. Now, on the face of it, the description of the form is very simple. One takes the root and applies the termination -*ti*. The quetion of any *vikaraṇa* does not arise at all in such simple description. Yet, Pāṇini and all the other grammarians have invariably followed the following descriptive procedure:—

What they have done is that they have stated the application of the *vikaraṇa a* i.e. *śap* and laid down its loss or zero. Actually since there is no infix between the root √*ad* and the termination -*ti* in the case of the form *atti* (the same is the case with all the verbal forms of the second conjugation), the laying down of such an infix and then negating it may seem to be a very strange process, even an illogical and unwarranted process. Such a process of description, however, is presumably occasioned by a conscious or unconscious comparison of the form *atti* (and of all the verbal forms of the second conjugation, for that matter,) with the one like *bhavati* (from √*bhū* 'to be') or *khādati* (from √*khād* 'to eat'), both of the first conjugation. And the comparison is in terms of the number of items to be included in the analytical procedure. The description of *atti* in the manner stated above assumes that, like the forms *bhavati* or *khādati* or for that matter like those of roots in any conjugation other than the second, this form also *must* contain three terms or items in its analysis. Thus, if the form *bhavati* has a root, a *vikaraṇa*, and the conjugational termination as three items in its analytical stage, the form *atti* also must be represented as having the same three items viz. the root, the *vikaraṇa*, and the conjugational termination. We, therefore, find that the form *atti* is described with a reference to the form *bhavati*.

Apart from the question whether such a description is right or wrong, logical or illogical, brief a otherwise, it involves first the creation of an entity which does not occur there, and secondly its negation. Such a description starts from the maximum structure of the type of the formation as available in the language and its comparison with similar ones, and hence necessitates the techniques of zero.[1] It must be stated here that this is the procedure of analysis originally adopted by Pāṇini; and all the post-pāṇinian grammarians have followed suit.

Such a state of affair, however, does not prevail in the case of the past passive participial formations. As we have seen above, what the grammarians have done is that they have assumed the structure of the past pasive participles as composed of only two morphemes, viz. the *prakṛti* which is the verbal root here and the *pratyaya* which is the past passive participial suffix *-ta* in the present case. And in no case of the past passive participial formations, do we find an example of a three-morpheme or a three-term structure being assumed. It is this fact which has led all the grammarians to describe even those past passive participial formations, which display an additional item viz. *i* (= the *iḍāgama* of the grammarians) and which could have been in that case analysed as possessing three terms,—viz. the root, the *āgama* *i* and the suffix *-ta* —, as being constituted of only two, and not three, morphemes.

1. For a discussion of zero, *cf. W. Has*, "Zero in Linguistic Description, '*Studies in Linguistic Analysis*, Special Volume of the Philosophical Society, Oxford, 1957, pp. 33-53; *vide* also *W. S. Allen*, 'Zero and Pāṇini' *Indian Linguistics*, Vol. 16, 1955, Poona, pp. 106-113. For zero in Pāṇinian description, *cf. M. D. Pandit*, 'Zero in Pāṇini' *JMSUB* (Humanities) Vol. XI, No. 1, 1961, pp. 53-66; also 'Zero in Pāṇini' CASS, Pune, 1990.

1.1.1. An Objection

But one may object to the above observation, namely, that the grammarians have assumed the structure of the past passive participial formations as being originally composed of only two morphemes, the *prakṛti* and the *pratyaya* and that of the conjugated verbal forms as being originally composed of three morphemes, the *prakṛti*, the *vikaraṇa* and the *pratyaya*. The ground for raising such an objection is : If we examine only the Pāṇinian *sūtras* stating the *vikaraṇa* and its *lopa* on the one hand, and the *iḍāgama* and its absence on the other, we find that he has followed in both the cases a consistent procedure in regard to the *sūtra*-arrangement. In both the cases, what he has done is that he has treated first the cases, in which both, the *vikaraṇa* on the one hand and the *iṭ* on the other, are not available (cf.the Pāṇinian *sūtras* about *lopa; adiprabhṛtibhyaḥ śapaḥ*, 2.4.72; *juhotyādibhyaḥ śluḥ*, 2.4.75; also cf. his *sūtras* about *iṭ : neḍ vaśi kṛti*, 7.2.8; *ekāca upadeśe'nudāttāt*,7.2.10, etc.) and he has gone to state the application of *śap* and *iṭ* only afterwards (cf. his *sūtras* for *śap*, *kartari śap*, 3.1.68; for *śyan*, *divādibhyaḥ śyan*, 3.1.69 etc., for *iṭ*, cf. *ārdhadhātukasyeḍ valādeḥ*,7.2.35). The numbering of the *sutras* will easily convince one that the *sūtras* laying down the zero of *vikaraṇa* come first, or prior to those stating the application of the *vikaraṇas;* so also,the *sūtras* dealing with the absence of *iṭ* come first, or prior to those stating the application of the *iḍāgama*. Pāṇini's method of *sūtra*-arrangement in both the cases of *vikaraṇa* and *iḍāgama* is thus consistent in the sense that he gives priority of treatment to those cases in which the *vikaraṇas* and the *iḍāgama* are not found. The cases displaying the existence of *vikaraṇa* and *iḍāgama* get a second place in his treatment. Similar is the state of affair in other grammars also, since, obviously, they have followed Pāṇini in principle. If, therefore, one applies the principle of assuming a three-morpheme structure as original in the case of the conjugated verbal forms, in spite of the fact that the existence of a three-morpheme structure is acknowledged by Pāṇini and others in later *sūtras*, he, as logical reasoning demands, must apply the same principle in the cae of the past passive participial formations also and come to the same conclusion. But in the present case, the two conclusions in the two cases of *vikaraṇa* and of *iḍāgama* are not the same. The observation, therefore, namely that the structure of the past passive participial formations is originally assumed to be consisting of only two morphemes and that the structure of the conjugated verbal forms is originally supposed to be constituted of three-morphemes is totally wrong and unwarranted by the evidence of the *sūtra*-arrangment. Actually the *sūtra*-arrangement of Pāṇini in both the cases point to a conclusion which is quite the contrary, viz. that he (and also others) has assumed, in both the cases of *vikaraṇa* and *iḍāgama*, a two morpheme structure as original; the concept of a three-morpheme structure comes later on in his grammatical treatment.

1.1.2. Objection Set Aside

The above objection appears quite logical, natural and sound, being based upon the solid foundation of the arrangement of the *sūtras* in Pāṇini's *Aṣṭādhyāyī;* and one cannot gainsay the similarity in the arrangement of the two types of *sūtra*-groups, one dealing with the application and zero of the *vikaraṇas* and the other with the presence and absence of the *iḍāgama*. Yet, what matters here is the mode of statement. If we examine the manner in which the negation of the *vikaraṇa śap* in the *adādi*-group is stated, we find that it is negated by the word *luk* which is one of the synonyms of the word *lopa* (elision) *cf.* the *sūtra, adiprabhṛtibhyaḥ śapaḥ,* 2.4.72, in which the word *luk* (= elision, zero) is to be borrowed from the previous *sūtra*, 2.4.58; as opposed to this the *iḍāgama* is negated by the use of the regular, explicit *na* (not) which is a regular *niṣedha* for applying the *iṭ* (which is laid down in the *sūtra, ārdhadhātukasyeḍvalādeḥ*,7.3.35); *cf.* the *sūtras* negating the application of *iḍāgama, neḍ vaśi kṛti*, 7.2.8

etc. This means that though from a superficial point of view there is no difference between these two statements, from the strictly technical point of view, the difference in the two statements reveals a difference in the approach to the two phenomena. When Pāṇini says that the *śap* in the case of the *adādi*-group is to be elided, he takes for granted that there is already a *śap* in the form *atti.* This means that, according to the Pāṇinian technique, the *vikaraṇa śap* is originally there,— or rather, has a right to be there — and then it is to be elided. In the case of the *iḍāgama,* however, Pāṇini flatly refuses to admit its existence in the basic form; the *iḍāgama* according to him is an outsider. This, however, is not the case with *vikaraṇa.* The *vikaraṇa,* according to him, is an organic part of the basic structure of the verb. All this shows that, in the case of the *adādi*-group, Pāṇini takes a three-morpeme structure, composed of a root, *vikaraṇa* and the *pratyaya* for granted; in the case of the past passive participial formations, on the other hand, as is clear from his straight-way negation of *iḍāgama,* he does not start with a three-moprheme-structure; he starts with a two morpheme structure, a root, and the past passive participial suffix *-ta.*

There is a strong reason for not adopting the three-morpheme structure as basic in the case of the past passive participial formations. If we study the technique of zero,[1] adopted by Pāṇini, we find that on morphological plane the technique is employed only in the case of morphemes, which are basically minimal meaningful units. And since the *āgama iṭ* conveys no meaning at all, it cannot be, according to Pāṇini, brought under the technique of zero. The *vikaraṇa,* on the other hand, is a meaningful unit, a morpheme; it implies or connotes the two senses, viz. of 'an active sense (cf. the word *kartari* in the Pāṇinian *sūtra, kartari śap,* 3.1. 68) and of 'the *sārvadhātuka* form' (cf. the word *sārvadhātuka* in the *sūtra,*

1. Cf. *M. D. Pandit,* 'Zero in Pāṇini', *JMSUBH.* 1961 pp. 53-66; also 'Zero in Pāṇini, CASS, Pune, 1990.

sārvadhātuke yak, 3.1.67, which is to be borrowed in the next *sūtra*, 3.1.68 quoted above). It is because of the basic difference between the two techniques that the statements about *iḍāgama* and *vikaraṇa* are different. And it is because of the difference between the two statements that the conclusions regarding the hypothesis of the basic structures in the two cases,—of the conjugated verbal forms and the past passive participial formations—which are drawn above, are different.

Also, the aproach to analysis of the past passive participles is not structural with sense that the starting point is not an inflected form or finished form ready for use.

It is on account of the assumption of a basic two-term structure in the case of the past passive participles that the grammarians have been compelled to posit an additional infix i i.e. *iḍāgama* in the case of forms in which it occurs. It is this assumption of a two-term structure which completely does away with the concept and techniques of zero in the case of the past passive participial formations. And the assumption of a two-term structure in the case of the past passive participle is the result of the departure made by Pāṇini and others from the structural and comparative approach adopted in the case of the conjugated verbal forms.

The principle of language-analysis underlying the description of the past passive participial formations is, therefore, the assumption of a two-morpheme or two-term structure at the base. It is with reference to this two-term structure, basically assumed, that all other structures are explained. And all the Sanskrit grammarians, without any exception, have followed this principle.

2. Principles of Descriptive Analysis

The Sanskrit grammarians, as descriptive analysts, have followed, perhaps unconsciously, certain fixed principles for the descriptive analysis of the Sanskrit language. Presumably the motive behind this is to present as scientifically and comprehensively as possible the description of the language. We discuss in the following sections some such principles which can be deduced from the description of the past passive participial formations.

2.1 *Objectivity*

By objective attitude is meant an attitude which includes the statement of a fact or phenomenon as it is and not as it should or should have been or not as it looks to the observer. In the context of language-analysis, objectivity consists in describing a form as it is used in the language and is acceptable to the speakers of the language. The question of right or wrong is not or should not be allowed to come in when a fact is to be viewed objectively. Normative rules aim at the evaluation of a thing from the point of view of or on the basis of certain conditions and to certain people or desciplines. The principle of objectivity is far removed from such normative stand. We may even say that one becomes more and more objective as he goes farther and farther from the normative rules.

In the above sense of the objective attitude, we can say that the Sanskrit grammarians were as objective as possible. They have described the language in terms, none of which contains or conveys any normative principles. For them, the forms *jīvati* (from √*jīv* 'to live'), 'he lives' and *mriyate* (from √*mṛ* 'to die'), 'he dies' are equally important from the point of view of descriptive analysis, irrespective of the fact that the one, namely, *jīvati,* conveys a good, that is, auspicious sense and the other, namely *mriyate,* conveys a bad, inauspicious sense. So also the frms *gacchati* (from √*gam* 'to go') and *śavati* (from √*śav* 'to go'), both meaning 'he goes' are treated as equally valuable for description without any consideration of the fact that they were used in different countries,[1] or that √*śav* means *vikṛti* i.e. death of the body, that is, something bad, inauspicious in a particular region.

Similarly, we do not find anywhere in any of the Sanskrit grammars a statement to the effect that since a particular structure of a word is used in educated or higher stratum of the society, it is a good structure; and in comparison with this 'good' structure, all other structures are bad and hence not to be used in the language. This shows thus that considerations like good or bad meaning or form, difference in regions, distinctions in the usage of forms depending upon the social status of the speakers etc. have not come in the way of grammatical description. For the grammarians the language is, as a whole, a colourless, odourless and tasteless entity unaffected by any ethical norms or personal likes or dislikes. And, one must say, this is a strictly scientific attitude in the sense that it is purely objective.

There is, however, another important point which needs to be considered in connection with the question of objectivity. One may say that the Sanskrit grammarians have not—indeed, could not have—adopted a strictly dispassionate—'man-on-the-mars'—attitude towards Sanskrit, since, Sanskrit being a sopken language in the times of most of them, they could not have dissociated themselves completely from their knowledge of its usage.

This is clear from their device of some of the *ādeśas* — moprhemic substitutes — like *bhū* for √*as*, *jagdha* for √*ad*, *vac* for √*brū*, etc. These substitutes clearly show that they were in the full know of the fact that people actually used these substitutes for the respective roots. The basis for laying down such substitution was obviously the similarity in meaning of the *sthānin* and the *ādeśa*. When they lay down such *ādeśas*, it clearly follows that they know fully the meanings of both, the *sthānin* as well as the *ādeśa*. This means that they knew the language sufficiently well. If they had not known this, they would have either stated that these substitutes or roots

1. Cf. Patañjali in his introduction to his *Mahābhāṣya* : *śavàtir gatikarmā kambojeṣu.*

had no corresponding roots or substitutes, or they would not have mentioned or recorded forms like *jagdha, bhūta* etc. as past passive participles from √*ad*, √*as* etc., or would have, at the most mentioned that roots like √*ad*, √*as*, etc. did not display any past passive participles. And, what is more important, such an explanation could as well be regarded as being fairly logical and conforming to the facts. But the fact that they thought in terms of these substitutes for respective roots shows that the grammarians were fully acquaineted with the usage of the language which they were describing. This technique of certain substitutes for certain roots, between which two—the substitutes and the roots — there is no phonological or morphological similarity or equivalence, certainly creates an impression of artificiality. But recording the identity of meanings of the *sthānin* and the *ādeśa*, the Sanskrit grammarians removed this impression, and by the same artificial device of *ādeśa*, tried to make up for the deficiency of the past passive participial formations of some of the roots.

It may, therefore, be said that though, from what may be called an ethical point of view, the Sanskrit grammarians were absolutely objective, from the point of view of descriptive technique, they could not afford to be as objective as they would have been if they had not known the language or if they had to describe a totally unknown language.

In spite of this fact it must be readily conceded that they have been sufficiently objective in their description of the Sanskrit language.

2.2. *Descriptive Analysis Must be Based on What people say*

There is a trend in modern Linguistics which insists that descriptive analysis must be based on what people speak and that the linguistic structures generated by a grammatical or descriptive process which is adopted for the purpose 'must be acceptable to the native speaker"[1] of the language. In other words, the descriptive analysis must be based upon what people actually use in their daily communication rather than on 'what some people think they should say".[2]

The above criterion, namely, that descriptive analysis shall be based upon what people speak does hold good in the case of Pāṇini's grammar, but only partially. Pāṇini does not seem to have had before him any written record or document of the Sanskrit language which is called as 'the classical Sanskrit', when he wrote his grammar. The Vedas were already there, no doubt. But we do not have any evidence to prove that he did have such record before him for classical language. Actually whatever linguistic and other evidence we get, gives us sufficient ground to suspect that writting was either not known or was in vogue only on a very limited scale in or before Pāṇini's times.[3] We may, therefore, generally presume that Pāṇini's analysis of the linguistic structures is based upon spoken usage and not upon any written documents. In this sense, Pāṇini fulfills the condition of a spoken structure being made the basis for descriptive analysis.

But this may perhaps not be said to represent the whole truth. There had been in existence the *Saṁhitā*-and-the *Brāhmaṇa*-texts in pre-Pāṇinian times. Though they were handed down oraly, and not through any written tradition, they showed no change at all in their structures. This was particularly true in the case of 'the *Saṁhitās*'. The priestly or the Brahmanic class, which preserved this literature and handed it down orally, was so meticulous about the

---

1. cf. *N. Chomsky, Syntactic Structures,* Mouton & Co., The Hague, 1964, Ch. 2, pp. 13--17 and Ch. 6, pp. 49-70.
2. cf. for details, *E. A. Nida, Morphology,* Ann Arbor, The University of Michigan Press, 2nd ed. p. 2.
3. cf. the word *lipi,* 'script' used by Kātyāyana in his *Vārttika, yavanāl lipyām,* on the Pāṇinian sūtra 4.1.49; this being a *vārttika* by Kātyāyana, who flourished after Pāṇini, throws little light on Pāṇini's time.

pronunciation and accentuation of the Vedic words that there hardly occured any discrepancy in respect of them.

If, then, we were to understand by written language a language which did not normally show any significant changes in its structures, and not necessarily a language which was tangibly represented through some conventional phonetic or other symbols, we must say that Pāṇini did work on the basis of a written language, as his special section on *Vaidikī prakriyā* shows. The written language in this case was the vedic Sanskrit. For the classical Sanskrit, we do not have any exidence to show that classical Sanskrit was also written down or orally handed down without any significant changes in its structures. And from this point of view, the statement that Pāṇini worked on the basis of a spoken language would be only partially true. Further, the question of the preference of a spoken structure to the written one arises prominently in the case where the spoken form does not conform to the phonetic structure of the written word; cf. for example, the English words, 'should, could, would', etc. in which the phone *l* is completely lost and the phone-group *ou* has given place to *u*. In such cases, therefore, where the phonetic structure of a spoken word differs considerably from the phonetic symbols used to represent that word in the script, the question of the selection between the two for purposes of a descriptive analysis assumes great importance. In the case of Sanskrit, however, in which the phonetic script very faithfully represents the oral pronunciation of the word, the problem of the preference of the sopken word to the written one does not arise at all, or even if it arises, its significance would prove to be practically nil. One may, therefore, say that in view of this peculiar close agreement between the scriptal representation and the pronunciation of a word in the case of the Sanskrit language, the question whether Pāṇini's descriptive analysis is based on speech or not is virtually of little significance. One can definitely say that, irrespective of whether the evidence for the written character of the Sanskrit language is positive or negative, Pāṇini's *Aṣṭādhyāyī* would have been the same.

Pāṇini on his part does distinguish the spoken language, or what is called *bhāṣā* in his *Aṣṭādhyāyī*, from the Vedic language which he refers to by such words as *chandas, yajus, mantra,* etc. The difference between the *bhāṣā* and the *chandas* extends from minor details (such as the absence of the *iḍāgama* in the *bhāṣā*-form *grasta* from √*gras* and its presence in the *chandas*-form *grasita* noted by Pāṇini in the *sūtra,* 7.2.34, *grasitaskaṁbhita*...etc.) to major features such as the entire disappearance of certain Vedic forms in the *bhāṣā* (as in the case of the form *catta* from √*cat* 'to beg'; *cf.* Pāṇinian *dhp. cate yācane*). It may also be noted that certain *bhāṣā*-forms are not available in the *chandas;* cf. for example the root √*kvaṇ* 'to produce sound' and its past passive participial form *kvaṇita;* the whole complex connected with that root is absent in the Veda. The fact, therefore, seems to be that the language which Pāṇini has taken up for descriptive analysis was partially spoken i.e. *bhāṣā* and partially written (in the sense defined above) i.e. *chandra, mantra,* etc. or the Veda. If it were only *bhāṣā,* Pāṇini would not have incorporated in his grammar a section dealingwith the Vedic i.e. written (understood in the above sense) language; if it were only written, he would not have described the various formations which are not found in the written i.e. Vedic language, but which are profusely available in the *bhāṣā*.

In the case of all post-Pāṇinian Sanskrit grammarians, however, one feature is prodominantly discernible namely, that they have, one and all, omitted the section on the Vedic language. But can we understand this feature to imply that they were working on the basis of a spoken *bhāṣā* alone? The answer to this question must be emphatically negative. For, a fairly large corpus of Sanskrit literature was available to these grammarians for analysis. Sanskrit attained far greater prominence after Pānini, and many of the grammarians, especially those flourishing after the sixth century A.D., had the vast, written, classical literature before them. Therefore, in the case of these grammarians also, we cannot say that their descriptive analysis was based to any significant extent upon what people spoke, that is upon a spoken language. As the matter stands, if we examine these post-Pāṇinian grammars very carefully and compare them with the grammar of Pāṇini, we would find that there is nothing in them which is substantially new either by way of addition to or subtraction from Pāṇini's grammar. What these grammarians seem to have actually done is either to find faults with Pāṇini or to follow him *in toto*. Nor again, it must be noted, has any grammarian characterised any Pāṇinian forms as old or obsolete. This means that, practically they were working on the same language on which, in a much earlier, period, Pāṇini had worked. Naturally, there-fore, whatever is true of Pāṇini's grammar would hold good also in the case of all these post-Pāṇinian grammars.

Apart from what has been said above, attention may be drawn also to the discussion by Pātañjali in his *Mahābhāṣya* regarding *śabda-upadeśa* and *apaśabda-upadeśa*. This interesting discussion provides an altogether different dimension to the whole controversy. After positing the three alternatives in connection with the content of grammar, namely,(i) that only standard words *(śabdas)* are to be taught in grammar, (ii) that only non-standard words *(apaśabdas)* are to be taught, and (iii) that both the types of words, namely standard and non-standard, are to be taught, Pātāñjali finally comes to the conclusion that the standard words alone are to be taught in grammar, because their number is smaller than that of the non-standard words.[1] This brings into foreground one important point. No one would normally create literature, if

1. cf. Patañjali in the introductory section of his *Mahābhāṣya : kim śabdopadeśaḥ kartavyah, āhosvid apaśabdopadeśaḥ āhosvid ubhayopadeśa iti? .... laghutvāc chabdopadeśaḥ.*

it is to be generally acceptable, by using what Pātañjali calls the *apaśabdas* or non-standard words like *gāvī, goṇī, gopotalikā* etc. This means that the problems of *apaśabdas* would not normally arise so far as writing was concerned; it could have relevance only to speech. When, therefore, Patañjali speaks of *śabdas* and *apaśabdas*, it seems that the languge for discussion before him is rather a spoken language than a written one. Of course, this whole discussion by Patañjali tends to invest words or *śabdas* with a sort of normative character, but that need not be understood as necessarily implying that they were written and not spoken. What the entire discussion seems to point to is an objective descriptive analysis of standard spoken words. It is this spoken character of the language, which Pāṇini has described and which Patañjali has discussed in his *Mahābhāṣya,* which is all the while emphasized by Patañjali by such expressions as *laukikaḥ prayogaḥ, lokeṣu prayujyate,* etc. Such expressions clearly bring out the consciousness on the part of the Sanskrit grammarians of the fact that whichever structure the grammar generates must have a reference to its acceptability by the native speaker.

The Kātantra grammar has an independent *sūtra,* which emphasizes the importance of the usage of the form by the people, and regards as very essential the principle that every grammar must have a reference to the native speaker of the language; cf. the Kātantra *sūtra, lokopacārād grahaṇasiddhiḥ,* 1.1.23; cf. the Durga-vṛtti thereon; also cf. Hemacandra's *sūtra, lokāt,* 1.1.3.

Therefore regarding the controversial point, namely, that the descriptive analysis of a language should be based upon what the people speak and not on what they write, we can only say that so far as Pāṇini was concerned he had before him partly written and partly spoken language; and the bulk of the spoken language was far greater than the written one, which latter could have been constituted of some texts of the Vedic literature. As for the post-Pāṇinian grammarians, on the other hand, they had greater volume of written literature and comparatively little of new, varied spoken Sanskrit. The paucity of any new forms of spoken Sanskrit, apart from the Sanskrit which was more or less standardised by Pāṇini, has, as indicated above, resulted in the fact that the post-Pāṇinian grammarians have very little to add in the nature of new formations or technique. Yet the fact that even Pāṇini (and others) has left out many Vedic and non-Vedic words in his analysis and derivation shows that even in his times the language was so varied and changing both geographically and historically that it was not possible even for a grammarian like Pāṇini to keep pace with the speed of variation and change. This implies that he was not working on a fixed or written language; but the language he was analysing was spoken on a very large scale in a very wide area. Only this fact would account for the absence of many formations in his grammar.

2.3 Formal Structure of Primary Importance : Every Other Considerations, Secondary

When one studies the different grammars, one finds that, so far as the past passive participial formations are concerned, the only term used to designate this category is *-tānta* (or *ktānta*), and that the section dealing with all these forms is called *ktādhikāra, niṣṭhānta-prakaraṇa* or *niṣṭhādhikāra.* What is however, particularly note-worthy is that the practice of so naming the past passive participial formations, started by Pāṇini, is followed invariably by all the other grammarians. So one can see that a purely and/or arbitrary nomenclature is used to designate these forms. The other details such as the definition of *niṣṭhā*, the different senses in which that term is used in the language, etc., come only later on. cf. for example the Pāṇinian *sūtras : ktaktavatū niṣṭhā*, 1.1.26; *niṣṭhā*, 3.2.102; *bhāvakarmaṇoḥ*, 3.4.69; *tayor eva kṛtyaktakhalarthāḥ*, 3.4.70. These *sūtras* will show that the nomenclature for the past passive participial formations is *niṣṭhā*, a purely arbitrary term, which is defined in terms of a formal designation, i.e. *-kta* and-*ktavatu;* cf. also the relevant *sūtras* of other grammarians (cf. Ch. 2). These definitions show that the emphasis, even in defining a grammatical category, is on its formal aspect. To put in simple words, the formations in question are firtst *-ktānta,* then *niṣṭhānta,* and then finally *bhāve* or_*bhūte* or *kartari*. Instead of such a cumbersome technical procedure, the formations could have been easily and strightway defined in a single *sūtra* such as *kartṛbhāva-karmasubhūte* (and / or *vartamāne*) *ktaktavatū* or something like that, in which the primary emphasis would have been on the passive or active and past or present sense and then secondarily on the formal aspect.

The peculiar technique adopted by the grammarians is hardly in consonance with what happens when the speaker of the language actually uses a past passive participial formation. An example will clarify the point. Take the situation created by the utterance of a sentence like *tair bhuktam* ('it is eaten by them'). The hearer or the reader of this sentence understands first the passive sense, then the past tense and finally perhaps the fact that the form *bhūkta* ends in-*ta*. This contrast between the technique of the grammarians and the normal response to actual speech-practice raises a questions : What was the principle which the grammarians had in mind when they adopted a method of definition which did not reflect the attitudes towards language of the general speaker and hearer? The only answer that suggests itself is that in the grammars the emphasis is shifted from the general understanding to particular knowledge, and there too, from non-formal considerations to formal categories. In other words, for the grammarians, a past passive participial form is first a form in-*ta* and then anything else; for a general speaker, on the other hand a form is, first of all, what it means and then its structure etc., For, a general speaker may use the present form *bhuṅkte* and convey a past sense (of course, depending upon the context). This would then mean that what the grammarians are aiming at is to build up a sound, scientific system of grammar, based on certain fixed principles, and that they are not writing a text-book of grammar meant for general understanding. For a grammarian the form of the word-structure is of prime importance; every other thing associated with the form, such as its grammatical category, its sense or tense, etc., is totally secondary. It is this example on a formal analysis of the language that explains the fact that the *-tānta* forms are nowhere defined by the name of a grammatical category such as 'nouns' or 'adjectives' or 'past passive participles', etc. They are first *kṛdantas,* then *niṣṭhāntas,* then *tāntas,* and then everything else.

And such an approach to linguistic analysis is quite natural. When, for instance, the forms like *bhūta, kṛta,* etc. are analysed, what is obtained is only the root and the suffix-*ta* which is common in other forms of this types. The forms do not present themselves as past passive participles in their initial stage. Therefore, to term them in the very initial stage of their analysis, by the name of a grammatical category would mean that the language is analysed according to a set, hypothetical classification, which is hardly logical. A language should be allowed to speak and afford its analysis for and by itself. No external criteria, such as the hypothetical, traditional, grammatical categories or nomenclatures, should be assumed in the pre-analysis stage. The only truth that these forms reveal to us in their pre-analysis stage is that they are forms in *-ta;* that they function as past passive participles is secondary for formal analysis. That only formal structure by itself, as isolated from any other—contextual, syntactic, semantic — considerations, is the subject of study in grammar is stated explicity by Pāṇini in his *sūtra, svaṁ rūpaṁ śabdasyāśabdasaṁjñā,*1.1.68.[1] Though,

1. cf. BD. on the Pāṇinian *sūtra,* 1.1.68: *śabdasya svaṁ rūpam saṁjñk śabdaśāstre yā saṁjñā tām vinā;* cf. also Kāśikā which explains it in greater detail; cf. also Patañjali on the Pāṇinian *sūtra,* 1.1.68.

it must be noted, none of the later grammarians has framed a *sūtra* of this type, every one of them follows this rule of formal analysis.

It is this principle, viz. complete adherence to formal analysis primarily, which has induced the grammarians to name or label the different categories of forms by either arbitary or formal terms;no non-formal lable like noun, adjective etc. is used anywhere. Thus, in Pāṇini, we see that the conjugated verbal forms are the *tiṅantas* and not *kriyāpadas;* the nominal forms are the *subantas* and not nouns or adjectives; the primary derivatives are the *kṛdantas* and not participles or nouns; the secondary derivatives are the *taddhitas* and not nouns etc. Actually defining or naming these formations by a lable other than formal may have resulted in a mis-nomenclature and may have adversely affected the scientific character of the Sanskrit grammars. However, in spite of this strict adherence to formal approach and analysis, the Sanskrit grammarians have been compelled to resort to non-formal categories also for a full and satisfactory explanation of the formal structure. To what extent? We shall see presently in the following section.

2.4. Formal and Non-formal Categories—Their Mutual Relation

In the foregoing discussion we have seen that the nomenclature *-tānta* or *-ktānta* given to the past passive participial formation is motivated by the desire for a strict adherence to formal appraoch and analysis. Yet, notwithstanding the facts that the principle of a formal nomenclature is valid in a majority of past passive partipial formations and that is generally adopted by the grammarians, there are cases,—and the number of such cases is also equally large, though not larger—where the forms are actually not *-tānta* and are yet grouped under the heading of *-tānta*-formations. Such cases are provided by forms like *śuṣka, kśāma, pakva, phulla, pīna, kṛśa,* etc., which do not end in *-ta.*

2.4.1. *Functional or Syntactical Considerations*

If we examine the cases in which the forms do not end in *-ta* and are yet listed as *-tāntas,* we find that beyond the superficial considerations of formal structure, the grammarians have some other considrations also in mind, which prompted them to list such non-*tānta* cases under the *-tānta*-category. What these considerations are will be clear if we compare two contextual situations in which both the types of categories, viz. *tānta* and *non-tānta,* are used. Compare, for example, the situation *taiḥ kṛtam* ('it is done by them') with *taiḥ bhagnam*('it is broken by them'). We find here that the form *kṛtam* is syntactically connected with an instrumental plural *taiḥ* with which the form *bhagnam* is also connected. In other words, the form *bhagnam,* a non-*tānta,* functions in the same way as the form *kṛtam,* a *-tānta,* functions. That is, functionally the two forms—a *-tānta* and a non-*tānta*—are on par with each other. The same will be found to be the case if we consider other non-*tānta* formations in *-ka, -ma, -va,* and *-la.* The principle on the basis of which the grammarians included the non-*tānta* formations also under *tānta*-categories may be stated as follows :

If two formations, such as a *tānta* and a non-*tānta* are syntactically governed by the same case and serve the same function, those two formations can be grouped together under the same category in spite of the fact that any one of them does not satisfy the formal criterion. It is in view of this that the non-*ta* suffixes are substituted in the place of the *-ta* suffix of the past passive participle and are made equivalent to it in respect of both form as well as function. One important point, however, needs to be noted in this connection, namely, that in the case of conflict between the formal and functional considerations, the functional considerations prevail over the formal considerations. Thus, even though the form *bhagna* is not formally identical with the form *kṛta,* it is included in the *tānta*-category only on the basis of its function being identical with that of *kṛta*. If, on the other hand, a form ends in-*ta* and yet is functionally or syntactically not identical with the *tānta*-formations, it is treated by Pāṇini and other grammarians in a special manner and is not included in the general category. An example of a -*tānta* which is strictly not a past passive participle is provided by the solitary form *kaṣṭa*, from √*kaś* or √*kaṣ*. The suffix -*ta*, that is applied here, is not the general, past passive participial suffix -*ta* (stated in the general rule, *ktaktavatū niṣṭhā*), but is laid down by Pāṇini in a special *sūtra*, *kticktau ca saṁjñāyām*, 3.3. 174, under the condition of *saṁjñā*, i.e. a special usage or fuction or name. And the Pāṇinian *sūtra* which prohibits the *iḍāgama* to √*kaś* or √*kaṣ* is *kṛcchragahanayoḥ kaṣaḥ*, 7.2.22. In the case of the *tānta* formation *kaṣṭa*, therefore, it is clear that it can neither be connected with a nominative (as agent, *kartari*) nor also with an instrumental (as an agent as well as, as an instrument, *karmaṇi* or *karaṇe*); nowhere do we find the usage *saḥ kaṣṭaḥ* (=he is tired)or *tena kaṣṭan* (= 'laboured or ploughed by him'). The formations *kaṣṭa* is thus not comparable either functionally or syntactically with the other -*tānta* or *non-tānta* formation,which functions as past passive participles in language. Moreover, the formation *kaṣṭa*, even though it is -*tānta*, functions, as an indeclinable simply on the basis of functional considerations; cf. the indeclinable *kaṣṭam* in the *svarādigaṇa;* cf. the Pāṇinian *sūtra*, *svarādinipātam avyayam*,1.1.37.

This whole discussion will thus show that the functional considerations, which are in a way non-formal in character, are also not totally left out by the grammarians in their insistence on the formal approach, analysis, and nomenclature.

2.4.2 *Semantic Considerations*

While studying the different *sūtras* stating the *nipātana* and morphemic substitutes, we further find that, besides taking into account the extra-formal category of function or syntactical relation, the grammarians have also resorted to semantic considerations in order to explain the formations; cf. the *sūtras* laying down the *nipātana* (discussed in Ch. 4) and morphemic substitutes (discussed in Ch. 3). Actually tha activity of grammar-composition restricts itself to morphohphonemics, morphology, and syntax of languge,[1] as opposed to that of linguistic studies in general which cover the vast field from phonetics, phonology embracing phonation, allophonics and phonemics to semantics. In grammar itself, which forms a part of the general science of linguistics, pure formal considerations, as we have seen above, are given priority.How then is it possible to allow semantic considerations to play a role in the formal description of a language? If they are so allowed, to what extent would they influence the formal description? These are the questions which have got to be answered before making allowance for semantic considerations in the field of grammar. If we study Pāṇini alone, we find that semantic considerations for the explanation of forms are resorted to in as many as 1000 *sūtras* that is to say, in more than one-fourth of the total number of *sūtras*. Even the apparently unrelated field of phonetic combination i.e. *sandhi* is not free from the influence of meaning.[2] This would seem rather unwarranted and raises a fundamental question, namely whether a grammar of a language cannot be composed without the help of semology.[3]

The only conclusion regarding the relation of grammar and semology and the influence of the latter on the former, that can be drawn from the above examples discussed in the

1. cf. *G. Trager, Studies in Linguistics,* 1958.
2. For details, *cf. M. D. Pandit,* 'Linguistic Principles in Pānini's Grammar', *Indian Linguistics,* Vol. 24, pp. 53-56.
3. For relation between grammar and semology, cf. *N. Chomsky* 'Semantic Considerations in Grammar', Monography Series on Language and Linguistics, No. 8, September, 1955, ed. by Ruth Hirsch *Weinstein,* pp. 141-158. *cf.* also *M.D. Pandit,* 'formal and non-formal in Pāṇini', ABORI, 1975.

chapters dealing with *nipātana* and morphemic substitutues is that, if a form is inexplicable on purely grammatical i.e. formal levels and if it is easily describable with reference to its semological import, the usual tendency among the grammarians is to resort to the semantic aspect of the word. Thus, if the form *nirvāṇa* is to be formally contrasted with the form *nirvāta* and is to be grammatically described, the only course open is to take into consideration the semantic difference displayed by the two forms. In such cases, the meaning of the form constitutes an inevitable aspect of its grammatical explanation and description. In simple words, if the formal change in a form is accompanied by or linked up with the semantic change, consideration of meaning has got to be included in the formal description in order to make the grammar as comphrehensive as possible; and conversely, if the difference in meaning brings about a change in the form of a word, the meaning must find a place in the grammatical explanation of the same. Thus, even though the boundaries of grammar and semantics are clearly demarcated, there yet seems to be a common province for both of them to meet and influence each other. The grammarians, therefore, have taken into consideration the effect of the meaning of a form on its formal structure when the structure is inexplicable on any other but semological level.

2.5. No Part of a Word-Structure Can be Described Adequately Without Reference to the Other

The foregoing discussion about the scope and limitations of non-formal categories in the field of formal grammar will show that the phonemics, morphology, syntax, and meaning of the word-structure cannot be described in isolation, that is without reference to one another. Of course, there are cases where a grammarian can be strictly formal and need not go beyond the phonological or morphological field. But there is an equally good number of cases where he is required to refer to other aspects of the word-structure also. The need, at a certain point in description, for resorting to such aspects of word-structures as are not strictly formal, is a natural consequence of the fact that a language in general and a word-structure in particular is not a departmentalized or regimented grouping of isolated structures or phonemes; it is an entity which functions as a whole, and, therefore, its part are not describable in isolation. They have to be considered only in their relation to the whole as well as to one another. Language is an extremely complex structure and it constitutes its own frame of reference. And, therefore, none of its part is adequately describable without reference to one another.

Almost all the grammarians including Pāṇini have recognised this fact and have included the meaning of the forms also in the grammatical description. The only exception is Jainendra, who has not incorporated meaning in the body of the *sūtras* in some cases; *cf.* his *sūtras* 5.1.126; 5.3.74 etc. where he omits the semantic part in the explanation while all other grammarians have inevitably allowed the semological considerations to creep in. Though the attempt on the part of Jainendra to exclude meaning for a strictly formal explanation of certain past pasive participles may be laudable, it inevitably creates the impression of a sort of imperfection or inadequacy of description. It should be noted, however, that this attempt by Jainendra totally to exclude meaning from grammar in certain cases is not fully successful as is clear from the *sūtra* like *nirvāṇo'vāte*, 5.3.66 etc., in which the meaning has found a place in the body of the *sūtras*. It should also be noted that the meaning which is excluded from the body of the *sūtras* is supplied in the commentary which only shows the inadequacy at a certain stage of the grammatical description of the forms without reference to meaning. The same is the case, as we have already seen, with Jainendra's attempts to exclude phonological considerations also from the field of grammar.

2.6. Dialectal Differences

Besides the positive or negative statements regarding whether a particular formation takes a particular termination with certain morphonemic changes or not, there are other types of statements also in the grammars which lay down on optional application of a termination to a root. Thus the root √*trā*, √*hrī*, √*vid*, etc. are said to be taking the past passive termination *-ta* optionally, with the result that they give out two formations—one in *-ta* and the other in *-na; cf.* the *sūtras* quoted before. Such option clearly implies that these formatins have been current in the language in more or less equal proportion. May be that one and the same person used both formations in different circumstances. But it is usually seen that a person, having his speech-habits fixed, uses only one formation in his speech, the other formation being left to be used by another. Such formations, may, therefore, be regarded as an indication of dialectal differences in the language. These differences are the result of four types of linguistic change,[1] viz. phonetic and phonemic change, and change through analogy and borrowing. Now the question arises as to whether the dialectal differences—and such optional forms are certainly the result and measure of dialectal differences—should be given a place in the grammatical description of a languge. The immediate answer to this question can only be in the affirmative, since, if grammar aims at the formal description of the structures used and accepted in the language, there is no reason why a formal description of such structures as are only dialectically different should not be included in the grammar. Yet, this answer presupposes many other factors also such as that one

1. For a detailed discussion of the four types of linguistic change, viz. phonetic and phonemic change, and change by analogy and borrowing, *cf. H. A. Gleason, An Introduction to Descriptive Linguistics*, (Revised Edition), Holt Rinehart and Winston, New York, 1961, pp. 391-400 *cf.*, also *C. F. Hockett, A Course in Modern Linguistics*, The Macmillan Company, New York, 1958, 321-340; also pp. 365-400.

form is accepted in the language as equally usable as another, that form in question is used in the language with the same statistical frequency as another etc. To illustrate, the form *vinna* is acceptable in the language to the same extent as the form *vitta;* so also, the former occurs in the language with practically the same frequency as the latter. In short, if two forms, which are optional occur in the language, they must find a place in grammatical description. The only point that occassions a difference in the description of such optional forms is that, if the linguistic circumstances under which they occur are the same, those circumstances can be comprehended in a single rule; if they are different, the environments can be noted down in independent *sūtras.* But the optional forms, which are the result of dialectal differences must be taken account of while describing a language. This in turn means that dialectal differences in connection with the formations cannot be totally neglected in the grammar of a language if the differences are significant.

From this point of view the Sanskrit grammarians are fully justified in describing the optional forms. The discussion of Patañjali on the *vārtika, sarve deśāntare,* recognises the existence of dialects,[1] and his ardent insistence on collecting all these forms from various places (cf. his words : *na caita upalabhyante/upalabdhau yatnaḥ kriyatām/)* clearly brings home the necessity of including and describing great and significant dialectal differences in the grammar of the main language.

The above-mentioned point can be viewed from another angle also. Though a descriptive analyst is not much

---

1. cf. Patañjali on the *vārttika, sarve deśāntare tad yathā / śavatir gatikarmā kambojeṣv eva bhāṣito bhavati ...... hammatiḥ surāṣṭreṣu, raṁhatiḥ prācyamadhyeṣu gamin eva tv āryāḥ prayuñjate / dātir lavanārthe prācyeṣu dātram udīcyeṣu //* Though all these examples given by Patañjali imply only the semantic aspect, he may be understood as making a general statement regarding the formal dialectal differences as found in different regions.

concerned with whether a particular form should be preferred to its optional one or not, the recording of these optional forms itself clearly indicates that he is here fully cognisant of the dynamic or changing aspect of the language. In describing the optional forms, a grammarian is unconsciously accepting the principle of linguistic change as his base.[1]

3. Principles of Morpheme-Segmentation

We have seen above (cf. § 1 of this chapter) that the chief principle underlying the analysis and description by the Sanskrit grammarians of the past passive participial formations is the assumption of a two-morpheme and not three-morpheme structure at their undeclined stage. To illustrate : when it is not declined by applying the declensional *sup*-terminations, the participle *kṛta* from √*kṛ*, consists of only two morphemes—the verbal root √*kṛ* and the termination *-ta*. It would be interesting to know how the grammarians have segmented the two morphemes—the verbal root and the suffixes *-ta, -na, -ma, -ka, -va,* etc.—from the ready-made structures available and used in the language. The present section seeks to find out the underlying principles of morphemic identification adopted by the grammrians.[2] We may start with the termination-morphemes *-ta, -ma, -ka, -va,* and *-na.*

---

1. The rate of increase or decrease in the use of a form may vary at different times in the history of a language or may be different in the case of two languages. This rate of change in the use of forms can be found out by calculating the proportion of optional forms. But this would require a historical study of the language, which is beyond the scope of the present thesis.
2. For principles of morpheme-idetification used by moern linguists, *cf. E. A. Nida, op.cit.*, pp. 6-61; *C. F. Hockett, op.cit.*, pp. 123-129; also *Language*, Vol. 23, 1947, pp. 321-343; *Z.S.Harris, Language*, Vol. 18, 1942, pp. 169-180; also *Language* Vol. 21, 1945, pp. 121-127; also Language, Vol. 22, 1946, pp. 161-183; *cf. R. S. Wells*, Language, Vod. 23, 1947, pp. 81-117; *C. F. Voegelin, Language* Vol. 23, 1947, pp. 245

3.1. Identification of The Morpheme -ta

3.1.1. Semantic and Formal Identity

For detecting a morpheme from the structure in which it occurs, it is obviously necessary to collect all strcutures in which there is likelihood of its occuring. After such data have been collected, the next step would be to examine the contextual meaning of all these structures and then decide whether the morpheme which is to be identified has influenced the meaning of the whole struture and carries an identical meaning in all the structures. A morpheme, which is to be identified, must, therefore, satisfy the condition of semantic identity.

The other conditon which the morpheme in question must satisfy is the formal identity. If both thses conditions—the semantic as well as formal identity—are fulfilled, we can detach the morpheme as the unit of the word-structures.[1]

The illustrate : in the case of the past passive participial morpheme *-ta,* one should collect as many structures, with *-ta* as an element, as possible. Suppose the strcutures *kṛta, bhūta, bhukta, vitta, dyūta, matta, pīta,* etc. are collected. One can then see that the *-ta* is formally identical in all these structures. It, therefore, fulfills one condition, viz. of formal identity.

If we examine all the contexts in which these formations in *-ta* are used, we find that this *-ta* invariably conveys the sense of past and passive. It, therefore, satisfies the requirement of semantic identity also.

We, therefore, can detach it from the word-structures and identify it as an independent morpheme which constitutes one element of the structure, and ascribe it the meaning of 'past, passive' participle.

---

1. cf. also *Bernart Bloch, Language,* Vol. 23, 1947, pp. 399-418; *cf.* also *E. A. Nida, Language,* Vol. 24, 1948, pp. 414-441; *cf.* also *H. A. Gleason, op.cit,* pp. 65-77; also, pp. 128-148; *cf.* also *L. Bloomfield, Language,* pp. 158-169.

This principle of formal and semantic identity helps in excluding the morpheme *-ta* or *-ita* as found in forms like *tārakita,* 'full of stars', *puṣpita,* full of flowers', *duḥkhita,* 'full of sorrow', *mukulita,* full of buds', etc. because though the -*ta* or *-ita* which occurs in these forms is formally identical with the *-ta* or *-ita* of the past passive participle, the meaning which it conveys there is not the same as that of the *-ta* of the past passive participle. It must be emphasized here that both these conditions have to be simultaneously fulfilled in order that the exact morpheme should be got at.

3.1.2. *Functional or Syntactic Identity for Morphemes -na, -ka, -ma, and -va*

Besides the above conditions, the functional identity has a significant role to play in deciding the morpheme. As we have seem before while discussing the forms in-*na, -va, -ka,* and *-ma,* it is on the basis of the function or syntax that the forms ending in these suffixes are grouped as past passive participles or *niṣṭhāntas* on par with these ending in-*ta,* although they are formally different from the latter. If, therefore, we find that the forms in-*na, -va, -ka,* and *-ma,* function in the same way and occur in the same syntactic environments as those in *-ta,* we have sufficient ground to accept them as being on par with the latter, even though they are formally different.

There is yet one more condition to be satisfied in the case of functional or syntactic identity. It is that the formal differences in the morphemes should be adequately explained or accounted for by well-framed phonological and/or morphological rules. In the present case, we do find that the change of *-ta* into *-na, -ka, -ma,* and *-va,* is well accounted for by the grammarians by suitable, well-framed rules.

The morphemes *-na, -ka, -ma, -va,* can therefore, be grouped as those representing the past passive participial formations.

It is on the basis of functional or syntactic considerations that the forms like *yajña* 'sacrifice' *muṣka* 'a testicle', a scrotum, *śuṣma* 'strength', *pūrva* 'east' etc. ending in *-na, -ka, -ma* and *-va* respectively, are excluded from the list of past passive participle, even though the change of *-ta* into *-na -ka, -ma,* and *-va* can be easily and conveniently accounted for by well framed rules. Also, it is these functional or syntactic considerations which exclude the formations like *bhavata, kuruta* etc. which end in *-ta* (which is identical in form with the *-ta* of the *niṣṭhā)* and yet which convey a different meaning and function in altogether different syntactic environments.

3.1.3. Accompaniment of Roots

The third and perhaps the most important condition for a morpheme to be one signifying a past passive participle, over and above the conditions discussed in § 3.1.1 and § 3.2.1, is that it must be a constituent of a structure in which the other constituent morpheme immediately preceding it is a verbal root or *dhātu* defined by Pāṇini. in the *sūtras bhūvādayo dhātavaḥ,* 1.3.1 and *sanādyantā dhātavaḥ* 3.1.32. This condition is implied by the Pāṇinian *sūtra, dhātoḥ,* 3.1.92.[1]

This condition of a *dhātu* immediately preceding the past passie prticipial morpheme, which is laid down by all the Sanskrit grammarians, automatically enables us to exclude such forms as *grāmata* (= *grāma* + *ta,* 'a group of villages'; cf. the Pāṇinian *sūtra, grāmajanabandhubhyas tal,* 4.2.23), *bālaka* (=*bāla* + *ka,* 'a child') *pāmana* (=*pāma* + *na,* 'having a skin-disease'; cf. for the word *pāma,* Pāṇini, *lomādipāmādi-picchādibhyaḥ śanelacaḥ,* 5.2.100), *madhyama* (= *madhya* + *ma,* 'the middle one'); *keśava* (= *keśa* + *va* 'possessed of hair') etc. or even forms like *tārakita* etc., which, even though they end in *-ta, -ka, -na, -ma, -va, -ita* respectively do not give out a *dhātu* as the prior morpheme after their analysis into two constituents.

---

1. cf. Kāśikā on the Pāṇinian *sūtra,* 3.1.91: *yad ita ūrdhvam anukramiṣyāmaḥ dhātor itya evaṁ tad veditavyam.*

To sum up : in order to identity the past passive participial morpheme, the Sanskrit grammarians have adopted five main principles. These principes are :

(1) There should be semantic as well as formal identity amongst the morphemes in question. These two conditions of identity must be fulfilled simultaneously.

(2) It there is only semantic identity without formal identity, the formal difference must be accountable or definable easily and conveniently by general formative phonological and/or morphological rules.

(3) Over and above fulfilment of the above mentioned two conditions, there should be functional or syntactical identity in the sense that the mophemes in question must be available in syntactically or functionally identical situations.

(4) The constituent morpheme immediately preceding the past passive participial morpheme must be a verbal root; in other words, the formations must be primarily derivatives from verbal roots.

(5) All these conditions need to be satisfied by the past passive participial morpheme simultaneously.

All grammarians seem to have adopted these principles of morpheme-identificiation and to have thereby determined the norms of the past pasive participial morphemes, which are five in number, namely, *-ta, -na, -ka, -ma,* and *va*. The only morpheme, which they have not sepearated, but which really speaking they should have separated since it is available in the language, is *-la* as found in a form like *phulla*. The obvious reason for this perhaps is that only one solitary form like the above *phulla* is available, and that, therefore, statistically speaking, it does not provide a sufficiently strong ground for framing a general formative rule. And this is perhaps also the reason for the *nipātana* of the form being mentioned in an independent *sūtra*. It must, however, be pointed out that all these principles are to be deduced only by implication; they are nowhere explicitly stated or defined by the grammrians. This may be accounted for by the assumptions that the old grammarians like Pāṇini represent a period in which the whole linguistic activity had virtually reached a climax and there was nothing left to be done by way of any spade-work in the field of linguistics in general and grammar-composition in particular. Pāṇini had all the linguistic material necessary for grammar-composition ready in his hand; and he made the utmost use of it in his *Aṣṭādhyāyi*. As a result of this, the *Aṣṭādhyāyi* turned out to be a very scientific and comprehensive work. Naturally, therefore, the post-Pāṇinian grammrians also had practically no scope for gathering new material and defining rules regarding morpheme-identification. In this connection, one may specially note the consequent, almost total absence of any rules about morpheme-identification in any of the Sanskrit grammars, including that of Pāṇini.

3.2. Identification of the Other Morpheme, viz. the Verbal Root

We cannot hazard any conjecture about the principles used in identifying the verbal roots, mainly because, right from Pāṇini onwards, every grammrian had a readymade *dhātupāṭha* before him. There was, therefore, no need for the grammarians to suggest any procedure for isolating the verbal root from any given verbal formation.

There is, however, the possibility that the norms of the verbal roots were determined on the basis of the primary derivatives themselves; there, too, the possibility of the past passive participial formations providing the base for finding out the verbal roots is all the greater, because the verbal roots are in their weakest grades in these formations. The past passive participial formations do not display even a single case in which the verbal root morpheme shows either *guṇa* or *vṛddhi*. It must have been this fact which led all the grammarians technically to reconstruct the past passive participial sufix *-ta* as *-kta* with the *it*-sound *k* and then invest this *k* with the power of negating any modification in the form or *guṇa* or *vṛddhi* in the verbal root; cf. the Pāṇinian *sūtra kṅiti ca,* 1.1.5 and the corresponding *sūtras* of other grammarians (cf. Chapter 1).

If this is really so, the value of the past passive participial formations is greatly enhanced in so far as they provide the basis for finding out the basic norms of the verbal root morphemes in their weakest, and perhaps technically speaking simplest, grades. Incidentally it is interesting to note here that, in a majority of cases the root-forms, that are listed in the different *dhātupāṭhas* and are taken as basic, are in their weakest grades. There may be cases of departure from this rule, but they are almost negligible in comparison with the large number of the other cases. The only procedure for finding out the verbal root morpheme, therefore, seems to be to detach the past passive participial morphemes. What remains behind is the verbal root morpheme.

Besides the past passive participial formations, there are the gerunds in *-tvā,* (reconstructed technically by Pāṇini as *ktvā,* with *k* as it and having the same power as the *k* in *-kta*) which also might have provided the basis for finding out the verbal root morphemes; first, because they do not necessitate *guṇa* or *vṛddhi* in the verbal stem, and secondly because the structures with derivatives in *-tvā,* in their undeclined stage, are also composed of two terms only. viz. the verbal root morpheme and the gerundive suffix morpheme. The structures with the past pasive participial suffixes as well as with the gerundive suffix *-tvā* may thus be regarded as having the minimum number of constitutent among all the word-structures in the language. It is due to this 'minimum' character in terms of the number of constituent moprhemes that these structures must have proved helpful to the grammarians in determining the verbal root norm. Obviously they are easier to analyse than any other multi-morpheme structures. To illustrate : it is certainly easier to analyse a two-term structure like *kṛta* or *kṛtvā* and fix the norm of the root than to analyse a three-term structure like *karoti* (= √*kṛ* + *u* + *ti*, with *guṇa* of *ṛ* into *or*) or a multi-term one like *cikīrṣayiṣayati* (a causal from the desiderative of the casual of the desiderative of √*kṛ*, to be analysed into *ci* + *kīr* + *s+a* + *ya* + *sa* + *ya* + *ti*).[1]

Though no principle in respect of the identifications of the root-morphemes are found to have been hinted at or implied by the grammarians, the roots themselves are well-defined by most of them and listed carefully in the *dhātupāṭhas* by some of them; cf. the different definitions of roots:—

Pāṇini	: *bhūvāayo dhātavaḥ*, 1.3.1 and *sanādyantā dhātavaḥ*, 3.1.32.
Kātantra	: *kriyābhāvo dhātuḥ*, 3.1.9 and *te dhātavaḥ*, 3.2.16.
Candra :	
Bhoja :	
Jainendra	: *bhūvādayo dhuḥ*, 1.2.1 and *tadantād dhātavaḥ*, 2.1.29.
Hemacandra	: *kriyārtho dhātuḥ*, 3.3.3.
Śākaṭāyana	: *kriyārtho dhātuḥ*, 1.1.22.
Sārasvata	: *bhvādiḥ*, 7.1.2 and the *vārttika*-type statement *sa dhātuḥ*, implying that those ending in desiderative and other terminations like *sa* etc. are also *dhātus*. (Incidentally, this also speaks for the loose and incomplete character of the Sārasvata-grammar).

1. For different types of word-structures, cf. *M. D. Pandit*, 'A Study of Non-Compounded Word-Structures', *VIJ*, Vol. I, Part II, Hoshiarpur, Sept. 1963, pp. 324-338 also 'A Concordance of Vedic Compounds Interpreted by Veda, CASS, Pune, 1989.

It can be seen from these definitions that, while the roots are only listed or enumerated in Pāṇini's times (cf. his definition of roots, viz. *bhūvādayo dhātavaḥ* 1.3.1, which is of enumerative type), they are grouped together on the semantic basis of signifying *kriyā* i.e. action, only later. In other words, while the approach of Pāṇini as reflected in the enumerative types of definitions seems to be purely formal, that of the later grammarians seem to be non-formal, that is, it seems to be particularly semantic. This latter certainly represents a stage farther from Pāṇini and a departure from the traditional formal attitutde towards anything grammatical. Jainendra and Sārasvata, however, closely follow Pāṇini in spite of the difference in the definition of *dhātu* in post-Pāṇinian grammars. According to the post-Pāṇinian grammarians, the chief principle governing the identification of the verbal root morpheme seems to be that it should signify some action. Thus, in other words, the basis for identifying the root-morphemes is the functional meaning of the root-morpheme, viz. action.

However, all grammarians including Pāṇini agree in identifying the transformed bases like desiderative, frequentative, etc. as *dhātu* by a reference to the transformational suffixes like *san, yaṅ*, etc.[1] A dhātu is thus defined by means of a reference to transformational morphemes, which in their turn have to be first identified on the basis of the principles of morpheme-identification deduced earlier. This second definition of *dhātu* obviously pre-supposes many things.

To sum up, we find that the only principle adopted by

---

1. As we understand from the *Kārikā*, given by *tattvabodhinī* which is commentary on BDs *Siddhātakaumudī*, viz. *san-kyac-kāmyac-kyaṅ-kyaṣo'thācārakvip ṇijyaṅau tathā/yag-āvva-īyaṅ-ṇiṅ ceti dvādaśāmī sanādayaḥ//*
   There are 12 different types of transformations which are all entitled to get the technical label of *dhātu* on the basis of the second definition of *dhātu*.

the Sanskrit grammarians, especially post-Pāṇinian, in the matter of identifying a verbal root morpheme or *dhātu* is that of functional meaning, viz. *kriyā* or action. The norm of the root-mropheme, however, could be determined by reference to the verbal derivatives which end in *-ta* or *-tvā*. These latter display a minimum structure of only two morphemes and show the root in its weakest, and hence simplest, grade without *guṇa* or *vṛddhi*. An important point to be noted in all this process is the shift of emphasis from the formal aspect which was evident in Pāṇini's time to non-formal, that is, semantic aspect in post-Pāṇinian times.[1]

4. Principles of Derivation

Besides the various point of view of looking at the past passive participial formations and their description by the Sanskrit grammarians, which have been indicated above, there is yet another point of view from which this whole subject may be studied. It is well known that the passive participial formations form a part of a larger category known as primary or verbal derivatives, termed by Pāṇini and other as *kṛdantas*. In this sense, these formations are primarily derivatives and only secondarily past passive participles. It would, therefore, not be quite beyond the scope of this thesis to examine the derivational or etymological principles on the basis of which the Sanskrit grammarians derived them from verbal roots or dhātu. Actually the section of past passive participial formations, or in general the whole section of primary derivatives or *kṛdantas*, in Pāṇini's grammar in particular and in other grammars in general, is not studied very deeply by those who study grammar in the traditional way. This is so presumably because it does not obviously

1. For a detailed discussion of the meaning of *dhātu*, cf. the chapter called *'dhātvartha-nirūpaṇam'* in the *Laghu-Mañjūṣā* of Nāgeśa Bhaṭṭa, published by K. P. Shukla, M. S. University of Baroda, 1961, pp. 85-112; cf. also *Vaiyākaraṇabhūṣaṇasāra*, edited by Pandit Sadashiv Shastri *Joshi*, Kashi Sanskrit Series No. 133, 1939, pp. 7-117.

involve a highly developed technique of grammatical description, as, for instance, in the case of the description of verbal and nominal forms or the *kārakas,* and also because it is believed to give rise to no principles of grammatical description which are of particularly great importance. But if one studies these sections carefully and seriously, he will find them to be of great significance in that they give us an insight into the principles of, and the grammarians' mastery over, the technique of derivation.

4.1. Roots in the Derivative Must be Obvious

However, in order to find out the derivational principles adopted by the Sanskrit grammarians from Pāṇini onwards, it is necessary, for the sake of comparison and contrast, to study them in grammars or any other grammar-like treatises in pre-Pāṇinian times.[1] The only pre-Pāṇinian treatises which attempt to lay down the derivation of some words, are the Nirukta of Yāska and the *Uṇādi*-sūtras of śākaṭāyana.[2] A

1. For a short discussion of etymologies in the *Brāhmaṇas*, cf. *G. B. Palsule, The Sanskrit Dhātupāṭhas — A Critical Study,* University of Poona, 1961, Ch. I, *cf.* also *Saroja Bhate, Pre-Pāṇinian Grammatical Thought,* Ph. D. Thesis submitted to the University of Poona, 1971, Chs. I, II.
2. The question of the authorship of the *Uṇādi-sūtras,* as incorporated in Pāṇini's grammar, is a controversial one. According to *K. B. Pathak,* it was Pāṇini himself who composed the present *pañcapādī Uṇādisūtras; cf. K. B. Pathak,* "Pāṇini and the Authorship of the *Uṇādisūtras*", *ABORI,* Poona Vol. IV pp. 111-136, also, "Further Remarks on the *Uṇādisūtras* of Pāṇini", *ABORI,* Poona, Vol. XI, pp. 90-93. On the other hand, Nāgeśa Bhaṭṭa, the author of the *Laghuśabḍenduśekhara,* who was discussed this problem in his commentary on the *Uṇādisūtras,* comes to the definite conclusion that Pāṇini is not, and cannot be, the author of the *Uṇādisūtras;* cf. his remarks on the *Uṇādisūtra* No. 1: *evaṁ ca pāṇinir na tadvyutpanna-tvavādīti spaṣṭam evoktam / cf.* also, ... *teṣām apāṇinīyatvāt pāṇiniśāstre tadārambho yuktaḥ//* etc. Not only this, but "the present *pañcapādī uṇādisūtras* have been collected by experts from the grammar of śākaṭāyana and others following he school of *Nairuktas* who maintain that all nouns are framed from verbal roots" (cf. *J. S. Pade, Tāmbūlamañjarī,* Introduction, P. XIV, The M. S. University Oriental Series No. 1, Oriental Institute, Baroda, 1958). According to *J. S. Pade,*

comparison of the derivational principle of Yāska and the Uṇādikāra on the hand and of Pāṇini and other grammarians on the other hand, therefore, will be useful in finding out the general derivational principles employed by the latter.

Yāska may be characterised as an extremist because of his firm view that a noun has to be derived from some root of the other, under any circumtances and at any cost. Yāska also insists that the etymology of a word must be given; the noun must not be left un-etymologised; *cf.* his words : *avidyamāne sāmānye'pi akṣaravarṇasāmānyān nirbhrūyāt na tv eva na nirbrūyāt, Nirukta,* II. 1. This attitude towards etymologising led him to suggest strange rather crude, and sometimes even incredible or absurd etymologies of some words. It must, however, be admitted that, in a few cases of derivation, he anticipates all the criteria that are fixed by modern linguistics.[1] But due to his extreme standpoint, Yāska generally fails to create a very favourable impression as an etymologist. His importance as an etymologist lies in the fact that he is perhaps the oldest etymologist of India who attempted to build up a science of etymology or derivation.

Of the Aitihāsika school of vedic interpretation, to which Yāska refers in his *Nirukta,* no treatise has come down to us;

---

who had discussed this problem in his edition of *Tāmbūlamañjarī (cf. J. S. Pade, ibid.,* pp VIII-XIX), śākaṭāyana, a pre-Pāṇinian grammarian, did compose some *Uṇādisūtras;* but they have not come down to us. The present *Uṇādisūtras* are the currupt forms of the former *Uṇadisūtras,* later improved by some post-Pāṇinian scholar.

1. For incredible or absurd etymologies, cf. Yāska's etymologies of words like *anna,* from *ā* + √*nam, āśā,* from *ā* + √*sad* etc. *(Nirukta,* III. 9); for a detailed discussion, *cf. Siddheshvar Varma, The Etymologies of Yāska,* Vishveshvrānand Indological Series No. 5, Hoshiarpur, 1953, p. 4 ff.; *cf.* also pp. 72-85; for primitive and erroneous etymologies, cf. pp. 115-122. For etymologies which would satisfy the criteria of modern linguistics, cf. examples of words like *sahasra, viṁśati, śraddhā* etc; cf. *Siddheshvar Varma's* remarks (*ibid. p. 4*) : "....... side by side with the overwhelming majority of crude etymologies. Yāska offers here and there a few derivations which impress us as if proceeding from a modern philologists."

cf. *Nirukta*, II. 16: *tvāṣṭraḥ asuraḥ ity aitihāsīkāḥ*. Who these Aitihāsikas were, we do not know.

The author of the *Uṇādisūtras* comes next in the line of those whose writings on derivation have come down to us. From the derivations of such words as *taru* (= a tree), *mala* (= dirt), *sthālī* (= dish), as also of such proper nouns as *gaṅgā* (= the river Ganges), *mithilā* (= the city named Mithilā),[1] which derivations are neither necessary nor obvious nor add anything more to the interpretation or meaning of words and which signify meanings for removed from their meaning in usage, it seems that this etymologist also sides with the extreme view of yāska and lays down crude, strange, uninterepretative, and meaningless etymologies of words.

Neither Yāska nor the *Āitihāsik* nor the *Uṇādisūtrakāra*, it must be admitted, has ever given the etymology of a past passive participial formation. And yet they can be taken for comparison with the grammarians like Pāṇini and others because the past passive participles, as primary derivatives, are analysed on the same etymological principle as any other primary derivatives.

In the field of etymology, next to Yāska and the *Uṇādisūtrakara* come all the grammarians whose grammars form the subject of study in the present thesis. All of them have derived many nouns, or, in Pāṇini's terminology, the *prātipadikas*, from the roots assumed and enumerated by them in their own *dhātupāṭhas*. This fact and the reference to the *Uṇādisūtras* by all of them,[2] which only shows the acceptance

---

1. For *taru* from √*tṛ* 'to cross', *cf.* the *Uṇādisūtra.*, *bhṛmṛśītṛcaritsarita nidhanimimasjibhya uḥ*, 7; for *mala*, *cf. mṛjeṣ ṭilopaś ca*, 115; for *sthālī*, *cf. sthācatimṛjer ālajvālajālīyacaḥ*, 121; for *gaṅgā*, *cf. gan gamyadyoḥ*, 128 and for *mithilā*, cf. *mithilādaya's ca*, 60.
2. cf. Pāṇini : *uṇādayo bahulam*, 3.3.1 and *tābhyām anyatra uṇādayaḥ*, 3.4.75.
   Kātantra : *uṇādayo bhūte'pi*, 4.4.67.
   Candra : *uṇādayaḥ*, 1.3.1
   Bhoja : *uṇādayo bhūte'pi*, 2.4.1
   Jainendra : *uṇādayo bahulam*, 2.2.1167 and *uṇādayaḥ anyatrābhyām*, 2.4.62.

of the derivatives derived by *Uṇādikāra* as well as his principles of derivation, imply that Pāṇini, and also other grammarians to a certain extent, are of the view that some nouns, though not all, are derivable from roots. They also imply that all these grammarians are fully aware of the controversy as to whether all nouns can be derived from roots. But the feature which distinguishes the derivations given by Yāska and the *Uṇādikāra* from those given by the grammarians like Pāṇini and others is that, while, in the case of the former, the roots are not only not obvious but are chosen arbitrarily, in the case of the latter, the roots are obvious and the root-norms are fixed and based upon a definite *dhātupāṭha*. Thus, to cite an example, while Yāska derives the word *anna* from *ā* + √*nam* 'to bend down' (cf. *Nirukta*, III. 9), Pāṇini and others rightly derive it from √*ad* 'to *eat*' + the past passive participial termination *-ta*/*-na;* the change of *-ta* into *-na* is very well accounted for on phonological grounds by the Pāṇinian *sūtra, radābhyām niṣṭhāto naḥ pūrvasya ca daḥ*, 8.2.42. The existence of fixed *dhātupāṭhas* has proved exceedingly advantageous to Pāṇini and others while its absence has detracted considerably from Yāska's importance as an etymologist. The result of the absence of a *dhātupāṭha* is that both Yāska, who proposes several etymologies for a single word (cf. his etymologies of the words *anna, indra, agni*, etc.), and the *Uṇādikāra* who derives, of course artificially, quite dissimilar or non-cognate words like *taru* 'a tree' and *tri* 'three' from a single root √*tṛ* 'to cross', to swim' etc., the root √*tṛ* having no semantic relation to either of the derivatives, give the impression of not being quite sure about their etymologies. No such element of ambiguity or doubt creeps even distantly into the derivations given by Pāṇini and other grammarians, for they throughout follow a regular technique and pattern of phonetic or morphological or semantic or syntactic or

---

Hemacandra : *uṇādayaḥ*, 5.3.93.
śākaṭāyana : *uṇādayaḥ*, 4.3.280.
Sārasvata : *sadoṇādayaḥ*, 8.3.1.

functional rules. We thus get the first principle underlying the derivational process of Pāṇini and others, namely, that the root from which a word is to be derived should be obvious in the derivative; and, as a corollary, that the whole derivational process should conform to a regular descriptive pattern. These conditions are conspicuously absent in the etymologies of Yāska and the *Uṇādisūtrakāra*. This same principle may be stated in other words as follows : there should exist a natural phonetic as well as semantic correspondence between the root and the derivative thereform; and the meaning of the form, arrived at through derivation, should be identical with that found in usage. If, therefore, the etymology suggests a meaning which is totally different from the one available in the language, the etymology is unnatural, hence unscientific, and should not be put forth. The process of derivation adopted by Pāṇini and other grammarians follow these principles throughout without any exception. To illustrate: the word *anna* is derived from the obvious root √*ad*, and the meaning it gives out is identical with the meaning in which it is used in the language; the phonetic change of *-ta* into *-na* is very well accounted for by a set of well-defind rules.

If, on the other hand, the meaning arrived at through derivation differs from the one used in the language, it should be possible to account for this fact with the help of well-defined semantic consistencies, as has been pointed out elsewhere; cf. the forms like *akna* versus *akta*, both from √*añc*; cf. the Pāṇinian *sūtra* which difines their meaning; *añco' napādāne*, 8.2.48 and the corresponding *sūtras* of other grammarians.

4.2. Terminations as a Compulsory Category

Attention may be drawn to one more interesting point regrding the comparison between Yāska on the one hand and Pāṇini and other grammarians on the other. If one carefully examines Yāska.s etymologies, one finds that, apart from the merits and/or demerits of the derivations proposed by him, Yāska does not speak of any termination at all in the case of the words he derives. He simply imagines a root, which may be obvious or otherwise, and a derivation therefrom. Yāska does not seem to think of the division of a word into its *prakṛti* and *pratyaya,* so far as the etymology of that word is concerned. True that one finds some suffixes like *ksa* (cf. *Nirukta,* II. 2: *ksa iti nāmakaraṇaḥ*), *asa (cf. Nirukta,* I. 17: *aso nāmakarahah)* employed here and there to which Yāska refers with the appropriate term *nāmakaraṇa* (=noun-framer); but suffix as a necessary formal category in descriptive analysis does not seem to have been recgnised by him as a general rule. Actually, for Yāska, application of a suffix is an exception rather than a rule. According to him, the task of an etymologist ends as soon as he finds out the root which might possibly be at the bais of the derivative and from which the the formation could be accounted for with the help of some derivational principle, popular or scientific, linguistically sound or unsound. It was this non-recognition of a termination as an independent, necessary category in descriptive analysis that led him to derive the past passive participial formation *anna* from an upasarga *ā* juxtaposed with the root √*nam; cf.* his words : *ānatam bhavati.* What is more surprising that even though he senses the correct root at the base (*cf.* his alternative explanation : *atter vā bhavati*), he does not consider a termination to be essential. It is also this fact that led him to derive the word *agni* from two or three independent roots, viz. √*i* + √*añj* or √*dah (=g)* + √*nī,* "one who moves, shines (or burns) and leads."[1]

As opposed to Yāska's procedure of derivation, Pāṇini and all other grammarians have analysed every derivative, including the past passive participles, into two parts, a *prakṛti* and a *pratyaya,* both of which are minimum constituents of a structure. Out of these, the category of *pratyaya* is independently recognised and is compulsory. In this, the

1. *cf. Siddheshvara Varma, ibid.* p. 25 ff.

Uṇādisūtrakāra also joins hands with the grammarians. All his derivations presuppose a verbal root as the *prakṛti* and some *pratyaya*. And this marks a difference from and a stage farther than Yāska.

The recognition of the termination or *pratyaya* as a compulsory category forms the second principle of derivations, followed by the grammarians, and can be enunciated as follows :

Every past passive participial formation is to be divided into two parts—the verbal root and the past passive participial terminations, viz. *-ta, -na, -ka, -ma, -va,* and this terminational part is the common element to many formations; also it constitutes a compulsory category.

4.3. The Past Passive Participial Suffixes have Meaning

There is one more important point to be considered regarding the past passive participial suffix in particular and the primary derivational suffixes in general. It we compare the derivations of the *Uṇādikāra* on the one hand and the grammarians Pāṇini and others on the other, both of whom recognise the participial suffix as a compulsory element or stage in descriptive analysis (as opposed to Yāska who does not recognise it as a rule), we find that the latter show a new point of difference from the former. While in the derivation of words by the *Uṇādikāra,* the terminations are devoid of any meaning, in the case of the derivations given by the grammarians, all the terminations in general and the past passive participial suffix in particular are infused with meaning. For the *Uṇādikāra,* the words *taru* and *tri,* both from √*tṛ*, are derived by applying the terminations *u* and *ri* which are without any meaning. It is accordingly rather difficult for one to understand in what sense the root √*tṛ* gives out the two formations; by what relations the root and the terminations are bound with each other; or, whether it is merely due to the whim of the etymologist that the two are juxtaposed. Does it mean, that, since no meaning is specified, the terminations do not convey any meaning or that the derivatives thus formed are semantically identical? Does it mean that the derivatives *taru* and *tri* mean the same thing? If they have different senses, the problem of the location of the difference always remains. There seems to be no guarantee in such derivations or the derivatives being semantically different.

All the questions implied above, however, get their answer in the grammars of Pāṇini and others. What they have done is that, in each and every case, they have laid down the meaning of the suffix *-ta.* Thus, a root, say √*kṛ*, get the suffix *-ta,* to give out the form *kṛta,* in the definite sense of 'past tense' (cf. the Pāṇinian *sūtra, niṣṭhā,* 3.2.102; cf. B.D. on the *sūtra, bhūtārthavṛtter dhātor niṣṭhā syāt*) which is laid down by the *sūtra, bhūte,* 3.2.84. That the termination *-ta* conveys the grammatical meaning of *bhāva* and *karma* (= passive) is also explicitly laid down in the *sūtra, tayor eva kṛtyaktakhalarthāḥ,* 4.3.70. It is on account of this technique of defining the semantic boundaries of the suffix that it becomes immediately possible to distinguish the past passive meaning of the formation *kṛta* from the past active meaning of the formation *gata,* which is also well-defined in the Pāṇinian *sūtras* 3.4.71 *(ādikarmaṇi ktaḥ kartari ca)* and 3.4.72. All the other grammarians have followed, of course rightly, the Pāṇinian way of derivation.

This method puts a sort of life into all the elements—the verbal root, the suffix, the whole process of derivation and the derivative—as opposed to that of the *Uṇādikāra* which looks like a dead, mechanical dissection of the forms.[1] The

1. The process of mechanical formal analysis in the *Uṇādisūtras* is very finely summed up by Patañjali, *cf.* his *bhāṣya* on the Pāṇinians *sūtra,* 3.3.1, *uṇādayo bahulam :*
saṁjñāsu dhāturūpāṇi pratyayāś ca tataḥ pare, kāryād vidyād anūbandham etac chāstram uṇādiṣu //

author of the *Vaiyākaraṇabhūṣaṇasāra* has laid down the whole process of derivation of the grammarians in only two lines, viz. *prakṛtipratyayau sahārtham brūtaḥ/ tayoḥ pratyayārthasya prādhānyam//*[1] This means that the *pratyaya* has, like the engine of a train, the capacity to change the semantic course of the formations.

We may represent the three processes of derivation adopted by Yāska, the *Uṇādisūtrakāra* and the grammarians, which have been taken here for study, symbolically as follows :—

F = Formtaion derived;

R = Verbal Root;

S = The derivational suffix;

M =Meaning

A. As a general rule, in his process of derivations, Yāska does not recognise the suffix as an independent, compulsory category; nor does he assign any meaning to the suffix. His derivation can, therefore, be symbolically represented as :

$F = R$, or sometimes

$F = R_1 + R_2 .. Rn.$

B. The *Uṇādikāra* recognise the suffix as a compulsory category, but without any meaning; his process, therefore, is :

$F = R + S.$

C. The grammarians, besides recognising the suffix as a compulsory category in descriptive analysis, infuse the suffix with meaning; their process can be symbolically represented as :

1. cf. *Vaiyākaraṇabhūṣaṇasāra*, edi. Pandit Sadashiv Shastri Joshi, Kashi Sanskrit Series No. 133, 1939, p. 69, *cf.* also Kāśikā on the Pāṇinian *sūtra,* 1.2.56; cf.also Patañjali under Pāṇini 1.3.1, Vārttika No. 4 : *saṁghātena hy artho gamyate saprakṛttikena sapratyayakena sopasargeṇa ca.*

First stage : F = R + S
Second stage : MF =MR + MS.

These formulas give us a correct picture of the principle and procedure followed by the Sanskrit etymologists.

By investing the termination with meaning, the grammarians have also given to the meaning a position in the formal analysis of words which is based on positional considerations. This is clear from the fact that the *pratyaya* is stated specifically to follow the *prakṛti;* cf. the Pāṇinian *sūtras, pratyayaḥ,* 3.1.1. and *paraś ca,* 3.1.2 Like the extra-formal categories, such as gender, number, etc. which all reside in the *pratyayas* and hence get a position in formal analysis, the category of meaning also is given a position or a location in descriptive analysis.

The past passive participial suffix, as we have seen in the introductory chapter, conveys various grammatical meanings.

The study of the past passive participial formations, as described by the various Sanskrit grammarians, thus, reveals the foregoing general principles of language-analysis, descriptive procedures, identification of the morpheme *-ta* and derivation. What needs to be specially noted is that all the grammarians have followed these principles invariably. In this sense, though we get a number of grammars in and of Sanskrit, the general trend of grammatical thought and principles is the same and flows continuously right from Pāṇini onwards up to the very late grammarians like the author of the Saupadma school. All have built up a generative type of grammar, generating the forms used in language from roots in the *dhātupāṭha* by constructing a pattern of general formative rules. In this sense, therefore, though we find different schools of grammar, so far as the past passive participial formations and the process of their derivation are concerned, they all belong to one fundamental school which has based its linguistic analysis on the principles discussed above. Whatever differences there may be in the various grammars, they are not fundamental; they are of the nature of details, and strictly from the point of view of the theory of grammatical-or, in general, linguistic—analysis, are of minor importance. What these differences are is discussed in the next section.

6

Particular Principles

1. Levels of Grammatical Description

Language basically consists of different utterances, short or long,which are nothing but sounds. These utterances are divided,for the sake of convenience of study and analysis, into sentences which are again split up in words, morphemes, phonomes, etc. These are all theoretical categories which facilitate the understanding of the language-structure and paves an easy way for grammatical description.

To put the same thing in a different way, first the sounds are identified and different phonemes are hypothised; groups of such "smallest individually meaningful elements in the utterances of a language"[1] make up morphemes which are interrelated by certain syntactic rules and are used in the language. These morphemes and their arrangement in the language is the subject-matter of grammar.[2] though phonology also serves as an ancillary tool. Morpho-phonemics deals with the phonological changes in the morphemes, which are brought about while arranging or juxtaposing two morphemes. All these three constitute the "central sub-systems"; the remaining two systems called "the peripheral subsystmes" comprise of (i) the semantic system "which associates various morphemes with things and situations or kinds of things and situations" and (ii) the phonetic system which deals with "the ways in which sequences of phonemes

---

1. *cf. C. f. Hockett, op. cit.* p. 123.
2. *cf. C. f. Hockett, op. cit.* p. 147, also p. 128-29.

are converted into sound waves by the articulation of a speaker, and are decoded from the speech signal by a hearer."[1]

The grammatical systems of the language are likely to differ from one another according as they are built on (i) phonological, (ii) morphological, (iii) semantic, or (iv) phonetic level.[2] Out of these, the two peripheral sub-systems, the semantic and the phonetic, cannot be the sole basis of grammatical description, since through the former grammar will degenerate into a dictionary while the latter will never be able to build up a grammar at all. It must, however, be admitted that both of them, especially the semantic one, influences the grammar to a certain extent.

The first two central subsystems, viz. the phonological and the morphological, are likely to influence each other to a greater extent, though, it must be emphasized that the chief concern of grammar is to study morphemes and their arrangements. So, the level of linguistic description, which can be characterised as strictly grammatical, is only the morphological level.

The present section aims at comparing the different systems of Sanskrit grammar from the point of view of the level of grammatical description. And it is in this context that we have some scope to set forth the difference between any two grammars on the same language.

2. The Problem of Nipātana

Before we proceed to compare different grammars from the point of the levels of grammatical description, we have to consider carefully the question regarding *nipātana*. The question regarding *nipātana* may be stated as follows:—to which of the three or four grammatical levels discussed

1. For a detailed discussion of this topic, *cf. C. F. Hockett, op. cit.*, Ch. 16, pp. 137-144.
2. For different meanings of "level", *cf. Emmon Bach, An Introduction to Transformational Grammars*, Ch. 4, pp. 57-59.

above, should or does the technique of *nipātana* belong? As will be obvious from the previous chapters, we have, in the present thesis, discussed only two main techniques of linguistic description from the section of the past passive participial formations; they are : (i) the technique of substitution— *ādeśa,* and (ii) the technique of *nipātana,* which, as we have discussed before, is also a kind of *ādeśa* of a full form for another full form. But, this may not be the whole description and explanation of the technique of *nipātana.* As a technique of linguistic description, it may be grouped under the technique of *ādeśa,* 'substitution'; but this explanation does not give any idea as to its proper place in the classification of grammatical levels. As has been seen above, there can be only four bases of linguistic description : (1) phonetic, (2) phonological, (3) morphological and/or syntactic, and (4) semantic. Out of these, the *nipātana* can certainly not be included in the categories of phonetic and phonological description, since, obviously, the whole technique and the formations of *nipātana* are not discussed on phonetic or phonological bases. The basis on which they are described is primarily morphological and only secondarily semantic, since in majority of the cases of such formations, meaning plays a very important role in the explanation, so much so that the formations cannot be explained without the consideration of meaning. The technique of *nipātana* may, therefore, be said to belong to the grammatical level of morphology-cum-semantics.

However, this again is not the whole truth. The *nipātita* form is not a morpheme in the sense in which a *pratyaya* is a morpheme. To illustrate: the *nipātita* form *nirvāṇa* is not a morpheme in the sense the past passive participial *pratyaya* *-ta* is. Because, although both fulfil the condition of being the 'smallest meaningful units', there is a great deal of difference between the two. While the morpheme *nirvāṇa* can be directly used in the language after applying the declensional terminations viz. the *sup-pratyayas,* the morpheme *-ta* cannot be so used. The latter, viz. *-ta*, will have to form a part of another morpheme which must precede it and which again must not be a *pratyaya* but must be a root and the two together, when juxta-posed, will be usable in the language after the application of the *sup*-terminations. This being the difference between the two, the *nipātita* form does not remain only a morpheme but assumes the character of a lexeme, which the *pratyaya*-morpheme can never do. From this point of view, a *nipātita* form, as a lexeme, must be treated on lexicographical level, and, as such, goes out of the province of grammar since lexicography can hardly be included in grammar.

Then the question is : why did the Sanskrit grammarians, including Pāṇini, discuss the *nipātita* forms in their grammars? Did they or did they not distinguish between the boundaries of grammar and lexicography? If we assume that they realised fully well the limitations of grammtical level, we cannot explain the inclusion of the lexeme-items, the *nipātita*-forms, in their grammar; if on the other hand we assume that they did not know the boundaries of grammatical level, we cannot take their works for serious and scientific study. But the fact is that some grammars, especially that of Pāṇini, has stood the test of time for the last several centuries. This fact itself constrains us to re-examine the question of the inclusion of the lexeme-items in the grammars. We cannot dispose of the question of the inclusion of the *nipātita*-forms in the grammars by merely saying that it was due to the whim of the grammarians, but we must find out some rationale for it.

One may concede that the *nipātita* forms are not only morphemes but are more than that—they are lexemes, ready for use in the language. One may also concede that their grammatical analysis into *prakṛti* and *pratyaya* is not given. But while accepting that these facts suggest their non-eligibility for inclusion in the sphere of grammar, one would do well not to forget that, even though the *nipātita*-forms are not analysed grammatically into *prakṛti* and *pratyaya,* their analysis is implied. As we have seen before, every *nipātita*-form in the section of the past passive participles has at least one corresponding form which can be explained or described by the general formative rules. Thus, the form *nirvāṇa,* which is a *nipātita,* has the corresponding form *nirvāta,* which can be regularly analysed and described as being composed of the elements *nis* (the *upasarga*), *vā* (the *root*), and *-ta* the past passive participial suffix. When, therefore, a form is stated by *nipātana,* it is to be immediately compared with its corresponding form which can be explained by general formative rules. In the present case of the form *nirvāṇa,* one can easily conjecture and lay down its analysis as *nir* + √*vā* + *na,* which is the substitute-suffix for *-ta*. Similar is the case with other *nipātita* forms like *bhitta,* etc. They immediately remind us of their corresponding regular forms the analysis of which points the way towards the analysis of the *nipātita* forms also. The argument that, since the *nipātita* forms are not analysed grammatically and are ready-made lexemes, they cannot be included in grammar, does not, therefore, sound so valid as it would have done if the *nipātita* forms had no corresponding regular forms which would help us in analysing the former. It must, however, be stated that so far as the past passive participial forms are concerned, the analysis of the *nipātita* forms is not explicit; it is only implied by the analysis of their corresponding regular forms. The only difference between a *nipātita* form and a form which can be explained by regular formative rules is that, while the analysis of the latter is explicit, that of the former is implicit, but could be easily conjectured. The difference between the two is thus not of kind but of degree. In this sense the *nipātana*-technique operates clearly on pure, though implied, formal level. To characterise it as merely lexicographical or extraformal would be to misconstrue totally the implications of the whole technique. Such being the case, the *nipātita* forms, even as lexemes, can be treated on purely grammatical levels. Similarly even though the *nipātana* of a form is stated with special reference to meaning, it can still form part of a grammatical treatise, or category, because the semantic content is invariably shown to be located in some formal counterpart in the *nipātita* structure of the word, whose derivation again is implied. Thus, the semantic content, viz. the sense of *'avāta'* ('not-wind') in the example of the *nipātita* structure *nirvāṇa,* is located in the formal element *-na;* the *nipātita* structure *nirvāṇa* again, in turn, can be implicitly derived according to the general rules of the formative process, on the basis of the corresponding non-*nipātita* structure, of the word *nirvāta.* The foregoing discussion will show that *nipātana* in any form, that is to say whether it is a purely formal *nipātana* or whether it is a semantic *nipātana,* is entitled to be included in grammar. The *nipātana* lies on the border-line of grammar on the one hand and lexicography and/or semantics on the other. The grammatical level on which it can be said to operate, and hence the level which can be ascribed to it, can only be morphological, since, obviously, the *nipātita* form is basically a morpheme, even before it can be said to be a lexeme.

3. The Levels of Grammatical Description Adopted by the Sanskrit Grammarians

After a careful study of the various *sūtras* and the past passive participial formations discussed here, from the point of view of the levels of grammatical description, we find that the grammatical levels adopted by the grammarians for linguistic description are mainly two : (1) phonological and (2) morphological. The formations in which the phonological substitution of *-ta* by *-na, -va, -ka,* or *-ma* takes place provide the example in this respect. The phonological circumstances in which the change of *-ta* to *-na* takes place are also defined by the grammarians fairly well and in great detail. The range of such phonological changes extends from the simple lengthening of a vowel to the complete substitution of one sound by another. It also includes the *samprasāraṇa*. Thus, the form *dūna* from √*du* shows the lengthening of *u*, while the form *kṣīṇa* from √*kṣi* that of *i*. These forms also show a wholesale substitution of the past passive participial suffix -*ta* by -*na*. The form *śīna* (from √*śyai*) with *ī* for the original *y* of the root √*śyai* displays the phenomenon of *samprāsāraṇa*. The question of the phonological phenomena of *guṇa* and *vṛddhi* does not arise at all, because, since no past passive participial formations in the language show either *guṇa* or *vṛddhi*, the grammarians have regarded the suffix -*kta* as *kit* and have thereby totally derprived it of the power of bringing about any *guṇa* or *vṛddhi*. We thus get, on phonological level, the following three phonological phenomena: lengthening, *samprasāraṇa* and phonemic substitution ; the two phenomena of *guṇa* and *vṛddhi* are totally absent.

On morphological level, we have morphemic substitutions of one base or *prakṛti* by another base. The substitution of √*ad*, √*as*, etc. by *jagdha*, *bhū* etc. respectively can be cited as examples of the grammatical process operating on morphonological level. The *nipātana*, as we have seen, also operates basically on morphological level.

Besides these two main levels on which the grammarians have described the past passive participial formations which have been taken up here for study, we also find that they have touched the border-line of function or syntax, which again, is a strictly grammatical level. The forms, which imply the operation of syntactic or functional considerations, are those like *śuṣka*, *pakva*, *kṣāma*, etc., in which the morphemes -*ka*, -*va*, -*ma*, etc. can hardly be equated, either phonologically or morphologically, with the past passive participial suffix-morpheme -*ta*. The only valid ground for including these morphemes in the group of the past passive participial suffix -*ta* is the consideration of function or syntax. Because the formations with these morphemes, viz. -*ka*, -*va*, -*ma*, etc.

function, and are syntactically related to other formations, in the same way as those with the morpheme *-ta;* they are regarded as being on par with the formations in *-ta.*

Yet another level, the border-line of which the grammarians seem to touch in the course of their description is that of semantics. We have already seen that forms like *dyūna* etc. have to be explained with special reference to their meaning. Indeed they defy the possibility of being explained on any other than semantic level.

Besides the forms which can be described on the levels mentioned above, there do exist forms which are *nipātita* i.e. stated without any grammatical or formal analysis, and which accordingly cannot be explained by resorting to the normal and general procedure of mormative rules (cf. for example, the form, *nirvāṇa).* Such forms pose a problem in respect of the level of their description. As has been shown above, they are primarily morphemes and, hence, they can be said to be explainable on morphological level. But such *nipātita* forms, as has further been shown, are also lexemes. Hence the description of these forms can be said to touch the border-lines also of lexicography. It would thus be seen that lexicographical considerations are, to a certain extent, included among grammatical considerations by the ancient Indian grammarians of Sanskrit.

We thus have in all the following five levels on which the whole process of the grammatical description of the past passive participial formations operates : 1. the phonological level; 2. the morphological level; 3 the functional or syntactic level; 4. the semantic level, that is, in which the explanation of the form is accompanied with a considerations of its meaning; and lastly, 5. the lexicographical level, in which the whole, ready-made, usable, finished formation is laid down, with or without semantic considerations.

Of these five, the first three, viz. the phonological, the morphological and the functional or syntactic, levels are strictly grammatical; the remaining two, viz. the semantic and the lexicographical levels are clearly beyond the scope of grammar; they are purely extra-grammatical. These two extra-grammatical levels have been resorted to for grammatical analysis and description because forms like *nirvāṇa* could not have been adequately explained without their meaning and lexeme having been stated. Mere reference to the substitution of *-ta* by *-na* would have left the explanation of the form incomplete. Hence the considerations of the meaning is necessary. In order that the meaning is included in the explanation, it is also necessary to lay down the whole form, or we may say, the whole lexeme *nirvāṇa.* In the absence of the statement of the whole lexeme, the grammatical description of the form by a regular formative process would have been elaborate and cumbersome in many cases. Thus, inevitability and brevity seem to be the two main motives behind the acceptance, in the field of grammar, of these two extra-grammatical categories, viz. the semantic and the lexicographical. At the same time it must be remembered that even these extra-grammatical levels are joined together with the formal or grammatical level by a common thread. Thus, the extra-grammatical meaning of *'avāta'* has a location in the grammatical category of the phoneme *-n;* it is because of the change of the phoeme *-t* into *-n* that the difference in the meanings of the two forms *nirvāṇa* and *nirvāta* arises. Also, the meaning of *avāta* is conveyed by the whole lexeme *nirvāṇa* and not by mere change of *-ta* into *-na.* Otherwise, the form *-vāna* alone would have given out the meaning of *avāta.* But this is not the case. The meaning of *avāta* is signified not by the mere change of *-t* into *-n,* nor also by the lexeme *-vāna* alone, but by the two lexemes *nir* and *vāna* put together. Where such a common thread joining the extra-grammatical with the grammatical does not exist, the grammarians have not taken resort to the extra-grammatical levels; cf. for example, the form *kṛṣṇa* meaning two things, viz. (i) Lord Kṛṣṇa and (ii) black. The grammarians need not in such cases explain the two meanings in grammar, simply because the difference in meaning is not located in the difference of any grammatical category in the form. Such cases celarly belong to exclusively extra-grammatical levels of semantics and lexicography.

All the levels mentioned above have been taken into account by all Sanskrit grammarians.

7
Concluding Remarks

Concluding Remarks

Given the various *sūtras* of the grammarians which describe the past passive participial formations, the data of the formations which are described by them, and the general principles of linguistic and grammatical description deduced from all this, we are now in a better position to make some general observations about the differences in the schools of Sanskrit grammar. As for the general principles of linguistic analysis and grammatical description, all the grammarians, as has been mentioned before (cf. Chs. 2, 3, 4), follow invariably the same principles of descriptive technique, viz. the phonemic and morphemic substitution, i.e. the *varṇādesa* and the *pratyayādeśa*, and the *nipatana*. In this respect, there seems to be absolutely no innovations in the field. No new method- no new technical device- of grammatical description is seen to have been invented by the post-Paṇinian grammarians; all, without any exception, follow the same principles which were adopted by Paṇini. The post-Paṇinian grammarians do not even seem to be inclined to strike a different path from Paṇini's.

What is true of the three techiques of grammatical description, viz. the phonemic and morphonemic substitution and the *nipātana*, is also true of the principles of morpheme-identification, language-analysis, and derivation (discussed in ch. 5). While studying the various Sanskrit grammars, we feel at every stage that what we are dealing with are not different grammars composed by different grammarians in different times, but the same grammar, that of Panini, with slight variations, here and there, either in the wording of the *sutras* or the description of the forms. Actually the impression that is created is not one of development or progress in grammatical description and technique, but of *status quo* or even stagnation in the field. What is still more surprising is that Paṇini's descriptive skill is conspicuously absent in post-Paṇinian period. Indeed, it is positively on the wane in some cases such as that of the Sārasvata grammar.

The same thing can be said in regard to new formations. Except for some 10 to 15 formations like *nirviṇṇa* etc. the post-Paṇinian grammarians do not seem to have collected any new data of the past passive participial formations; they seem to be working on the same data on which Paṇini had worked several centuries before, without either adding to it in any considerable measure or subtracting from it any obsolete formations.

Does this *status* quo or stagnation in the field of linguistic and grammatical thought, as reflected in the post-Paṇinian grammars, imply that most of the post-Paṇinian grammarians were devoid of any descriptive skill or originality? Were they intellectually so indolent as not to have invented new descriptive techniques or collected new data, and thereby registered some improvement on Paṇini? A possible exlanation of this state of affairs may be hazarded as follows:

In this connection, one must, first of all, take note of a very significant fact, namely that, between Panini on the one hand and the whole group of post-Paṇinian Sanskrit grammarians on the other, two great figures have come on the scene. They are the *varttikakāra* Katyāyana and the *Mahabhāṣyakāra* Patañjali. These two cannot be called grammarians in the strictest sense of the term because none of them has written an independent grammar as such of the Sanskrit language; but they are certainly grammarians in a broad and general sense. What Kātyāyana has done is to fill up whatever deficiencies there have been in Paṇini's grammar according to him. He has done this by writing voluminous *vārttikas*. Patañjali, on the other hand, has provided scientific, logical, and linguistic grounds for whatever Panini has stated in his *sutras*. He has also tried sometimes to justify Panini against Kātyāyana. Thus the total bulk of the grammatical work produced in the period between Panini on the one hand and the whole group of post-Panini grammarians on the other, is several times greater than Panini's own *Aṣṭādhyāyī*.[1] The result of this painstaking, voluminous, and comprehensive grammatical work of these two great grammatical luminaries was that there was hardly anything worth while left for the later Sanskrit grammarians to accomplish, either by way of providing new bases, techniques, or linguistic and grammatical principles or by way of making any significant additions or omissions. Pāṇini's *Aṣṭādhyāyī*, together with Kātyāyans's *vārttikas* and Patañjali's *Mahābhāṣya* may be said to have already exhausted the the entire field of linguistic theory and grammatical technique.

But there is also another side to this picture. We do get evidence which shows that the post-Pāṇinian grammarians taken here for study have not followed Pāṇini. Such evidence is provided by a critical study of the different levels of grammatical description reflected in the different grammars. Take, for example, the past passive participial formation *sphīta* from *sphyai*. While Pāṇini describes it by the method of substditution i.e *ādeśa* of *sphyai* by *sphī* (cf. the Pāṇinian *sūtra, sphāyaḥ sphī niṣṭhāyām*, 6.1.22), Śākaṭāyana descibes it by adopting the methodd of *saṁprasāraṇa* of *y* of *sphyai* into

1. Actually the study of grammatical thought from the period of Pāṇini to that of Patañjali forms part of an independent thesis : *S.D. Laddu, Evolution of the Sanskrit Language from Pāṇini to Patañjali (primary Formations)*, thesis submitted to the University of Poona, Poona 7, 1966, pp. 1-454.

i (and tdhen into long ī.) Stated in linguistic terms it means that, while Pāṇini describes the form *sphīta* on morphological level, Śākaṭāyana describes it on phonological level (cf. Śākaṭāyanaś *sūtra*, *sphāyaḥ*, 4.1.129). It must, however, be conceded that such cases are very few. It must also be pointed out that this difference in the two approaches, viz. morphological and phonological, is not consistently followed and maintained throughout Śākaṭāyana, who seeks to strike a path different from Pāṇini's but has not succeded in doing so to any appreciable extent. In the majority of cases of past passive participial formations, Śākaṭāyana has blindly adopted the Pāṇinian method and even wording.The same can be said of other post-Pāṇinian grammarians.

We may, therefore, put it as follows:—

1. The differences in description which the post-Pāṇinian grammarians display are very few.
2. Even when a different line of description is sometimes adopted, it is not maintained consistently and as a part of an innovation in technique. It is but haphazard.
3. So far as the technique of description is concerned, the post-Pāṇinan grammarians cannot be said to be unanimous. They differ among themselves. Nor is it possible to group the post-Pāṇinian grammarians into such clear-cut classes as (a) those following Pāṇini in each and every case and detail, and (b) those not following Pāṇini under any circumstances.
4. Most of the post-Pāṇinian grammars seem to have been written not for introducing any new principles or techniques of grammar, but only to satisfy the apirations of the authors and perhaps also to meet the practical needs of their respective times. Also, there were secterian considerations behind writing these grammars, *cf.* for example, Kātantra and Cāndra grammars.

It must, however, be emphasized that the fore-going

conclusions - if they can at all be characterised as conclusions- are arrived at on the basis of a partial study of only the section of the past passive participial formations, and that too, mainly so far as it concerns the two main techniques, viz. the *ādeśa* and the *nipātana*. The conclusions based on a comparative study of all grammars in their entirety may perhaps come out to be totally different from the ones drawn above. One, therefore, cannot claim the above conclusions to be final in the sense that they reflect the final fruit of a comparative study of all Sanskrit grammars in their entirety.

Appendix — A

Topic Index

N.B. The order followed in arrangement is that of English alphabets.

a

b

c

d

f

g

i

l

m

n

P

Appendix — B

Index of the Sūtras

Index of the various *sūtras* discussed in the work.

N.B. The order followed is of the Sanskrit alphabets.

Bibliographical References

(a) Research articles and books

Abhyankar K.V., *A Dictionary of Sanskrit Grammar*, Gaekwad's Oriental Series No. 134, Baroda, 1961.

Agrawala V.S., *India As Known To Pāṇini*, 2nd Edition, 1963.

Allen W.S., 'Zero and Pāṇini', *Indian Linguistics*, Vol. 16, 1955.

Bach Emmon, An Introduction Transformational Grammars, New York, Chicago, San Francisco, Holt Rinehart & Winston, 1964.

Basu, S. C., *Aṣṭādhyāuī of Pāṇini*, Vols. I, II, Motilal Banarsidass, Varanasi-Delhi, 1964.

Buck Carl D., *Comparative Grammar of Greek and Latin.*

Burrow T., *Sanskrit Language.*

Belvalkar S.K., *Systems of Sanskrit Grammar*, Bombay 1916.

Bhate, Saroja, *Pre-Pāṇinian Grammatical Thought, University of Poona, Poona, 1971.* (unpublished)

Bhavsar S.N., *Stymologies in the Brāhmaṇas*, University of Poona, Poona, 1970. (unpublished)

Bloch Bernart, *Language*, 23, 1947.

Bllomfield L., *Language*, 1933.

Brugmann Karl, *Kurze Vergleischende Grammatik der Indogermanischen Sprachen*, (Zweite Lieferung) Strassburg, 1903.

Chatterjee K.C., *Cāndravyākaraṇa of Candragomin*, 1961.

Chatterjee K.C., *Technical Terma and Technique of Sanskrit Grammar*, Calcutta, 1948.

Chomsky N. *Syntactic Structures*, Mouton & Co., The Hague, 1964.

Chomsky N. 'Semantic Consideration in Grammar', Monography Series on Language and Linguistics, No. 8, 1955.

Dalai, B.K. Indian Lingustics BKP. Delhi, 2007.

Ghosh, B.K., 'Aspects of Pre-Pāṇinian Sanskrit Grammar' *B.C. Law Volume*, The Indian Research Instt., Calcutta, 1945.

Gleason H.A., *An Introduction to Descriptive Linguistics*, Holt Rinehart and Winston, New York, 1961.

Gonda, J., *Remarks on the Sanskrit Passive*, Leiden, 1951.

George Sergiu Al., 'The Semiosis of Zero according to Pāṇini', *East and West*, Vol. 17, 1967.

Haas W., 'Zero in Linguistics Description', *Studies in Linguistics Analysi*, Special Volume of the Philological Society, Oxford, 1957.

Harris, Z.S., *Language*, 18, 1942; 21.1945; 22.1946.

Hockett C.F., *A Course in Modern Linguistics*, The MacMillan. Co, NY. 1958, also *Language* 23, 1947.

Joshi V.L., 'Treatment of Laon-Words in Sanskrit Grammar, *IL*, 32.1971.

Macdonell A.A. *Vedic Grammar*, Indological Book House, Varanasi-Delhi, 1968.

Mehendale, M.A. *Some Aspects of Indo-Aryan Linguistics*, University of Bombay, Bombay, 1968.

Mīmāṁsaka Yudhiṣṭhira, *Sanskrit Vyākaraṇa Śāstrakā Itihāsa*, Prācya Vidyā Pratiṣṭhāna, Ajmer, 1963 (Part I), 1962, (Part II).

Nida E.A., Morphology, Ann Arbor, The University of Michigan Press, 2nd Edition, 1963.

Pade J. S., *Tāmbūlamañjarī*, M.S. University Oriental Series, No. 1, Oriental Institute, Baroda, 1958.

Palsule G.B., *A Concordance of Sanskrit Dhātuupāṭhas*, Deccan College, 1955.

Palsule G.B., *The Sanskrit Dhātupāṭhas—A Critical Study*, University of Poona, Poona, 1961.

Palmer L. R., *The Latin Language*, 1961.

Pandit M.D., 'Mathematical Representation of Some Pāṇinian *Sūtras*,' *JUPH*. 23, 1966.

Pandit M.D., 'Pāṇinian It-Saṁjñā —A Symbolic Zero' Silver Jubilee Volume, *BDCPRI*, 1965; also 'Zero in Pāṇini', CASS, 1990.

Pandit M.D., 'Pāṇini—A Study in Compound Word-Structures', *JMSUBH*. Vol. 12, No. 1, 1963.

Pandit M.D., 'Pāṇini—A Study in Non-Compounded Word-Structures', *VIJ*. Vol. I, pt.2, Sept. 1963.

Pandit M.D., 'Pāṇini va Gaṇitaśāstra', (in Marathi), *Saṁskṛti Sugandha*, 1970.

Pandit M.D. 'Some Linguistic Principles in Pāṇini's Grammar', *Indian Linguistics*, 23, 1963.

Pandit M.D., 'Zero in Pāṇini', CASS, 1990

Pathak K.B., 'Further Remarks on the *Uṇādisūtras* of Pāṇini', *ABORI*, Poona, Vol. XI.

Pathak K.B., 'Pāṇini and the Authorship of the *Uṇādisūtras*', *ABORI*, Poona, Vol. IV.

Renou L., *Terminologies Grammaticale du Sanskrit*, Paris.

Shukla K.P., *Laghu Mañjūṣā*, M.S. University of Baroda, Baroda, 1961.

Trager G., *Studies in Linguistics*, 1958.

Varma Siddheshvar, *Etymologies of Yāska*, VVRI, Hoshiarpur, 1953.

Voegelin C.F. *Language*, 23. 1947.

Wackernagel J., *Alt-Indische Grammatik*, Band I, II, III.

Wells a.s., *Language*, 23, 1947.

Whitney W.D., *The Roots, Verb-Forms and Primary Derivatives of the Sanskrit Language*, 1945.

(b) Texts Utilised

Grammar

Pāṇini : *Aṣṭādhyāyī of Pāṇini*, Ed. by S.C. *Basu*, Motilal Banarasidass, Varanasi, 1964 (Vols. I & II).

Kāsikā, Kāśī Sanskrit Granthamālā, No. 37, Chowkhamba Sanskrit Series, Varanasi, 1952. *Siddhānta Kaumudī*, by Bhaṭṭoji Dīksita, ed. by Vāsudev Laxman Śāstrī Panśīkar, Bombay, 1915.

Kātantra : *The Kātantra*, ed. by Julius *Eggeling*, Bibliotheca Indica, Calcutta, 1874.

Candra : *Cāndravyākaraṇa of Candragomin*, ed. by K.C. *Chatterjee*, Deccan College, Poona, 1961, (Vols. I & II)

Jainendra: *Jainendra Mahāvṛtti*, ed. by Ācārya Abhayanandin, Bhāratīya Jñānapīṭha, Kashi, 1956.

Hemacandra : (i) *Haimaprakāśa Mahāvyākaraṇam*, Vol. I, ed. by Upādhyāya Kṣamā vijayagaṇī, Bombay, 1937, Vol. II, ed. by Śrīvijayakṣamābhadrasūri, Bombay, 1954.

(ii) *Śrī Siddhahemacandra Śabdānuśāsanam*, ed. by Muni Hemāṁśu Vijaya Jain, Advocate Press, Ahmedabad.

Śākaṭāyana: *Śabdānuśāsana of Śākaṭāyana*, ed. by Gustav Oppert, Madras, 1893.

Bhoja : *The Sarasvatīkaṇṭhābharaṇa of Śrībhojadeva*, ed. by K. Sāmba Śiva Śāstrī (Vol. I, 1935, Vol. II, 1937, Vol. III, 1938); ed. by V.A. Ramaswamy Śāstrī, (Vol. IV, 1948) Trivandrum.

Sārasvata : *Śarasvata Vyākaraṇam*, ed. by Pandit Śivadtta Kudāl, Revised by Vāsudev Laxman Śāstri Panśīkar (4th edition), Bombay 1926.

Vopadeva : *Mugdhabodham Vyākaraṇam*, ed. by Śiva Nārāyaṇa Śiromaṇi, Calcutta, 1911 (only upto Taddhitas).

Patañjali : (i) *Patañjali's Vyākaraṇa Mahābhāṣya*, Vod. I ed. by S.D. Joshi, 1968, and Vol. II, ed by S.D. Joshi in collaboration with J. A. F. Roodbergen, University of Poona, Poona, 1969.

(ii) *Mahābhāṣya of Patañjali*, ed. by F. Keilhorn, Vols. I, II, III, BORI, Poona.

(iii) *Vyākaraṇamahābhāṣya*, ed. and translated into Marathi by V.V. Abhyankar, Deccan Education Society, Poona. *Vaiyākaraṇabhūṣaṇasāra*, ed. by Pandit Sadashiv Shastri, Kashi Sanskrit Series, No. 133, Varanasi, 1939.

Yāska : (i) *The Nighaṇṭu and the Nirukta*, by L. Sarup, Motilal Banarsidass, Varanasi, (Reprinted) 1962.

(ii) *The Nirukta*, by Pandit Satyavrata Samasrami, Calcutta, Vol. I, 1882, Vol. II, 1185.

(iii) *Nirukta*, translated into Marathi by V.K. Rajwade, BORI, Poona, 1940.

Vedic Texts

Ṛgveda Saṁhitā (Vols. I-V) ed. by Vaidika Saṁśodhana Maṇḍala, Poona.

Śatapatha Brāhmaṇa, ed. by A. Weber, Chowkhamba Sanskrit Series, Varanasi, 1964.

Taittirīya Brāhmaṇa, ed. by A. Mahadev Shastri, Vols. I-III, 1908-1913.

Other Texts

Jaiminīya Upaniṣad Brāhmaṇa, ed. by B.R. Sharma, 1967.

Kāvyaprakāśa of Mammaṭa, ed. by S.S. Sukhthankar, (ullāsas I-III), 1933.